MW00378502

NIGHT

IN THE

WORLD

Night in the World

a novel

SHARON ENGLISH

Freehand Books acknowledges the financial support for its publishing program provided by the Canada Council for the Arts and the Alberta Media Fund, and by the Government of Canada through the Canada Book Fund.

The author acknowledges the financial support for this work provided by the Canada Council for the Arts, the Ontario Arts Council, and the Toronto Arts Council.

Freehand Books
515 – 815 1st Street SW   Calgary, Alberta   T2P 1N3
www.freehand-books.com

Book orders: UTP Distribution
5201 Dufferin Street   Toronto, Ontario   M3H 5T8
Telephone: 1-800-565-9523   Fax: 1-800-221-9985
utpbooks@utpress.utoronto.ca   utpdistribution.com

Library and Archives Canada Cataloguing in Publication
Title: Night in the world / Sharon English.
Names: English, Sharon, 1965– author.
Identifiers: Canadiana (print) 20210368276 | Canadiana (ebook) 20210368284 | ISBN 9781990601026 (softcover) | ISBN 9781990601033 (EPUB) | ISBN 9781990601040 (PDF)
Classification: LCC PS8559.N5254 N54 2022 | DDC C813/.6—DC23

Edited by Deborah Willis
Book design by Natalie Olsen
Cover image © buddhawut/Shutterstock.com
Moth image on page 1: *Daphnis nerii* © Didier Descouens
Author photo by Kevin Connelly
Maps by Sharon English
Printed on FSC® recycled paper and bound in Canada by Gauvin

The sun, the darkness, the winds, are all listening to what we have to say.

GERONIMO

~

Song

There are those who are trying to set fire to the world,
We are in danger.
There is time only to work slowly,
There is no time not to love.

DEENA METZGER
Looking for the Faces of God

CENTRAL TORONTO

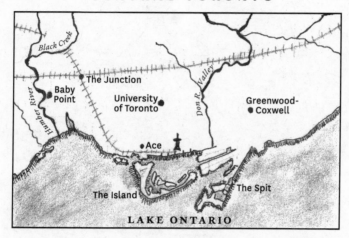

TORONTO ISLANDS

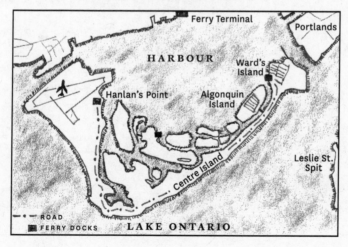

Part I

Ripe for Dreaming

1

THE NIGHT BECKONS when he stirs from sleep, troubled by worries about Leverage and Naomi. The uneasy day ahead. As his eyes open the dog is already approaching, nails clicking against the floor, to meet the warm hand extended. A few strokes of the soft face. Another moment accepting he's wide awake. Then he rises.

They head downstairs, the usual routine, he doesn't need or want to turn on lights. A pearly illumination from the street shows him the way to the back door, his boots and coat. Turn the bolt, twist the knob, pull. Cold wafts in and Reg darts out.

He stands calf-deep in snow while the dog relieves himself. Wind swells the trees along the yard's edge into creaking. In the west, toward the river, a bank of cloud almost white in the city lights, though it's hours before sunrise. The worries continue to flit through his mind, like brambles tugging wherever he goes, and he shrugs the trench coat tighter again. And something else now, something new. Not a problem or difficulty, like the others. Not even tangible.

This new thing is like an absence that crouches or a hole filled with darker darkness, waiting for him to step inside. It's come with his mother's death but isn't Death, not exactly. Even while he stands here in the calm of a January night, with Reg sniffing nearby, Justin can feel it, close as a shadow. It's something other, a force that knocks things loose.

~

ADDRESSING THE ASSEMBLY at his mother's funeral that afternoon, Justin Leveridge doesn't break down. He's running on a few hours' sleep, an extra Xanax and lots of coffee, and has the sensation of a hot towel wrapped tightly around his neck – the beginning of illness, or erratic nerves. Yet his mind, like a helpful assistant, passes him the words he needs. He says the right things. Kind things. He talks about his mother's intelligence in raising him and Oliver alone after their father died. How she learned to invest and make more from little, and her love of late-night online poker, which she played for money and was usually ahead. He makes people smile.

And gradually he becomes aware that the eulogy he's giving, while factually true, is a pale distortion, like so much else these days. Nice, expected, and even sincere, but so wretchedly scripted and contained that it's barely alive, like a storm caught and corked in a bottle.

He looks out at the audience. Naomi's staring down at her hands. Oliver's expression is solemn. The concerto that tinkled guests to their seats has begun to replay. Only Gwynn, his girl, gazes back with love. His breath catches and he tries to wind up.

"Mom. What can I say? She drove me nuts sometimes – I'm sure some of you can relate?" A hand through his hair. "She had her opinions, and she was usually right about them. She pushed me early on, believed in me, and I wouldn't be the person I was today without her." Something building inside; not building, *burning*. His mother popped. And he can't say anything with feeling. Like how he could never quite tell if she loved him or just admired how he'd succeeded, a sound return on time spent. Always that cool distance with her even when she was close and happy. Does it matter?

He swallows, looks to Gwynn again. "We'll miss her always, won't we, dear? We loved Grandma. We loved you, Mom."

Stop there. Live with that.

Before people exit the room there's the final farewell. In the open casket lies her body: powdered and rouged, hands crossed modestly over thighs. She's wearing a dress he's never seen and nylon stockings too. Justin stares at this schoolbook idea of dignity until he senses the shuffling of shoes next to him.

At the reception he has plenty to do even though Naomi and Aunt Fiona have seen to most of the arrangements. With his brother he stands receptively by the flowers and guest book, growing glassy-eyed from fatigue and all the hugs, handshakes and thank-yous. He speaks with people who knew his mother or aunt, some of his staff who made it, and he hopes he manages each conversation with grace. He's assumed the robes of an ancient office today; he wants to stand tall and proud as her son.

He meets Oliver near the entrance, changing his shoes for boots. His brother glances up at him.

"Good speech," he says.

"You too."

Oliver had spoken of their mother's strength. If she was so strong, why'd her heart give out?

"See you over there?" Oliver asks. A dinner Fiona's hosting.

"Of course. And we should make a plan too, you and me." Confusion on Oliver's face. "Talk about the will, the house, all that?" *Shit* he almost adds, because that's what it is: another mound of details and processes to tackle, mostly on his own.

"Right."

With a nod and a tight-lipped smile, Oliver heads out the door as if the conversation is over. Justin watches his younger brother slip on the pavement, catch himself, vanish into the parking lot. Didn't he come with someone? His ex showed up, though they didn't sit together. Justin shakes his head.

It's almost seven now, and the sky is the colour of wood smoke, that urban murk that passes for night. Snow still falling thickly. On the way here, traffic proceeded cautiously on roads edged by white embankments.

I'm thinking about *weather*, he realizes. Isn't that amazing? Death yawns open, your last parent disappears, and you hold an emotionally mute service that feels somewhere between a holiday luncheon and a graduation ceremony — no wailing, no keening, no rending of cloth or prostrating before gods. Bundle up the family and drive off like it's any other day, with your usual sack of concerns. Tomorrow, someone will call about the ashes.

EARLY MORNING. Pushing the recycling bin, Justin puffs up the driveway. He feels like an old bear prematurely woken. His belly aches and he's been awake for hours. Planning. Strategizing. Making mental lists and notes. He can't stop himself — there's too much happening.

He wheels the bin into place and gives it a shove. Catches his breath. Bears are right to hibernate. He doesn't want to go back inside. Because that means starting the whole thing over: another day.

What does he want?

He wants all the calls, and the questions, and the emails, and the expectations, to drift far far away. Let the wind disappear them into that grey horizon. He wants to lie close with Naomi, and Gwynn. To slip into *living* again.

He inserts the key, turns and pushes. Warm air on his face, winter behind him.

About his mother's death he doesn't really know what he feels. At the funeral as he spoke there was that nuclear surge within, but he dialed it down. The day felt too staged, Grieving Son a role. And since then, nothing. True, authentic, hot-in-his-veins *feeling* seems completely out of reach, a luxury experience.

Since when?

16

A good long while.

To avoid disturbing Naomi he goes down to his basement office and lies on the sofa under the duvet, his hands on his sore belly. Dozes until his watch alarm beeps.

When he re-emerges the sun's in the kitchen and so is Gwynn, eating toast.

"Morning, Chickadee. Your mom up?" She nods, her head lightly bobbing. Justin kisses her then listens to confirm the whine of water. He takes down his favourite cast-iron pan from its hook. "Are you singing inside?"

Gwynn nods again.

"Cool. That's what I like to hear."

He adds minced onion to melted butter, not too much or neither of them will eat the omelet; then fresh tarragon, egg batter and shaved parmesan. When Naomi joins them, her wet hair pulled into a clip, he divides the meal onto three plates and sets them on the table while Naomi gets out vitamins, reviews the contents of the lunch box and adds a granola bar.

"Do you smell something off?" she asks.

"Just the onions."

"No. Off."

He shrugs.

As she eats, Justin relaxes. He asks Gwynn to sing the song she was making up and he and Naomi laugh. *George Aborge, George Aborge, George Aborge got the lowww down!* is the essence of it, name upon name. *Gina Bellina, Gina Bellina, Gina Bellina got the lowww down!*

Then breakfast's done, there's the dash for coats, boots and bags, and his girls are out the door.

She texts him twenty minutes later.

He keeps working.

When she returns from dropping off Gwynn at school, he's making another piece of toast for his aching belly.

"Oh!" she says, that stiffly bright tone. "I thought you were busy."

"I am," he replies, calmly buttering. It would defy mathematics to count the number of times he's told her how he loathes this passive-aggressive behaviour. *Chick speak,* he privately calls it. He loathes the tedious, vacuous, unnecessary texts too, this trickling demand for responsiveness to the most mundane and fleet-footed of thoughts and occurrences, expressed simply because Naomi's bored or anxious or because she can.

"I heard your ping but I figured if it was important you'd call me," he says.

I heard your ping? God!

Naomi's looking at him. "I'm worried there's mold in here," she says. "I've been smelling it for weeks. There's all that condensation in the sunroom. It wouldn't surprise me if the whole thing's rotted."

"Alright, let's take a look."

The sunroom, a spacious addition built some years before they purchased the house, used to be their favourite space to eat or curl up with books or laptops overlooking the backyard, under skylights that showed clouds and pattering rain. About a year ago these windows became permanently fogged, then began to drip. After a heavy summer storm, chunks of plaster fell to the floor and water stains appeared, first on the ceiling, then on the walls and under the windows. They decided to have the entire room rebuilt and hoped it could be done before winter set in, but the house has heritage designation, and the plans got tangled in the permit-approval process. For months now the skylights have been sheeted with plastic and the room cleared. Casey, Justin's go-to carpenter, has moved on to another job.

Naomi points to a crack along a windowsill rough with dark matter — black mold, certainly. The sills are actually spongy to touch. With a kitchen knife Justin easily lifts away rotten wood, slides the knife down and brings it up covered in damp sooty stuff.

Naomi rears back, a hand to her throat. "My god, honey. There's tons of it."

He tries to reassure her that in the spring – only a few months away – the room will be dealt with. He's been pressing the right people.

"So you say, but who knows what else could interfere?" Which is true enough. "I can feel it, Jay, deep in my lungs." She starts to pace. "I wake up in the morning with this craggy ache in my chest and my head. It feels like something's got inside me, literally. I can feel it there right now, like pollen, like I've got allergies, which I've never had in my life! And Gwynn feels it too. From what I've read, once this stuff gets into you it can take ages for your body to get rid of it."

He kisses her cheek. "I don't know what else we can do, my love. We can't tear it down yet." He strokes her shoulder. Another kiss. "I got to get moving. I'm meeting Stanko."

But Naomi follows him to the upstairs bathroom, saying they must figure out something. He starts the shower and undresses, turning aside to remove his underwear. It's been months since they were intimate, and like always when these troughs occur, he starts to feel a peculiar modesty around her, ashamed and protective of his hungry body.

"We could get it caulked, I suppose. I could ask Casey." He aims the gotch at the hamper.

"Would that help?"

He says yes, he thinks so, and will make the call. Then he steps into the tub, wishing she'd follow him now. Shuts the glass door.

Steam. Water. A memory: Naomi's long hair wonderfully slimy between his fingers as he worked in the conditioner – when? Some afternoon or late morning after lazing in bed, in a time of freedom he'd not recognized. Before everything got so relentlessly, inescapably wound up tight.

Driving to Ace, he considers black mold: yuppie asbestos.

Stanko's late. Sitting in the booth nearest the kitchen, Justin checks his phone. Another text from Naomi: she'll pick up Gwynn from school today. Dutifully he replies. Then taps out a message to Casey. Checks email again.

Never, never a moment anymore.

When his landlord arrives, Justin orders them cappuccino. Waiting for it fills the first minute of their meeting, while Stanko slips off his coat and checks his phone, neither of them willing to initiate the social niceties that would admit a weaker status. Justin drums his fingers and wonders if he should have taken another Xanax. Stanko appears to be reading a pleasant message.

"Did you hear from Alex?" Stanko finally asks, putting down his phone and looking up with a smile. Opening volley.

"Was I supposed to?"

"Yes. He'll be calling you today, I expect. I took him through."

"Though the kitchen?" Motherfucker. "When?"

"Sunday morning."

Outmaneuvered again. Gone is the appealing prospect of showing Stanko the damage himself today, in the presence of the men who had to clean it up — who *always* have to clean it up, *his* crew. He's been imagining the circle of men tightening, their gazes leveled . . . the glint of knives in their hands —

"You should have called me. I'd have come down. That plaster landed on my grill. That's a seven-thousand-dollar piece of equipment, by the way."

Stanko sugars his coffee and sets the wet spoon on the table. "You can talk to Alex yourself, no problem. That's why I asked him to call."

Justin stares at him in disbelief. Everything with this man is always *no problem, of course, perfect*.

Back when Ace first opened, Justin rented from Stanko's father, a dour, war-damaged old man. Yet the elder Mr. Stanko dealt directly, and bore to certain principles. When you battled him you *connected* with something. Stanko Jr. is smoke. Stanko Jr. is cloud. He's a man for these times.

"Alright," Justin concedes, "but no more patches! That's pointless."

"Alex says he knows the source of the leak. He'll fix it. He's very good, I trust him. If he says patches, that's fine with me."

"It'll be a waste of money. The roof needs to be replaced. I lose business whenever this happens, and then we go through this whole routine. This affects you as well as me."

"I know, I know it's wearisome, but everything's so old," says Stanko mournfully, diverting to an Eastern European fatalism he possesses only second-hand. "Roof, road, sewers, streetcar tracks, building." He casts a tender look around the room. "This place was built as a store! It was never meant for hundreds of people every day, all this activity. What can you do?"

Justin leans in, glaring with as much ferocity as he dares. "Fix it properly this time. Honour your long-term tenant and invest in your own infrastructure."

Stanko merely shrugs. The discussion's over. He hands Justin a card — one of Ace's. Penned on the back is his contractor's number. "The last fix from your man hasn't even lasted the winter," Justin says doggedly, even though Stanko's sliding out of the booth.

He's offered a greasy grin. "So, we try again."

Alone, Justin picks up his phone and heads into the kitchen. Staff have stapled thick plastic sheets across the crumbling ceiling. What is it about ceilings in his life?

Out the back door. The alley offers nothing to abuse, not even a discarded bottle to kick.

He shuts himself in his car and turns on the stereo. Alice in Chains fills the space, and from inside the music he beholds the rear of the building. The kitchen, a single-storey, flat-roofed add-on to the original Victorian-era structure, was built sometime in the 1970s when the location was converted to a restaurant. In winter they have to climb onto the roof and shovel off the snow. The roof leaked in the same spot when he rented the space thirty years ago, and the eaves leak too: at the corners great knobs of ice bulge out and drool down in two long fangs.

California I'm fine, sing Alice in Chains. *Somebody check my brain.*

This leaking won't kill him, but Leverage might: he created it at great cost and it's beautiful, but doesn't thrive. It leaks. Every month it costs more than it takes in, and every moment he's aware of this like a weeping wound.

Leverage was his plan to reclaim something of his old self: his enthusiasm, his original vision. Living by positive commitment, not just routine. Yet from the beginning, the tone of the project was different than Ace had been, which he should have seen coming. The times are different, he's different.

California's alright, somebody check my brain.

He wants to call Naomi now. He misses her, misses how they were. Yet he can't call. Last fall when he was opening Leverage, his stress hit the stratosphere and still he avoided calling her, started keeping more and more to himself. She doesn't have the same interest in or patience with him anymore. He's not making her happy. He's difficult, and for the emotional hardships Naomi's apparently experiencing, she's put him on rations.

On the car seat beside him lies a copy of *Now* magazine, still folded to the theatre section and the ad. He picks it up again. *The Black Rider: The Casting of the Magic Bullets.* Underneath the red-lettered title looms a white-faced devil, a black bandit's mask painted across his eyes. From inside the darkness he grins gleefully, eyes greedy for mischief, as only a devil would. Justin stopped reading *Now* years ago when it became bloated with left-wing diatribes and righteous green-washing and toothless hipster posturing. It's limped into the digital age, slimmed down by half, ribs showing. But that ad, when his eye happened to fall on it, slapped him. He'd heard of the avant-garde musical, created by William Burroughs and Tom Waits and some German guy, though he's never seen it performed. He ordered two tickets, feeling a little spike of the old excitement — like the anticipation of seeing a great rock concert, which he never does anymore because that life is gone. It'll be a treat to take Gwynn, and a welcome change from another night of Netflix or Disney DVDs.

Naomi won't be joining them. Because she's going away again.

For a while now Naomi's been saying she needs space: to rediscover herself on the other side of becoming a mother, to decide where to concentrate her gifts. And fair enough, Naomi stopped working when she got pregnant and had been only half-working from the time they moved in together. A degree in commerce, some years in retail — she's never really found her groove. It's not him, she says, it's her.

Except when it *is* him.

Mindfulness meditation this time. In the woods.

They've just lost his mother. Yet she asked him if it was still alright for her to go, so of course he said yes, it's important to you, et cetera. He doesn't want her staying home to be his nurse. He wants his wife.

Naomi, apparently, wants something else.

2

HE'S BUILDING AN EGG. It must get finished.

It stands upright before him: a ribbed wooden frame, wider and taller than himself so he needs a stepladder to reach the crown. But he's stuck. He bends forward, calculating and recalculating cuts: two-eighths of an inch, three-sixteenths of an inch, scribbling the fractions with a flat carpenter's pencil on scrap wood. Soft yellow light that might be from a candle illuminates his work; past the egg there's only darkness, a hint of damp stone.

Time's running out.

What was the next step? He scans the nails and pieces scattered about, frantically confused, and his heart starts to gallop. His own shout wakes him, ringing in the darkened room like a shot.

Oliver wipes his eyes. Grief swells in his throat. The egg-that-must-get-finished is gone.

~

OLIVER'S OFFICE IS at the back of the gym. Past the front desk and the windowed cubicle used by Foroud, where Oliver drops off another empty and cleaned casserole dish belonging to his boss's wife; past the workout machines and free-weight zone, the lockers and fat coils of undulation rope; past the wooden rings hanging from black straps and carabiner fastenings, the jumping boxes, trip-hazard ab rollers and single tractor wheel. Tucked behind the punching bags that dangle like swollen cocoons and sway when no one's touching them — that's where Oliver retreated when everything went to shit, and where he's stayed put since.

He unlocks the dented metal door, turns on the computer, sets down his mug, removes his coat and boots. The rotating portable heater. His Obus Forme, going linty.

"You are here?" Foroud at the door, stating the obvious.

Oliver tries to grin as Foroud reminds him of the time off he should take. He doesn't want or need it. Work means structure and routine, tasks with some value. He waves him away, but kindly. Foroud and Nasrin attended the service. And how many employer's spouses would bring you foil-covered pans of ghormeh sabzi and oily, fragrant fesenjoon after your mother's death?

It's mid-month, a busy time at the gym. Oliver has to chase down remiss members for payments and print paycheques for staff. He lucked into the job by being in the right place at the right time. It's a handy and uncomplicated place to work. He can walk here from his apartment. Gets his membership for free.

Of course, he has no idea what he's actually *doing*.

He used to be a journalist. Has an above-average memory for detail and data. When he punches in Justin's number, later that morning, he doesn't even need to use Contacts. He meant to get back to him yesterday, but just couldn't face it. Maybe a decent night's sleep would come upon him, he reasoned hopefully. Give him more spirit. It didn't so he won't find out.

"Hey Bro." Justin sounds gravelly. "I'm supposed to ask you about the cat."

"Oh?"

Shit. He was hoping the issue of the cat would have gone away, dealt with somehow after he left that dinner at Auntie Fiona's.

When she spoke of Mimi at the table he pretended not to have heard. He even hoped, a bit shamefully, that his relatives had formed a low enough opinion of him that he wouldn't be considered a prospective parent.

"Yeah," Justin says. "Look, it doesn't matter to me, but Fiona called us this morning, no one else has offered and she can't take her. Neither can we."

His aunt also phoned him, yesterday. He hadn't called her back either.

"That beast can draw blood."

A snicker from Justin. "Yeah, she's a *cat*."

Oliver shuts his eyes. Feels himself growing smaller and smaller. He has never been responsible for a pet, dreads unsustainable vet bills and lives in an attic apartment. He's away from home all day. Mimi will hate it.

"You don't want her in a shelter, do you?"

"Of course not." Though at least there, Mimi might attract the right person. Or a terrible one. What would his mother want? Would she even approve of him taking Mimi? Mimi, who would pad up his mother's chest as she lay on the sofa or bed, and nuzzle her lips? *Kisses. Kisses from my princess* . . . Princess! His mother never cozied up to anyone like she did to that cat, and a small sucky part of himself would like to abandon Mimi for that, as if the cat's to blame.

"I'll do it," he says, and stands up from his desk so the decision feels real. "I'll try to get out there tonight."

"And you'll come down to Ace tomorrow? For sure?"

"And I'll come down tomorrow, noon."

"Bravo."

"Smartass," Oliver mutters as he disconnects. Mom's cat. God help him! He better not fuck this up.

HE RENTS ANOTHER CAR from the same agency he used for the funeral and drives out to Oakville after work, over an hour in traffic. Wet, icy snow whirls out of grey darkness. Now he wishes he had taken time off; his back throbs, reminding him not to get careless, and he's getting trancey from the half-ration sleeps he survives on, with no breather today.

He exits into a residential area, a place without sidewalks because there are no pedestrians out here. The night lies deeper between houses still festooned with Christmas lights. His mother lived in this suburban neighbourhood for over thirty years, ever since she moved them from the island. He endured his adolescence here. Tonight the streets feel lonelier than ever and he becomes intensely aware of his solitude, the mechanical flip of wipers.

She died alone — sudden cardiac arrest. Slumped in the upstairs hallway, a basket of folded sheets and towels upended nearby. Like she'd just climbed the stairs, his aunt told him, after she found her. Two sets of stairs, actually, which he'd worried about for years: a three-storey house with a large yard was too much to manage even with the help he offered. He tore out of the office when the call came, rode the subway to its western end then took a cab, though there was nothing to be done and he knew the ambulance would be long gone. He went to his aunt's, spoke to her awhile, tried to soothe, then walked the short distance over and let himself in. Empty rooms, the spook of his own reflection in the dark windows.

He wept when he finally saw her again: laid out like a picture, framed in wood. She was gone, and it felt like someone had reached into him and removed an artery. Inside he's still weeping.

The house is cold when he enters. Aside from the thermostat being lowered by his frugal aunt, nothing seems touched. No sign of the cat, though her food and water bowls are topped up.

He searches closets and then the basement for a carrier, locates it, a box with a metal grill at the front. Climbs the stairs to the main floor to find the cat sitting at the top of the second-floor stairs, eyeing him.

"Mimi girl, we're going home."

Her tail swishes.

"That's right," he says, slowly approaching. The tail works faster. When he reaches out she rises, sniffs then moves under his hand, nudging his fingers with her cheek, the thick tail now encircling his wrist as he murmurs reassuringly. He scoops her up and she dangles from his grip like warm rubber, all the way down to the carrier.

At this point Mimi seems to realize that "going home" is bullshit. Her hind legs come up and the rest of her goes crazy: twisting and snarling, kicking and biting and trying to claw his skin. She's not a cat, she's a bundle of snakes. He hears himself shouting that it's okay as he tries to push her into the prison, and when she wriggles from his hands he snatches at her, connects with a flank, rolls her over, hoists her up by the belly and squishes her under one arm. Tries to kind of pour this writhing bundle into the carrier held between his knees. Her claws grip the grill so he can't close it without catching them. He pries one paw loose and then another, and back again until his fingers bleed. Finally bolts the door.

He slumps against a wall, sweaty and breathless. His eyes sting. His hands are trembling and he wipes blood on his jeans. He was an animal with her. A predator. "I'm so sorry, girl," he pants. "I'm so sorry." Mimi lets out a hollow wail.

Together they crawl back to Toronto through blowing snow, the Queensway to the Expressway to Lakeshore Avenue, where the water is a black precipice drawn up against the city. From the passenger-side floor, Mimi continues to cry. It's after ten when they pull up at his place and he carries the cat inside, then returns to start lugging in her things. He's climbing up with a sack of litter on his shoulder when the door to the second-floor apartment opens. His neighbour emerges then ducks inside to let Oliver pass on the landing.

29

"Hey Rosh, thanks."

"No problem. You've gotten a cat?"

"Inherited one."

"Oh." Rosh's smile drops. "Do you need a hand?"

Reaching the third floor, Oliver slides the bag to the floor outside his door and starts back down. "It's okay, just one more trip."

"Sure, well good luck! The transition can be touch-and-go, but it won't stay that way. Or maybe you know that."

"I know nothing."

"We grew up with cats, so feel free to ask. They can seem kind of mystifying at times."

"I can't wait."

He's ashamed of his sarcasm as soon as he's outside. Rosh moved into the second-floor apartment a few months ago, and though they've not run into each other much, Oliver's been wondering about him ever since. "Oliver Leveridge the writer?" Rosh said when they first introduced themselves, the only person in a long while to recognize Oliver's name — and it's not like he ever had much of one, either. He should have at least stopped to chat.

After the final load has been hauled in, Oliver locks the door and removes his coat and boots. He makes spaces for Mimi's bowls and bed and poo-shed, then opens the cage. She races out of sight.

He cleans his wounds with antiseptic, then changes into flannels and gets a beer. Lifts the robe from its hook, claps on his trapper hat and steps onto the deck. The apartment is on the top floor of a house in an east Toronto neighbourhood that's not yet distinguished by a name, like The Beaches or The Danforth, or East York, Little India, Port Lands. Someone at the gym said Greenwood-Coxwell has been proposed, but he thinks that's too charmless to be true. He ended up here when his Little Italy life fell apart. The walls slope, yet the old wainscotting and moldings hold warmth, and when the trees are in leaf, a happy green light pours in. The apartment also has one exceptional feature: this deck, large enough to be almost another room, and facing south. From this height just before the land drops down, he can see all the way to the lake — a rare thing in Toronto, especially for a decidedly non-premium location. He can't see the island, of course, but he can feel it from here, and that glimpse of watery blue is heart balm on dreary days.

As he watches his breath billow and takes sips from the bottle, his nerves start to settle. Snow has already sheeted the rental car parked below. It's been the wettest January on record, he keeps hearing, and the new year's just begun.

For the first time since morning he thinks back to the dream: the egg. It's come to him before. He remembers the same images and panicked wakening back in the Little Italy apartment when he and Connie were still together. Trying to make something he couldn't — taking on more than he could handle, and getting hopelessly lost. Just like back then.

Connie came to the service, along with a few of their old friends. She was the only one he'd contacted, because she knew his mother; he's been long out of touch with everyone else. Seeing them enter the funeral home, facing them . . . he felt queasy. Although for years he'd not been able to admit it, the truth is that circle of friends and colleagues didn't abandon him en masse when the going got rough; he'd shoved them away. Only with Connie has he managed to sustain a tender if distant friendship.

Before going to bed he searches for the cat and finds her crouched between the sofa and the wall. She growls and won't look at him.

~

THE STREETCAR skates arthritically from Bathurst subway station, venting tepid heat. A bright and clear Tuesday morning. Cold whitens the pavement, drifts in vapours under traffic. At Queen Street West Oliver exits the car, which clatters and clunks over the intersecting tracks before regaining its whining momentum. On numb feet he walks briskly toward Ace.

It's been a while since he came this way. Many long-term restaurants and stores along the strip are gone, new names and images under the familiar arched windows and dormers, rusticated brick and masonry. He feels like a traveller returning, a thought that bemuses him. Traveller from the country of Failure? The nation of Dropout? Ace, the restaurant-bar Justin opened in the late eighties, has the same cantilevered sign, the double doors. Oliver's pulse quickens as he steps inside.

Hardwood floors, exposed brick, a busy but not overcrowded lunch in process. It's always felt like a cozy saloon in here. After a call from a hostess, Justin descends from his upstairs office. He looks tense and preoccupied — the Commander Oliver's long come to expect.

"Let's get out of here," he says. "I need a walk."

"Rough day?"

"Not especially." His lips pinch as if that's a dumb question.

The sun casts dim shadows that glide in front of them on the sidewalk. Justin wants to show him Leverage, Ace's new sister establishment up the street. It was practically all he talked about with their aunt and cousins. He strides, hair blown back and long winter coat shrugged closed over a protruding stomach. His style has never changed: black jeans with black boots and dress shirts, a full head of hair worn thick and below the collar, now streaked grey. Handsome, earthy, and looking a bit too well fed, Justin's the image of the aging musician who's found success. Versace combat boots now, not Doc Martens.

Oliver's mind has gone blank, succumbing to the usual intimidation he feels in his brother's presence. He steps around a broken chunk of ice and bumps against Justin, who eyes him without comment.

When they were young, Oliver liked to think that he and his

guitar-playing, punked-out older brother were cut from the same cloth. Justin got the cutting edge, of course, while Oliver hoped he'd just be cool enough not to be embarrassing. He was the good student, the son with no obvious talent, so he went on to university while Justin — always connected, always planning — launched Ace, made it a success, and at some point arrived not at the fringes of local culture, but its centre. Even so, there was a time when it seemed that Oliver, in his own way, would meet his brother there.

Leverage has no customers, not even a lone drinker at the bar. Justin gives Oliver a tour, observed by staff who attempt to seem occupied. The rooms feel stiff, like the shiny hasn't been rubbed off yet. By the front windows they sink into oversized pleather chairs, Oliver leaning to one side to ease his back while he reads the chalkboard. He really must make time tonight for his exercises again.

A waitress appears, trembling with energy. "Just bring us the sandwich specials, we can share them. Thanks, Kirsten." Justin sighs once she's gone. "It should pick up. Everything takes longer now — everything."

"It must be tougher than ever to break in these days."

"It's always been tough — that's just business." A knowing, slightly patronizing smile. "But people keep moving downtown, the city's growing like mad, so that's ultimately good." Same old Justin: seeing the world through the lens of personal benefit. Tory-voting Justin.

"And this is still Queen Street West," his brother continues. "Ace is still jammed on the weekends."

"It's a fixture," Oliver agrees, wondering if that actually matters anymore.

Ace has been a definitive part of the Queen West strip since Justin opened it. It's still the only establishment that celebrates the city's music scene: Toronto music is always on rotation, while framed posters and photos of local musicians and bands hang everywhere — not so up-to-date as they could be, and leaning heavily toward rock, new wave and punk over other genres, but they have authenticity and retro appeal, for Justin is in some of the photos, and the posters are mostly signed. Ace can justifiably be called a landmark: to Justin's youth, to local pride. Even if the stage closed years ago, the bands replaced by branding.

Justin's complaining about the red tape involved in running a business these days. He's drowning in bureaucracy, he says. Costs. Oliver dislikes Leverage already, and not only because of its lame pun on their family name. It feels shallow: concrete floor, traffic signs on the walls, randomly stenciled words and chains — an idea of edgy. Grunge with boutique beef.

"I should have bought the building — Ace's building — when I had the chance and Stanko was willing to sell," Justin's saying.

"Why didn't you?"

"Timing. It was the nineties, the recession. I thought his price was too high. Not exorbitant, not completely fucking insane, like now, just high." In the light from the window, the skin under his eyes looks brown and riddled with tiny bumps. He's grown jowly, and there's something tired and rote about even his complaints, Oliver thinks.

When lunch arrives, Justin brightens a little. He tucks into a pulled pork sandwich, then leans forward and peers at his brother. "So you're still at the gym, okay, gotta pay the rent. But what about your writing?"

"Oh, that's done with." Oliver opens a napkin on his lap, affects a casual smile.

"Really?" Justin frowns. "That's too bad. I don't know if I ever said this, but I admired what you wrote. I mean the last stuff about water. Ahead of its time, it was."

Oliver nods. Justin hadn't said anything of the kind, actually. Not ever. He *had* once offered the unasked-for advice that Oliver should try not to be so dark. "People won't buy gloom" was Justin's insight when Oliver spoke of the difficulty in selling his work.

And how would Justin have spun an article on water pollution to lend it more sizzle?

It doesn't matter. He doesn't want to talk about it. He'd like to be able to talk about their mother, but which mother would that be? Justin always seemed to have a totally different relationship with her. She shared Justin's interests in stock markets, his politics; she was Grandma, part of their family, while he's a satellite. Maybe, when you have two sons, one inevitably becomes the daughter, for that seems what he's always been: the angel in the house, the son who drives and lifts, paints and rakes. Or just the baby child.

"How's Gwynn taking things?" he asks. He barely knows his niece, who must be seven or eight by now.

"Oh, she's fine," Justin says. "A bit sad, you know. But she'll be okay."

"And you?"

Justin's eyes meet his — startled? — then slide away. He combs a hand through his hair. "Mostly, Bro? I'm just fucking tired. Tired of this world. But *that's* not going to change." He pushes his plate aside, looks around the empty room.

"Only if we do," Oliver says, but his brother seems lost in thought. The old Justin would have risen to this bait, been ready for an argument. Even a political debate would be better than silence.

Perhaps a personal conversation between them is simply no longer possible. After all, how long's it been? Since before Gwynn, possibly before Justin's marriage. As children their age gap often got in the way, but for a few brief years as adults they became brothers for real; then that faded. There was no break, no big crisis that pushed them apart, just the gradual assumption through time of their respective natural positions. Justin's a big-canopied tree on a hill, which has only a distant relationship to its kin in the valley.

Justin pushes his plate aside. "Not to rush you, Bro, but we do have ground to cover." He brings out a file from his leather satchel and slides a document across. Oliver picks up the will and stares at the gothic font. It looks like a film prop. He's never read one before, and given zero thought to its contents. He scans the first page: florid legalese, all-caps shouts, his mother's name bolded, Justin's, his own. There they are, what's left of their family: united in black and white at the end of days, before their final separations.

He sets the paper down, reluctant to take in more, and just nods while Justin starts to talk about their mother's investments and savings, about putting the Oakville house on the market. Oliver knows this needs to happen but it feels premature, almost prurient.

"Alright, that was easy," Justin says, and to Oliver's relief, seems done. He leans back in his seat and gazes at him with a soft smile. Waiting for something.

"What?" Oliver says irritably.

"The next part's going to be weird for you, Bro."

"It's *all* been weird."

Justin takes a breath, smiles again. He's genuinely nervous, Oliver realizes, and his own gut tightens.

"There's the house on the island. She never sold it."

Oliver stares in disbelief. No joke, Justin's saying, explaining how this impossible statement can be true. Oliver listens yet can't really hear; there's surging in his ears, the room wavers, his breath comes in little puffs.

"Hey Bro, you okay?"

It *can't* be true. He removes his glasses to wipe his face. Tears. He can't stop them. A napkin in his fist, damp. It's too much, it doesn't make sense; his heart hurts and his breath hitches.

This past was closed, knotted, forever shut. They left it behind when Dad died. Mom took them away, and that house and life slid into the abyss of childhood dreams. Home for real, a place of beauty and belonging – he's never found that again. As an adult he came to accept that long ago, and set aside such hopes.

3

IN THE PHOTOGRAPH, Hilted Arches perches on a leaf. It's black and brown and deep dark green, with markings like pale lichen — as if a little spot of soil had grown wings. Gabe doesn't actually need the image; she knows Hilted Arches. When she closes her eyes, she can picture the white reniform spots and the fine and curious pattern of dark "arches" along its fringe.

Melanchra. Melanchra . . . adjunct? Adjuncta.

Her eyes flutter open. Turn the picture over: correct! Check the box on the list. Check the time: past eleven?

She rubs her face and sits up straight. Just one more stack after this, then bed. Really.

Next!

This moth shimmers like moss lit from within. The Hologram, one of her favourites. *Diachrysia balluca.* Another check. And that makes two hundred.

When she picks up the next stack she reverses them, so she sees only the scientific names written on the back.

Parallelia bistriaris. The Male Looper. A veined leaf. Quick look to confirm, check.

Tegeticula yuccasella. Yucca. An ermine robe.

Cucullia asteroides. The Asteroid, another fave. Body of a broken twig.

Cosmopterix pulchrimella. Chambers's Cosmopterix. Four wind-whipped, white streaks. Crazy looking thing.

Chytonix palliatricula.

Gabe recognizes the name. She knows that she knows this moth. But no image comes to mind. The name doesn't *mean* anything to her, that's the problem. Who the hell knows Latin? There's nothing in the words to connect to, so it's like reading a serial number, a bar code.

With a sigh Gabe flips the card. The Cloaked Marvel — of course!

It's late, she should get some rest, but the names, the freakin' names, she's got to get them straight. She swivels to look at the wall behind her. Pictures of moths cover it entirely, rising from the quarter-round just above the carpet and fanning into branches: hundreds of index-card-sized photos of small creatures perching on leaves, twigs, bark. In black felt pen the common name appears on the border of each, the binomial name on the reverse. Gabe's gaze sweeps along the thick Noctuidae branch to which *Chytonix palliatricula* belongs. Though she can't remember the tribal name either. Tribe Xylenini? Orthosiini?

They find no purchase in her mind, these scientific names. Only by this rote repetition has she been able to press them into memory, bit by bit. And even then, it's like pressing pieces of paper to skin, sticky notes.

Now her whole life depends on that paper.

~

IN THE MORNING Gabe scrapes ice off her car, letting it idle to warm. Temperatures will rise to eleven degrees in Whitehorse, Yukon, today, while here in Peterborough, Ontario, it's sunk to near minus-thirty. Gabe grunts as she reaches across the windshield, straining against tight yet indispensable layers of clothes, pausing to wipe her nose. The cold engine chutters and chugs. The sun looks like a stained penny lost behind the clouds, and offers no heat.

Downtown, a group of people without the luxury of being deterred by deep cold, mostly young men, has gathered on the steps of the shelter like on any other day. The dealers have struck up stiffened poses in their usual doorways. At a red light, while exhaust billows from the dripping tailpipe of the pickup ahead, Gabe watches a man without gloves talk on a phone. His dry grey hands make her wince.

Twenty minutes south of the city, she pulls up to the park entrance. A chain has been strung permanently across it, hers the only vehicle. Some years ago the Serpent Mounds Park closed for winter and never reopened. The Band cited failing infrastructure and lack of public support. The guard booth is rotting, the electronic parking arm broken and the road impassable from storm damage.

After a couple last swigs from the thermos, Gabe cuts the engine. Wind whistles and moans around the car. She pushes the door open.

With snowshoes clasped to her boots, she hikes into the former campground, following a buried vehicle pathway through the woods. Posts used to mark the defunct site grid, but someone has removed them, perhaps for firewood. When she arrived last November the ground was littered with beer bottles and other refuse, and she brought along bags for cleanup whenever she visited. Now the place looks magical: a great white blanket danced over by rabbit feet, deer hooves, bird claws and coyote paws, and her. She warms up quickly by lifting her feet, her breath like steam, the nip of the air on her cheeks a spirited lover, teasing. It's so joyful to be here that she stops, grinning — seized by the sheer magic of this place, this day, her body's vigour and the fortune that's hers to be alive and here right now. From a cedar to her right two large dark wings lift: an osprey, heading into deeper cover.

The same hike almost every day since she returned to Ontario. Rice Lake has always acted like a magnet on her, like she's in orbit around it.

She emerges from the trees near the Mound, raised to overlook the lake. In the snow it looks like any other hill. Gabe climbs to the top, reaches into her pocket for the container of birdseed, opens it and scatters the contents with murmured thanks. Then the other pocket, the bag of cornmeal. Her gesture made, she turns and sweeps her gaze across the expanse below.

The lake is frozen and snow-covered, its southern shore lost in a motionless white haze. In the middle distance the wooded islands look stony, like archaic temples or hoary dreams of the slumbering land.

The Serpent and other mounds in the park were raised by the Mississaugii centuries ago. They chose this place for their dead to rest: not in a heaven above, but a heavenly embrace right here. This place has been beloved for millennia; perhaps that's why she, whose Irish-Black-Acadian ancestry is a trail of forgotten crumbs, feels more at home here. It's easy to slip out of time and current worries on these visits too: to imagine the lake as young and fresh, the Mound builders just over the rise preserving fish, tending fires. Or to scry in the mists and oak leaves' dry rattle a future when all today's turmoil has been resolved, and healing and peace brought to this beleaguered world.

But now is not that time.

This is the time of crisis. Rupture. Grief. This maelstrom has been building for a while, and though she's fumed and ranted about the forest fires, plastics, acid rain, chemical pollutants, radiation, destabilized weather, and loss of so many species forever, and though the downward human spiral has made her vision blur and bones ache with sadness and rage, she's dithered away her time. And now — hello — she's thirty-five. It's time to get serious — do something that matters, for fuck's sake, in a corner where she might make a difference.

She was never a strong student. Finishing her undergrad became a running family joke — *What's the major now, Gabe?* She can still hear Jenn's groan when Gabe told her the news: that she was moving back from Halifax to enroll in grad school.

"For *moths?*"

Yes, dear sister, moths.

"Have you even paid off your student loans?"

Yes she paid, every goddamn dollar, and that's left her with squat, after working full-time for years. Jenn came around; she always did. And in November Gabe left the apartment that was two blocks from the ocean, and her job at Parks Canada, and all the great friends she'd made out east. Traded that life in for "coming home," as Jenn called it: to the city Gabe gladly fled after high school, and the house she'd grown up in, now renovated by Jenn and her family, and a bedroom in the basement vacated by one of her sons.

A wind comes off the lake, dusting Gabe with snow. Her feet and fingers are going numb; she's been still too long. Her thesis supervisor expects her later this morning, to discuss Gabe's project proposal — a Dr. Hegyi, whom she has yet to meet in person. Gabe claps and stomps to get her blood flowing, then with a last loving look at the lake, heads down to retrace her tracks.

This is not the year to linger, to meander dreamily as she's always loved to. She's got to take off these snowshoes and hit the concrete.

THE CAR, the highway, the wider highway. Fields replaced by industrial parks, malls, new housing developments jammed right up to the road, and then, an invisible threshold where the city takes over and she's inside Toronto, all grandly entangled schemes gathered around the traffic grid.

The campus, the parking lot, the laneway to the Earth Sciences building, more coffee? Bad idea. She's nervous enough. The staircase, the grey hallway lit by fluorescents, the department of Ecology and Evolutionary Biology, office doors all looking alike.

"Dr. Hegyi?" This door stands ajar and Gabe raps.

"Yes!" An arm waves her in. "Just a moment!"

Gabe sits in a chair near the door while Dr. Hegyi types. Cycling helmet on the desk, a carrier bag next to it. Snow flurrying outside. Seriously?

"I'm thrilled to meet you, Gabrielle," Dr. Hegyi says, pushing back from the screen still looking at it, then turning to her, standing but not getting much taller, and reaching out a hand. Tamara Hegyi, honey bee specialist and director of the university's Bee Evolution, Ecology and Protection (BEEP) Lab, has the plump cheeks of a child, a girl's sweet smile, short greying hair, and rimless glasses around bright eyes. Gabe guesses that she's not much older than herself.

"I go by Gabe," she says.

"Gabe it is. Now I was just responding to Professor Brimer, I made him aware of you and he'll be joining the committee. Which is one down, one more to go, but Brimer was the crucial one, the one we needed the most. Not that the other member won't matter! Of course they will. Now he mentioned several studies he thinks you should include in your literature review. I asked him to forward them and oh — I didn't copy you on the email. Well I'll send them on. Now I've read the draft project proposal you sent, and it's just fine."

Dr. Hegyi pauses to smile at her again.

"That's a relief."

"Yes, no worries, Gabrielle — Gabe, you're on the right track. And I didn't get a chance yet, but I'm going to send it back with comments. You've a clear idea what you want to do, that's good, so to get ready for the committee we'll just flesh things out a bit more on why and how. Are you looking at disturbances, spatial or temporal dynamics, that kind of thing."

"I didn't realize those aspects would come into the work at this stage," Gabe says carefully, wondering if she even understands what "spatial dynamics" means. She's proposed a straightforward species count in two distinct bioregions where little is known about the state of moth populations. The same could be said for the rest of the country, in fact.

"Oh, it's not too soon to be thinking about them," says Hegyi, who hasn't told Gabe what to call her yet. "It will add value and complexity." Gabe nods. "Now the catches, I wasn't clear what you were planning to do. Are you going to collect the moths for study?"

"Trap, count and release," Gabe says. "That I'm pretty used to from all the Moth Nights in the park, though we didn't count them. Plus I've been doing it on my own for ages."

Hegyi smiles. "Fantastic. I'm so happy that the park you worked at offered such a program. So you will not be collecting at all?"

The question is unexpected. She's never "collected" moths, for the simple reason that when you collect them, they die. She's never understood why anyone would want to do that.

"Uh, no, I didn't see a need to," she says.

"Well, the committee may disagree."

Gabe opens her mouth, closes it. Still tripping over her surprise. "Can we work around that, then?"

"Maybe. If you present good reasons. I mean, persuade them."

"Moth populations are in decline, species are dying out . . ." And it's just, like, wrong?

"That's a start, yes."

"So, correct me here, but I didn't think collecting was going to be necessary. I've been reading studies, and some do kill moths, but not all."

"The kinds of studies you're hoping to conduct *do* collect," Hegyi says. Her sweetness has gone; was saying "kill" too blunt? "How can one be accurate otherwise? See," she continues, "that is the challenge in our field. Obtaining accurate data, assuring that what you contribute has integrity, can stand up to scrutiny, because you are building important knowledge."

"Of course."

"So, we will work on this together!" Her smile returns, eyes shining with enthusiasm.

The meeting ends shortly after, and Gabe wanders down the hallway but cannot find the stairwell door; she must have gone the wrong direction. There's an exit sign up ahead, so she takes that and emerges into a crowded common area. Gabe watches hundreds of students funnel slowly through two open doors. A light has been activated above them, signaling that the lecture is about to begin. As the doors swing closed Gabe glimpses students settling into padded theater-style chairs, opening laptops and notebooks, chatting to friends, texting. Then the sound from within the room muffles.

The light traps she uses for moths lure them down into a bin that is lined with paper eggshell cartons, snug places for moths to stay until released. In the traps used by collectors, moths fly in just the same but land in a jar of alcohol solution. From the outside the traps look identical; the moths trust the light, either way.

4

THE THEATRE WHERE *The Black Rider* will be performed occupies an old factory off Dupont Street. Warehouses, lumber yards and light manufacturing still intersperse houses that once would have been owned by employees before gentrification ignited the market. Justin pulls into a parking lot pooled around the feet of two hydro towers gripping wires. The headlights sweep across a fence gnarled with leafless vines, railway tracks visible through the mesh.

Gwynn puts her hand in his as they walk up the street, talking excitedly. Father and daughter out together, it's a treat for them both. They turn a corner and there's the bright entrance. The show's sold out! In the crowded lobby where they wait to be let into the house, Gwynn is the only child. People notice. Gwynn likes this. Justin stands tall with his arm around her, unabashed, and the patrons who curiously regard them seem to decide they're cute, not weird, and smile at the little girl with her dad.

The doors open; everyone enters and gets settled. The mood is jittery. Oh, how he misses the stage at Ace! Nothing compares to live — nothing. Whether it was managing bands or hosting shows, he used to love it all: how from the chaotic, dubious and rough beginnings — the rehearsals in shitty spaces, the bickering, the fuck-ups and endless feuds — would rise something unprecedented: like a shimmering animal gained life and took charge and then, when it at last faced the audience, roared.

The house lights fade to a blackout. Justin takes Gwynn's hand as they sit in total darkness, waiting.

The darkness continues. It starts to become an ache, a breath held for too long.

What's happening? Is this intentional?

Whispering, coughing, and agitated shifting begin. The audience struggles like swimmers needing to surface. In his midrow seat, centre of the action, Justin likes the play already. Of course he's on Xanax, with two Tylenol 3s as a buffer — just in case.

Lights snap on. Half a dozen actors form a line across the stage, their faces blank, eyes on the audience. They're in white face, like puppets or dolls, with red cheeks and lips. There's something eerily familiar about them but he can't place it.

Beside the stage a band comes suddenly to life and the grinning, bandit-faced Devil enters in black suit and white gloves, his dark hair slicked. He moves down the line of actors with a mechanically smooth motion, like a figure on a conveyor belt. Like he's tireless, Justin thinks. The Devil starts to sing, a cheerful invitation for the audience to join him, and the doll-faced people twitch to life, assuming expressions of confusion, wonder, hilarity, desire. Action begins with a white-collar hero in a suit, a bureaucrat or banker stupefied by obedience, unmanned by office slouchery. He's desperate to win the hand of his Beloved. Sleek Satan appears, and the hero wagers his soul for a real man's sure fire. Gaily the hero sets off, happy to have found the easy way out and believing in the power of purchase. His soul had been like an old key he carried in his pocket. Where is the lock? Who knows or cares? That's an ancient house. His future in-laws are more terrifying, his fiancé a girl-woman with a body that won't settle: in one scene she's a giantess absorbing her man between her legs, in another a shriveled, mewling baby mouthing gibberish. The Devil's allure lies in short-cuts. The piano keys trill. The band charges. You can only sell your soul, not buy it. The Devil chases down the hero and rides him like a horse. The Devil flog-fucks the hero like a horse. His bride screams and swoons and looks ready to gulp blood. The titular magic bullets find their tragic mark, and all things wind to their dreadful, dreadful end.

The lights go out. No one stirs. In the darkness Justin remembers: his mother's body in the coffin, lipstick and face powder. A fake figure he didn't know and wanted to forget.

Outside, he and Gwynn return to the car in silence. He feels like he's on much stronger drugs — mushrooms or acid. He's not even sure he can drive. Everything looms weirdly and with hidden significance: a tattered bag on a branch, a cone of light over a shed — each radiates its Something-ness. The wind hisses over a lip of snow and electricity follows them from above, humming. Justin grasps Gwynn's mittened hand, that little key the one stable thing left.

He promised her ice cream at a local place that stays open year-round. Somehow he gets them there and they sit at a window table. Cars fume by the curb, waiting for people to return with their treats. Gwynn doesn't use her spoon. She holds the tulip sundae glass by the stem and approaches it with her tongue. He rubs his eyes. They're itchy, like they have hairs growing on them. The Tylenol 3s. He wishes he'd brought more, though.

"How'd you like the show, honey?"

She continues licking. Her eyes look flat. She seems obsessed with the ice cream. Maybe she's been traumatized, just like Naomi feared. When he told her about his plans earlier — cheerful and thinking she'd approve of his creative initiative with Gwynn — Naomi fretted about the effects of "too mature content." That micro-managing, protective-hen reaction — it's a fucking vice! He'd stayed calm and reassured, then gone down to his office. His chest hurt. Maybe his heart would give out next.

"Sweetheart?" He taps Gwynn's hand.

She strains forward to lick the top of the sundae then sits back suddenly, her lips rimmed with chocolate sauce. "It was tre*men*dous!"

Justin nods, passes her a paper napkin and asks what parts she liked.

"I liked the music. I liked the piano player. He was goofy. But I liked the devil the best. He was so funny! And handsome."

She picks up the neglected spoon and digs in.

Back home, he kicks off his boots and heads for the cellar, knowing exactly what he's in the mood for: a bottle of Amarone. He opens it and turns off the living room lamps, lights candles on the mantle and coffee table, then puts on Tom Waits's *Rain Dogs*, forwarding to the title song and cranking it.

Gwynn comes in wearing pajamas and her New York Yankees cap. Justin takes a long swig of the wine, then starts to dance. Back bending, arms rising, his hands becoming claws. He shakes his head and makes a beastly groan.

He's a troll.

The troll goes stomping around the room, grunting. With a squeal Gwynn crosses his path and teases him to catch her before darting away.

Oh how we danced and we swallowed the night
For it was all ripe for dreaming . . .

Reg barks and worries, jumping up to paw at the troll, who gets down on the carpet and goes eye-to-eye with the dog. He draws back and starts to yip. Gwynn straddles the troll's back, shouting *Mush!* He slumps around the room with the rider then bucks her off and rears up bellowing. He takes a thick kindling stick from the wood box and a pewter plate for his drum.

"Me! Me! Me!" shouts Gwynn, trying to grab the plate. He dances away, banging on it and laughing. His drum!

The song ends. Justin troll-walks to the stereo and starts the CD from the beginning this time. Everything changes. The troll vanishes, another creature appears. He spins around cawing and flapping his arms. Gwynn stands on a chair in a military pose, the cap low over her face, and barks orders at him, pointing with a wooden spoon. He caws back. She hops down and takes his hands and they dance circles, falling onto the carpet to throw their legs in the air, flipping onto all fours and wriggling their bums as they butt heads, ram shoulders, back up and rush together to stop at the last second, frozen, staring into each other's shining eyes.

The music travels out of the house.

~

THREE DAYS PASS. It's calmer in the house with Naomi gone. After Gwynn goes to school Justin sits in the basement office and works for hours, though mostly, he does bullshit.

Phone calls, banking and the ceaseless data-rain of emails — that's the bullshit. *Work,* the stuff that earns actual *money,* has become ever more difficult to reach. Getting to *work* now first requires this maddening traverse through the tripwire bureaucratic and electronic perimeter ever-thickening around him. He's spent by it: the hours of tap-tapping on the keyboard or waiting on hold or navigating websites and phone menus. Drained. He needs a break before he actually goes to Ace to *work.* Breaks he doesn't have time to take.

He addresses a health code violation given in error to Leverage and still not removed from the system. He follows up the City's inspection of Ace, which resulted in the need to re-modify its bathrooms (again) to meet accessibility and safety codes. Apparently the last contractor didn't know or understand the latest codes, and Justin can only be so pissed about this because it's just not fair: the codes are forever complexifying and he can see a future when every contractor must employ a bylaw official on site, where engineering schools offer adjunct degrees in bylaw law . . . And all this stuff is thinky-dinky detail, it doesn't approach the tasks required to run his businesses: the ordering and staffing, the menu planning.

And if only the bullshit ended here.

But it's in his home and family life too. You can't just send your kid to school anymore; there are parent-teacher meetings to attend, emails and e-newsletters and even texts to absorb, events, interviews, consultations, volunteer time — and this is only grade four, for fuck's sake, not bilateral diplomacy. There's also the parenting issues Naomi wants them to keep abreast of, articles and links she forwards so he can thoughtfully weigh these strategies and threats and worry how to protect Gwynn best and plan her future to avoid the many, many pitfalls that lurk, including his own selfish mistakes.

There's the sunroom building permit, inching through City bureaucracy. And now there's his mom's estate, which he's trying to keep out of probate. There's the tenants in the bungalow, the Littmans — total island weirdos. It took Oliver all of a day to ask to see inside the bungalow again, could that be arranged? Justin did so by serving the Littmans an eviction notice. Island houses aren't supposed to be rented, he is not becoming landlord of that dump; one way or another, ejecting the Littmans will simplify life. And they've not only asked for time above the two-month period, they want half a bloody year, purportedly so that the move doesn't affect school for their children. Emotional emails containing too much information have been arriving from Mama Littman. He's had to seek legal counsel on how to proceed.

As to *why* Mom kept the bungalow all these years and said fuck all about it, he's stumped. She wasn't sentimental — or so he's always thought. If the house was a money maker, she would have simply said so. He found nothing in her papers to suggest a reason. Reading about the house in the will for the first time, he'd felt winded. That house! For years he'd barely thought of it; in his mind it was tangled up with losing Dad, a pain like a leg broken and set wrong, but what's done is done. Yet, did she think her son was incapable of understanding? That he lacks sufficient emotional complexity, as Naomi's angry silences suggest? Does he?

Around noon he drives to Ace. Xanax stabilizes the ride.

In his office he listens to music and reviews accounts. The kitchen roof gets patched, while Leverage seeps blood.

He comes home, spends time with his daughter, takes the dog out and goes to bed. A few hours later he's awake and marking fresh snow as he walks the quiet streets of Baby Point with Reg. Mercedes and Lexus, Lexus and Mercedes. You can only sell your soul, not buy it.

FRIDAY, his late night at Ace, Gwynn with their sitter. Justin visits the downstairs bar just before closing.

Kurt, their most recent hire, brings him his beer. "Queens of the Stone Age," he says with a grin.

"What's that?"

"I heard you listening to them. When I passed your office."

"Huh."

Justin takes a sip. He doesn't like Kurt very much. Doesn't trust his golden-haired hipster demi-cool, or his actor's smile.

"It's better than gouging my eyes out," he says, and Kurt laughs. Justin's not sure he likes that either. The guy's a player. Why did he hire him? One of his personal rules is to protect the staff from bad influence.

"You're a fan, then. Got time to listen to something?"

"I'm just ringing out."

Upstairs in the office Justin puts on his new love: *Splinter,* Gary Numan's comeback CD. Kurt hears Nine Inch Nails echoes right away. "Exactly!" Justin says delightedly. "I've been going back to Numan's earlier stuff ever since I heard this. I hadn't listened to him in ages, I never made the connection, but it's so —" He opens his hands, overcome by feeling.

We were dust in a world of grim obsession

We were torn from our life of isolation
We were pulled from our path of least resistance

The music stutters, violently backfires, becomes gasping echoes of itself, then surges to life. It's the music of resurrection wrapped in breakdown and ruin.

We are yours, we're waiting for you.

They have another round. While the CD continues, Justin throws open the fire escape door so they can smoke. It's almost like old times, leaning against the cold metal outside. He shares some stories of Ace's glory days with Kurt. Opening it had been his mother's idea — yes, he says, nodding, I take no credit, it's true. Because he'd never have thought of something that farseeing, he thinks; he was just another feckless music-scene crawler hanging out in clubs and trying to "manage" bands. Terra Nita. Juvenile Luck. Wanting to be part of something that mattered — and it *did* matter, for a time: the scene blazed into greatness, offering more music than the culture could handle, yet where else could it go? Independent releases. Interest and disinterest from Americans. Tours of the prairies and Atlantic Canada, and video rotation on MTV. His mother had co-signed the loan for Ace and persuaded him to offer food as well as live music. The restaurant took off, yet the combination of bands and dining died, over time.

"It was probably inevitable," he says, "given what's happened to live music. The scene's crushed." And what did he do to help? Closed the stage. Chose the safer path. Image of the grinning white-faced Devil, dancing him into oblivion . . . He stubs out his third cigarette. His throat's getting raw from them and he likes that.

Kurt smirks. "Death by iPod shuffle. Death by Spotify and Google Play."

"It's humiliating, isn't it. The thousand-cuts death from an opponent without a face," Justin says. "But hey, I've been hogging the conversation long enough. Give me another smoke and tell me about you."

It turns out that Kurt's fighting his own battle: scattered family, student debts. No means and nobody coming to his rescue. "That's what makes me laugh when I hear all this talk of 'community' these days," Kurt says. "Like people actually have it, know it. What a joke. Community is all bricks, no mortar. Soon there'll be no family either, just people living solo, side by each, with your own personalized AI companion."

Justin listens feeling tremors of recognition. He snorts, blows smoke. "You think?"

"If people in charge get their way, yeah."

He's decided he likes young Kurt. Or finds him bracing, which is perhaps even better. Since they're feeling so loose, Justin wishes aloud that they had something stronger.

It's two in the morning. Kurt says he knows a place Justin might find cool.

He pulls out his phone and texts the sitter: must deal with a leak in the kitchen, will be very late. Can you sleep over? Her parents are just up the street. She replies in seconds: no problem.

On Kurt's directions, Justin drives them north to Davisville. Mount Pleasant Cemetery opens on their right, its tombstone paths wending from Yonge Street toward other shores. Uptown isn't where he expected to be headed to this secret destination, so the trip's already worthwhile. They leave the car in a public lot and foot down a lane under the sharp moon, vapour coming from their mouths.

At the rear of a brick building they approach two figures flanking a steel door. The men look them over. Just you two? Kurt offers the cover: a red fifty folded over more notes.

The doors are opened and banged shut behind them. They're in a warm corridor lit by sconces. Ahead: low, pulsing music.

They emerge into a cavernous space, more noisy than crowded, in which the music and voices cloud. Brick walls rise several storeys to a sloped roof raised on thick squared beams. About halfway up, a catwalk runs under a gallery of canvases hanging from chains. People are standing up there with drinks, leaning over the railings to watch the floor below.

Justin follows Kurt through sitting areas sectioned by Japanese screens. It's a pretty crowd, everyone shimmering as if dusted with money. He's grateful to be wearing his Prada trench coat, a gift from Naomi.

Kurt indicates a man to see for their purchase. Justin hands him several hundred to get what Kurt feels is best, which turns out to be one small packet of coke, plus crystal, plus some pills.

"Want to ditch your coat?" Kurt tosses his onto a sofa behind one of the screens. "Don't worry, no one will fuck with you here."

Justin sits. The place actually feels like someone's home – the dealer's, perhaps. Down a hallway he can see two bowls for pet food on the floor.

The bar sells full bottles of liquor or wine only and no beer.

"Are you kidding me?" Justin glares at the woman serving them.

"Pretentious cunts," Kurt says, once she goes to fetch their order. He's acquired an even grimmer mood since their arrival. When their Prosecco and water arrive, he sets to work on the blow.

Cocaine. There were a few years Justin had a lot of fun tooting up. Different times. Freer, and oddly, more innocent. Yes, he'll stand by that thought. The seventies – even the early eighties – were still innocent: sex without death, drugs without guilt. And music – oh, the music! Created by people who were passionate about artistry and who actually took chances. Real music, not the cannibalized, regurgitated mixes and mash-ups cynically marketed today.

Kurt chops and gathers and chops again. Justin thinks about Robert Fripp and his work on *Heroes*. The coke is only mildly alluring; Justin prefers the Prosecco and pretty faces. Whenever someone new comes into the room, the people up on the catwalk are quick to study them with feigned nonchalance, though whoever they seem to be anticipating (a celebrity?) never arrives.

An Asian woman in a peacock-blue peacoat enters, scans the room and heads their way. She's lovely. Snowflakes halo her dark cropped hair, tip her leather boots.

"Hey Kurt!" she says, smiling.

To Justin's surprise, Kurt greets her rudely and doesn't invite her to sit. "Fucking mooch," he mutters after her short visit's over. He offers Justin the mirror. "She tries that again and we'll have to swat her."

Justin inhales a line, coughs, and swallows. Showers of sparks fly into his head.

"Amen," Kurt says. He toots his line, swallows, and grins.

Blinking, Justin gazes at the room with renewed interest. Blinders he wasn't even aware of have fallen away. Look at the colours! The people!

"Another?" he says to Kurt.

"Give it ten."

They finish the bottle, do a second line, then decide to find Blue. She's at the bar sipping water. Kurt kisses her cheek and introduces her as Leelee.

"Not to you," she says, the smile gone.

"Oh? What are you to me, then?" He wraps his arms around her and rocks his groin against her hip.

"Apparently no one," she replies, but her eyes engage Justin's and she strokes her neck.

They bring her back to the sofa and put her between them, pour her wine from the new bottle and feed her a line, which turns her all wonderful. Now they have a party with twirl and spin, not just two guys dribbling the energy back and forth. Kurt hands them the pills, explaining that they complement the coke, and though Justin is skeptical (things are *so* pretentious now, back in the day they just drank beer with their coke), he's not going to be a drag. He takes two, washes them down. Their little party gets intensely festive then.

HE'S BEING CARRIED on waves of sound.

He's been exploring the room — for how long? There's no windows. It might be day or night. He might be dreaming. People recline on the sofas, the women's jewellery and breasts slouching. A little crowd hives against the bar.

Something keeps buzzing against his thigh. Ah — the phone. An unfamiliar number, not the sitter's. He puts the device away. There's only one other number he cares about. Because his heart's a dog, waiting for its master. But she's many miles away, his bride, sleeping under strange trees. He's on a long leash tonight.

He climbs the stairs to the catwalk, his eyes alight. He moves as a proud warrior, and whatever his gaze touches springs to attention: women sense and appreciate, men nod their respect. These people aren't a tribe, yet the old affinities and longings flow deep.

Leelee's beside him and he's talking to her at length in front of a painting, hearing himself use the words "roller coaster" and "malfeasance" in the same sentence. Really? They're touching too. Did her hand reach for his arm, or did his arm pull her hand toward him? A gemstone earring winks in her upper ear, just below the helix. Back in the day a stud in your upper ear stood for something: you were a rebel, you had opinions. Back in the day. Then there was the further back, the time of tribes, when a piercing would have to be earned, a rite of passage, sign of womanhood and wisdom. Justin thinks about this as he talks. Tomorrow night Leelee might wear a mood ring or a princess-cut diamond — whatever!

He touches her shoulders, feeling he should reassure her through these waves of perception. Where did it go, all the meaning in things? Who poured it out? How can they gather it again?

Leelee leans in and nips his earlobe because he's stopped paying attention. In response he moves his hand to her bum, then takes it away. She kisses his cheek, tongue-flicking the skin. His chest is swelling, his heart pounding.

Outside he finds Yonge Street and flags a cab, not caring about his car. Once he's heading safely away, the fear falls behind. He had a good time tonight and wasn't a bad boy. He's still very high and the city multi-colourful. He loves riding through it as the sky pales. He loves arriving home.

The sitter's asleep on the couch. Upstairs he checks on Gwynn then slides into bed, thinking of Naomi. The part of her body he knows best these days, besides her face, is the shallow pool between her shoulder blades when he spoons her. He likes to put his lips there.

No state is permanent. He and Naomi can still be happy. When she comes home tomorrow, he'll deposit all his kisses in that pool.

HE WANTS TO LIFT HER over his shoulder. Instead, he carries her bags inside. There's colour in her cheeks and she looks relaxed. He kisses her tenderly and long, holding her, his beloved, his wife. She's warm and surrendering, though not like when they were young; she withholds not so much her body as her heart, he feels, like it's a gem she's keeping close.

He tells her that he's got dinner covered. Why doesn't she see Gwynn, then meet him for a drink? He knows better than to demand face time with her anyway until she reconnects with her daughter.

In the living room he opens wine, lights candles, puts on Emmylou Harris. When Naomi's back and settled in, he starts telling her about *The Black Rider*. It was the best theatre — maybe the best performance — he's seen in his life.

"Better than Devo in '79?" she asks.

"Ha! Life-altering concerts aside." He smiles, so grateful for her memory of his stories. He kisses her brow. But how to do the play justice? The bride's pinched face, her parents' tormented-souls wailing. That grinning, thrusting devil slapping the hero's fat ass.

"It was incredibly artful, yet totally raw," he says. "It felt like it turned us inside out."

"Ouch."

"Yes. But amazing. You know how when you see a great band, a really fantastic band having a fantastic night, and the music shatters all the bullshit that accumulates over everything, all this crust, this dead matter that strangles us?" He's gesticulating, trying to convey the play's effect. It was like realizing he'd been breathing through a tube. Gulping air. It was like the coke. "A hand grenade tossed into the room," he says. "Blam!"

Naomi smiles. He wishes she'd laugh. Always these days she seems to be wanting yet not wanting him. It makes his heart sore.

"Sounds pretty wild," she says. "What did Gwynn think?"

"She loved it. The kid's got good taste. I wish you could have seen it too. Hey, I could find out how many more shows are running. Maybe we could go?"

"Maybe." Naomi tucks her feet under her. "It's a bit of a stark contrast to the headspace I've been in."

"Tell me about it."

Naomi sips her wine. "I thought Gwynn was coming down?"

"She will soon enough."

Naomi stretches her legs and points her slim bare feet. Takes another drink. It occurs to Justin that maybe this is it: he and his wife have nothing to talk about anymore except their child. The chasm's permanent. Still he abides, while she fidgets and resettles, refusing to believe it.

"Babe? Tell me about your time. I want to hear all about it."

"The retreat was great, really great. Just . . . kind of the total opposite experience, I think." She pauses, and he tops up her wine.

"Thanks, Jay," she says, and his heart swells. Don't you see, Naomi? Things can be so easy if you just love me. Just act like I'm *here*.

She describes the retreat centre, cabins in snowy woods, a main lodge. Days spent learning to do nothing, working on her "practise" of doing nothing . . . confronting all the distractions that draw one's attention from the moment, from living. To Justin it sounds like they actually paid for a similar experience. The idea excites him.

"But it's not the same, Jay," she says. "On the retreat you try to reach a place of accepting yourself and training your mind not to be so possessed by those distractions. We weren't allowed to speak during the time, even at meals. But at the end, the most incredible thing happened. We'd been together for a week, right? Twelve of us, never a word. Then when the final meditation was over the facilitators — the only ones who ever spoke — thanked us and said we were now allowed to talk to each other. It was an odd moment because during the last couple of days I felt like I was starting to get somewhere, finally, and didn't want to break the spell. I was still frustrated and felt like the whole thing was incredibly hard, but not all the time. I seemed to be moving out of the swing between resistance and acceptance to this other place beneath them, if that makes sense. It was really interesting.

"Anyway, the retreat was over. Then you know what happened? We all stood up and spontaneously embraced. No 'Hi, I'm so-and-so,' little hug and kiss or handshake. Just 'Hi!' And then falling into these full, long embraces, everybody, like it was the most natural, easiest thing to do. People were strangers yet not strange. Just . . . other selves, almost, you know? We'd harmonized through silence."

Justin slips down to her on the couch, wanting to take her hand but waiting. He still thinks they had a similar experience and wishes she'd see that. It's not like his was less valuable because he didn't struggle through a sanctimonious week.

"And now, it's really over," Naomi says. "I drive home and *whoosh*, here I am again in the big 'what next?'" Her eyes drift down, brow tightening into a vulnerable, lonely expression that Justin knows well — one that lies at the core of Naomi and his love for her, though she seldom shows it.

Yet he doesn't know what to do with this sadness that's taken hold of his wife. This lostness she keeps searching for ways to understand. "The 'big what next' is that you come home to the ones who love you, and the rest will follow," he says, and slides his arm around her.

Naomi's head inclines toward him, but the rest of her stays still. She doesn't even raise her eyes. In a moment she leaves to check on Gwynn.

The next morning he feels rundown, a scoured sensation. Yet he makes his girls pancakes, playing the jolly chef and hamming it up as he serves. After they leave he descends into his office to begin shovelling through the day's bullshit. Lonely, sore. Always sore these days.

The jeans he was wearing on the weekend are still lying there in a pile of clothes. He checks the pockets for the unused packets of crystal. Thumbs them a moment, then puts them away in his desk.

5

THE FERRY TERMINAL for Toronto Islands has changed little with time: it's still a rough, concrete pen, open to the pigeons and bitter wind, with four gates. Moored at the wharf are the same boats that brought Oliver between shores as a baby and boy, and carried his father through his childhood too. Of these only the fleet's youngest and smallest vessel, *Ongiara,* makes the winter run. The others, battened down until spring, float like phantom bergs against the dusky sky and ice-filled water.

Calling Ward's Island, a crewman unlocks and opens the gate with a clang. The huddle of passengers flows through, and Oliver passes the man a paper ticket. The *Ongiara's* flat, open deck, which can transport vehicles when necessary, holds only bicycles tonight. Oliver veers to the narrow starboard cabin, overheated as always, and sits on the wooden bench near the bow. People and chatter push in around him, the horn blasts, and they rumble out of dock.

He pulls off his fogged glasses to dry them, presses aching fingers to his cheeks. The hull bangs and scrapes against ice. Peering out, he watches slabs of it bob heavily or get heaved up and away by the boat's slow passage through the inner harbour; this trench will be re-broken daily for the several-kilometre trip unless the harbour freezes solid. He wonders when that last happened? In the old days Islanders skated on the harbour during winter, were accustomed to weeks-long freezes without boat service. He remembers playing hockey out here with other kids: the crack of a puck in knife-cold air, trees creaking like they'd snap and the dormant-looking city seemingly a world away. But winter has been ebbing for decades — this year being the exception that proves the new rule, the "new normal" that's anything but.

He turns back to the cabin. The passengers — all Islanders, commuting home from their workdays — are gabbing as loudly as ever over the engine and grinding racket. They have teenaged children picked up from high school with them, dogs, groceries. Some call out to their neighbours, laughing, while others have their heads together in talk. A woman with wild grey hair wags a finger at her friend, making Oliver grin. Day in and day out there's a festive mood to this boat ride home, which has to be one of the most unique commutes in the world.

As they close in on shore he leaves the cabin to wait on deck. In the gathering night, the island is a rim of deeper darkness marked by scattered lights. It looks so slight, so fragile, a narrow lap of earth they could easily slip past. Yet it calls, as it has always called. And he answers as he's always answered: with all his heart.

The boat brings him in.

At Ward's Island dock the crewmen toss ropes and knot them tight around the pier cleats. They lower the mechanical boarding ramp and unhook the guard rope, then stand on either side in their winterized hi-vis jackets. Oliver is first and he is ready. He passes between them and up, crosses the docking platform to the road, and strides into the night.

Everything changes once he's left the boat.

It's darker, windier, colder. The island is a long, low sandspit lying between the open lake and the city's dense geometry. Through bare-limbed trees Oliver can see both perspectives as he walks: to the south, the dark open water of Lake Ontario seems to stretch to infinity, the far shore — by day visible as an intermittent, roughly penciled line — so distant that it belongs to another country. And to his right in the north, a tower kingdom rears up at the lake's edge, jubilantly lit, as if the bulrushes were transformed by magic.

Cyclists puffed like birds in winter clothing pass him, their bikes hitched to grocery trailers, bags dangling from handlebars. He's glad when the last exiting passengers are gone, glad to be alone.

Everything changes here. *He* changes here. Home, centre — the place he came into the world. The place their family was whole. Though he was only ten when they left, he's come here countless times since; could walk this place in the dark; knows its body like no other. His father, too, is here. The coloured lights shining through the trees, the boat masts gleaming like icicles, the little woods and bays — all are inseparable from the sound of Dad's boots as they walked to the ferry, the way he cooked morning eggs doused in pepper or lifted their canoe. The paths they took together remain rooted like willow tendrils. And his father also, like a shaggy old willow with a gnarled trunk, one of the battered trees by Hanlan's Point — that's how Oliver imagines him, living out the life that was cut so short.

The road curves and straightens, following a channel separating Ward's from Algonquin Island. "The island" is actually not a singular body but a collective of more than a dozen diminutive islands semi-connected since European settlement. The road starts at Ward's ferry dock and continues past Algonquin, Snake and Centre Islands to Hanlan's Point, some seven kilometres west. No one will be out that far tonight, though. The yacht clubs, marinas, bicycle rentals and cafés are closed until spring. Centre Island theme park is closed. There are no stores, no cars. Ward's and Algonquin hold the only two settlements remaining after the City designated the lands a public park.

As his feet move the lake heaves against the shoreline ice, a deep and rhythmic pulse. This is how the island gets into you, one of its thousand ways. In summer the land is snug and green, with sandy places, woody places, and places that barely ripple, where sober, heavy-lidded turtles bake in the sun like dinosaurs. In those months the meadows turn shrill with frogs and crickets, but the greatest presence of all is the birds: water birds, shore birds, tree birds; birds nesting under bridges and eaves; birds migrating in from the north and south and resting on their journeys. Birds of summer followed by birds of winter. And birds living unseen through every season, known only by their calls at night.

None are audible now, only the lake's chthonic pounding.

On those nights he and Justin used to camp out in the backyard, staying up late with the lantern between them. In the house their rooms were on separate floors and his brother, a decade older, lived on another schedule, but things changed in summer once they set up the tent. He remembers Justin strumming his guitar or lying on his belly with a book, his long body all angles at that point, or propped on an elbow telling tales. Mostly, though, he remembers the songs: Dylan's "Buckets of Rain," Orbison's "In Dreams," Young's "Old Man" and the Elton John classics played on cassette for them to sing to.

He arrives at the pretty wooden bridge that arcs across the channel to Algonquin, where the bungalow that was lost still exists and is now, astonishingly, back in their hands. Why did his mother deceive them? And what did she intend by keeping it?

Midway across, he pauses to look down on the frozen channel. Several houseboats, the same that have moored here forever, are wedged into the ice. He remembers pausing here the day they left for good, setting down his bag while his mother and Justin walked ahead. Late June, close to his eleventh birthday. The unfairness of leaving, the unfairness of the wasting disease that killed his father, the impossibility of going on. He wanted to leap into the water and die, though he wondered if he really would, or get rescued. Then he realized that if he drowned, he'd never get to think about his father again. That seemed even worse. Being united in spirit mustn't have occurred to him; his sense of connection was entirely bound with living.

In the bungalow even after his father passed he'd still surrounded them in the woodwork made by his hands, the creak of the floorboard where he'd stand at the bedroom door in the morning, *Rise and shine, Ollie. Time's moving.* In Oakville, they arrived to a house that smelled of paint and his father's armchair was gone, sold or given away. Oliver's bedroom window looked out to a yard of new sod bordered by a solid fence, beyond it a surreal vista of razed ground where the next suburban phases would be built. A lunar land, a world of dust.

Half a year and his world had imploded. He lived in shock, a numb weight replacing tears. As was their wont, Justin and his mother expressed few outward signs of grief: a sad shrug or sigh at the mention of Dad, a sudden quiet. Otherwise they'd talk over dinner in their usual lively manner, while he sat between, tracing the metallic threads on a plate or counting seconds as he held his breath or mentally connecting the peppered dots on the rug. Their firm grip on themselves — admirable in a way — has always made him uncomfortably aware of his own flux, the currents constantly in motion within. He recalls little else of that first year.

Later, he understood that his mother couldn't stay on the island. She needed distance to cope, wanted to be close to Aunt Fiona, her sister. He came to appreciate how she placed pictures of the four of them together on bookcases and in the front hall — they were never moved — and how she planted a garden in that new sod, re-created a life from early widowhood and a pair of squabble-prone sons. The suburb, too, revealed unexpected life. The next development phase got delayed, so in the intervening seasons he adopted the strange bare ground as his own, wandered its ditches and hillocks of earth that began to sprout wildflowers, mapped the fire-hydrant markers on the otherwise featureless future streets. He discovered that birds came even to this place: ducks and gulls and occasionally swans graced the puddles that gathered over the depressed ground.

In short, he too moved on. Recovered a life.

And eventually, sometime in his early twenties, he returned here as a visitor and lost son. Kept that old life private, always tells people he's from Toronto, which isn't wrong. Yet is. He's an Islander, born into a history that city people like Justin's old Scarborough friends or Oliver's colleagues at the gym have never heard of, habituated to a world as socially peculiar, in its way, as an Amish village.

On the far side of the bridge, his heart starts to thump. He turns west and passes down a narrow pedestrian lane. Others branch off to the north, and he takes the third street in. Older and dimly familiar homes are nestled in the trees and gardens along with newer places built in the local style: cedar shingled, with woodstove chimneys puffing smoke. Boats are laid up beside some, along with bicycles and grocery carts. A few steps more and he's there.

The bungalow's set back in a deep yard, one of the smallest homes on the street. And it looks exactly like it did the last time he saw it: neglected.

There's no garden anymore, just the snow-covered lawn. The enclosed porch that his father built is stuffed with junk, while heaps of god-knows-what bulge under tarps in the side yard. Only the chestnut tree and spruces out back, where they used to pitch the tent, have flourished.

Looking at it now, it's hard to imagine the four of them living here, in a place the size of a cottage.

The tenants are Islanders, of course — that's how his mother got away with renting the house out for so long. Real estate on the island operates by its own rules, governed by the Island Trust. With such a limited number of homes, the Trust requires owners to commit to the community: long-term rentals and absenteeism are forbidden, and interested buyers must submit and pay to keep their names on a very long list of applicants to be contacted when a home comes up for sale. But then, Islanders' kids grow up and want to stay, aren't on the list or can't afford to be; discreet rental arrangements are found. And all these years he thought these *tenants* were responsible for the torn screens and cracked panes, the sagging roof and steps gone unmended. The lack of care made the loss of the house seem not only cruel, but tragic, given that it's an island heirloom: an original, wartime home rescued from Hanlan's Point before the City bulldozed that community to oblivion. His father's eldest brother floated it here to this yard. His Dad purchased it later, moved Justin and their mother over from the city just months before Oliver was born.

Curtains are drawn and lit from within. Why keep it but not take care of it? If he was hoping to find answers tonight, he was wrong. He still doesn't have a clue. Maybe he won't.

But he does know something, now: he can still see himself in that house. He's got to come back here.

On the return ferry, he calls his brother. Once Justin told him about the house, Oliver barely took in anything else about the estate or the will. He's not even clear on the division of assets.

"Oliver!" Justin says, not the usual "bro." Loud music, voices.

"Sorry, you're obviously at work."

"Not a problem!"

"Look, I was just wondering if we could talk again about the house – on the island – and Oakville too? I'm probably going to start working on that place soon, but I have some questions about the bungalow –"

"Littmans will be out end of March." Squeal of a chair pulled out, a belch.

"Well I wasn't –"

"What are you doing right now? Wanna come down?"

"I'm just coming back on the ferry."

"Oh fuck, really? You must be freezing your nuts. Come to Ace! I'll wait for ya."

It's after eight and the last thing he wants to do is head to Ace. But maybe the timing will work in his favour. Justin seems more relaxed than usual, so perhaps they can just have a drink, keep the conversation friendly but to the point.

WHEN HE ARRIVES a hostess calls up to Justin's office. The call takes a while and she frowns and repeats several times.

"You can go on up," she says at last.

He squeezes through the crowd toward the stairs. It's only Thursday night yet feels like a disco in here: women with straightened hair and unnaturally white teeth, wearing tight pants and Bolero jackets; men with painstakingly groomed facial hair — not hairy, not bizarre, not like in the eighties, when looking like a raccoon-eyed androgyne or super-gelled space-alien was a Statement. He feels out of touch, and self-consciously scruffy in his parka and salt-stained boots.

On the upper level there's different music playing in the bar and also coming from Justin's office. He pounds on the door. It's opened by a handsome, fair-haired man.

"And you are?"

"Oliver."

The man narrows his eyes. "Ah! The brother," he says, with a theatrical ripple of his body, like he's been struck by a wave. It's weird.

From inside the room comes an echoing cry: *brother!*

The door swings open and there's Justin at his desk wearing a big silly grin, his dark eyes shining. He looks totally high.

"Baby Bro! Whaddya know!" He grabs Oliver's arm and pulls him into a rough sweaty hug. "Kurt, I want you to meet my brother. Doesn't he have a sweet face?"

"Poetic."

"Yeah, he got Dad's looks." Justin drapes an arm over Oliver's shoulder and he tries to smile, but it's more like a squint. He can hear other people talking nearby but can't see them.

"Let's have a round!" Justin says. "Oliver loves Guinness, get him a Guinness." He waves Kurt away.

Bar noise pushes into the room and is sucked out. From behind Oliver comes a peal of laughter: outside on the fire escape two women dressed in short skirts and heels are sharing a joint and falling into each other with hilarity.

"Oh man." Justin watches them with the air of one pleasantly oppressed. He shakes his head.

"I'm sorry, I didn't mean to interrupt —"

"Hey, how are things at Mom's?"

He's not been back at all since getting Mimi. "Okay, I guess, though I've just started."

"Gonna be hard when you finally have to say goodbye to that old Oakville place, eh?"

"No." He has no idea why Justin would say that.

"Aw, c'mon, I know you claim differently, but you were attached to that place. Like secretly. Like it's your guilty secret: you *really* want to live in the suburbs." He giggles at his own joke.

"Yeah, that's right. You got me." Oliver takes a seat. What a terrible, terrible idea this was. He'll drink quickly.

"Well, you spent all that fucking *time* there, living with Mom."

"I left when I was nineteen."

"*I* left home when I was fucking eleven. More or less." Justin swivels his chair back and forth. "You realize that? *I* effectively left as soon as we moved to that shit hole, the island. I went where I wanted, where I needed to be."

"Good for you," Oliver says. He can't help it. He *really* shouldn't have come.

"Yeah," Justin says, his attention already shifted. "Where the fuck is Kurt?" He stands up. "I need some air. Come! I'll introduce you."

"That's okay. Look, it's obviously not the right time and I'm really not in the mood."

"I know, and that's your problem. But I understand, see?" He throws an arm around Oliver again and pulls him along.

"Hey ladies, give us a toot."

Oliver declines the joint, earning a good-natured sneer from his brother. Since when does Justin party at work? What the hell is going on? The handsome hipster returns with beers and hands one to him with a wry expression that shoots right up Oliver's spine.

Justin takes a drink, leaning into him so heavily that Oliver slops his own. "So this is Thelma, and this is Louise," Justin says, indicating the Asian woman and her white, red-haired friend. He pushes Oliver against the railing and lowers his voice. "Look, we're heading out as soon as we enjoy these. I don't know about these chicks, personally. They're with Kurt." He pauses to stare at them. "Whatever. They're feeders. But it should be a good time. This club is pretty unique."

The women, who've been comparing the brothers, announce that Oliver's "cuter" while Justin's "more manly." "Not *more* manly, just differently manly," explains "Louise." She speaks in that urbane, creaky voice Oliver associates, unpleasantly, with humanities grad students.

"Aw, you two are the ones who are adorable," Justin says. Shifting his arm from Oliver's shoulder to neck, he bends down to nuzzle her nose, dragging Oliver with him. Oliver's glasses go askew. Blood rushes to his face.

He extracts himself and calmly adjusts his glasses. Takes a deep drink.

Justin's touching him again, talking about the club. "Not tonight," Oliver says, trying not to sound terse. "I'm heading home."

"Home?" Justin throws up his hands. "Oh for fuck's sake, come on out with us. On me."

On me. It's the same old line, from those years when they did hang out, after he returned from grad school in Montreal. The pre-Naomi, pre-Connie days: a time of being not only brothers, but friends. In that brief era they saw concerts, explored the city and (though it wasn't Oliver's thing) went clubbing. Justin's energy back then was irresistible: he was generous, fun, affectionate, and knew where he was going.

"I've got a busy day tomorrow."

"Who the hell doesn't?"

Justin heads back into the office, Oliver following. He starts to say that he'll call, but his brother's not listening. "I got something for you, from Mom's safety deposit box," Justin says. "You're gonna love it." Digging in his pocket, he brings out a handful of keys and jangles them. "And I sure as hell don't want it."

Keys to the bungalow.

"Algonquin Island," Justin mutters, angrily working the ring open. "That thing was firewood fifty years ago — they all were, those places. The island's a sandbar. Hello climate change? It's doomed."

"Dad loved it there. That was his home."

"Yeah it was. And then he upped and croaked. Maybe you should think it through before chasing after this little dream."

"I'm not *chasing* anything."

"You're wanting to go back there, sink your inheritance into that place. You're a fucking open book."

Prying off two keys, Justin passes them to Oliver, whose fingers close over them firmly.

His brother shakes his head. "Don't say I didn't warn you."

Then he turns to Kurt, who's been leaning against the wall the entire time. At a nod Kurt opens the door, and Justin and his entourage leave.

6

DR. HEGYI, Gabe's supervisor, enters the seminar room chuckling and talking animatedly with an older man, grey beard and glasses, lined face, he must be seventy at least. From her web search Gabe recognizes him as R.M. Brimer, specialist in tropical insect evolutionary biology and genetics and in conservation entomology; editor of the *Journal of Insect Physiology;* active Professor Emeritus – and their "crucial" committee member, Hegyi said. Still carrying on, the two split up and take the seats at each end of the oblong table, clearly used to the routine. The third Supervisory Committee member, a Dr. Ochoa-Rodriguez, enters a beat later and remains standing as he greets the others by first names and joins their effusive discussion. No one has glanced at Gabe, who chose a middle seat. At last Ochoa-Rodriguez drifts toward Brimer, pulls out a chair and sits.

They keep talking. Rehashing some meeting or departmental communication in a shorthand of obscure references and acronyms. Gabe feels her face growing warm. Academia's like joining a team, she reminds herself, and she's the rookie. That's why she works as a photocopier and PDF formatter ("research assistant") and exam grader ("teaching assistant") for stipends that wouldn't house a horse – at least not in this city.

When the three conclude their discussion, Hegyi acknowledges Gabe and introduces both men with surnames and "Professor," while she is Gabrielle Flynn.

"Gabe," she says with a smile.

"Yes! Well now, the purpose of today, Gabe, is to give you support for this wonderful project you've proposed." Brimer nods. His khaki, safari-style shirt is bleached by the sun, its sleeves rolled up on arms coated in silver hair. His hand rests on a leather-bound daybook on the table, beside it a folder and reusable coffee cup. Ochoa-Rodriguez stares at his iPad screen.

"Now we've had a chat already," continues Hegyi, "and I believe we're all very satisfied with the basic scope of your project. For a Masters level, with the time and resources available, this is nicely honed, and as you persuasively demonstrate in your proposal, your research will address clear gaps in knowledge about the diversity and robustness of moth populations in these regions. Our questions centre more on approach. Richard, do you want to chime in here?"

"Sure," Brimer says with a grin. He's not much taller than Hegyi — certainly shorter than Gabe — and has the gaunt yet energetic physique of someone thriving on passionate dedication. Brimer's lab oversees research projects around the world; his bio lists hundreds of publications and a dozen honours and awards. She was not only surprised and grateful, but also quite terrified to learn that such a person has made time for her.

"First off, it's *great* to see an interest in moths for a change, as opposed to butterflies," Brimer says. He tents his fingers on the table. "I *was* hoping you'd include an urban area, somewhere in the GTA for example. I think it would be interesting to compare findings and would help give your research an added tie-in, for example to inform conservation efforts, green-space planning. It's important to be thinking along these lines in this field." He looks at her intently for a moment. "Who is your audience, beyond scientists? Since it's our job, really, to inform decision-makers —

or at least, try to." He grins again. "But this focus is still fine, absolutely." Hands relax. "And I think with some rethinking, you can improve site selection to capture more interesting data. For example your choice of locations seems fairly random within each bioregion, there's no discussion of what led you to choose each site."

What led Gabe was a road map. She looked at where she'd be staying during her fieldwork — a fishing cabin owned by friends of friends, farmers on the south side of Rice Lake — and where she could reasonably drive on the days of trapping and counting. Her project has to have six sites, three in each region, the traps set on rotations throughout the spring and summer. She hopes gas costs will be offset by the rent she's barely paying.

"I was really thinking about places I could get to, public lands where leaving the trap wouldn't be a problem, road access, that kind of thing," she says.

"Pragmatics, I get it. Necessary. Still, you might consider an ecologically rich area versus an area that's seen more disturbance, for example. Maximize the contrast of sites."

"Yes, that's a good idea."

There's discussion of the various site features Gabe might consider, then lively speculation about other factors her study might track: moon luminescence, temperature, wind speed. Ochoa-Rodriguez, who's been researching the impact of climate change on insect populations, describes how he's used traps mounted on towers to study insect life within and above the forest canopy. Brimer and Hegyi are sharing stories about field trips, study strategies, and Gabe thinks about the University of Toronto library, the fourth largest in North America, where she found entire books on the moths of regions that would fit into southern Ontario — *Moths of the Maltese Islands, Moths of Madagascar, Moths of Hampshire and the Isle of Wight* — yet not one book about the moths of any Canadian province. Her project should be so simple.

"Well, perhaps these are possibilities for another time," Hegyi says, to Gabe's great relief. "You've heard our suggestions about reviewing the sites, making some changes if possible. We can move on, I think?" The men nod. At a glance from Hegyi, Brimer chimes in again.

"The main issue really is your collection method," he says. "I can appreciate completely why you'd want to avoid collecting when possible, we never want to if it's not required. But I just don't see this idea of yours working. Even *if* you've got extremely keen ID skills, almost nobody in this field can ID all the species all of the time, on the spot. It would also take you a great deal of time. Then you've lost your evidence."

"It's also impossible not to lose moths when you're opening and shutting the traps," Ochoa-Rodriguez adds.

"Not many, though. And I'm actually used to IDing on the fly."

"And you can probably do that for many of these moths," Hegyi says, "but we find it difficult to imagine that you won't compromise your research if you don't collect."

Gabe's face must say something, for no one else speaks. After Hegyi flagged live counts as a possible issue, Gabe revised her project proposal to include a few paragraphs explaining that this method was chosen because of species decline, so as not impact certain fragile populations. She hoped this would satisfy the committee.

"I'm uncomfortable with that," she says after a moment. "I'd like to find an alternative."

Brimer shrugs. "I don't see what."

"Well . . . there must be something."

Ochoa-Rodriguez leans forward. He has a serious, gentle face that Gabe instinctively likes. "One of the approaches that I find helpful," he says, "is to use freezing for the species you can't identify, but only those. That way you don't have to alter your trap, you count all the moths you can ID at the time and jar those you decide need to be collected, based on ambiguity of IDing them correctly."

"Or the massive time and energy," Brimer interjects. "But that's possible, I suppose. Still doesn't deal with the lid problem, so you still lose your evidence with all that opening and closing."

"But you do minimize the impact on the populations."

Brimer scoffs. "A few nights' collecting in a season doesn't make any difference! There's no proof of such impacts at all."

Is that true? She'd not researched that, actually; the argument against collecting had seemed so self-evident to her.

"This whole issue of collecting can ignite such *anxiety*." That grin again, his hands raised and fisted. "When in terms of real impact, it's almost completely peripheral to graver concerns — like habitat loss." His eyes strike hers, then dart to Ochoa-Rodriguez.

"That's true," the other man says. "But it's an alternative."

"So, would this be an acceptable option, Richard?"

Brimer shrugs again. "Not really." He glances at Gabe, the others. "But I can probably deal with it. I'll bow to the wisdom of the committee."

Gabe looks at Hegyi, who as her supervisor is really the deciding vote. She ponders a moment, then nods. "I think if you feel strongly about this, Gabe, we can accept this option."

The hour allotted to the meeting is almost up. Thanks to Ochoa-Rodriguez's negotiating on her behalf, the kill jar has been moved off the table, group decimation downsized to death by freezing for the unlucky oddballs who fall into her traps. Gabe herself feels frozen by what just happened.

Hegyi thanks everyone for coming. Brimer nods and says he looks forward to Gabe's revisions. Ochoa-Rodriguez has turned away; the moment of solidarity she felt with him passed. The meeting ends on a cordial if cooler note. Mustering her manners, Gabe respectfully offers thanks and takes her cue to go.

ON ST. GEORGE STREET, the main thoroughfare on campus, Gabe joins a queue of students in front of the street canteens. The food sold from these trucks is mostly salty, greasy, empty calories boxed in wasteful containers, but she has no will to care. She's hungry, lonely, confused and depressed. The food calls to her like a favourite blanket.

Holding the warm container, she veers without a plan past the flank of Robarts Library and away from campus, across Spadina Avenue and into a neighbourhood of narrow, Victorian-era houses on quiet, warren-like streets. The day's sunny and cold but not frigid, the snow on the sidewalks firm — an excellent day for walking, which she's fallen out of doing ever since she first met with Hegyi and the term ramped up. Although the MSc degree requires her to take only one course, she enrolled in two, thinking she'd still have plenty of time for research and her own dedicated learning. She didn't factor in the two jobs, guest lectures and seminars she's expected to attend, and the sheer scale of the learning curve itself. Toss in the Peterborough–Toronto commute, seventy-five minutes on a good day (which most aren't). Visits to the lake have ceased.

A parkette tucked between houses offers bench seating. Now that she's away from campus, it's pleasant just to hold the container on her lap. Across from her stands a mountain ash, which is actually a rowan tree. Orange berries cling to a few of its branches, left by the birds; a chickadee will find a meal here. At the summer moth nights she hosted for guests in Kejimkujik Park, not part of her job at Parks Canada but something she took on, she loved to see the wonder and joy on people's faces. Often it was hard won, moths being small and subtle, after all, and not inclined to show up or perform on cue. But with patience they always did: flying out of the seemingly empty darkness to whir and flit about the lights by the hundreds, touching down on the sheet like acrobats posing so she could share their charming names, point to their shocking colours and shapes and patterns. Where did they come from?

a child would always ask. Right here, Gabe would say. All around. *This* is night in our world: full of dream-spun colour and life.

The sure celebrities of any evening were Saturniidae, the Giant Silk Moths. Promethea, Rosy Maple, Io, Cecropia, Buck, Pine Imperial, Luna, and Polyphemus . . .

Polyphemus was the first moth she herself loved. On hot mid-summer nights when she and Jenn were children, her family would gather in the backyard until late. You could legally light fires in the city back then, roast marshmallows, watch stars. She was always enchanted by the moths that flew to their porch lights, always scampered after them, and one night her father pinned a white cotton sheet to the clothesline and lit it with a black light bulb clamped to a tripod. It was an invitation, and Polyphemus arrived. Alongside the other moths, flies and strange miniature creatures that crawled or perched on the sheet, Polyphemus was as our Sun to the stars. It didn't even look like an insect, for it had *fur*.

She drew as close as she dared, looking to her father for assurance, trying not to squeal with excitement. If a cinnamon-coloured teddy bear sprouted wings – magical wings – that might describe Polyphemus. Velvety, rippled and banded, the wings stood wider than her outstretched hand. But most astonishing of all were the markings, for on each forewing sat a tiny, transparent circle: a window. How could that be? And what lay on the other side? Was it a different world, like Alice found? Her father touched the wings carefully and they fanned open. Oh! Two great eyes peered back, their irises lemon-yellow, their lids twilight blue. Fairy eyes. Owl eyes. Eyes made to see in darkness, watching her.

Gabe sighs. Things were going to be straightforward, she thought, back when she applied to the program. But what had she expected, enrolling in a scientific degree? She liked the committee members, really; they were just trying to steer her so her efforts would matter. She feels an innate admiration for anyone who devotes their life to insects, the perceived pests of the natural world; it's like helping criminals or the incurably insane. And of course one should aim for accuracy in research.

Perhaps if she studies her index cards hard enough, the freezing will be minimal.

Alternatives? No savings, no rich parents, no real funding, no job, no more apartment.

This is the road ahead, Gabe, the only road. Knuckle down and buckle up. She opens the container and stares at the glistening mess.

7

WAITING TO PICK UP Gwynn from school, Justin listens, as he often does, to a pair of women talking. It's crowded out front here, so they stand close to his vehicle on the sidewalk; he can hear every word. The conversation's pretty inane, sure, but that's not what makes his skin crawl. It's their pitch, the *way* they speak – that awful Mommy Voice he hears everywhere: a strained and shrill inflection, like the speakers are cinched into undersized pantsuits. It's *so* unattractive and *so* freaking sad. These women are being asphyxiated, but do they know it?

After Gwynn was born, Naomi stepped into one of these suits. He didn't ask her to; he expects responsibility, not self-repression. Yet she seems to feel it's as necessary and inevitable as wearing a three-piece on Bay Street, and nothing he says makes a difference.

The Mom Suit: this attire is less formalized than its business counterpart, though it comes with as many rules and regulations. A stiffness has crept over Naomi, and all that breathing and stretching in Pilates and meditation hasn't softened it – in fact, it's getting worse. Tighter. Harder. Not the hardness of strength, but brittleness.

The new Naomi has all these sensitivities. She's always stressed, and takes offence. Is it the toxic mommy blogs she reads? Has he been overindulgent, too compromising, and fed a growing neurosis? Or has he failed to be present or understanding in the right ways?

The change in Naomi has crept over their family. A husk has grown up around them. On the inside there's life, but it's so wound up! So often when they're together he feels like he's trying to loosen the receptacle without shattering it. Nuclear family indeed.

The women he's been listening to have ended their conversation and parted. Justin checks his phone. A text from Kurt: the thumbs-up icon. He'll have to hit the bank before going to Ace.

So he's been doing coke. He's not proud of that, and it won't last. But for now, coke supplemented with a little crystal here and there is helping him cope. And he's discovered how much he's been doing just that: *coping*. Not living. Not thriving. Just edging through the days, a soldier hoping to make it back to the ditch without explosions, losses. What amazes him more and more is how he's managed to live this way for this long. The toleration.

Naomi's left town again. It's part of her "program" to do these retreats, so she claims. To go away. And this time he just thought — fine. He's losing patience with her wall of cool. And with the depth of her non-starter approach, too, her daunted dithering when it comes to getting back on the horse — working again. His cautious suggestion that extra income would be timely, given the precarity of Leverage, made her practically twitch.

Long ago he told her she could always count on him, and to that he will hold. But it seems to him now that he's the one being held.

~

"*THAT* ONE. The streaky blonde."

He follows Kurt's gaze. Blonde heads abound, and they're all streaky.

"There. Making the porn face. The lips!"

"Ah."

The woman in question is managing to combine a pout with a smile. Her breathing seems off. He's reminded of a small-mouthed bass, actually . . . and the word *bimbo*. A seventies concept too tame for these times, however, almost sentimental.

"She looks stuffed," he says.

"It takes practice. Look around."

"A Socially Transmitted Disease?"

"Supposed to invite cock, I think, but it makes me afraid."

At Kurt's signal they move through the crowd, ploughing toward the bar. Who are these people? That buttery blonde on the stool there, easily sixty, looks like a pale dumpling squished into leather pants and jacket. She's like the matriarchal model for younger, salonified replicants scattered about the club. The male patrons are mostly black-haired. Indian, Persian, Asian and unknown, wearing jackets with loosened ties, like they've been on the prowl since work or worked late — the price of living in a sky box.

They wedge open a place against the bar. Kurt baits his hand with a fifty.

Sheppard and Yonge: along the crest of a ridge, condominium towers serried above the roaring 401. As they ascended the exit ramp earlier, passing beneath them to merge with local traffic, Justin felt his personality diminish, weakened by this collectivist zone. Arriving at a plaza somewhere. The club between a dry cleaners and pet food chain, people lined up outside, instincts with wallets.

The Kid — Sherwin — parked them out back so they could do a bump. Then they were lions. They didn't have to stand in line.

"Bimbo?" Kurt muses. "That word's made a comeback. Been 'reclaimed.'" He laughs at Justin's face.

"I guess nothing is too low in these times," Justin says. "I never went for that type myself, except this stripper once. And she wasn't really one, she just had to play one for work." Kurt's too young to get that joke. "She was cool, and bimbos were never cool. That's why I never understood the appeal."

"What was she like?"

"Smart and fun. A fun person." Justin smiles. "She was from the Sault, but I met her in Montreal when I was on the road with Juvenile Luck. Then she showed up to a gig here one night at the El — the Mocambo — with a girlfriend. They'd taken the bus down for it. I think she was really hoping to fuck the singer, but that was a long line. We ended up getting busted by a bouncer in the bathroom."

Grinning, Kurt clinks Justin's glass with his own. A cool pebbled tumbler with a satisfying weight and twenty-two-year single-malt within. They lean back, watch the crowd. The coke sets him on a throne. The cover band, like a live jukebox, plays a stream of classics to keep the energy steady. Leelee and her friend have been swallowed on the dance floor.

"You know what's really weird about that night? That was the night I first met my wife. She'd come to the same gig." Hoping to fuck the singer too, he's always thought, though Naomi denied it.

Oh, Patty Lowes — where is she now? Stunning girl: glittering eyes, beautiful skin, black hair you could keep warm in. Bold enough to leave the Sault, but for where? Hull? St. Catharines? Probably got married once or twice, has a couple of kids, works to pay the bank like everybody else and is bored out of her fucking tree.

Prince is right: you're better to go crazy.

Kurt leads them to a banquette occupied only by coats, which he shoves aside. Two men at the next table are ripping up chicken wings. The coke gives him a ravenous feeling but not for food; his hollow stomach buoys him, he needs only air and these amber drops to moisten his tongue. It's wonderful.

A dark-skinned guy wearing a houndstooth jacket and heavy, Geek-vintage-style glasses slides in beside Kurt, emanating blandness. Their Man, Justin assumes.

What happened to Naomi? What happened to the woman who yanked off her panties in his car on their third date, when he'd been assuming he was just dropping her off at home? Their first years together were so free-spirited. Naomi wasn't looking for marriage and neither was he. And then he realized he needed her, would be a fool to lose her. She accepted everything he offered: living together, marriage, a child.

There was a time when she said he was her hero: it was he who made her grow up and realize there was more to life; it was he who'd enabled so much for her. She didn't say "hero" jokingly, either. She was serious.

The bump's wearing off. Under the table Kurt passes the freshly purchased packet as if reading his thoughts, and minutes later in a washroom stall Justin chops himself a short line and rejoins the stars.

The women are back and a centre of gravity is forming at their table, pulling in strangers, forming a mini-party zone. Suddenly he's meeting half a dozen people, laughing. Kurt gets to his feet and does a back bend like the guy from the *Matrix*. His long hair brushes the carpet and then he springs up to applause, pink-faced.

Leelee holds her hand over her mouth when she laughs and it's cute, but Justin likes her Latino-looking friend better — Teresa? Melissa? He thinks of her as Cynical Girl. Mouthy, energetic. On the trip up she amused him with her verbal slugs at other drivers, pedestrians. When the band takes a break, he suggests they leave, is everyone okay with that? Hell yeah, says Cynical Girl while the others are still indecisive. We've done our time here, we've given this place all it *deserves*. She grabs her coat.

It's a chilly night, not so cold as damp, and Cynical Girl huddles into him as they wait for the Kid by the curb. "*Awesome* to have a driver," she says. "He just hangs around?"

"That's what he's paid to do."

"Nice."

"Our chariot!" Justin shouts when the Kid — *Sherwin*, he reminds himself again — arrives. Okay, he's acting a little giddy, but the Infiniti is so black and shiny and warm inside — how happy it makes him! They tumble in, leaving the dealer with the retro glasses and two other women standing outside. Cynical Girl flings her leg across his. Retro leans toward the open window, asking where they're headed.

Justin looks at Kurt. "What about your place? I've never even seen your place. You be the host!"

Shouts for "Kurt's Place!"

"That's 'cause it's the size of a box. *You're* the property owner."

"You have properties?" Cynical Girl says. "You're like, Monopoly Man."

Hands thump the roof. The car seethes with little dramas all happening at once and there's the Kid's puddy-coloured, honest face turned to him from the driver's seat, awaiting direction . . . "Boss?"

A hot tongue's in his ear.

"Take us to Leverage!" Justin says. "Staff'll be gone by the time we're there."

Kurt relays this outside and off they go, racing downtown. It's like tobogganing to music. Why are all four of them sitting in the back seat? Don't know and don't care. He's never ridden in the back seat of his own car, especially with a woman's warm leg on his.

Oh to be free! Gwynn's at a friend's until Sunday and there's nothing, nothing he needs to do.

Cynical Girl laughs, flung against the door. She pokes fun at Kurt, but never at Justin. He's her ballast.

"You're better off *not* calling yourself an actor in this town," she's telling Kurt. "Like, introduce yourself with something that sets you apart — fucking anything's more interesting than 'actor.'"

"He's studied yoga," Justin offers.

"Him and a million others. Come on! Did you go to school — I mean university?"

Kurt's eyes widen as if from a private joke and his lips turn up in a slow grin. "I did. I studied *architecture*," he says, with mock self-importance.

"You're a motherfucking architect? Dude, hello? Why the fuck are you trouncing yourself with this 'actor' identity? You're an architect!"

"I'm two credits short."

"Fuck that. Do you have an acting degree?"

"And I owe forty grand."

"So? You're going to let the University of fucking Athabasca-Saskatchewan, fucking Farmers' Wheat Pool Wankers hold you back?" She and Justin laugh and laugh, he has tears running down his face. "That's crazy!" she shouts. "You shouldn't be paying for your education anyway!"

At Leverage the Kid parks out back and Justin enters through the kitchen first to ensure the place is empty and the front blinds drawn. After sending the Kid home with cab fare, he brings the others inside and turns on lights, feeling a swell of pride. Behind the bar he unlocks the cooler and takes out two bottles. *This is fantastic! Is there music?* He counts four flutes. Someone pounds on the front doors: Retro and his posse.

"Let them in," Justin tells Kurt. Adds four more flutes. There's only seven of them, but he likes a round number.

HOLDING TWO WARM WAISTS, Justin dances. The women are barefoot. He's taken off his shoes. They tooted the coke then smoked the back-up crystal and now he can't stop moving, his nerves so wired his teeth are chattering.

"Water! Remember to drink water!" Cynical Girl says, passing a sloshing glass.

"Thanks, honey."

He closes his eyes, twists her fingers in his as they move.

In the bathroom she pushes him against the door. With a low giggle, she reaches under his shirt and he cups her breasts through her blouse. It's all friendly fun, dipping his fingers in the warm river of her back, and just earlier he was talking about Patty Lowes for the first time in years. It's like his life is winding backwards or reset- ting . . . the path of responsibility bending round to rejoin a former route. Something big is changing in him. The design's unclear, but he can feel the old stitches unravelling —

There's no bouncer here tonight. Cynical Girl rubs his cock through his pants, squats.

"You don't have to do that," he says, stroking her hair.

But she insists she does and so he surrenders. He sits on the toilet lid while she kneels on his jacket. His cock is hard, yet kind of numb. Watching her, he sips his bubbly wine. *A king on his throne* — funny.

Can't sit still though so he pulls her up and leans against the wall to watch in the mirror. She watches herself too, seriously, as she works his cock. She seems to be thinking. Suddenly she stops.

"There's no security camera, right?"

"Are you kidding? No! That's illegal."

"You never know."

He sighs, thumbs her hair, and with a gentle movement of his hips encourages her to continue. "I understand, my dear," he says. "I understand."

THE BAGGIE OF CRYSTAL is down to a few nasty bits. A lone woman dozes on a banquette while Kurt talks intensely with Retro, who keeps stretching his arms way behind his head in this uncom- fortable-looking way.

Where's Cynical Girl?

Almost delirious with drugs and wine and ordinary fatigue, Justin lopes toward the bar and slams into a table. Getting off his knees, he hauls himself onto a chair to catch his breath.

Have to pee.

Bathrooms — locked?

Justin rattles the knobs then pushes into the kitchen and leans on the steel door. It opens with a gravelly noise like a cave unsealing and sparrows burst from the pavement. For a moment he thinks they've flown out of it.

It's morning: shimmering light, steaming earth. Rain has come and melted the snow.

Hand clasps his phone: 5:54, no messages.

As he's pissing into a puddle, bracing himself against the wall with the other hand, a car rolls up the lane. A police car.

HE GETS KURT to send the others away, turns off the music, cleans himself up, checks over the bathrooms, tidies the tables and chairs and rubs down the bar until a watery reflection of his face frowns at him from the wood surface. He fills a carafe with water and sliced lemons and carries it to a table where Kurt sits scrolling through his phone. Sun slants through the blinds.

"Did you check the bathrooms? No puke or condoms or whatnot?"

"Done. They're clean."

Only now does Justin tell him about the cops. How the car stopped, and two officers emerged. Was he the driver of the Infiniti? He must have looked terrible.

"Soon we'll all have cameras stuck up our asses." Kurt rubs his eyes, glances again at his phone. "My friend's posting pictures of a house he bought back home, fully reno'ed, big trees outside, two-hundred-and-twenty grand. His mortgage costs less than half my rent."

Justin makes no comment. Such humiliations are borne these days.

"I dunno, Regina's not looking as dull as it used to. You coming down?"

Justin nods. The high diminishes in a lurching way, like a jet hitting turbulence and losing altitude. Less high now than when he talked to the cops, he's still far from sober: he can't stop his leg from jogging under the table, his heart palpitating as he sips the water, and his emotions trail behind him in the clouds. That conversation with the cops — *Have you been driving, sir?* — he can't even take it in yet. The incident patrols the ground below him.

The lemon slices pick up the sunlight shining into the room. For a moment or two he's floating with that fruit, which ripened under a tropical sky. Of course! *That's* why food nourishes: it absorbs the energy of the sun. The *Sun*. It absorbs the energy of the rain and the earth. It even absorbs things that have died, and passes on their life. And he's never thought about this once in all his years. How absurd, when he's had so many stupid thoughts.

More than anything he wants to go home, but there a shadow will pounce: he'll have to consider the blow job, the drugs. He hates secrets. He has the honest person's instinctive fear of lies.

"You got anything on today?" he asks Kurt.

"Nope, got Saturday off this week."

"No great plans?"

"Just tiny ones."

Kurt sets his face on his hand so the skin pulls his cheek. In the sunlight his pupils are golden. "I'll probably read. I'm reading that biography of Steve Jobs."

Justin shakes his head.

"What?"

"Biographies. They're mostly gossip. We should be reading about our own lives. They're being written every moment."

"Then tell me how to find the delete button."

Justin's mind whirs, like a battalion of guns tracking a target. But the guns are heavy, unsuited to these modern threats. Bureaucratic warfare: unwinnable struggle against a hidden enemy. You can't blast away debts, economic policies, taxes, laws, socially engineered fear —

"I have more stash," Kurt says. "We could go to Leelee's."

That's a terrible plan, Justin thinks.

THEY ARRIVE FOR BREAKFAST: coffee, toast and sliced bananas. Leelee's in a green kimono and flip flops, with a friend or roommate or lover, a woman dressed in a long black T-shirt and red knee socks. In the living room there's only a couch to sit on so everyone bundles together and Kurt gets them high. Justin hoped Kurt had coke, but it's more crystal.

The toot fires him into the ether just the same, though with a pounding headache. He looks down on the city. His house? There, that Monopoly piece.

The women are chattering like animals gone mad and he can't sit, he jumps up and strides into the kitchen, heart racing. Yanks open the fridge a few times to enjoy how the jars rattle on the shelves. Through the archway he can see the others: Kurt playfully sucking Leelee's nipple while her friend kicks him. It's too much — should he go outside?

He steps onto the balcony, which is many floors up. This building's just another game piece and he needs to *move*, he's a warrior-god who must ride the wind, shout and swing a hammer. He goes back inside. Leelee's friend comes in and wriggles against him, dancing to music he's not realized was even playing and it's Astor Piazzolla. As she dances she makes eye contact, smiling, and runs her hand along his waist, first one side, then the other, back and forth. She's not nearly as comfortable to be with as Cynical Girl, but graceful, and he enjoys her touch, enjoys feeling that his waist is desirable. He starts to play with her too, raking his fingers down her arms, turning her, now her waist, her lower back . . . His head jerks away from her smooches, but his hands find her hips as she performs a little thrusting for him, laughing, her nipples poking against the cotton shirt like sharp new roots.

"Oh my god," she cries, collapsing on his shoulder. "Maybe we should fuck now, when it's feeling like this."

"So fuck me now," he croons. He's joking, really, and when she tugs on his hand he pulls her back, wanting to dance longer. They move around the kitchen in an improvised tango, swaying against each other, shoving aside chairs with their feet, laughing. Then she tugs at him again.

In the bedroom she pulls off her T-shirt. It's a dark room, a purple blanket or poncho draped across its window, and her body is pale, her shape strange — unfamiliar ground, though still, ground. He touches her. She's soft, with a woman's soft belly. He'd like her to feel good.

She tells him what to do: lie down, crush my ass in your hands.

She's dry as the desert inside.

"That's okay, it's okay," she says breathlessly, and pulls out a bottle of lubricant and condom and puts them in his hands. He wets her, warming the gel between his fingers first, then sheaths himself. She mounts him, and he does what she asks but he needs to move more. He flips her onto her stomach and gets behind, heart pounding.

To be wild animals again.

Though not totally; there's no stamina involved, his erection is preternaturally enduring and, pushing inside of her again, he seems mostly outside, observing himself: willing vassal of the senses with her cunt ring catching his cock hammer.

And so — and on — they wild each other.

And so — and on — he looks down on them.

More gel!

— into the tractless forest —

She's been moaning and yelling and grunting and squeezing his balls for ages and he finally comes in a single hard jolt.

He peels off the condom, glances at her where she lies panting, one arm across her torso.

Dressing, he checks the time. Sudden recall: Reggie's not been fed or walked since — yesterday.

He takes a piss, rubs his face with water, soaps and dries his hands thoroughly. She's asleep or just shut-eyed when he leans into the room to say goodbye. Kurt raises himself up to offer another small hit to get him home, but this time he declines.

Outside, he walks to the nearest corner then calls a taxi. Sunshine on cracked pavement. A bus barrels past like it's fleeing a catastrophe.

Reggie's trembling with joy when he arrives, but there's guilt in those eyes too.

"It's okay, buddy, it was my bad. I'm sorry." Justin pulls the dog's ears wearily, hugs him. The main reason he stopped using coke years ago wasn't the drug's cost, but its other price: the crash that follows. You don't just smash into the ground, you plunge underground.

After letting Reg into the yard and refreshing his bowls, he locates the miserable turd pile on the laundry room floor and removes it. He sheds his clothes right there and chucks them into the washer.

Running a shower, catching water in his mouth. Tastes like metal. Lungs and nose burning. In the stall under the spray he feels no guilt or fear of what's to come, only emptiness. He plops down with his back to the tiles, not focusing on any thought or object. One thing alone remains in his world: craving.

8

ON THE SECOND SUNDAY in February, Oliver heads to Oakville in another rental car to start clearing their mother's house. Four weeks out from the funeral, he's run out of excuses. The task feels like ascending a mountain by taking it apart; at some point it will be over yet he'll have gained nothing but empty space.

He dials up the thermostat. Warm air gusts from the vents, softening the stillness that's settled here.

The last time he saw her was the week before she died. His monthly Sunday visit. In summers he came biweekly because he cut the grass, but in winter once was enough for the Costco run and vacuuming and other tasks she'd line up. Then, usually, dinner and a TV movie, chance to unwind from the day's inevitable petty furies.

"Two bags of litter."

"I know."

"Make sure it's unscented?"

"I know."

"Not the plastic tub one, either."

"I *know*. It's called Kwality Kat."

"That's the stuff in the tub."

"No it's not! Kwality Kat is the one you always buy."

At home, the whole routine would start over.

"Put one beside the litter box —"

"I know."

"And the other —"

"On the shelf behind the fucking stairs!"

"Ooh la la, someone needs a good night's sleep."

At least she never got really angry. He used to imagine he'd prefer some messy, revealing rage to her infuriating self-control, until he got to know people whose parents didn't possess it.

He wanders room by room, wondering whether to begin with the most private areas or least, and since he can't face the basement, opts for the middle bedroom she used as a den: computer desk, bookshelves and filing cabinet, a cornered and dusty exercise bike (is there any other kind?), assorted yoga balls sulking. He's brought cardboard boxes for books and anything else worth keeping, and many plastic bags for the rest.

He didn't check in with his aunt. He contemplated visiting her to ask about the bungalow, in case she knew anything about her younger sister's intentions. Decided against it. It's doubtful Fiona would, and if she did, she's honed tight-lipped reserve to a high art. Oliver pulls books off the shelves without glancing at the titles, getting on with the job. Pointless to go there.

Justin has no interest in the bungalow. The will splits the estate in two, and through emails over the last week, they established that they'll sell this place and divvy the sum, then Oliver will buy out Justin's share of the island house. The other money left in the estate should provide amply to fix it up. His brother was an ass that night at Ace, but was right about one thing: he *is* going to move to the island, as soon as he can make it happen.

Why the hell wouldn't he?

There's nothing left for him in the city; that's been obvious for a while, so he'd be better off just accepting that. He can commute to the gym or figure out something. Maybe find a better home there for Mimi, the cat who eats the food he puts out and leaves turds and hairballs. Lately, when he's awake and up in the night, she'll emerge from under the bed and perch on his upholstered chair across from the sofa where he's reading, her tail twitching, green-rimmed eyes staring at him.

What?!

"Loving the Alien" comes to mind. Except he's living with one.

Two bookshelves cleared. He leaves the boxes open to look through later. Checks the time. Decides to change course and start on the bathroom. Opens the vanity drawers: tubes, bottles, drugstore watches, soap rinds in assorted scents and colours. He's the angel in the house. He's seriously overwhelmed. His mother was cheap with herself but shrewd; perhaps she hung on to the bungalow as an investment? Maybe there was nothing personal in it at all, and though he longs to believe she kept it for him, or to honour his father, that might be wishful bullshit. And he'll never know. Angel in the house, forty-something bachelor who torched his career, was he too much a loser, a baby, to be given even this confidence? He upends the first drawer and sweeps it all into a bag.

Connie told him he shouldn't be doing this work alone, that he should ask Justin to come help. Not going to happen, he texted back. Have his brother on his case? Once all this estate business is sorted they should just go their separate ways. Justin can carry on being Justin — which these days, apparently, means being a sleaze-bag. And he — he will leave, and live quietly through the seasons in his father's house. That will be enough.

~

HE'S BUILDING AN EGG. It must get finished. The ovoid structure stands before him, partially ribbed and planked. Hurry! He bends forward, calculating and recalculating cuts, scribbling frantically.

Yellow light. Silence and scent of stone.

Hammer. Nails. Saw. The next rib. His pencil marks look like hieroglyphics —

Oliver starts awake. Mimi's roaming the bed and muffled sounds — not the usual night street noises — are coming from outside. Voices. He hears footsteps on the inside stairs below his apartment, the door to the house closing with a thud.

Even in a building where people live side by each in relative anonymity, one acquires a sense of normal and abnormal disturbance. Without turning on the lights, he rises and goes to the living room window. He doesn't know what he's expecting to see, but it's certainly not the scene playing out on the front walk: Rosh, his downstairs neighbour, is standing handcuffed and hunched between two cops. A third stands in front of him, speaking. Reading him his rights? The porch light illuminates Rosh clearly, his dark hair pillow-awry. Under his open parka he wears a white T-shirt and pajama bottoms, and he looks frightened and outraged at once. Straightening up, he shouts at the policeman who's talking.

"Show me!"

Oliver can't hear the officer's reply. What the hell's happening? Should he go down and see? Or would that make things worse — embarrass Rosh? The officers turn Rosh and yank him toward one of two waiting cruisers. They fold him inside. Then the cars drive off.

Oliver watches them vanish around the corner. The street's empty, quiet again.

It's four a.m. He lies on the sofa, pulling the blanket close. He's trembling and cold. What he just witnessed replays again and again. Why didn't he go down? But why would he? The images are joined by others, things he's seen on the news or in films but never in person: Jews dragged from their homes, the Rodney King beating, midnight disappearances.

And he just stood there, watching.

But what does he know about Rosh? A long Sri Lankan-looking surname on the Unit 2 mailbox. A man who remembers bygone environmental journalists and grew up with cats. Who seems kind, and intelligent, and good company. Oliver has no idea what he does for a living, though. He's away a lot, the apartment often dark.

Arrested for what?

The next day at work, he tries an internet search but can't remember how to spell the surname. Skills rusty. Shameful.

No lights shine in the second-floor apartment when Oliver gets home early that evening. He keeps the music off while he assembles a pizza from frozen crust, slides it in to bake, starts washing romaine for Caesar salad. Toward eight he hears what he's been waiting for: footsteps on the stairs. He removes the pizza and goes out the door and descends as Rosh is still opening his, a cloth shopping bag hanging from the crook of one arm.

Rosh glances at him. "Oh, hey Oliver."

"Hey." He stops. "How are you?" Rosh looks ragged: chapped lips, dark circles under his eyes.

"I've been better." He turns the key, pushes open the door and looks at Oliver again. Understanding comes over his face.

"You heard what went on last night?"

"I did. And saw."

Rosh crumples a little.

"I was already awake," Oliver says, not wanting to add to Rosh's upset. "I looked outside."

"That must have looked bad. Probably freaked you out a little."

"Well, yeah. But I was worried too."

Rosh nods. "I'm pretty fucked up now. I spent the night in jail. First time . . . Got home this afternoon still wearing my PJs. They called me Mr. Suds, because of the pattern on the flannel. You know they plucked me out of bed?" He nods at Oliver's astonishment. "That's right, in the apartment and right into my room. I woke to a man pointing a gun."

"My god."

99

"Yeah. And I'm sure this door was locked." His fingers brush the hardware. "If they knocked or rang, I didn't hear. Shit lock, though. Maybe they popped it."

"What about the downstairs door?"

"I thought it was bolted but there's no damage, so maybe I or someone else left it open? I don't know. They told me they had a search warrant, but I never saw it." *Show me.* He says he thought the gunman was a thief at first. Several more policemen were in his apartment. They claimed they had a warrant to arrest him and did.

"That's incredible. Horrible." Oliver can barely believe it, yet he saw it, and what's more, he knew at the time that something wasn't right. Felt it. But why would the police act this way? What did Rosh do?

"I'm gonna head inside," Rosh says. "I haven't really eaten since dinner yesterday. I had a bail hearing today. *That* was weird. But really, just so you can sleep tonight, I swear I'm not a psycho."

"Wasn't that Ted Bundy's line?"

Rosh's eyes widen.

"I'm joking. Sorry."

"Nah, I was just thinking, shit, I'm not even an original psycho. I'll have to work on that." He grins. "They're just trying to scare me, I think. Shouldn't happen again, he says naïvely.

"Look, I know you said you're not writing anymore, but you of all people might appreciate this. If you've got a minute?" Rosh steps inside his apartment and sets down the bag.

From the threshold Oliver peers into Unit 2, which he's never seen, wondering what "this" Rosh wants to share and starting to feel unsure about getting involved. His neighbour shrugs off his coat and heads to a bookshelf. Oliver looks up at the ceiling, the structure that supports his own floor. He sees himself living his life up there, oblivious to what lies beneath.

Rosh returns with a DVD. The cover shows a hand-drawn oil well. Over top, the title *Fracking Up Your Future* in a distressed font.

"This is just the demo," Rosh says. "It'll have a more professional look."

"You made this?"

"Am still making it, but we've done most of the filming now, been showing up at protests. Caught their attention, basically."

Oliver turns the DVD over. There's nothing on the back. What was it like in the jail cell? What was the charge? Who's the "we" making the film?

"Really interesting," he says. At the same time, he feels himself recoiling. His pizza's getting cold, and Rosh looks like he's going to wilt. "Look, I just made dinner. Want me to bring you a plate?"

"That's really kind of you." It was in fact a diversion. "But I'm okay, I picked up some things."

Oliver returns the DVD. "Maybe you can tell me more about it sometime." A polite yet neutral closer.

"That would be great. I'm sure you'd have some insights."

"I don't know, I'm not so up to date —"

"Yeah but you were in the field."

"Sure. Come up for a beer maybe, once you're feeling better." He starts backing away. When he scoots up the stairs, his heart's pounding.

HE REHEATS THE PIZZA and sets it out with his salad, but it's a hasty dinner, he suddenly can't sit still and finds himself pacing the rooms.

Fracking: a word that combines *cracking* and *fucking.*

Bore a hole, pound it open. Choke with industrial spew. Wait for retching. Take what comes up.

Water carries the chemicals used in fracking. Water poisoned and turned into a weapon. Water that pays the price.

Pacing. The cat leaping from the sill and dashing off. Water was there with him from his earliest moments of life: as rain on the bedroom window, spray on his cheeks when he ran on the beach.

He watched gulls break the lake's surface and lift it up, wriggling silver.

Trapper hat on, beer in hand, slide the balcony door open and greet the cold. Close the door before the cat escapes. As he leans against the railing, staring toward the invisible lake, his old life comes rushing back. Montreal, where he and Connie met in an undergrad English class. Their half-a-season relationship and ludicrous breakup on his balcony the night they were supposed to see The Smashing Pumpkins. She melted into the city and he went storming out later, tacked the tickets to her apartment door, probably got drunk. By the next semester they were friends – and had thus established the on again/off again, romance-to-friendship pattern that defined them for the next dozen years.

That was a time when things seemed to flow into his life: friends, lovers, roomy once-grand apartments he could afford, luck, even money when he needed it. But more than anything, optimism: it was the 1990s, and the world's burdens seemed solvable. People had risen up to demolish the Berlin Wall. The Doomsday Clock was inching backwards, and the environmental movement achieved the first Earth Summit. Fresh energies seemed to be welling up everywhere. He returned to Toronto, where his freelance career modestly supported him. Features of his started to appear in *Esquire*, *The Guardian*, *Harpers*, and many publications now defunct. The *National Post* took every article he pitched before offering him a column, where he profiled new "green-oriented" careers in an upbeat, entertaining manner. He was a young political lightweight. He'd known that great harm was being done to the Earth, but not *felt* it back then. He believed that things were on the right track, solutions being found and implemented, because it was easiest to. He rode the wave of opportunity thinking it would last and keep serving him. He believed that working hard would be enough.

One day, something new came through the spigot. It trickled into his life so naturally he thought *he'd* found *it*.

December 2004. He and Connie lived in Little Italy, in a gorgeous two-bedroom-plus where they'd been stable for five or six years. Connie was in a similarly promising place with her writing. Life seemed good. In the paper one day, he read about the sentencing of the Koebel brothers, the only public officials ever charged in connection to the Walkerton drinking water disaster. People were angry: coming so long after the tragedy, the trial and mild punishment were a feeble justice. At that point he'd been mulling over writing a book – a project to up his game – and water management had become a global concern. He read up on the Walkerton incident, Canada's worst recorded E. coli contamination of public drinking water. It was a sordid tale: hundreds of residents in the town of Walkerton, Ontario became very sick, and some died, because of bureaucratic ineptitude, deception and plain tight-fistedness. The story had been huge in its time, shocking.

He was intrigued. Another journalist had published a solid book about the tragedy, so that work was done, but Oliver sensed a different angle or story still needed to be explored.

Researching local drinking water management, he was startled to learn that his own city takes its drinking water from the lake. How had he never given that a thought, even during the Walkerton crisis? He'd just assumed that his tap water came from some wild reservoir safely beyond the city's reach; that it sluiced through the forests of the Oakridges Moraine, a pristine effluent on some protected bio-throughway heading south to pipes of gleaming steel. *Of course* Toronto's water comes from Lake Ontario: the lake's huge, and right there. Though he'd come to think of the lake as more of a public toilet than public fountain. The city's treated sewage gets dumped into it, and hot water from nuclear plants, and industrial wastes from factories huddled around the shore. Freighters chuck their cargo residue in it. Pesticides run off from agricultural lands. Overfishing had exterminated the lake's great aquatic populations by the end of the nineteenth century;

he couldn't imagine what, if anything, still lurked beneath. However much the lake was protected in the age of green awareness, he thought, it was still a dump.

How had he not once thought about these things, he wondered then. Perhaps he'd just been fooled by optics: the beauty of the R.C. Harris Water Treatment Plant, for example, Toronto's grand, art deco temple to clean drinking water. Dramatically situated on a grassy bluff overlooking the lake, the temple's large windows offer views of a tiled interior worthy of a spa, where pools of water are lovingly massaged by handsome filtering equipment. It certainly inspires trust.

He secured interviews with workers at the plant. Innocently yet inexorably, it seemed to him afterwards, he was drawn toward the thing that would be his undoing.

The interviews went nowhere, at first, until he crossed paths with a night-shift operator named Patrick who was taking a smoke break when Oliver emerged from a meeting. Lean, grim, with stringy hair hanging from under a baseball cap, Patrick had the look of a small-time dealer. On impulse Oliver introduced himself. Patrick agreed to talk, though gave him a wary eye.

"So, off the record, are you confident that Toronto's drinking water is healthy?"

"Off the record? No."

Oliver was excited. Nobody he'd talked to at the plant had had anything critical to say of its operations. "Why not?"

"Because it's full of industrial chemicals? We pour them in every day."

"Okay, but there are protocols for that, safety standards. Are they not being followed?"

"Everything's being followed to a T. This place is one-hundred-percent airtight." Patrick took a drag, gave Oliver a sidelong look. "But who sets these standards, and on what information basis? You realize this isn't a simple thing, right? That there's politics in public health?"

"Of course." Oliver was growing bored. This wasn't leading anywhere.

"So," Patrick continued, "picture this, if you dare. Rubber-lined trucks show up with the fluoride, for example. And then? Glug glug glug. A few tests to make sure everything that could officially harm you is dead, plus everything that could actually help you, too."

There was nothing surprising there, Oliver replied. If the plant was following protocol, he had nothing to investigate.

"Guess you're not very interested in health, just scandal," Patrick said.

"Well, I wouldn't —"

"Tell me something, out of curiosity." Patrick stepped closer. The wind lifted his hair like a Medusa. "Do you actually know what fluoride is?"

"It's a naturally occurring element."

"It's a known neurotoxin, friend. It's a byproduct — actually a *waste* product — of phosphate production. It's not a pharmaceutical. Not a medicine. It's scrubbed from the insides of smokestacks so that it's not vented so much into the air, where it has this nasty habit of sickening and killing things. Instead, it's put into drums, driven here, and we dump it into your water."

"But not just like that."

"*Exactly* like that." Patrick lifted his hands, holding an imaginary tool. "I'm scraping the walls of a smokestack that's been belching from aluminum production. I'm putting this crud into your glass of water now. Happy? Okay, machines do the scrubbing, but my point is there's no middle treatment, no alchemy, just dilution. But hey, trust the experts, it'll give you a great smile." He grinned. "You want a hot topic? It's yours."

Patrick flicked his butt to the wind and left. Oliver never saw him again. He felt irritated for wasting time with an obviously disgruntled individual.

And yet. Patrick's words, the images he painted, wouldn't leave his mind. *Known neurotoxin. Industrial waste.* In the tap water.

To satisfy his curiosity, Oliver checked into it. He quickly learned that Patrick's description, while a bit lurid, was more or less sound. None of the literature denied where the fluoride added to drinking water comes from; instead, it spoke of its benefits at low doses, emphasizing that fluoride is *naturally occurring*.

So is radiation, Oliver thought, but we don't expose ourselves to it all day, every day.

Reading further, he entered a thicket of debate about a chemical he'd never questioned, drawn back in time to the introduction of fluoridated water in North America. He discovered that drinking water was fluoridated only after thousands of lawsuits had been filed, and sometimes won, against industries venting fluoride into the atmosphere. The lawsuits came from plant workers suffering injuries, farmers with cattle and crops destroyed by fluorine gas. The most publicized incident was the Donora, Pennsylvania smog disaster of 1948, when a great cloud of fluorine pollution settled over the town for days, sickening and killing thousands.

Why had he not stopped reading? He'd obviously been sidetracked. But water had found him; he was sinking, and couldn't help himself. The conflicting studies and claims about fluoride's safety gripped him. Fluoride lowers IQ. Fluoride is linked to bone decay. Baby formula made with tap water gives infants hundreds of times the natural dose of fluoride in mother's milk . . . He traced the political-corporate alliances that worked to crush lawsuits. He was amazed by the spin used to turn fluoride, publicly understood as toxic waste until the 1950s, into a child-friendly medicine. Fluoridating tap water is an outright violation of the public's right to medical consent, one lawyer-critic wrote, "the arrogance of power writ large." Fluoride tablets and toothpaste are readily available for those who desire fluoride, after all.

The first column he wrote about fluoridation for the *Post* was also his first to meet rebuke. His editor called it a "loony-magnet issue" and ran the piece only after Oliver had placed the fluoride discussion in the context of other water purity concerns. When his editor went on vacation, though, Oliver slipped through a profile of several local anti-fluoridation activists whom he'd interviewed and come to respect. One was a university professor, who wearily explained that fluoride was a money-making scheme foisted on a misled public and dimwittedly supported by corrupt, bullying dental "experts." Emails and letters poured in from dentists; readers called him a conspiracy theorist. His editor hit the roof — and that was his last appearance in the *Post*.

His career would have recovered. But the fighter in him had been ignited, and he didn't know when to back down. He was an Islander; he'd come into the world surrounded by water, listening to water, and it pulled on him like blood. Water connects, and he was starting to see how other connections — between industry, science, government and health education — had led to serious abuse. His old "Eco-Spotlight" column embarrassed him.

He pitched alternative presses. Some of his fluoridation articles were picked up, but most editors said it wasn't what they were looking for. Friends and colleagues tried to caution him. Connie, a journalist also, grew uncomfortable with the newly politicized, increasingly bitter and underemployed Oliver. Only later did he recognize that her reaction came mostly from concern. At the time he resented her and the rest of his colleagues for "playing it safe." He didn't understand how necessary a good reputation is, and how fragile.

"You're not listening," he remembers her saying, over and over. *I don't believe in you,* he heard.

He no longer wanted to attend the latest launch of somebody's book about recovering from drug addiction or being a lesbian parent. Connie went to all the launches. She was liked. She supported others, felt happy for their success. "You should think about your friends," she said once, when he caught her at the door, dressed and perfumed, and snarled a complaint at another night's absence. "Where'd they go?"

Then their split, his move to the east side.

He learned a lesson then.

Yes, he'd been wrong to approach such a touchy subject full-on. He'd gotten obsessed. Fluoride, after all, was just one issue among the many affecting water. If he could write about *all* of them – like his ex-editor suggested – then he'd stay safely away from the fringe zone and reach a receptive audience. This was the most important thing.

In that period of adjustment, he conceived of the book he'd write: the definitive exposé on water quality in Ontario. He'd already done much of the research. It would be his comeback.

For many painful months, he gnawed on that ambition. He joined the gym, where Foroud didn't employ a right-hand man yet, and for money did odd gigs, writing commercial newsletters, editing a journal. Justin had withdrawn from his life long before that, or one of them had; he had a baby daughter by then. All Oliver's energy went into his book. During that year following his move, its structure began to emerge. Surprisingly, the story was personal: the first chapter was about the island. With growing excitement, he started to see how he could craft the story to move people – for everyone recognizes the beauty of water. Once that opening chapter was drafted to his satisfaction, he emailed it with an outline and proposal to several publishers. He applied for and received a small grant.

He was still bitter, though. Life was lonely and tough, and he hid his hardships from everyone, smiling when his mother asked how things were going and talking about "the book" to assure her his career was back on track.

Connie visited now and then, probably to reassure herself that he was still alive. She'd started seeing someone, and though she didn't say so, it was obvious that this new relationship was getting serious. He could feel it in the atmospheric change between them: a sense of final remove, of orbits disentangled. They were friends.

One day she brought astrology charts and a book with the word "evolution" in its title. Late in their relationship she'd started studying astrology — an appalling move that helped shore up his belief that they didn't think alike, she was not the woman for him, and so on. She sat him down, laid out her charts on a box he'd still not unpacked.

I've been looking at your transits.

The Uranus opposition, that's what she'd diagnosed: when a person approaches forty, the slow-moving planet Uranus comes opposite one's natal Sun position, an event that acts as a mid-life planetary kick in the ass. Truly it was a *watershed time*, she cooed, an opportunity to *shed his skin*. The universe would guide him well, if only he could *stop feeling so victimized* —

He all but threw her out. Didn't speak to her again for months.

The accident happened not five minutes from home. An early spring morning, clear and cold. The roads were dry, but as he rode his bicycle under a bridge into its shadow, he hit black ice. A car following hit it too. They slid together in the lane, a slow-motion ice duet: car spinning, bike skating, like a planet dancing with its moon. His foot caught a bumper and he slammed into the concrete pier.

Uranus: lightning planet, planet of surprises. He woke in the hospital, unable to turn over unassisted due to an agonizing, knife-like pain in his back: a ruptured disk, from which he's still not fully healed, seven years on. Months of physio and frailty frightened him to his roots. Typing: twenty minutes at a time, at most, lying on the floor. Walking: like an old man. Having buses pull away on him because he couldn't hurry to the stop.

On the balcony, Oliver downs the last of his beer. Seven years in the shadow of that loss. The work on his book ground to a stop. Even after he grew stronger again, even when one of the publishers he'd contacted expressed interest, he found he just couldn't continue. Day-to-day living took everything he had.

Without giving himself time to think he lifts the recycling bin from its corner and heads inside and opens the filing cabinet's lowest drawer. Thick file folders. Whenever he's contemplated doing this it seemed too radical, like home tooth extraction; now it feels right, inevitable. He can almost feel the relief of the hanging file folders, emptied of their bulk.

Cleared. Ventilated.

This too is dead. Time to bury it.

He picks up the first folder and slips out its contents, intending to toss it in. Already his mind's conjuring a fire somewhere. But a sentence catches his eye:

I grew up on a little island.

It's the first chapter, which he barely remembers writing.

Its ponds, channels, and white sand shores were my home. I could wander its woods and meadows and swim its lagoons without fear. I learned a kind of trust that everyone should. I was lucky . . .

Was this really him?

Pushing the bin aside, Oliver sits on the floor to read.

9

RICE LAKE, ONE A.M. Darkness hides the lake, where three days of February rain broke the ice and wore it away. Darkness hides the woods, and the Mound, and her.

The Mound hides bones.

The lake hides an old bridge.

The woods hide the future generations. Hundreds of them.

The moths of the future aren't formed yet. Last summer and fall, they were caterpillars. They lived to stuff themselves with food. One by one as the air began to cool, each caterpillar stopped eating, spun its own shroud, and sealed itself in. And then, in this self-made abyss, it consumed itself. Enzymes dissolved organs, tissues, flesh; it lost all shape, even identity. It became presence without form — like darkness itself.

It kept one thing: an intention.

While the cold lasts it endures, living without breath, awaiting its moment.

~

A LOW RHYTHMIC TRILL breaks the silence. Two repeats, a pause, then three more calls: a screech owl in the oak stand down the hill. Gabe listens, but the owl is quiet now.

She's been sitting atop the Mound for hours, should get home and to bed — yet what a night! The wind is from the south, steady and dry and smelling of thawed ground. It's so warm she's left her winter coat open. Walking here carefully in the dark, she felt her boots sink into the ground a little with each step. Earlier today in a sunny courtyard on campus, she spotted the first snowbells, their heads bent like supplicants or half-asleep dreamers emerging from the soil.

After months of winter this soft night beckoned her here, yet it's unnerving too. February's not spring; if the weather trend persists, it could summon the moths and other insects to hatch too soon.

The owl hoots again: a set of three, always the same pattern. The world is made of such patterns, and people — modern people, at least — are just beginning to appreciate this. Centuries of determined movement toward casting the light of reason upon everything, mapping and naming and explaining all, have reached a place of shadow: a realization that the patterns are bigger, denser, wilder than imagined; that reason is but a headlamp; that we have seen through a glass, darkly. At the same time, Earth systems and patterns are changing. Weather, species — all are in flux, on the move. The culture of the light has left wounds, poison, destruction. Great actions are needed; that is clear. How to change and how to mend are not.

Lately she's thrown herself into the stream of guest lectures, seminars and events on offer at the university and other venues in the city, trying to learn as much as possible before her fieldwork begins. She's getting to know some of the other students, particularly her fellow TAs for BIO 150, and they've become a little team, informing each other about upcoming talks, attending and discussing them in the grad lounge afterwards or over beer. Habitat conservation, resource management, infectious diseases, invasive species, genomic diversity, evolutionary biology — in every single area, they hear, the problems today are *critical, urgent.*

It's hard to take in these changes. She wonders if those not rooted in an Indigenous culture truly can. And how do you *live* with emergency ringing in your heart and head, so that even moments of joy and beauty — like this night — are always tinged with apprehension? She's coming to appreciate the comforting structure that science provides: every study follows the same steps, abstract, literature review, materials and methods, et cetera. Tidy. Ordered. The skills-building sessions she's attended have helped her adopt the right language and style, while this immersion in research and the academic milieu teaches a way of thinking and approaching the vast realms of scientific study so such work becomes tenable. Her first couple of assignments have been returned with respectable grades. She feels encouraged.

And also?

Off track.

In all this activity, the reams of studies, books, talks, labs, and classes, in the dedication of energy, resources, passion — certainly there with profs and students alike — there seems to be something crucial missing. It goads at her; she can't put her finger on it and wonders if it's simply that she came to this work late, got set in lazy ways out east? Maybe it's going to take more time and effort for her to adapt. She hopes getting into the fieldwork will help.

With a sigh, she sets aside these thoughts and stretches her legs. The screech owl seems to have departed. In the south there's a moon glow behind thinning clouds. As the light strengthens, a serpentine shape appears on the shore. The snow's all but melted in the park, but a ribbon has lingered along the beach, snaking the waterline sand like a ghostly companion to the Mound on which she sits. She wonders if ancient peoples here once saw the same phenomenon: Snow Serpent, lake's guardian.

When she stands she bows toward the image, brings her hands together in thanks to the Mound builders for creating this place, for their love. Flicks on her flashlight then decides it's not necessary. She heads back the most direct way, by the disused road.

The streets of Peterborough are utterly vacant at this hour. She pulls up at the family home, thinking briefly about her parents, living in a condo complex for retirees in Victoria, BC. They flew here at Christmas, which had a special warmth this year with Gabe "living at home" again, and she could tell they were both excited for her, proud she'd taken this step. Jenn and her brother-in-law also, despite their teasing about Gabe's track record and the fact that she and her eldest nephew are in university at the same time. Hard to believe that she is this old and feels so young and unformed, while Jenn's children are already leaving the nest.

Downstairs she turns on the little salt lamp by the bed, cracks open the window, undresses and snuggles under the duvet. The moth tree she created has grown, its branches now outspread to touch two other walls. All these photos she took herself over the years. During the day she reads black marks on screen or page, left to right, top to bottom, but in the living world there's no such thing as one direction — even this "tree" is more like a web. There are only patterns, of shape, colour, and design . . . The eyes of an owl appear on the wings of the Polyphemus; the Snowberry Clearwing resembles a bumblebee. Which came first? And what sets the patterns? The patterns seem to be *what* nature creates and *how* it creates, a musician riffing on structures and phrases.

That's about as much as she understands tonight.

10

THE STYLIST IS SHORT AND STURDY, a bulldog-type with tat-covered arms and grey, spiritual eyes. He circles the chair, lifting Justin's hair and letting it fall.

"Can you make it look cool, and a bit different, without it looking like I'm trying to be twenty-five?"

The stylist runs the hair through his fingers and rubs it like he's testing cloth. Justin has never felt his hair being so tenderly appraised. "Absolutely," the man says. "You've got a lot to work with."

The cut takes an hour. A girl (young woman, Justin mentally self-corrects) who has a ruby-coloured brush cut brings him a double espresso from the place next door. She's friendly. Everyone's friendly. He savours his drink like the caffeine hit's enough. In the future, it *will* be enough.

It's been a wretched few weeks.

He hit bottom that day after the after-hours party at Leverage. That woman. Women. Maybe "bottom" isn't the right word, though. He should be wary of dismissive judgement, which brings guilt and repressive weirdness. On that side lie Mommy Suits and Daddy Suits and the security-crazy anxiety cinching up his life — and

Naomi's, and frankly everyone's, as far as he can tell. The whole world seems to be spiraling into that trap.

Still, that night was a mode or a road he doesn't want to travel again. He's fighting back. There's been no more illicit sex and no more nights with Kurt. He has not, in fact, seen Kurt at all because he's barely gone into Ace. He's too afraid.

With darting snips, the stylist deftly tailors the cut to Justin's head. The effect is pleasing: the shaggy dog look has gone and he really does look cooler, "a bit different." He feels like he's been seen.

It's just a haircut, but he has to start somewhere.

After paying and tipping he slides on his Ray-Bans and steps outside. It's a bright day and cold again. Nonetheless, he's starting to sweat.

Medical accounts of crystal meth that he's read online explain the drug's effects in chemical terms: dopamine and the psychological-reward system. The analyses cite studies based on lab rats and mice. In their language, a user's brain is like software being overwritten by crystal's new code.

These are uncertain analogies, Justin thinks, popping two chiclets in his mouth while he waits for the light. Talking about the mind like it's a program, testing on rodents and applying the results to people. Being neither mouse nor machine, he's skeptical. A rodent's wants are unique to itself, while a computer has none.

In the car, hands trembling with the keys.

It's been exactly seven days since he last did crystal, and the strength and persistence of the cravings alarm him. By the time he drives to Gwynn's school and parks in the smoldering vehicle queue, the calm and safety he felt at the salon are gone. He eats sour chews from a bag, joggling his leg. Women pass on the sidewalk, speaking in tight, high-pitched mommy voices to children. The women *sound* like children. He finds himself staring, then fearful of staring. Did he break the three-second rule?

The passenger door whooshes open and he starts. He's expecting women with claws, men in uniform, the screeching demons of his dreams.

Gwynn climbs in and buckles up.

"How's my Bunny Bear?"

"Okay," she says.

He waits to give her space to say more, but she doesn't. She's in a mood, it seems. Well, he can't blame her, all day in that place.

He starts to drive. Traffic. Cyclists. Scratchy-scratchy cravings. He's fighting back. But he needs more strategy. Today the haircut filled the midday danger time, yet he's no better than –

"Dad!"

"What?" He hits the brakes. The car behind stops and honks. "Piss off," he mutters, glaring at the driver in the rear-view, then at Gwynn.

"What are you yelling about?"

"Nothing."

He makes the turn into their street carefully. Takes a deep breath.

"Just . . . your lips were moving."

"Ah. I see. Well, I was just thinking things over, Pumpkin. I hear you talking to yourself in your room all the time."

"But you shouldn't do it outside."

Justin nods. His daughter's head's getting filled with junk values. But that's okay – that's where he can help.

"Come to the grocery store with Dad?"

"Okay."

"That's my girl."

On the way, he delivers a lesson on the commonly misguided distinctions between "crazy" and "sane."

~

THREE MORE DAYS. In the mornings he focuses on damage control: there's something wrong with Leverage, just wrong, and one branding package can't fix it. Naomi urged him to try a marketing consultant, so he's put out feelers. One candidate suggests he develop an online delivery business. Retail's all going on the web, she says, clothes, food — everything. Like this is news.

Jittery for a toot, he tries to summon again the optimism he felt at the salon, but his mind keeps turning on figures. Two credit lines maxed. There's the money from his mother's estate, but the thought of pouring it into Leverage makes him miserable. That money should be for Gwynn, or a project with better prospects.

In the evenings he cooks and keeps his nose clean. Ten days. Puttering in the kitchen, his thoughts grind on buying another packet, just a small one, to get him over this hump. He loads the dishwasher, remembering that other kitchen in the morning light of another world where he stomped like a wild god and danced with a demon woman into tawdry, shitty, yet deliciously crazed fucking.

He presses the start button then joins Naomi and Gwynn for a video. They watch the screen and he watches them.

Steady on.

At night, the mad critics of his sleep scream.

Liar! Scumbag!

Coke head! Hypocrite!

He sits up in bed. Sometimes his movements wake Naomi. Depending on her mood she'll either rub his back or clamp a pillow over her head.

You'll be living in a garage. They'll hate you.

He dresses. The dog waits by the front door, tail wagging.

They set off down the street. Reg trots ahead, pausing to look back. Justin follows slowly, uneasily, like he's passing through foreign territory. Showpiece homes set back from the street, spot-lit masonry. Baby Point — why'd he agree to it?

He knows he must come clean with his wife. Can't hide it, can't do that to her and to them. He's constructed and demolished that conversation endlessly, never satisfied. Naomi can be remarkably open-minded, it's one of the things that drew them together, and that gives him hope. She even instigated his infidelity once. It was when Gwynn was a baby: Naomi had a hard time breastfeeding and then Gwynn was such a screamer. Naomi's sex drive zeroed, and at their thirteenth or fifteenth month of celibacy she basically ordered him to get laid, for his relief and hers. After some doubt, he followed through. Simple friendly sex, nothing more, but it brought him to a powerful realization: he wasn't into anyone else anymore.

He was in awe of Naomi after that. Like she'd known. In Mexico, after the worst had passed with Gwynn and they took their first vacation again, he watched his wife swing in a hammock, ocean-wet hair like a mermaid's, and thought she was the most beautiful and wise woman on the planet. He was convinced like never before that they'd make it.

Oh, home is woman. How many times has he told her that? The receptive vessels in "w," the circle of life in "o" — it's all right there. Without these containers, home is just another space a man passes through.

Damp wind, racing clouds. Justin shivers. He whistles to Reg but he doesn't come. He's gone around the corner, the street to the river. Justin follows, descending to a T-junction at the woods, the path through them in shadow but he knows it's there, he drives past here often. Reg is snuffling around it.

"Reg!"

He crosses. The trees swell, sound of an ocean. He steps closer to them. There's light at the bottom of the path and it's not far. He edges down the slope with the trees lifting about him and the dog ahead and finds himself at the edge of a small parking lot, lit and empty, beyond it the water.

The river's smoking. Here and there rocks break the surface and on each stands a seagull, motionless, like idols marking a trail. On the bank he watches them for some minutes, waiting for one to move. They never do.

"Come on, boy."

They return to the street, and Reg stays close this time as they pass the darkened houses, two grey shadows cast by the moon. In living a lie he's becoming that wraith gliding before him, no solidity. It's not what a man should be. But he's been waiting for something: an idea, a concept, like the melody of a new song, because if he just tells her everything without that, he'll be offering nothing but his mistakes.

Yet he really should talk to her. Soon.

It's the honorable choice.

True, but also cold, surgically sharp. Survival rate unknown.

Just love. Speak the language of love.

Is this the voice of his conscience, or one of the mad critics in disguise?

The longer you wait, the worse she'll feel betrayed.

Maybe the insights will come in the process.

THE NEXT DAY, fully resolved, he drives to Ace in the afternoon. At a light without thinking he calls Kurt, who sounds like he's just woken up. Coke isn't immediately available, money and calls are required, ETA perhaps tomorrow. Crystal he can get in a couple of hours.

"That shit's like swallowing a firecracker," Justin says. "I hate it."

"You just need to pace yourself with it."

"That's not possible."

"I'll bring you a little until the coke comes," Kurt says, hacking. "Then switch over."

Fine. A little is all he needs.

In his office Justin puts on *Wish You Were Here*. The record makes him feel sad but brave, because the songs are true and relevant. Then he reviews the quarterly statements. Ace as usual is doing well; they've actually increased profits over the last few months. Meanwhile there's Leverage, sucking it all away.

When Kurt arrives, Justin places a hand over the packet laid on the desk and moves it into his breast pocket without looking away from the screen. He wishes Kurt would leave now. Instead, he invites him to stay. He will not show weakness, and Kurt already knows too much.

"Have a seat," Justin says. "I want you to explain something to me. Share your honest opinion on what you hear."

Kurt inclines his head, his long suede coat spread over slim legs.

Without revealing the financial details, Justin describes how he sees Leverage in terms of the market, all the reasons why it should be succeeding. "So I come now to my question. What, in your opinion, is the problem?"

"The place lacks backbone."

Justin studies him. "It's a cocktail lounge. It's shallow by definition." Though he never meant Leverage to be that.

Kurt shakes his head. "It's fake. Confused. Like you with your new haircut."

"I like this haircut."

"It's a fine cut, sure. Leverage is a fine place — but it doesn't stand out. What *is* it? A swinger's club has opened up the street. You know what that means? I'm not saying that place will last, but if you want to attract *new* people, you must offer something really new."

Justin frowns. Naomi said the same thing back when he was planning Leverage, and he'd not gone with her ideas. "You mean a 'concept' place," he says.

"Yes."

"I hate those."

"So?"

Justin laughs. "Wow. That's cold, man."

"So's money." With a shrug, Kurt sinks back in the chair. His eyes are dark vestibules inviting no approach.

DRIVING HOME a few hours later, still with full intent. The packet's just his parachute, should he need one.

Yet once there, resolve weakens with every habitual act and word. Another evening and another tormenting night are going to pass . . .

At nine-thirty, after Gwynn's in bed, Justin stops loading the dishwasher and in a state of near trance descends to his home office and locks himself in the bathroom. Lighter, glass pipe.

The room fills with smoke. The counter disappears, then the mirror.

It comes rushing back: his might, his willpower.

Sometime later, back upstairs – hunting for her. Wet windows and fairy lights outside.

He heads toward the bedroom. No one there. Confused, he shuts the door and takes out his phone.

"Naomi."

"What are you doing calling, you goof? What's this smoke downstairs?"

"It's me."

"It reeks. What the hell is it?"

"I'm not the man you married."

"Where are you? Did you go out?"

"Stop talking and listen! You need to see what's going on."

Heart pounding, Justin gets to his knees.

"There are shadows here," he whispers.

"Where and what are you doing?"

"They're taking over. Naomi, things have gotten out of hand!" His voice cracks. "I'm doing drugs, that's what the smoke is." Roaring in his ears. "Naomi, I'm –" Fucked up? No, speak the truth! "I've come to the end of something, some old me. I even slept with someone a few weeks ago when I was high, when you were away."

Silence.

"I've been lying. I stayed out all night getting wasted and having sex. This is what's happening to your husband around here!"

Naomi takes a long breath. Her voice sounds small and distant. "Since when?"

Justin shakily rises. "Since I don't know when, I'm not a fuck-ing timepiece. Since things started to feel so fucking impossible. Since Mom died." Is that true? Because she always believed in him? Protected him? Or is he just playing for sympathy?

"But this isn't a confession!" He races on, pacing now. "This is me, extending an *open hand* to you. I hope you understand what I mean by that and what it's taking for me to say this. An open hand. I can't take this secrecy and pretense . . . I can't take this isolation! I get more affection and companionship from Reg than you." She didn't even notice his hair!

"We need to turn things around here or we're going to die. I want it all in the open, no more shadows." Panting, he runs out of words.

From Naomi, a gasp or hiccup.

"Yeah, get it out, let's get things out between us at last."

She doesn't reply. Justin looks at the phone: the call's been ended.

Thumping downstairs, he can't find her. Gone outside? He wanders into the yard and stands in the rippling night. Back in his office, he starts as a bulgy cube tumbles down the stairs: a duvet in a plastic tote. She slipped back in and is tossing down pillows without a word.

He strides up the stairs and up again to the second floor. She's outside their bedroom: eyes black, mouth a taut line. Strangely, her nipples also stick out underneath her white bedtime shirt. Naomi never walks around the house that way; she thinks it's unseemly for them to be seen in their underwear in front of Gwynn, so she must have changed after seeing Gwynn to bed, then gone downstairs to the basement to complete a last task.

Now she's a tigress. With a warning hand raised, she halts him. Her voice is low and flat with controlled rage.

"Stay the fuck away. Gwynn is sleeping, so no noise. But, if you come any closer right now, I swear, I might just beat you."

"Okay," he whispers. Seeing her so raw like this, his heart burns with love. "But listen, you need to know that I'm dying for us to be close again, that's the heart of this, my love. It's *destroying* me." He steps toward her, his voice rising. "That's the whole reason I need to —"

Naomi darts forward and grabs him by the throat.

"Shut up shut up shut up!" she hisses, fingers pinching his windpipe so his mouth gapes. "No talk now! I'm going to bed." She releases him, and points to the floor. "You — that's your place. Down there."

She leaves him in the hallway and locks the bedroom door.

11

HE'S PUSHED HIS Angel work to the evenings, rented the car for the next few weeks to get through it all. It's not like he has a social life anyway. And during the day there are auction houses, interior painters, handymen to contact. On one of their email exchanges Justin advised hiring packers. Who *does* that? Oliver thought. There are drawers of panties, slippers, socks and stockings, closets with worn-out jeans and gardening shirts, each item holding their mother's shape. Photographs, letters, ribbons awarded, pressed flowers, figurines. He even found a stash of Justin's old LPs in milk crates (which he's not said a word about, yet).

In a chest one evening Oliver finds something he didn't know existed: a keepsake album devoted to his writing. Pieces he published as an undergrad. All his columns from the *Post*, his younger face above the byline. Articles he forgot entirely. The *Canadian Geographic* feature on sustainable fisheries, which won him a National Magazine Award. His mother attended the ceremony with him and Connie — it was Connie's idea to invite her, he wouldn't have thought of it because he's dense that way. Afterward they ate a late dinner downtown: he remembers his mother in a dark blue dress, silver hair cut close as always and gems in her ears, her eyes merry in the candlelight, the waiter's attentiveness. It was possibly the only time the three of them ever did anything festive like that; he never had the money for it. Why the hell didn't he do it more often anyway?

He takes the album home, along with some photographs. The house sits on a corner, and he parks in the usual spot these days at the side. Up on the third storey, the desk lamp he left on illuminates one window. Lights are also on in Rosh's apartment. They've not spoken since that evening last week and he's still haunted by what happened, has noticed himself listening for sounds of trouble when he wakes in the still hours.

He heads up the front path then stops, puzzled.

On the side street near where he parked sits a black SUV. The vehicle's windows are tinted so he can see nothing of the driver, but someone inside is using a phone, and the pale blue light is what caught his attention. He's seen this before. Last night from the balcony? Two nights ago? It strikes him that he's seen it many times lately: same car, same spot, blue-screen glow afloat within. Perhaps another insomniac or night-shift worker has moved into the neighbourhood.

Inside he locks the front door then climbs the stairs with his box of mementos. "Oliver, hey." Rosh stands in his door, smiling. He's dressed in jeans and a thick wool sweater and slippers. Low music pulses from within. "I picked up some beer today. You got time for one?"

He has to push through the automatic negative that's become his default. No time. No friends. No fun. "Sure, just have to feed the cat."

"Right! How's kitty doing? I've seen her perched in the window a few times."

"You can meet Mimi, if you want to come up."

In the kitchen he opens a new tin for her as she paces around his feet. Two scoops of glop, more crunchies. Rosh comes in behind him and hands over a six pack, then crouches a respectful distance from the cat. To Oliver's surprise, Mimi removes her face from the bowl and pads over to sniff Rosh's fingers. He even gets a little lick. In a moment he's petting her head.

"Geez! Maybe she should move in with you."

"Giving you some push back, is she?"

"I think it's called distain."

Rosh grins. "She'll settle down. She probably just blames you. And she's showing off."

She really was. Mimi was strutting about like a runway model, whisking her tail around Rosh's hand and purring.

Oliver opens their beers. "Things seem to have been quiet," he observes. "No more 'unexpected visits.'" He uses air quotes.

"No more home invasions! No." Straightening, Rosh takes his bottle. "To peaceful progress and understanding neighbours," he says, holding it out.

"To your film." They clink.

Rosh leans against the counter. "It's a bit of a story. Do you know the Wild Water Alliance?" Oliver shakes his head. "We were a pretty small organization, and we no longer exist anyway. Got shut down last year."

"You mean forcibly?"

"Well, they audited us."

"Ah." This he does know about — a strategy for making certain activist or nonprofit groups go away.

"It was coming. We got harassed by CSIS for years. We were friendly with whistleblowers, collected their data. But there's nothing like the CRA to pull the plug."

"How are you making your film, then? Crowdfunding?" Oliver leans against the wall, mirroring Rosh's stance. They're a similar height and build, could probably swap clothes.

"Depends on how you define 'crowd'?" Rosh says. "It's more like, we were partway into filming already, so we felt obligated —

and determined — to see it through. Lots of volunteer hours." He describes how a handful of ex-employees and volunteers have continued the project, travelling to film protests against fracking across the country, interviewing experts willing to speak on camera. He paints an amusing picture of himself learning to shoot and edit film, since they can't afford professionals for any but the most essential sequences.

"We've filmed some protests that turned ugly — one in Windsor last year, where police got really physical with protesters, lots of punching and pepper spray, and no reason for it at all. And I think that's when we really got on their radar, started getting tracked. They charged me with 'conspiracy to commit mischief.'"

"But why the midnight invasion?"

"Honestly, I don't know. Because it's scary?" Rosh holds Oliver's gaze a moment. "A show of force? As I said, they claimed to have a search warrant, though I think that was bullshit."

Oliver wonders if there's more to the story. The whole thing seems kind of extreme. "Do you think the charges will be dropped?"

"I sure as shit hope so!" Rosh flashes a mock-terrified smile, fingers to his teeth. "Apparently they've constructed a good case. But my lawyer's optimistic. No previous criminal record, good citizen, et cetera. We won't know for months, so we just wait and see. Carry on, you know?"

"Fuck." Oliver doesn't know what else to say. He can't imagine having to wait for that kind of decision.

Rosh laughs. "Hey, don't worry, I don't mean to bring you down. My life really isn't this shitty most of the time. Just a run-of-the-mill psycho wanting to create a better world. Tell me more about you? How did you inherit Mimi?"

"Oh. My mom passed away last month."

Rosh stands up straight, eyes wide. "Oh my. I'm so sorry."

"Thanks." Oliver feels his voice waver as he says it, something about Rosh's sincerity, an authenticity to his emotional presence, and perhaps just saying the words? *Passed away*. Like his mother went out with the tide.

He walks toward the living room, nodding for Rosh to follow. Finds himself rambling on about Mimi's adjustment to the apartment, which leads to his job at the gym. Rosh is curious about it and that gets them talking about the neighbourhood, which Oliver knows better, and what led each of them here. They discover they're close in age (though Rosh is a few years younger) and that he also went to McGill, where he studied organic chemistry.

"So how did a chemist end up . . ."

"In deep shit? I was on the inside, working for the enemy: Enbridge."

"Wow." Oliver's impressed. "And now?"

"Freelance."

"That's tough."

"As you would know."

"Yeah, I packed it in. Too much strain." He sighs, thinking about that album, the manuscript of his book that he shoved back into the filing cabinet. Drains his bottle.

"Well, you know, if you're ever interested, we could use a writer on this project. Zero pay, tons of glory." Rosh opens his arms.

FEBRUARY SLIDES INTO MARCH, and Rosh's invitation comes at exactly the right time: when Oliver can't stand the thought of another evening spent in his mother's basement, where the Angel has descended to unseal Mason jars of nails, matches, and elastics, cans of hardened paint, varnish and glue, to find more broken phones and clock radios. The experience reminds him of his dream: the cave, the panic. He needs a breather or he'll break down himself.

He meets Rosh after work on Queen's Quay, near the foot of York Street, where the Greenpeace flagship vessel, *Arctic Sunrise*, has docked. It's the start of March break for schools and just into daylight savings; at five-thirty the sun's still shining and the weather temperate, dry, with an energizing nip in the air. Tourist boat operators, winter-lean and hungry, have set up their booths and sandwich boards all along the Quay and its docks. Behind the *Artic Sunrise*, the inner harbour's come alive with vessels of all shapes and sizes: showboats, yachts, double-decker cruise ships blasting party music. There's even a steamship replica and three-masted schooner. As they stroll toward the gangway, casually chatting, Oliver feels like he's emerged from weeks — even months — of submersion underground. It's exhilarating.

Crew members dressed in clean orange overalls with *Greenpeace* stitched on the breast pocket welcome guests on board. The event's for membership appreciation — and for media, since the icebreaker just returned from a high-profile blockade of a coal ship heading to a lakeshore power plant. On deck there's complimentary food and beer, local stuff in sea-green bottles. Rosh greets a few people and introduces Oliver, but doesn't abandon him. "Let's check things out!" he says with a grin, motioning Oliver to follow.

The members and their guests have almost unlimited access to the ship. Oliver's never been on a real oceangoing vessel before, one that's sailed the polar waters and wild North Sea. They descend into the humming hull, where the air smells oily and the crew has set up a makeshift basketball court. They turn brass door handles to peek into spare sleeping quarters, white cubes with riveted walls. It feels like being inside a safe. Back on deck, they edge as far forward as is allowed, until they're floating above the water and the breeze makes their bottles whistle. They visit the bridge: polished cabinetry and glass-domed dials. Peering through the curved windows, Oliver tells Rosh he feels like an H.G. Wells-type time traveller visiting the future. Electric lights mark the lakeshore as far as they can see, veering around to the smokestacks of Hamilton Harbour. They watch a fireball sun sink behind black funnels.

Speakers announce the start of the speeches, and when they arrive on the back deck, a man at the podium is extolling the *Arctic*

Sunrise's achievements. We're working to protect Canada's forests and waterways from further exploitation, he says. We're standing up for a healthy future for all. The faces in the crowd appear calm, resolved. It's easier, Oliver thinks, to feel certain and inspired when you're standing with others. But it's really not. Each of these people, he suspects, wonders like he used to whether this work truly matters, will make any difference. Despite the speaker's assertions, the chainsaws and forest fires haven't lessened since the environmental movement began; they're spreading. Canada still has no national strategy to protect the Great Lakes or drinking water anywhere from pollutants.

A sudden boom bursts his brooding thoughts. The tourist schooner — flying the Jolly Roger — has fired its pretend cannon as it passed. The crowd on the *Arctic Sunrise* shout and a woman beside him utters a pirate's *Argh!* The speaker, laughing, says it's time to return to the party.

It's when he and Rosh are back on the bridge, listening to sea stories from one of the crew, that Oliver notices the ladder. In an alcove, metal rungs climb the wall and disappear through a small dark hole in the ceiling. Looking up, he sees a faraway light.

"The Crow's Nest," he tells Rosh. He noticed it earlier: a windowed cabin raised high above the deck. "Wanna see?"

"You go, I'll watch your back. I got a text to return."

"Deal."

They wait until no one seems to be paying attention, then Rosh gives him a thumbs-up and Oliver starts to climb.

As soon as he's inside the tunnel, he realizes this was dumb. It's pitch black, smelly, and claustrophobically tight — though not tight enough that he couldn't fall. He climbs reaching in the dark for the next rung, hearing only his breath. It's like being inside a hollow tree, he thinks. Though the circle of light below shrinks, the light above doesn't seem to get closer. It's dead fucking quiet. Maybe he should reverse? He looks between his feet: Rosh, small and faraway in the circle of light, is thumbing the screen of his phone. Screw it, he's not returning without a story about what he found up here, at least.

At last he pokes his head through the opening. The cabin's not lit, but the deck and city lights illuminate it perfectly well. Standing a few feet away and gazing outside is a woman. She quickly turns.

"Oh hi. Company," she says.

Oliver apologizes for startling her. The cabin's really just the hole in the floor with enough room around it for one or two people.

"It's fine. Is it just you? There's space." He heaves himself up and edges away from the opening and her as much as he can. "Isn't this great?" She gestures to the views of the skyline and lake. It's a gull's perspective up here, hovering above the deck. Oliver looks down at the crowd, then out toward the island.

"Beautiful. Thanks for letting me crash the private party."

"It's not, I'm happy to share it. I'm Gabe." They shake hands, and he recognizes her as the woman who growled like a pirate earlier. Warm dark eyes, pretty face.

"Do you work on the ship?" he asks, knowing she doesn't. It's just something to say.

"Ha, I wish!" She leans on her arms like she'd launch over the deck if she could. One of her feet twitches behind her. "I've actually been thinking about it, up here. I'd probably go a bit bananas sleeping in one of those berths, too confined for me, but some things would be amazing. Storms . . . sea life . . . the stars. Being out there, going to all the unseen corners of the world."

Her straight black hair shimmers a little, reflecting the coloured lights as she turns her head. Oliver feels like he's just travelled a thousand miles with her. The cabin doesn't feel so cramped.

"And did you check out that basketball court? Can you imagine a game when the ship's pitching?"

"An added challenge," he agrees, rather lamely. Her smile is beautiful. He's still sailing with her on those far-flung seas.

"And that would be the best time!" She raises a finger. "If the ship were under my command, there'd be mandatory basketball during every squall, tempest and gale."

Oliver grins. "And floor hockey."

"And ping-pong. Any game with balls and running. And a ship's band, too."

"Jazz? Marching?"

"Hmm. Marching's too serious, though I like the costumes. Maybe rockabilly."

Oliver laughs, they both do, then they turn to the windows again. He opens his mouth to ask her another question, but she's already talking.

"So neither of us work on the ship. What brought you here?"

That's easy to answer, so he volleys the question back. She tells him about being a grad student in ecology, coming here tonight with others in the program. "I'm new and still meeting people. It's so nice to get out — I've not even been down here before, to your lake." He's not surprised to learn that she's not from Toronto; her manner's too soft and open for local. Her dark features are unplaceable.

"Grad school. I remember those days," he says, curious to know more.

"Yeah?"

"It was a while ago, journalism."

"It's been a while since I've been in school too."

"How's it going?"

"Oh, that's a complicated question! I *think* it'll work out. I'm . . . learning a lot about things I'm not sure I ever wanted to learn, gaining skills I never really wanted to hone, but it's good for me, really, it just feels like boot camp. And I'm in pretty poor shape." She grins. "Rambling now."

She's so relaxed with him, even in this elevator space. He likes her voice, her energy, even her style: basic jeans and jacket, boots, and a gauzy, lightly patterned blouse, the only feminine part of her outfit. It catches the light when she moves, like her hair.

On deck below the party crowd has thinned, and caterers have begun clearing the food. Rosh will be wondering where he is. How can he keep the conversation going? He stands beside her. "Do you notice how people look more separate when viewed from above, even when they're standing together in groups?"

"It's because you notice the space between them," she says.

"Exactly."

"Though to me, when I look down from up here, what I notice most isn't the separateness of people, but their similarity. They all look more alike."

"That's true too."

They talk a little more. How long has he been up here now? His mind races. "Look," he says, "I've got to get back to my friend before he wonders what the hell's happened to me —"

"Oh, sure thing." Does she sound disappointed, or is he just hoping she does?

"But we're going to go for a drink, and it would be excellent — if you want — to have you join us. And your friends," he adds.

"Really?" Her eyes brighten. "Well, let's head down and see. Maybe your friend has changed his mind."

They descend together, him first, and he has to suppress his impulse to ask how she's doing now and then. She made the climb by herself, after all. The tunnel is just as long and oppressive, and by the time they reach bottom he's convinced that she'll leave.

Rosh is still on the bridge, talking to a crew member. They turn and look as Oliver and Gabe appear.

"Well?" Rosh says. "Did it lead to Victorian England?"

"Not exactly. Rosh, Gabe." He's grinning like a fool.

They return to the back deck and thank the crew for the party. Down the ramp, onto the shore, along the boardwalk. It's up to him to make this happen. A drink? Sure, Rosh says — thank god.

It's still early and they stroll along the Quay, discussing the event. The Westin Hotel with its executive-style lounge appeals to none of them. But Gabe spots a bar across the street: it's small and characterless, more like a convenience store, yet open and actually busy.

Oliver finds them a table and gets it cleaned, and the three of them sit.

Gabe smiles at him.

For a moment all he can do is stare at her. Blood rushes to his cheeks and an energy hums in his chest, one he's not felt for so long that he's forgotten how it actually feels. He's like an old dusty bell, silent for years, finally struck.

12

YOU WANT THEM until you've got them. That's been Jenn's assessment of Gabe's love life, offered at intervals through the years. *You want them until you've got them, then you don't know what to do.* And after umpteen flings, serial relationships, and a handful of "big" loves, Gabe's come to agree.

She's an excitement chaser, a romantic lightweight. Something in her is inherently flighty, and no matter how much she wishes or believes she's ready to dig down deep and see things through for the great long haul, it never happens. She won't be caught.

It took a married man to bring this thorny insight fully home. Hugh was her last go at love. A naturalist colleague at the Park, witty and charismatic, blue-eyed and grey-bearded and more than twenty years older, Hugh, she thought, would act like a counterweight: lend her emotional maturity, help her come to her senses. She broke her own rule against involvement with anyone who isn't free — though of course he'd deceived her about that, at first, through conversational omission and the convenience of having a wife in another country. By then she was hooked, wholly in love — or so she thought. Really, she just became more determined to land him. *You want them until you've got them.* Even convinced herself she'd be doing him and his wife a favour, setting them free of each other . . .

Two years on and off she spent chasing Hugh, trying to justify her own stupidity. Her friends who knew about him thought she was insane. She didn't even tell Jenn the whole story until she moved back here, because it shamed her. Hugh turned out to be not a counterweight, a balancer, but her own counterpart: dangling intimacy like a lure, then moving out of reach; causing pain to his family and her through his wavering; self-involved and personally reckless; committed fiercely to his work, yet unable to bring to those who loved him this same devotion.

Mirror to her own future self.

"Maybe you really are just waiting for the right person," Jenn says kindly. They've huddled on the back step to share a cigarette. It's March 20, Jenn's birthday, and here Gabe is crying and wiping her nose as she bemoans her idiocy again.

"Nah, there's plenty of 'right' men. I'm the problem. It's like you got the sensible 'count-your-blessings' gene and I got the 'grass is always greener' one."

Jenn ponders that.

"Not that you're boring, I mean," Gabe adds. There's nothing the least bit dull about Jenn, though her sister's life does at times baffle her, the way it has integrated so completely with the lives of her husband and children, her lean body swelling and contracting to create this family, forever altering Jenn's dimensions and lines. How has she retained herself?

"Family's *never* boring, not when you're really in it," Jenn says. "Nothing is, I think. It's just a matter of where you decide to hold your ground, so to speak."

"Hold against what?"

"Against the part of you that wants to flee, give up, can't be bothered. All that." She takes another drag, passes to Gabe. "I think your problem has always been space."

"Space."

"Yes. You think you'll have it by running away, be safer over yonder. Then you find yourself alone and you're lonely."

"I know, I know. It's pathetic!" Gabe stubs out the butt on the patio. "Give me another."

"No. It's cold and I want my cake."

Gabe grins. "You're not supposed to know about that."

The cake's in the fruit cellar down the hall from Gabe's room. She retrieves it and brings it into the kitchen, sets coloured candles in the thick icing, stage-whispers to her nephews and brother-in-law. He switches off the lamps and sets a match to the candles, then he and his sons carry the cake into the living room, singing. Gabe brings up the rear. The lambent globe crosses the room until it illuminates her sister's smiling face. Jenn looks a young woman again.

Gabe cleans up later, enjoying the excuse this evening has given her from schoolwork. Her phone buzzes on the table, drawing her to sit down. Eventually Jenn appears carrying the much-reduced cake.

"He's texted me three times now, the guy from the boat."

"I thought there were two?"

"Just the one who wants to meet up."

"The one you liked?"

"I liked both of them."

Jenn rolls her eyes.

"I don't mean *that* way —"

"Oh, *I* know that."

Gabe makes a sour face and returns to her screen. Truly, she's got too much on her plate to be meeting up with anyone except her group of students, yet she's already responded and could recite his replies, she's read them that closely. He was so very attractive. Smart, attentive, funny, and vulnerable . . . He felt Real, as did his friend.

Jenn squats to open the crisper, knees cracking, and starts moving things around to make space. Every week food enough for a commune comes into this house, all of it plastic-wrapped, packaged or bagged, even the bananas. It drives Gabe crazy. Give her brown rice and veggies, and she'll last for weeks.

"Want a hand with that?"

"You can't hide forever," Jenn says.

"Who's hiding?"

What a strange night that was: the ship and her excited school friends, the crowd, the wind, the gulls hovering to snatch scraps. It brought her back to Halifax, walking the pier, all the people she left behind and the mess of the last couple of years there. Hugh. Then a freaking cannon fired.

It was dark and quiet in the crow's nest.

It's true: she has been hiding. Then *he* came through the trap door. Oliver found her. Boom.

GABE OPENS THE MENU. Numbered dishes go up almost to two hundred. She turns page after page.

"See anything?" Oliver asks.

"Too much. It's overwhelming."

"Perhaps I can make a suggestion?"

"Please!"

"Well, there's the tempting 'sweet and sour bone and fish sauce,' or the mysterious 'fresh bulb and return meat.' Ah, but you're vegetarian. How about a nice bowl of 'baked backwash with mushrooms'?"

"Bullshit!" Gabe hits his menu with hers. Oliver calmly points to the items, and they spend the next while giggling over other translation-fouled phrases. It helps calm her screeching nerves.

He orders all-vegetarian with her, which is nice. The restaurant's noisy and crowded and stuffy, with staff shouting across the room, bussers weaving with bins, a din of pots and sizzling from the kitchen. Before them, loud paper placemats on a white plastic covering, clamped in place like at a picnic table. After the library's hushed cerebral gloom, this place rocks. Plus a romantic dining experience would put her over the edge.

Oliver's been cheerful and fun so far — also perfect. Once they order he leans toward her, voice pitched low and mock urgent. "So I have to ask you a question. It's been on my mind since we met, and you might as well tell me the truth." Dramatic pause. "What's your deal with bugs?"

Gabe exhales. Slowly grins.

"I know that this might be personal, and we're still practically strangers, but I'm really curious."

"Great! Ask me what you want to know."

He assumes an interviewer's cross-legged pose. "Well, let me see. This thing you have for moths, for starters. Is it exclusive? Do you, for example, also work with butterflies?"

"Just moths."

"Do you not like butterflies?" Sad face.

"Of course I do. I just prefer moths."

"The things that flutter out of cupboards, smash into lights. Cindery little fliers, squeezing into rice jars, chewing holes in sweaters —"

"That would be them!" She smiles. "Actually, only *one* type of moth caterpillar eats wool, out of thousands of species. Moths also make silk, the caterpillars do. And some moths are pollinators. People just tend to overlook these benefits."

Oliver sips his beer, smirking. He's got a bookish look: neat features, glasses. His face is attractive yet ordinarily so, except for the eyes: they're almond-shaped, darkly sensual, and seem always on the verge of some intense, withheld expression. It was the eyes that caught her attention when he popped up through the floor, like a creature emerging from its den.

"So tell me, as a slight shift in topic," he continues, "what's hot these days in the land of moths?"

Gabe laughs. "Now those are words rarely heard together! Hot? Hmm, well, a few new species are discovered every year."

"Is that what you hope to find?"

"I highly doubt it. They're usually located in rainforests, mountains, remote places. I suppose what I'd love to find is that, by some miracle, moths are actually thriving."

"They aren't?"

Gabe shrugs. "They certainly don't seem to be, generally. Their habitat's dwindling like, everywhere. Or being contaminated. No home, no future."

"Except for the Gypsy moth."

She hopes he isn't being serious. "Yes," she says through gritted teeth, "the Gypsy moth is a 'pest.' It's spreading and messing things up, so *it* — not us — is a problem. We must all battle the Gypsy moth! The thousands of other species are more or less invisible. Who cares about them?"

Their appetizers arrive steaming. "Sorry," she continues, "it's just kind of getting to me, all the focus on invasive species, all the research being devoted to them. I can't tell you how many studies I've waded through about the Gypsy or other so-called problem moths. It's all about how they're like, *unruly*, how they need to be managed. When they're simply moving where the habitat has opened up, or where people have brought them. And yes, it does become a problem, because all Earth systems are getting out of balance."

Oliver nods. "People just want to get rid of them, the invaders. Like refugees. Keep 'em out."

Gabe considers this: invasive species, invasive people. It's never occurred to her that the rhetoric around each can be eerily similar. "A lot of entomologists make their living around pest management, though, and it's part of habitat conservation, so it's complicated."

"But that's not what you're studying. You said you hoped to find out that moths are thriving, but you already know they aren't. Is that it? I mean, are you looking for something in particular?"

"What am I looking for," Gabe says. "The million-dollar question. I appreciate that." She takes another bite of spring roll, then rests the chopsticks on her side plate. "So, my project's pretty much a straight up diversity count. It'll provide information on what's out there in those regions, a benchmark, really, since there's not much awareness. But what am I looking for personally? Why do this?" Oliver's leaning in to hear her, those eyes like wells she wants to drop only the purest, most truthful words into. Her voice lowers with shyness. "I think what I want is to feel that I did the right thing for the moths. I've always loved them. I think they're the most strange, beautiful, extraordinary beings. They opened up the world for me, and they keep it open, so that as soon as the lights come back on, I don't forget how marvellous it really is. Somewhere in the last year or so, as things got worse on planet Earth and my life seemed to get more and more pointless, I realized the moths needed to be my priority. I can't stop the destruction that's happening on a global scale, I can't even 'save' them, certainly not alone. But if I give *more* of my life, let *them* be central, feel the urgency *they're* facing . . . It seems like that's the only path toward balance, toward a real future, you know? Maybe this study and degree are just steps, too, I can't say for sure. But this seems to be the right direction."

She nudges the plate of rolls toward him, wishing he'd stop gazing at her now. His rapt attention draws her out, then makes her self-conscious. "Here, these are yours."

Obediently he takes the cue, pours sauce on his side of the plate, dips half a roll, eats.

"What about your work?" she says after a moment. "I wasn't clear on it the other night. Do you work with your friend?"

"Actually I don't know him very well." Oliver wipes his mouth, clears his throat. He seems to be pulling himself back from an emotional brink; she can feel the tremor of it in him, and a corresponding tremor in herself. She even pushes her chair back a little. "Rosh is my downstairs neighbour," Oliver continues, "and we just started hanging out. As for my work, it's — complicated, also. My mom passed away earlier this year, and I've been pretty occupied with her estate."

"Oh. I'm sorry —"

"Thank you. I'm okay. At least, as okay as one can be with such a change, I think." His eyes slide away and his head nods forward slightly, as if pulled. Gabe feels it too: a stormy spiraling or welling up of confusion, sadness. Then Oliver takes a breath; the moment's passed in a second.

"But there's been a lot to deal with since, practically speaking, and it's made me reconsider my own direction. Things have been kind of tough for a while, like years, and strangely, Mom's passing seems to have shifted that, I think."

"Was she unwell?"

"No, nothing like that. Ah — here's dinner!"

They stroll afterwards to a park near Queen Street West. The trees aren't yet in bud, but the temperate spell has continued, the ground's dried a little and it's liberating to be outdoors without winter coats and boots. Oliver tells her about Toronto Island, and the lake, and the city's history with the waterfront. A noise grows and fills the air: starlings, roosting in the trees above the path, chattering hundreds. Gabe pauses and shuts her eyes: it's like standing under a waterfall. When she opens them Oliver's watching her tenderly. She gazes back.

It's after sunset and cyclists disappear into the gloom ahead. Stairs take them down into a wide grassy bowl. At bottom they look up at the wooded hillside. Yellow light spills through the branches from an old Victorian building, grey brick, ornate, the only such structure in the park. Oliver says that it was once a college and houses the elderly now.

"It's like a castle," she says. Its windows seem to shine from far away, another time and place. She thinks again of the crow's nest, their meeting in that sort-of-turret floating above the deck, how utterly surprised she felt when he was suddenly there. It had taken her breath away, and she'd babbled to steady herself.

"So do you come here often?"

"It's been a long time, actually, since I lived on the west side. My brother used to live near here too, way back. His restaurant's just over there on Queen."

"Are you close?"

"Not exactly."

She almost moves a hand to his back then, to the hurt she senses in the hollow between his shoulder blades. Instead she turns and looks back toward the path.

"Want to head out?"

She nods with relief. "Yeah, I've got a bit of a drive." They talk about grad school on the return walk to her car, the thesis she'll be writing, and he assures her she'll get through the learning curve just fine. When she asks about his writing, he speaks of it like it's on hold, supplies a few details about working at a gym, all of which puzzles her a little. She opens the door, tosses her bag on the passenger seat.

"Next time, if you're willing to endure me again, I'll tell you about my own writing tragi-drama."

"Can't wait," she says with a laugh, and gives him a light hug. Scent of skin, brush of warmth on her cheek. He closes the door when she gets in, stands on the sidewalk and waves.

Then she's alone, at first happily as she threads through the city to the Don Valley Expressway, then the 401 East. Night has fallen. Suburbs pass as a continual stream of lights, only vanishing after she turns north to Peterborough.

There, the downtown has donned its evening cloak of creepiness. Shapes huddle in disused entryways, and intersections are marked by lone or coupled people standing, scowling as they wait. For what? Perhaps a ride, or a deal; perhaps something that won't arrive today if ever. Young faces, hardened. Older faces, ravaged. They break her heart. In barely two decades the city she grew up in, where her parents would take them to the cinema downtown on weekend nights, has slipped into this decrepit state. Were the cracks present then? Of course they were. Perhaps they could have been repaired, but they were not.

In bed shortly after, she lies staring into gloom. How often she's lain here feeling adrift and unsure, aching for the people on the streets, for this city and this world engulfed with so much want and sorrow. She rolls over and places her hands on her heart, feels the warmth there and remembers the many moments from the evening that made her smile and hope. Thanks to Oliver, she carries a little lamp inside of her tonight.

13

JUSTIN WAKES TO his phone alarm. Sunlight roars into him. Cravings whisper.

Can't. Won't.

Two Xanax and a splash of vodka in orange juice. Steady on.

He keeps expecting a scene when Naomi returns from taking Gwynn to school. Is braced for it with an apology. But the tigress has vanished; Naomi won't engage. Not the morning after, not that afternoon, nor that night. He's frozen out. Life continues this way for days.

Naomi doesn't work rage like a human being. She's a machine. Nothing troubles her daily efficiency, no gremlins derail her schedule or even cause a hitch, a dropped dish or forgotten duty. Whether Gwynn is home or not Naomi's life clanks on, except its soul has been removed.

No eye contact, nothing personal in her address to him. Home is state bureaucracy.

He flees to Ace like a suffocating man. When he brings Gwynn home from school the family-engine runs until bedtime, then he's two floors beneath them in a silent house.

Apathy isn't natural to Naomi, though. It wears her out before long, which he's been counting on. She finally calls him at work and asks to talk. Gwynn has been sent to stay overnight with a friend.

Now, she demands details.

They sit at the dining room table, Naomi with a pot of tea, he with wine and the boost of a small toot to help stay the course. He shares everything she wants to know (except that, of course).

For the first time, Naomi's anger softens. She hunches, her face pale and long hair pulled back tightly, forced into a simple band. "It's just . . . this is just . . . so not like you," she sputters. Such deep disappointment, such withering grief. His throat tightens, his eyes brim. "I mean, you have a wicked temper, for sure, but you're the affectionate one," she says, with a bitter laugh. *"I'm* the bitch."

"You're not a bitch."

"Oh come on!" Her eyes sharpen. She sniffs, tears dropping down her face. "I know that about myself. I nag you and I can be cold."

"Okay, yes. But not really. I mean, that's not truly *you*, my love. It's just . . . the way you've been coping."

"Damn right." She wipes her eyes. He watches her struggling to gain perspective on the hurt, but it's like trying to lift a stone slab. "All the fucking effort I've made, and it feels now like you've just gone and blown it all away. I can't believe you'd be so reckless."

The sex is what she keeps coming back to. Who was she — or they? How did he know them? For how long? She's fishing for something bigger than a single night of excess, and she ignores what he's saying about how he feels about his life, that he's been realizing how stifled he's felt in every way and how he needs to re-establish his priorities. Repeatedly, he has to assure her that the sex was just an extension of being high, it wasn't about their relationship specifically —

"Ha! I'm glad it wasn't about me 'specifically'! It's not like I should be a major consideration."

Justin shuts his eyes in concentration. "I meant that I wasn't trying to hurt —"

"Of course you were trying to hurt me. And you have! If you want to be so honest, you can start by admitting your revenge sex."

The phrase riles him — or is it the portrait of himself? Justin stares. "Okay," he concedes, "it's true that I've been really pissed off at you. I feel like our marriage and the way we operate as a family have gotten out of focus, and I really, really want to fix that. But there's also more to it, about me, my own . . . changes."

"So you 'fix' things by fucking someone else, act like a fucking moron by calling to tell me about it after getting high in our bathroom? What fucking planet have you rocketed too?" Now she's on her feet. "Maybe it's never occurred to you that I could be unhappy too? I've only told you like ten million times! But I don't take it out on you by this bullshit!"

"You never said you were unhappy with *me*, just frustrated with your life."

"That's brilliant! Yes, Justin, you have nothing to do with my life. And all that talk about getting us into couple's therapy was just me spouting nonsense."

Now he's on his feet. She never told him that, she said therapy was a way to "communicate more effectively," which isn't the same as being unhappy with *him*. But she insists she's told him and told him, yadda yadda yadda — if he'd actually been paying attention —

The argument's a maelstrom now, sucking in all the debris of their years together. They circle each other, lobbing accusations, criticisms of each other's parenting and immaturities, grudges going back to the first years of their relationship — a narrative of dissatisfaction, limp intentions and mistakes. Whenever Justin feels like he's turned them toward an upward path Naomi undermines him from some new angle, and already she's twisted up everything he said to her so carefully when they began, and as he tries to explain it again she recites a checklist of his contradictions and lies.

And this drags on for, oh, hours, it seems.

With his head and gut pounding, he rears up for a furnace blast. "Go take another class in the woods! Go call your newfound friends! You're a fucking poser. No direction, no ambition, no risk-taking. No *real* help for this family. Indulging your fucking wishes and whims, your precious anxieties. Germs! Mold! Stress! You want hardship? Go work in a fucking mine for a week. Call up Casey, ask him how he's feeling after freezing his nuts off to take apart that sunroom — so you could breathe better, you poor thing! You're worried about Gwynn? Worry about your uptight micromanaging bullshit! You're a neurotic, self-indulgent yuppie cunt. And you're fucking crazy!"

With an ear-splitting screech, Naomi snatches the Russel Wright teapot from the table and wings it at his head. He ducks and the spout clips his ear on its path to the wall. "You fucking dip-shit loser! You're a fucked-up, hyper-inflated, self-pitying wanker! I hate you!"

The pot has smashed. She loved that pot. She bolts from the room.

Despair fills him and he whirls about. Madness!

His eye falls on the basket of wood. He grabs a handful of tinder from the tin pail and chucks it on the grate. Clanks open the flue.

Squatting, he begins to teepee the kindling. Upstairs, Naomi thumps around.

He doesn't know what he intends, but as the flames catch and grow, their heat starts to extract his own poison. He feeds them more wood, sits back. The house has gone quiet, and his desire to pursue Naomi — that's gone too, for now.

Justin turns off the lights and hunkers down on the floor wrapped in a blanket.

The fire burns well. It's a good fire.

~

ANOTHER MORNING, roused by the grinding of coffee.

Naomi in the kitchen.

Talk radio.

Down in his study, Justin lies on a foam mattress. Naomi looks after herself and Gwynn only these days. No longer does she pour his coffee into one of the dainty, hand-painted espresso cups she bought, Italian of course, each with a unique design and colours to charm the morning.

Justin draws the duvet over his head. He's survived many battles with Naomi, some quite prolonged, and because of that he's aware that this isn't a fight anymore. It's a rupture.

The phone alarm chimes. Gwynn will be awake soon.

He heaves himself up. Naked, he lets the duvet fall and takes unsteady steps to the desk chair currently serving as his garment rack, picks up underwear and jeans and gives them a shake. Dressed, he opens the sliding door: cool, fragrant air, bird twitter, the poplars shushing in the softest of spring mornings.

Naomi speaks only when he greets her. He dumps out the spent grounds, and as he's working the machine, she leaves the room. For a moment his actions continue and then he just stops, arms dropping to his sides.

Nothing, nothing in his life has prepared him for what seems to be happening in this house.

He doesn't remember his parents arguing. Did they hide it? Repress? They were opposites yet there was no perceptible tension or toxic build up. Mom got upset with Dad mostly when he did something to endanger himself: crossed the ice on foot from downtown, worked too long and hard (in her opinion) to help out a neighbour over the weekend, forgot to eat or to dress for the cold. She was protective of him in a way she wasn't with anyone else, even her sons. Did she sense the fragility in him, the susceptibility?

Other than tuning him out, Naomi's strategy has been to call in the troops. Her old roommate came over for dinner one evening with his boyfriend; on another Justin returned to a *House*-watching party, with several shiny-eyed, wine-soaked women giving him complicated smiles when he stepped in to say hello.

Today, according to an overheard phone conversation, Naomi's having a friend over to talk about "how to get something more sunny" in their household lighting arrangement.

Apparently, Naomi's been thinking deeply about that.

LATE ONE EVENING, after more days of silence, he encounters Naomi in the kitchen. Approaching his wife from behind, he speaks. Acquiescence ripples through her shoulders and without reply she follows him downstairs and sits on the sofa he offers. He pulls up his desk chair/clothes rack and faces her.

It's true that he's been deceitful, he says. He's failed to honestly represent his frustrations for the last number of years. He's let himself be engrossed by work and his own stubborn refusal to change. He's blamed her for constructing a prison around him when he'd not stood up for himself. None of this is the way he wants to be — with himself, with her. Accepting the Wrongdoer's Chair, he says all this.

And he speaks about the kind of marriage he needs and thinks they might yet have: a more authentic, truly sharing relationship of exploration and openness, where neither would feel compelled to pretend that these roles define them completely, roles that stifle them both.

Naomi cocks her head. "Are you saying you want an 'open' marriage?"

Justin winces. No! He needs to explain his ideas better, yet he doesn't quite know what he's trying to describe. Something he's never experienced: a relationship based on the best of the old values and what makes sense for them and these times. A relationship where the terrible he-she power struggles and pain of the centuries have been laid to rest. Is that even possible? He can imagine it, so it must be. A relationship of profound surrender — yes, *that's* where he wants to meet her. An image comes to his mind: long grey beach wrapped in fog, a place without borders.

They will co-create it, define it mutually, he says. He doesn't and can't have all the answers and needs her perceptions, her womanly insight. To further make the point, or gain points, he also casually mentions the list of marriage therapists he's working up.

Naomi nods. Her expression's encouraging, considering instead of critiquing. "Openness is about honesty, not doing whatever you wish," she says at last.

"I don't want to do whatever I wish."

"I believe you. But you want to be able to sleep around and have that be alright as long as I know. You're bored." She shifts, crosses her legs. "You love me and Gwynn, but you're bored. It's classic, so classic that I can't really blame you for feeling that way. I'm just pissed off about how you went about — or didn't go about — taking responsibility for yourself."

"That's — no! I'm not just *bored*." How can she so reduce everything he's just said? But don't his actions, in their crudity, speak otherwise? So much of what he wants seems a reaction to what he doesn't want.

He reaches for solid ground. "What I *do* know is that I want to be your husband in every way, with trust and acceptance enough that we can talk about our desires. But frankly, I don't think either of us is mature enough right now for whatever an 'open' relationship might be. Most of all, what I want is to do things with *you*."

"Things? I'd like to do more things with you too, but I doubt you'd come to Pilates or meditation." With a wry smile, Naomi shakes her head. "You know what I feel these days? I feel like I'm in a time warp. I'm working my ass off to get stronger, get more clarity, and you've . . . slid back to the party zone."

This puritanical contrast is hardly fair. *She* plucks from the wine cellar almost every night, though now isn't the time to point that out. "You used to love the party zone." He tries a smile. "We met in the party zone."

She gazes at her nails. Rolling the chair forward so their knees almost kiss, he peers into her face, trying to collect her, lift their beached ship off the shore.

"Honey," he says gently, "*everything* has its price. Monogamy, polygamy, celibacy, whoredom, drunkenness and sobriety. Risk has a price, and so does safety."

"That's hardly new."

"We need to operate as a team, but we can't do it if our idea of ourselves is so . . . so small. We need to enlarge us."

She meets his eyes, then looks away. "I really don't know how working on one's personal growth could be defined as anything but big. Maybe I just don't see things in your grand way." She stands, reaches up her arms and stretches.

"I should go to sleep," she says, not moving, her face half-turned toward him.

Justin rises and kisses her shoulder. She allows it, her body inclining closer.

He kisses her again. She's turning, offering her brow and cheeks, which he kisses fervently, his arms enfolding her. Then she's pulling away, mumbling that she has to go. He automatically follows and she whirls.

"Enough!"

He stares at her, bewildered.

He hears her upstairs, then heading to the second storey. He goes up to the kitchen, opens cupboards blindly, finds a glass and pours water into it. Dare he have a toot at this hour?

And then she returns in her thin white undershirt and pajama bottoms, flits around in an agitated way, opening the same cupboard doors, turning on the tap full throttle to rinse out a mug.

"I still can't *believe* you tried crystal," she says. "I can't believe that after living with me for over a decade, you'd be that self-destructive."

He shrugs. From all he said tonight, she continues to pick at this?

"I mean, at least do coke," she adds with a sarcastic laugh. "Or drink whiskey."

"Crystal is like coke-light."

"More like coke heavy, coke dangerous. From what I've read, it's mind rot." Moving around behind him.

"Stop doing that."

"Stop doing what?"

He takes a breath. He has to leave right now. Silently, he walks toward the basement stairs. But when he's on the second step she fastens her fingers in his hair and pulls.

With a yelp Justin claps his hands over hers, arching back and twisting.

"Stop doing what?"

"Let go!"

Naomi's face looms over his, ugly with rage. "You're such a two-faced shit! You know that I found your little stash? Oh yeah, you just wanted to try crystal out, it was just a temporary thing. Liar!"

The pain in his scalp's electrifying. He starts to fall backwards, one leg kicking out.

Gwynn. He chokes out the name, an instinctual appeal to sanity.

Naomi opens her fingers and he half-slides, half-stumbles down the stairs. At bottom he slumps against the wall cradling his throbbing head.

From upstairs, metallic clattering.

Justin crawls toward the foam mattress and curls up on it. He hopes that she's searching for the sharpest weapon, for truly there is nothing left and it seems only fitting that his wife, whom he's so betrayed and enraged, will end his life.

14

FROM THAT FIRST NIGHT he's imagined bringing her here. Gabe's busy and it took some persuasion for her to agree — nail-biting days, that. But she did. And meanwhile he organized what was necessary: contacting the Island Canoe Club, obtaining a membership near the end of their annual cycle — this following exchanges with the Trust to confirm that one of the Leveridge sons will be taking up residence in the bungalow later this year. The Littmans are moving out this coming weekend, in fact. He thought about showing Gabe the house, decided it's better to wait until next time, assuming there is one.

They ride over on the deck of the *Ongiara*, gulls gliding ahead of the advancing prow. Buffleheads and long-tails paddle aside. Gabe turns and turns to take it all in.

"I'd no idea."

"What?"

She shakes her head. Grey clouds scud on a raw, damp wind. The buffleheads call to each other with their soft voices. "That this city could feel almost wild."

It's just past four on Thursday. He worked a half-day so they could do this trip before dark; he'll make up the time later. Only a handful of passengers disembark with them, filing past a slightly larger number waiting to board. Gabe moves in a state of wonder, pausing on the pier to watch the departing ferry rumble away. "That boat!" she says with a laugh. She's wearing a wool toque, red, with a whale stitched in black on the brow.

He leads her along the road to Algonquin, superbly pleased. The quaint cottages and willow-lined lanes, the old fire hall (now the canoe clubhouse) with its little bell tower and shiny red door, then the new fire hall in blue, with clock and weathervane — all elicit gasps of delight. He points in the direction of his house. *His house.* Privately, he notices how very sodden the island looks: the ground oozy, water pooled in shallow dips and depressions.

The canoe racks are tucked behind a wooden screen by the bridge. The combination given to him works on the first try, he unlocks the shed and tosses out life vests and paddles. Gabe selects an orange canoe that he also unlocks and inspects before they hoist it onto their shoulders and carry it to the channel and set it into the green water directly from the bank. There is a dock, but it's submerged. They climb in carefully and push off.

The road vanishes behind shoreline grass. The houses on Algonquin drop behind. A slender egret regards them from the bank, its body still as carved white bark.

Gabe's quieted. The city skyline opens on their right then vanishes behind the pines of Snake Island. Their paddles dip in tandem, pulling them into a cold mist. He's not canoed here since the old days with his father. Strange that he should be here with this woman, and precious too; first the bungalow, like finding lost treasure, and now *her*. A night heron glides across the channel, stringy legs dangling as it rises to settle atop a fir. With a smile Gabe twists around to see if he noticed, and he nods.

Long ago, one of his favourite channels lay near here. The islands used to be full of them: willow-guarded tunnels where shy birds like bitterns waded and great turtles hunkered in the mud.

The channels held secrets, held the past. Lying in bed at night as a boy, he'd listen for the rustle of Indian braves canoeing to spear salmon, weapons glinting in moonlight. He was sure he heard their spirits many times.

He turns north into the first side channel they come to, hoping.

It's there! Narrower than he remembers, and choked with lilies and logs. He turns them west and heads in. Plastic water bottles, old rope, shredded grocery bags entangled. Bumping and maneuvering, they thread through to a kind of natural centre where the logs have concentrated. A nest.

"Let's hang out here," he suggests. They pull in the paddles and the boat holds.

The mist has become a fine rain. "You warm enough?" Gabe gives a thumbs-up. She's half-turned toward him, solemn and thoughtful, observing chickadees and finches in the thickets. He points to a lilac tree. "From an old garden, when there were houses out here." He tells her about the waves of building and settlement over the years on the island: the village that used to occupy Centre, the hotels on Ward's Beach and amusement park at Hanlan's Point. The razing of them when the city hatched new plans.

"What about before all that?"

"Before? It wasn't even an island, then, but a peninsula, connected to the mainland by a thin strip of beach. The colonial elite used to ride their horses there. In old maps the beach looks like an arm stretched out into the lake, with the island its hand, curled to make the inner harbour. And before that, before Toronto, Indigenous people — the Anishinaabe — came out here, though not to live. They used the islands as a retreat."

"They came for holidays?"

"And for ceremony, I'd think. Because it was so beautiful. I used to hunt for arrowheads — and pirate booty." He grins. "There were shipwrecks off Hanlan's Point later, back when the harbour had become a major port."

Gabe wipes the rain from her face. "What happened to the peninsula?"

"A storm washed it away completely one night, back in the late 1850s."

"Wow. That must have been something."

"It destroyed a newly built hotel. But people had known about the possibility for a while. A lot of sand had been removed from the peninsula for city construction over the years, so the beach was weakened. The Harbour Commission had actually been trying to shore it up. They held a public competition for solutions and awarded prizes to the best proposals." He shrugs. "They were too late. In the end, the land decided."

Gabe lowers herself from her seat and lies back, facing away from him. The canoe moves by degrees one way, then reverses. A pair of cormorants pass above. Rain falls soundlessly.

"This feels like the overgrown woods of an enchanted castle," she says.

"You seem to have a thing for castles."

"I guess it's my romantic side. My Dad's Irish — well, third-generation Irish. Not that they came from castles, but I think that's where the longing comes from, for ancient places, different ways, old stories."

"And your mom?"

"Acadian French and Black. That side's pretty opaque."

"Well, I'm afraid this castle's gone, and not coming back." He runs his fingers through the coppery water, which is cool and undulating like thought. A fat carp glides past and into the canoe's shadow.

"I wouldn't say so. I think the city itself is the castle. It's fallen under enchantment, and its inhabitants can't remember where they came from anymore. They wander the rooms, unaware of what's all around them outside — the real world, the Earth. They look out at it like it's a picture on a wall. Its voice is silent to them. They toss their shit out the window and move on to the next room. I think that's us."

She turns to look at him and he nods agreement, but doesn't know what to say. He tried to get people's attention once. They didn't want to listen. Treated him like a nut. His own passion destroyed what he had.

He wishes he could touch her now. His chest aches.

"Shall we keep on paddling?" she asks.

"If you like."

THE DATE FEELS SUCCESSFUL, their connection strong, yet when they part nothing in her manner indicates that he's more than a nice guy to hang with on a weekday afternoon. No drink or dinner, Gabe's got to take off. He accepts her hug with a smile like before, his body tense when he holds her. Is the hug slightly longer and closer? Maybe. Wave and keep smiling.

The eastbound 501 drops him at Greenwood. Since daylight savings ended the evenings feel gorgeously long. He strolls north under a glowing sky, thinking idly of Mimi, who's always lurking in the kitchen when he returns, even when he tries to be quiet. Does Gabe like cats? Turns onto his street and there's that damn SUV again, blue screen light of someone sitting inside. He's seen it in the middle of the night many times; the car and passenger seem to be here constantly. Who sits in a vehicle 24/7?

If he thought about it more, he'd just go inside. After all it's none of his business; maybe the car's a man-cave sanctuary for a guy with a crap relationship or crazed roommate. But he doesn't really want to go in, he's disappointed that Gabe left early, so he marches up to the driver's side. The window's cracked open and he raps on it.

The glass partially lowers, revealing half a man's face, looking at him.

A few pretenses rush through Oliver's mind. *Do you have a light? Know the time?*

"Hi," he says. Friendly firm tone. "We live here." He points at the house, pleased with this invocation of the weightier *we*. "And we've noticed you're parked out here basically 24/7. I don't mean to be a jerk, but it's making my girlfriend nervous. Do you mind telling me why?"

Eyes stare at him coldly. "Fuck off," says the hidden mouth. The window re-seals.

OVER THE WEEKEND Oliver goes to Oakville and puts in time and goes to the gym and catches up. He decided a while back that his visit to the bungalow would happen in the stillness of early morning, after the Littmans have gone. Just to see.

On Monday he boards the day's first sailing, the sole passenger heading over. Six-thirty a.m.: thick white haze hangs over the lake, and the island is a veiled serpent stretched on the waves. It feels like crossing dimensions and time. When he glances behind, the city's faded to a charcoal sketch of itself. Fingering the key's little teeth in his pocket, he watches the yellow guiding light on Ward's Island dock.

Commuters enter the boat behind him when he leaves. The odd dog walker appears and disappears on the road. Trees stand motionless, their black trunks wet. Water pools on the asphalt and brown grass; sometimes it appears both wide and deep. He must research climate resilience strategies for living here. The homes on the island don't have basements, can't have them. The bungalow has only a crawl space. He's brought his camera.

The bungalow's porch and side yard have been mostly emptied of junk, yet it's like the stuffing's been removed: the place looks even smaller. Seeing it in the day, he notices leaf litter clogging the eaves and green mold or moss seaming the shingles. A plastic bag's wrapped tourniquet style around a drainpipe.

Oliver opens the screen door and enters the enclosed porch. Sees it as it was, with the orange-plaid sofa and wood chairs, side tables and potted plants. He faces the lane: this view! Remembers bicycles on the lawn, one upended on its seat where his dad would be fixing it, dressed in his weekend overalls. Rosebushes. The lilac tree. What happened to it? Doesn't matter.

The front door's still the same: oak with etched glass. The hardware's been replaced, badly, and the wood's scratched and pretty beaten on the bottom edge, but otherwise the door seems intact. He unlocks it. Takes a breath. Pushes it open.

Low ceiling, cramped space. He forgot just how modest the old island homes are. And dim. His eyes need to adjust a little. Still, he feels like he's standing in somebody else's house — like he walked into the wrong place. Of course he was smaller himself then. His sense of scale different.

And it was clean. And tended.

There's still a woodstove, though he can't say it's the same one. Stains or burn marks on the hardwood floor. Bulging plaster walls, cracks running across them. A deranged person painted the walls dark brown, though maybe it was an attempt to hide them.

The kitchen — holy fuck. Above curling linoleum, mushrooms sprout from the water-stained ceiling: dark skinny stems with saucer-shaped caps, hanging upside down from the tiles like bats.

He wanders about, shaken. Justin's old room on the main floor: it would perhaps fit a dresser and double bed. Was it really so? The built-in cupboard he recalls, its doors gone. No hardwood here, just ugly tile. Was there carpet over it before? Ascending the tight stairs to the second storey, starting to use the camera like a shield now, clicking and recording. A warped sense to the floor. Forgot about the sloped ceiling in his parents' room, they must have slept in a double too, and then his: the antique crystal doorknob still in place, and the robin's egg blue ceiling light with a snowflake pattern . . .

But even these gems and his own nostalgia can't mask the truth: the place is a shitshow. It was let go for far too long.

APRIL: water streams, gathering the messages left by winter. Sluicing dog shit and pigeon feathers and straws, trickling into sewer grates — water whisks away all the old, the cold, the stuck. It dirties itself with city filth, yet goes down singing.

He wakes in the night at the usual time. Not from the egg dream, which hasn't repeated in weeks, nor from noises that shouldn't be there. Tonight he wakes to rain. Wind is moaning and sweeping against the house, and when he tries to look outside, the windows ripple like Van Gogh paintings. He cracks open the balcony door and peers over the railing. No SUV, which is a relief. Whatever that guy was up to, he had a nasty vibe.

Back in bed, tired yet wired. Mimi, a dark hump, now occupies the far lower quarter at night and will complain if his feet infringe. He lies on one side, the other, as worries and fears both familiar and new crawl out of their holes to enact spectacles of doom. It is ever thus in the thin morning hours, when the Shadow Show begins.

You don't have what it takes . . .

He thought it would be so simple, he would move there and slowly fix it up . . .

Rotten. Rotten like your life . . .

The Shadow Show dances from personal to global, and his thoughts shift uncontrollably to the things he learned when working on his book: the lake in India that explodes, the rivers that catch fire; the externalities and collateral ruin of professionals doing their jobs, seeing yet unseeing. He imagines giant toxic phalli being shoved into the earth, and the groundwater, the beautiful water . . . Back when he was writing he couldn't understand why people weren't up in arms about what was happening, yet now he does. Who *wants* to know these things? They seize you by the balls, if you let them. Life's hard enough! Everyone has their own shit to deal with. The world seems impossible.

So much damage, corruption, apathy, weapons . . .

Lies entanglements layers . . .

In the morning the Shadow Show players will step back into the rock walls that grip them more or less securely as he beats though the day doing necessary things, working uncomplainingly, waiting in lines, not breaking down from the loneliness of it all and the hunger for justice.

She'll never love you.

Nothing to do but lie here and bear it. This is their time.

LATE THE NEXT DAY, he returns from the gym to find the SUV back. With its tinted windows and the sunlight he can't tell if his friend's within. He heads inside and starts up the stairs to the landing. At Rosh's door are two men, one kneeling in front of the lock and the other observing, a small tool bag between them. They turn at the sound of his approach.

Oliver stops. "What's this?"

"Replacing the hardware."

"Oh good." Rosh must have got their landlord on the case. He continues up the stairs to his door.

Perhaps it's the two men present for a one-man job, or these particular men, with their clean black jeans and hoodies. Or maybe it's that the face of the kneeling man seems familiar? Oliver turns back around, puzzled. He's not seen Rosh since the night of the Greenpeace event; he mentioned going out of town for filming. And come to think of it, their landlord always does jobs like these himself.

He can't see what the kneeling man is doing because the other blocks the view. So he watches. The men exchange words in low tones. The standing man turns his way, frowns.

"You going to do my door as well?" Oliver asks.

"Not today."

"Well, I've got the same problem."

"Talk to the owner. We'll come back."

Oliver feigns annoyance. "I'll call her right now."

"We'll still have to come back."

He starts to scroll through his phone, his heart pounding. Their landlord isn't a woman, and though he's still not sure, his nerves are crackling. The men glance at him. There's tension between them. The kneeling man rises. They seem ready to abandon the job not done.

Oliver steps forward, putting all the authority he has in his voice. "*I'm* the owner," he says. "And I didn't call you."

The man who was kneeling narrows his eyes. It's the same man — from the SUV. "What's your problem?" he sneers. "We're doing our job here."

"No, you're not, you're leaving or I'm calling the police."

The men exchange a look. The SUV man nods toward the exit and they start down the stairs, Oliver behind them.

In the foyer the setting sun turns the men into shadows. As the front door opens, one of them spins and wallops him in the eye. He reels into a wall, whacks his head. His legs give out.

By the time he staggers upright, the men are gone. No vehicle, no trace.

15

THE DATE WITH OLIVER on the island leaves her fluttering
and confused. So at first it's fine not to hear from him when final
assignments and her literature review for the project are due, and
when the fieldwork that felt so distant is starting next month. Even
her basement room contains too much stimulation. The sounds
of normal life, of people walking around overhead, going outside,
activities in the kitchen, disrupt her concentration; she finds herself rising to make coffee or chat, which are not allowed. And the
moth web makes its own kind of noise, holding too much fascina-
tion, temptation to dream.

Robarts Library becomes her post. In this gruelish fortress of
passageways, recesses, cubicles, staircases, numbered doors, Gabe
retreats to a corner. Bare concrete, lights strung in rows, shelves of
spined tomes tucked close. She shuts out all but the screen.

That's the idea, at least.

Though it's less a shutting out than a splitting off. While the
sun arcs across the sky she types and pours over notes, thinking
sentences and paragraphs on bathroom breaks, each writing task
a puzzle assembled from pieces she must find and shape and fit

precisely. Hours mark productivity goals. She feeds and empties her body, keeps working.

But she can't completely quiet her heart. At the edges of her blinkered concentration flicker images and sensations. Oliver's cheek against hers as she hugged him; the muscles of his back moving under his shirt as he lifted the canoe; the smell of his skin when he leaned close on the ferry, his hand resting on her arm for a moment as they spoke. Her body thrums with erotic energy whenever she recalls these moments, and greedily, she keeps recalling them.

After that first dinner she searched out his writing on the net and found two articles from a while back, one a long and harrowing feature on fluoride pollution published in *Mother Jones*, the other about lead poisoning in Canadian schools. Each strongly researched and written, people-centered, moving, and pulling no punches either. He was really good, and the writing so important. What happened? On the island, after they'd finished canoeing and were walking toward the ferry dock, he told her that he'd burned out as a journalist. Freelancing was a slog, he couldn't make a go of it. "That's really too bad," she said, understanding yet also disappointed. She told him about the articles she'd read, how powerful they were. He was pleased yet sad. Said that maybe he'll return to it someday.

"Someday is now!" she blurted. "You got talent."

"And I'm not twenty-five."

"Exactly. You'll be even better now. Seasoned."

"Too seasoned."

Old Man talk. It irritated and kind of appalled her. How could he just give up on himself, on the work?

He seemed to notice or reconsider. "It would take planning to start again," he explained. "I'd want to be certain of myself and what I'm tackling, and I just don't know. I have a lot going on now."

Certainty? She forfeited that for a new direction. And who today has "certainty"? He seemed to her not so much lost as mired in defeat.

Days slip past in her cement cubby. Almost a week, and still radio silence from Oliver. Did she push him away? Worry starts to hurt her belly. No — it's been aching for days.

She decamps and rides up to the thirteenth floor, wrestling with whether to let him go if that's what he wants. When they parted he suggested dinner at his place; he apparently likes to cook. And she responded how? With a laugh. Gaily, she thought, coyly noncommittal.

Jerk.

From the south-side windows she looks out upon the modular city: gridded streets lined with Lego-block structures, the smoke-stacks of the Hospital District, the CN Tower needle. The built environment halts abruptly at a bluish expanse: the lake. That was where he took her, to his Oliver-world. And it had felt like returning to her own centre. Not the island itself, but being there with him, perhaps being anywhere he was? There was such a rightness to it, a naturalness, like they'd been doing this their whole lives. *Home.*

It freaked her the fuck out.

She can't afford to fall in love, not now! Can't she shelve the possibility for later? After the degree? Maybe he'll have his shit together by then, and she'll have a sense, at least, of the landscape of her own life. It's just a white blur now; she doesn't know where she'll end up or even who she'll be when she gets there. Hegyi's talk-ing about internships, even PhD programs.

Tap-tapping of keyboards, ventilator hum.

~

WHERE HOME-COOKED dinner dates can easily sprawl toward beds, popping by for a drink on one's way out of town has a safe, upbeat focus. Her breezy text to Oliver elicits a quick reply, though written with a care, even formality, that seems to characterize everything he does.

He texts her the address. "Warning — I look like a pirate," he adds.

"Peg leg and eye patch? Gold teeth?"

"Ghastly. But it's not damaged my hosting skills, I think. I'm really looking forward to seeing you."

She stops to pick up beer. Her nerves are singing when she pulls up to the house, gut tight, can't even suck a deep breath. The sun's going down. *Home.*

It's an older house, painted brick, long porch. He opens the door. He wasn't joking: a dark purple bruise covers the socket of one eye, so completely it looks almost painted on. The cheekbone below is swollen and red.

"Oliver!"

"Sorry. Hi."

"What the hell happened?"

"I got decked."

"Yes, I figured that." He's a brawler? Did she read him *that* wrong?

"We had a break-in here. Or so it seemed. I kind of got in the way."

"Holy shit! Are you okay? Is your place okay?"

"Yeah. It was actually Rosh's apartment they were going for. Come on in, I'll tell you the whole grisly story."

She hesitates, still shaken with surprise and doubt. Then she steps forward and hugs him tightly. He's taller and wider and she's on her toes. His arms encircle her stiffly, not really returning the hug. *Has* she offended? Or is he really not the man —

He draws her closer. His back softens, bends, and he lets himself rest there in her arms even while she's resting in his. The doubts vanish. His body feels strong and incredibly good and she loves his smell and the feel of his hair in her hand. Her eyes close. There is nowhere else.

After they part, she peers at his face and touches his cheek below the swelling.

"My god."

"It actually looks better than it did a couple days ago." He smiles and strokes the tip of her nose with a finger. "I'm so happy you're here."

He leads her up a set of stairs to a turn on a landing where there's a little stained-glass window, and then up a second set. The stairs creak. Her hand follows the wooden railing. She feels like she's ascending to a wizard's chamber, or a lover's or wanted man's, a girl in a story entering the place that will change her life, for good or ill; the place of doom.

He's just a guy with a black eye, wearing T-shirt and jeans, Gabe. Be cool.

She thinks she understands now why he didn't call or text: he was suffering, they're new to each other, so it was right to suffer alone.

Or he's got an anger management problem he's trying to hide.

Or she did come off as erratic and aloof — not infrequent accusations of exes.

In his apartment she hands him the beer, sees it go into the fridge. Yes, she'll take one, thanks. A gorgeous black cat — what? — brushes her legs, and there's introductions but she forgets the name. The cat swirls its tail round her calf not even looking at her, just possessing her. Then Oliver's showing her the space, objects whir past and they're in the living room and something's said about a balcony but she sits on the sofa, aware that she's talking though barely. Oliver sits in a chair practically across the room. Says he wanted to get in touch with her, but given what happened, and that she said she was busy, he figured he'd wait. All perfectly reasonable. He describes what happened to his face — a weird, disturbing story. The house stormed by the police, then these men. His friend Rosh and now him targeted. A film about fracking. But he's fine, he says. And all the while, there's the sunset through the window behind him, growing crimson. The sofa feels terribly isolated. Can you not sit so far away, she keeps thinking, pulling her socked feet up, sitting knees to chest, then knees apart. But he doesn't hear so finally she says it.

He looks startled. "Where should I be?"

"Over here, damn it!"

He sets down his beer. Uncrosses his legs. Stands. Finally he's beside her with an arm behind but not touching.

"Is that better?"

"A little." She smiles, agitated, pulse racing. So much for a "cool" drink.

Oliver looks at her calmly, solemn and sane. Those eyes, those beautiful eyes, eyes to wander in forever . . . The knot in her belly loosens and she leans in and kisses him. His breath meets hers, his soft lips, lightly at first, tenderly, then pressing, opening . . . She feels she's sinking and rising, sinking and rising. She's pushing against him, he's pushing against her, they're turning together . . .

"Wow," he says, a bit breathlessly, when she pulls away.

"Yeah."

She opens her hand and he reaches for it and their fingers entwine. Fuck being cool. This is a zillion times better.

16

RECLINED ON THE FOAM MATTRESS, couch cushions piled under his back and his tablet propped on his belly, Justin searches online for that Oakville realtor his mother used to know. One more message from Oliver about getting the house on the market and he'll lose his shit.

That overwrought pitch.

That passive-aggressive, self-involved, sissy-man tone.

Oliver's always been one Great Big Wound waiting to be poked. Well, take a fucking number, Bro. You aren't alone.

THESE DAYS his feet take him up the river path night after night. Reggie retires early with Naomi, two floors up. But when he wakes in the small hours and gets ready to go, the dog always appears: soft jingle of metal tags, nails on the basement stairs. "Good boy," Justin murmurs, stroking the furry cheeks and nuzzling his grey brow. They slip out the back.

It's at this hour under stark moonlight or murky sky that he feels his best. The pain of looking at things as they are, peeled of wishes and excuses and even resentment, is hard yet not so terrifying. In his upside-down life, this moon-time is like clarity during a fever.

Of course he's also sober.

On that front things could be better but are mostly reined in. He allows himself crystal every third day only. Xanax calms the cravings in between. Unfortunately it gives him a gooey feeling in his head, like his brain's turning to gum, a limp, pink, gum-wad brain for a gummy world. To counter the goo he drinks, which has required some finessing: vodka with Xanax makes him depressed, rye makes him sweat and red wine gets him drunk. He's settled on light beer. Despite the nanny warnings on the package against consuming Xanax with alcohol, he's found that this combination lets him think straight and still enjoy coffee without getting the shakes.

He did find a new source for coke, but decided it's too stupidly expensive. The line-snorting, high-roller type — been there, tried that twenty-five years back. Coke's too caught up with bullshit, with idolized wealth and glamour fake as silicone tits. If he's going to fuck himself up with chemicals, he'll take them common and rough. Crystal meth it is.

One day on, two days off. A neat, three-day cycle. And so the spring days have passed, in the psuedo-Switzerland that has become their home in Baby Point.

Naomi's never spoken about the last fight. Never asked if he was okay after she *mauled his scalp*. The next morning she was walking around the kitchen like nothing had happened, hair combed, face composed, and if *that's* not proof of Mom Suit madness he's not smoking junk.

She seems to him these days to be more mannequin or android than woman: the vital elements removed, access to neither fire nor ice. She addresses him like he's a lower life form, a machine she drops messages into. *I'm taking Gwynn to school today. Gwynn needs to be picked up at three.* And he nods, even as his eyes sometimes tear up at the cruelty of this treatment, to indicate message received.

Withdrawal: a woman's weapon. Can't call it abuse – no cuts or broken bones. All effects internal.

At home he subtly watches her, and when she's out he checks closets for packed suitcases and other signs of flight prep. Who knows what she might do? Her folks live out west, and he's personally known more than one man who's come home to an empty house. It's always the man. (Abandonment: another feminine form of violence).

There's one good thing about this situation only: he's grateful, immensely grateful, that he didn't lay a finger on her in self-defense, didn't so much as grab a wrist, for he considers no behaviour beneath her now. The Mom Suit mannequin has won in Naomi. He's afraid to keep his stash in the house in case she finds it and turns him in.

And yet, he'd forgive her the assault if only she'd ask, because he understands rage. All his life he's felt like punching someone, and a couple of times, long ago, he did. Men. Never women; that way Oblivion lies. The point is, he's had to *deal* with that fury, discipline it, be fucking "mindful." Naomi's not been so compelled. Girl don't know her own beast.

Legal counsel has been a thought. His own disaster prep.

They've come to the T-junction. He and Reggie cross the road to the path and start down through the woods. A bird calls. Something rustles in the undergrowth. He doesn't even look up. These night sounds are starting to feel as natural to him as the ever-present hum of traffic.

Perhaps, he thinks, there really is something the matter with Naomi. All those physical sensitivities she's developed, wheat and dairy and mold and scents, might they be symptoms of a larger issue? Her beast could harbour anger of proportions he's not fathomed. What woman alive isn't profoundly pissed off at what's happened to them and this world?

He has to consider that Naomi might be diseased.

The water's still running high. As he's strolling up the path, an egret glides out of the darkness and down the river corridor toward him, its outspread wings steady. Suddenly he knows: he won't involve the law. This is his marriage, not a business arrangement. He won't think that way and won't panic.

Switzerland won't last — and he should try to take charge of their direction. He will suggest again to Naomi that they see a counsellor.

An idea: what if he sold Leverage? Used the money to stabilize their financial situation. Not have to dig into Mom's estate. Would that be so bad? Could he handle open defeat?

Lights from the condos and Old Mill Spa complex recede. More trees here, Jack pines. The image returns to him, the one he keeps seeing: his mother stiff in the coffin, clownish makeup. One day he was yakking with her on the phone and the next was told they'd never speak again. One day she was swimming in the river and the next she was gone. Kaput. Done.

The initial question enlarges: why stop at Leverage? What if he just — changed course? Sold Ace too and became a man without these concerns, whoever that man might be.

RETURNING FROM HIS WALK early one morning, he hears Naomi on the phone. He's heading upstairs to see if Gwynn's awake, and he must be moving very quietly these days for her not to notice him. Maybe he's becoming what he feels: invisible.

"That's just it, he wants us to, but I've pretty much decided," she's saying from the bedroom, the door ajar. He freezes.

"Yeah, I know, that's why I think maybe we should. But it could throw me off, you know? I mean obviously it would be good for *him* to go . . . I know, I wonder that too. You should hear the way he talks about it. *We need an action plan!*" She quotes him, her voice low and booming like he's an idiot.

He feels punched.

He retreats into the basement. Heart pounding, he looks about desperately for something to counteract the tidal wave of hurt. His desk: estate files, mail, a book on investing, a book about the end of the oil economy . . . something's always ending these days. Toss it all away — better yet, get himself away. He could summon a taxi. He could shout "The airport!" Leave without even a suitcase, land somewhere cheap and dirty and live a crazy life.

Instead, he breaks his rules.

Using a fresh pipe, he sits on the toilet lid with the fan on, his iPod on, and two candles burning. Fuck Day Two. Fuck the cycle. He crumbles a nice hunk of crystal and lights up. In a few moments he doesn't need to go anywhere, he's soaring in his own plane again, alive to everything passing by the windows: a corner dust feather shivering in a current he can't feel, the silver nail heads visible in the baseboard (not Casey's work), a drop of water paused mid-birth from the faucet, and his own bent bony knees, the strangest sight of all. Doesn't remember taking his pants off. Doesn't care. There's so much freedom now, riding the wind! He can almost laugh about Naomi and her egotistic need to disrespect him. She's pathetic! Let her go her own way, find another sucker to feed her vanity.

When he enters his study again he strides to the desk, a warrior swinging his hammer. Flips through the mail. Crap! Notices a shelf: it's where he shoves things he doesn't want to look at but can't throw away. Wedged under magazines is a stack of envelopes. He drops the other shit into the wastebasket and snatches them.

They're notices from the City about parking tickets. Slitting one open, he reads:

On conviction you will be required to pay the set fine plus court costs of $16.00. If you do not pay the set fine and costs, an administrative fee of $20.00 will be added if the fine goes into **default**, the information may be provided to a credit bureau and the **renewal of your permit will be denied**. Should you wish to **dispute** —

Inspiration!

All these years and he never knew about the twenty-dollar icing on each parking ticket that defaulted. They've all defaulted, because he refuses to pay them anymore. Because parking tickets are a sneaky, dishonest form of taxation and make him blood-thirsty. He's lost thousands of dollars to fines over the years, mostly incurred during workdays when he can't waste time searching for legal parking spots — scenarios common to everyone that the City counts on. Of course he does eventually pay: to renew his licence plates, he's forced to pay these fines. He just presents his credit card to the bureaucrat behind the counter, glances at the receipt with open disgust (sometimes sharing the amount out loud just to gauge the personality of the clerk), and tosses it in a box for his accountant.

But he's never been to the ticket dispute office. The address is listed.

With coat and phone in hand he's out the door. In the drive-way he apprehends a problem: he's too high to drive. Not that he couldn't, he's so wired he could drive the Grand Prix. But knowing this might make him cocky.

Call the Kid? No time!

Opening the door to Naomi's Audi just because, he swings him-self inside. He always carries the spare key for her. Ha!

The parking ticket dispute office lies in the Hospital District (clearly a joke there), inside a chaste, grey-stone building that might be made handsome if someone cared. There's a vacant metered parking spot right in front, and he pulls in listening to Nine Inch Nails' *With Teeth*. Trent Reznor used to be too heavy for his taste; now he wonders where his brain had been. Back where he left his balls? And when did that happen? Was it when he chose comfort over culture, and closed the stage at Ace? Agreed to live in Baby Point? When bullshit exceeded work, and books about the economy became the only books he read? Was the weakness nourished by political correctness — or did that just make him question himself more, and in that questioning, doubt his way and eventually lose it?

A modest side-entrance leads to narrow stairs. After swallowing a pinch of crystal, Justin takes them two at a time. This is good — storming city bureaucracy, dealing with the bullshit head on! Don't all problems start when you move away from "connection to Source," when you let others take charge of your life?

Outside the office he encounters a quarterback security guard who stares at folks as they come in, then two baggy-eyed men, both with pot bellies and sloped shoulders under their cheap, coffee-spotted shirts. They ask the questions.

"You want to pay a ticket?"

"I'm here to discuss my tickets."

"You are disputing a ticket?"

"I have many tickets, and I want to talk about these administrative fees, which I don't intend to pay. Is that a dispute?"

It is, and because his tickets are past due and therefore defaulted, he needs a full record of them printed before he can proceed to the Disputes Area. With a tag from a counter machine between his fingers, Justin's directed into a large, windowless, very crowded room that's fronted by a service counter protected by bullet-proof glass.

"Heavy security for a parking ticket office," he comments to the woman sitting beside him. One droopy eyelid lifts, a blurry pupil rising about as far as his nose before returning to her phone screen. On it is a game that looks like a version of whack-a-mole.

Thirty minutes pass.

In response to the digital counter display, people proceed to the glass and speak through holes in the shield while black CCTVs observe. A woman with her boy kicking in his stroller. A man representing his cousin. Many stand-ins are present for those unable to get away for hours during a working day. The waiting raise their faces to the red numbers, showing meekness and patience — not from contentment, but resolve. The display digits change unpredictably rather than in sequence, designed to frustrate dashing out for a coffee or a bathroom call.

The bodies of the waiting – oh, the terrible bodies, Justin thinks, looking about the room. If there is a Creator, what does it make of such waste of potential? Slumped, sleepy, flabby. Puffy or puckered. Bony, sallow, saggy. Not a crew prepared to raise even a stink, let alone hell.

Forty-five minutes.

He's too high to feel hate, but he thinks hate, hate for the system that puts people in this position. That "system" is really so many, he reflects: municipal parking bylaws entwined with surveillance systems, policing and provincial licensing regulations linked to government budgets, economic and urban planning strategies in which living requires cars requires roads requires driving laws signs parking lots gas oil asphalt road salt and drilling and diplomacy and military deployments for oil to drive to work to make the cheque for the tax debt bills to eat so you can drive to work tomorrow.

Ha!

How could you fix any part of it without addressing the whole? The tangle's too dense ever to be pulled apart.

Yet is that really true?

"It's amazing what happens when you can't grab somebody by the collar anymore," Justin remarks to his new neighbour, a Black man who's been sitting contemplatively for some time, arms on his knees.

What was that story – the Gordian knot? Believe in the knot, and nothing will change. People will be sitting miserably in these rooms coughing up lifeblood the world over forever.

His neighbour stirs. "There'll be no collar grabbin' here," he says. "Got to show your passport, get through border check when you come in."

Justin chuckles.

"They got a metal detector in the next room," the man tells him.

"Seriously?"

His companion nods. "Justice of the Peace area."

"Really? I think that's where I'm headed." A metal detector! A *real* official!

Armed with his printout of amassed tickets, he eventually graduates from the big room. A corridor leads to a desk, beside which stands the detector and two apparently-armed guards who ask for ID and the printout, plus is he carrying a bag? Bags are searched.

This is like travelling to America! Have there been suicide bombers in the ticket dispute office? How could there not be? And are these post–9/11 theatrics now protocol in government offices across the land? A warrior should have known. He's not been paying enough attention.

In an antechamber, he approaches a glass-free counter and is handed a form that asks him to calculate the total costs of the tickets he's disputing. He counts the lines on his printout: twenty-nine tickets of different amounts.

"Is this a math test?"

"What's that?" says the startled man behind the counter. Justin repeats the question.

"You mean you can't do it?"

"Why am I *supposed* to do it? Don't you have calculators? This is basically a bank, right?" He pushes the sheets across.

"If you have a phone there'll be a calculator on it," the man says, genuinely trying to help. It truly is vile how a human being can be reduced to such timid acquiescence. It's like hobbling a horse.

"I left it in the car."

Without a word, the man pulls out his own phone, calls up the calculator, and hands the device across. Justin decides to tag this one a victory.

Twenty minutes, forty minutes . . . It feels like waiting to see the principal. He's a healthy citizen of the wealthiest city in this country, in one of the world's wealthiest countries, in a time of economic downturn, of environmental degradation, of never-ending international conflicts – of spreading fury, displacement and general uncertainty! And he's sitting in detention with a pack of doughy peers, awaiting their moment to fight parking tickets.

A Justice of the Peace!

PEACE.

What thoughts he's having! Three hours of his life used up, yet crystal, junk cousin of coke, gives him such endurance. (Just to make sure, he's been sneaking his hand into his pocket and pinching more crumbs.)

Grinning in his seat, Justin feels invincible and a little unhinged. Something is truly happening – his old self, that punk kid, is reviving. He can see now how he lost touch. At this moment there are six other men in the room. It seems to him that each is enclosed by an invisible cage through which they interact with the world. Yes, he can make out the transparent bars: they enclose the body about six to eight inches away from the skin, but bulge out into a square around the head. Do women have such cages? He thinks not; it's men who live parallel lives. Women are more like cage openers . . . yes, though many have lost that skill. Women are afraid of themselves these days, afraid of fat and wrinkles, afraid of feeling and of not feeling, afraid of men. These are terrible times, terrible; he doesn't blame Naomi for being crazy with them.

Look, a voice says. Something has hitched onto his plane. It speaks in his head.

You see the illusion. And Justin sees: how in the office, the electric lights strive to push back the shadows. Outside, the lights extend from city to village to frozen shore, tentacled across the planet.

You see, the voice says –

"Justin Leveridge?"

The man behind the counter opens the inner door and Justin

steps through. He's escorted right up to a small office. Inside waits a petite elderly gentleman behind a heavy desk. He has a bit of white hair and a mustache smudging his upper lip, and wears a navy jacket with shiny wrist buttons and a breast-pocket crest, colour-stitched. His frail hand extends and Justin takes it, feels a slight recoil, and realizes the man was signaling for the papers. He passes them across and sits down in a padded chair opposite while the man reads.

On the desk lies a bible. A bible! There's also an adding machine. Truly, this is empire.

"How are you?" Justin says, because the silence is irritating and his eyes are starting to burn. The room has a big window and all the lights blazing.

"Oh fine, fine," the Justice answers without glancing up, his lips barely parting. He's rapidly yet calmly scanning the papers one by one, lifting each and setting it aside with care. His watery blue eyes move back and forth behind his glasses. "Your total looks correct," he concludes. "So what is it that you want to do?"

"Wipe it out," Justin says, and explains his reasoning. He tells him about Ace, thirty years on Queen West, and offers a business card.

The Justice of the Peace reads it. "That's a very long time to last in the restaurant world. Hard to achieve." He's considering options.

"It is, and really this year was entirely typical in terms of tickets. I've paid out I don't know how many thousands since I opened, at least two or three annually, which is like, eighty, ninety thousand dollars! I can't do it anymore. I'm being bitten to death." Justin speaks forcefully yet with control, or so he hopes.

The old guy's gaze is neither hard nor soft. He says he can remove the administrative fees, types into the adding machine, writes down a figure and shows it to Justin, a new total.

"That's better, but I was hoping for the principal amount to be reduced too."

"I can't do that."

"I was hoping for a pardon, actually. What do you call it? Debt forgiveness. That's really why I came here."

"I can't do that. I can only reduce the extras. You save a lot." The Justice taps the paper for emphasis.

The burning's spreading. "With all due respect, I don't actually *save* anything when I'm being fined against my will. I still have to pay over two thousand dollars."

The man shakes his head. His voice is neither energetic nor tired. "This is all I can do. You agree to it, or you pay the full amount."

No compassion, no honour. How could he have expected them? Gloom creeps into him, a feeling of chewing on grizzle for too long. "That's really not fair."

The man's mouth opens to flash his little teeth. Is the old timer showing some spirit? "It's not a question of *fair*, this is just the situation. You've received the tickets, you didn't protest them in court —"

"To do that I'd have to go there in person, during business hours. I'd have to take time off work for each individual ticket! Who can do that? Almost nobody."

"Yes, well, that's the process, and if you found it important enough, that's what you'd have to do. Now the tickets have defaulted and here we are. You said yourself that the tickets were given when you were working, so they are part of your work, maybe one that you can reduce in the future."

"The process is manipulative! I just spent half a working day waiting for this conversation."

The Justice sits back in his chair, a hint of a smile, or maybe a wince, on his face. "If you're not accepting it, then fine, but that's all we can do."

Justin stands, wipes his brow. This man's brain needs dashing in, but it's impossible to get violent with a fellow so wrung of physical potency. Perhaps that's the idea.

The Justice of the Peace picks up his pen.

"Acceptable?" he asks.

How can you argue with what isn't a person, but a function? With a nod, Justin holds out his hand for his receipt.

HE DRIVES TO PICK UP Gwynn from school, a yellow parking ticket fluttering on the windshield. The crystal's starting to wane. He remembers Naomi's words about having already made up her mind, and her mockery of him. A sadness of smothering proportions awaits.

Gwynn kicks off her shoes in the car and sets her socked feet on the dash, a position Naomi does not allow because feet should not be put on furniture. She looks like an animal beside him, her face secreted behind her hair. He loves catching this bit of time with her before he heads off to work in the evenings, back when he was still doing that.

"Tell me about your day, Trinket."

"Are you sick?"

"Why do you say that?"

"You look it."

He shrugs. "Guess I better eat more vitamins."

"Your face is wet. There's a stream —" She touches the rill trickling down his cheek and squeals.

"It's not nice to tell a sick person they're revolting," he says. Her disgust stings.

"You said you *weren't* sick."

"No, I *said* 'I guess I should take more vitamins.' Get your freakin' story straight."

She huddles against the door. They approach the house, pull into the driveway. He puts the car in park but keeps the engine running.

The house looks like it belongs to another family. Such is a man's fate when woman bars the door: though technically he's allowed to enter, he's blocked from what really matters. He'll never get into the Keep.

Gwynn opens the door and turns to look at him. "Aren't you coming?"

"No."

"Where are you going?"

Down, Justin thinks. The crystal is leaving his blood, and he's back in his cage.

17

BY CHANCE HE'S OUTSIDE, setting the recycling by the curb, when Rosh arrives home. He waves and smiles as he pulls up and Oliver raises a hand. He didn't tell Rosh about the assault over email, just the break-in. And he didn't plan on laying this news on him the second Rosh returned, but here they are.

Rosh parks, steps out with a relieved sigh, pushes sunglasses up into his curly hair and stretches.

"Welcome back. How was the drive?"

"Good! I love the time to — whoa." He freezes. "What the hell happened? Did you start training at the gym?"

Oliver mentioned it's a boxing gym that night they had a beer. Good memory.

"I'm afraid not," he says. "This was your buddies' calling card."

Rosh closes the driver's side door and leans against it, listening intently as Oliver explains. "My god, this is so terrible. I can't even take it in yet, Oliver, I need to hear everything again. Are you free in a bit? I'm going to haul this stuff inside and I've got to quickly call Charlotte, our ex-director. Then I'll change and refresh so I can focus. But I won't be long."

"Take your time. You should also check your place, just in case they returned at some point?"

"Right. I'm not really worried about that, though, I had everything that they'd want with me. But I'm glad I saw you." He looks at Oliver a moment, then shakes his head. His eyes glint with anger. "This is so fucking wrong! I'm so disgusted right now I can't think." He turns and pops the trunk and starts lifting out hardback equipment cases, a knapsack. Oliver almost offers to help, then thinks the better of it.

"See you in a bit," he says.

"Yes."

Inside, he climbs the stairs slowly. His sleep's crappy to begin with and his eye hurts at night. Even his back has started acting up again in the same old spot. Yet despite these aches and injuries, he feels better than he has for a long, long time. Clearer somehow. There's Gabe. But even before her visit something had changed, after the men were here. At the gym the next day Foroud came into the office and thumbed his chin, squinting at the bruise. He touched it carefully here and there, then nodded with satisfaction.

"Your eye's going to be fine. You did good."

"I did nothing but fall over." He's never trained for boxing, hit a person or been hit. Foroud once sparred with Micky Ward.

"No," he insisted, "you got up. You stood up! To them. You did *good.*"

He stood up. He did good. Oliver still doesn't really understand what that means — something in the world Foroud knows. But maybe that's why he didn't tell Rosh about the punch earlier or want to report it to the police, as Gabe thought he should.

When he comes upstairs, Rosh brings a tube of anti-inflammatory cream still in the box. "I've used this brand and it works," he says, offering it. Oliver's touched. He hadn't thought to treat the swelling with anything but a pack of frozen peas.

"How's it feeling?"

"Mostly fine. Your place okay?"

"Yeah."

"Come out to the balcony?"

"Gladly." Rosh stoops to coo at and pet Mimi, which amazes Oliver again.

Outside, he points to the street. "Someone's been lurking around down there for weeks, sitting in a car all hours of the day and night. Have you noticed?" Rosh hasn't, but then, he'd have to stand at his living room window, and maybe he's not an insomniac either. "I kind of confronted the guy one night, and I'm pretty sure he was one of the pair trying your door."

"No way," Rosh says, not doubtful but dismayed.

"The car showed up after your arrest."

Rosh sighs, takes a seat in the wicker chair. He looks spent. "Fuck. This just gets better and better. Surveillance and break-ins— that's more harassment, of a sort. What I don't understand is why they'd attack you."

"I just pissed them off, I think. Got in their way. You think this is connected to your film?"

"Yes, but not just the film. I will tell you." Oliver sits as well. Rosh takes a deep breath, and when he speaks, he looks at Oliver squarely. "Remember how I mentioned before about Windsor, the blockade where the police got violent? Filming that seems to be what started this whole . . . escapade. The audit happened pretty soon after. I don't know if I mentioned that Charlotte, our director of the Alliance before we were shut down, was audited personally as well? She made, like, forty grand a year, has two teenage kids. Good thing her partner's a lawyer. Anyway, after the CRA closed us, we stayed active informally because we'd started to make the film, as you know.

"So. I'm in Fredericton at the end of January this year, and I'm leaving the Lord Beaverbrook hotel. The National Energy Board was holding hearings there about Energy East, the proposed pipeline?" Oliver nods. "It was a public meeting. Opponents were giving presentations. We filmed. So this RCMP officer comes up to me outside and introduces herself. She's plain clothes, but straight up about who she is. She knows my full name, including how to pronounce it correctly. And she's acting all kind of familiar, like we've met before, like I know her — which confuses me, right? I'm trying to recall but can't. She asks if we can have coffee, chat about my project. Well, I'm surprised, and I think about it, but decline. Say it's been a long day. It's a polite yet very tense conversation. Creepy, to be honest. It wasn't long after that the police showed up here."

"What's happening with those charges?"

"Still waiting on a court date."

"Did you know her, then? This officer?"

"I think we met at a protest. There's a lot of undercover surveillance now. I went through my pictures but couldn't find one of her." Rosh runs a hand through his hair. "I so wish this hadn't happened this way, that you'd not been dragged into this."

Oliver shrugs. "I did choose to get involved. I didn't have to."

"Right, and that's twice now you've been understanding, and I assured you the first time that nothing else would happen again."

"You said you weren't nuts too."

"Maybe you'll change your mind when you hear the rest of the story. Maybe we should drink more beer again first."

"Great idea. Back in a second."

"Me too, I need my parka."

It's past nine, overcast and damp but mild enough to sit outside in their coats. From the Greenwood Yards the faint squeals of subway trains returning for the night have the reassuring tone of friendly human industry, puttering on. "So the film," Rosh says, "is about fracking, obviously. I don't know how much you've read about it, but there were calls for a moratorium against fracking in Ontario. Moratoria have been passed in several provinces, so it looked hopeful for us, for a while."

"And now?"

"Oh, it's toast. Provincial government said they won't support it. At the same time they claim to be studying fracking, not making any commitments to anyone — which is crap. We have our environment minister on record lying about the extent to which shale rights have been sold and about plans for drilling. There's all kinds of seismic exploration happening along Lake Erie. The whole lakebed is shale, and huge sections of it have been bought."

"They're going frack *under* the lake?"

"You bet! Someday I'll be able to visit my parents in Port Stanley and gaze out on the platforms and watch the fishing boats pass them, while there's still fish to catch. Won't that be a treat? Isn't that the future we're all hoping for?" He grins devilishly. "Oh, it's going to be grand. They're planning wells all around Chatham, London, Niagara . . . The deals are coming to the table soon. Probably right now."

Rosh tells him to look up the geological maps the energy companies have created, information easy to find online. "You'll see that basically all of southwestern Ontario is up for grabs. It's all shale, right? From Windsor through to Toronto and up to Georgian Bay, that's what we live on. The drills will be coming, coming by the thousands. And if they fire up the offshore drills in Lake Erie, contaminate all that water for production —"

"It'll flow into Lake Ontario. Here."

"And out to sea eventually. One world, one great watershed."

Oliver didn't know any of this. The news settles in as a deep, dragging ache.

"Okay . . . so we have land rights bought, plans underway, bullshitting politicians. Sounds like business as usual."

"Exactly, but here's the unexpected thing." Rosh leans forward, holds up a finger. "As part of their considered moratorium on fracking, the provincial Ministry of the Environment commissioned a major study of fracking hazards. The research team was first-rate, and supposedly independent. They investigated dozens of fracking sites in Canada, and guess what? They concluded that fracking poses *significant risks* to human and other biological life, particularly near bodies of water and densely populated regions. The report is absolutely clear. In fact, it's pretty well damning."

"Great news, then."

"But who wants to know this? Not business!" Rosh mock-bites his nails. "The study was submitted to the Ministry last year and poof! No release. How do I know this? I received a leaked copy from a friend inside. I got it in late February, and now we're coming to the point. I think that's what the guys were after. Ostensibly at least? Because they should realize that everyone in our group has a copy on their computers now. So I think really, they're trying to intimidate us again."

Oliver stares at him. The story's graver and more horrible than he dreamed. To brush up against it even in this way imparts a bone-level dread, the same queasy feeling that seized hold after he witnessed Rosh's arrest; the intimidation's working very well, at least for him. At the same time — just as profoundly — he shares Rosh's outrage and admires the man's courage. Behind the rhetoric of environmental protection and care, a toxic future's being quietly installed.

"What if they return?" he asks. "Or what if the police come again and press more charges?"

"It's possible, I know. Things are getting ugly. And expensive. And more and more time consuming. We've been discussing what to do about it." Rosh stares at his feet. Oliver can see how the situation galls him: he has the hurt, morally bewildered look of a person who's tried to do the right thing, who never expects to be deemed an enemy.

Oliver has an idea. "What about holding a press conference? Going public with the study?"

Rosh shakes his head. "We're just a defunct group. It's too tough to get media attention. Actually what we're hoping to do, first, is work the study into the film. It's a lot to take on at this late point, when we should be moving to post-production. It's hard on the group. People are a bit divided over it."

"But it sounds crucial."

Oliver's reminded of his old boss at the *Post*, who accused him of "getting too political" when he wrote that first column on water pollution. The different forms of pressure exerted to keep people silent, from the casual, almost-subliminal dismissals and labels cast on certain topics and those interested in them, to social censure, job loss, and then — a step into another realm. He still wonders what it was like to spend the night in jail, be given a taste of what new life could be waiting. He thinks he'd be scared shitless.

IN THE MORNING he tends to his bungalow plans over coffee, loading the pictures he took. Now that he's had time to digest the house's condition, he feels optimistic or at least motivated again. The reno will probably be more like a rebuild, okay. He will have money for that from the Oakville house and his inheritance; he can move forward. Through one of the trainers at the gym he's connected with an architect about his hopes and plans. She's sent him a list of questions, and he attaches some of the photos with his answers.

Vaguely aware of rain starting to patter against the windows, he presses send, then begins another note to his brother. Last word from Justin was that the Oakville house was scheduled to be assessed, prior to going on the market. Oliver writes about his visit to the island, more to let Justin know that things are progressing and he'll need money than from a belief that his brother cares. He updates Justin on the items remaining to be sorted, donated or claimed at their mother's, which isn't much, and the few touch-ups and fixes scheduled to make the home appear fresh. Itemizing all these things stirs ire. Justin, the wanker, hasn't shown up even to take away the things he said he wanted. "All of this has taken months of time and effort. It'll be a relief to wind this up," Oliver writes, then erases because that's snarky, then inserts it again. Another click to send, and close window.

He's reading the day's news when there's a bright flash. Lightning? He looks up and listens for the thunder, hears nothing but rain, and burrows back into the story. He's following the pipeline protests out west, wondering if they'll inspire similar events in Ontario when the time comes. On a map of the country, a thin red line shows the proposed transnational pipeline path: it squiggles through British Columbia and Alberta, swoops across the prairies, loops into southern Ontario. In Quebec and Atlantic Canada lie grey disconnected strokes.

He imagines a similar map of shale rights to the lakebed. What Rosh told him sounded too immense in its scope to be real, yet he knows it must be. It is. He just can't bring himself to look.

A brilliant flash fills the apartment.

BOOM! Thunder shudders the house.

Oliver instinctively ducks — that second of not knowing what's happening. There's a thud from the bedroom: Mimi jumping to the floor.

The thunderclap opens into a long, eruptive rumbling. Then a moment of silence, like dust clouds billowing from wreckage, and rain starts teeming — as noisily as hail hitting the roof right above him. He goes to the window. Two people on the street running. A car creeping past. The rain drives into the pavement like white-tipped arrows, hard and straight.

A quarter hour goes by like this, while he makes and eats his breakfast, watching the trees rippling. Foroud calls: he can't drive in from Whitby right now, the storm's bad out there. Oliver needs to open the gym. He gets out his old cycling raincoat, stuffs an extra pair of shoes and socks in his pack and slings it on with the coat overtop. No rubber boots, so he pulls plastic bags over his socks.

His usual stroll to the gym becomes a full-out trek. On Greenwood near the Danforth he veers into the first real shelter he's reached, a storefront doorway. What a fool's errand! Who's going to come to the gym?

It turns out a few soggy diehards show up for morning classes. Oliver keeps a local news page active while he works in Foroud's cubicle. Online traffic reports show great puddles collecting on the low roads, the start of flooding. Power has gone out in vulnerable places. After an hour or so the rain eases, coming and going, and by noon it stops altogether, though the wind intensifies. He walks home later to garbage bins lolling and debris whirling.

With Mimi fed and the morning's wet shoes tucked under the rad, he applies more cream to his bruise and settles in for a dull night. The rain's gotten to his mood. Nobody responded to his morning emails, and the text he sent Gabe was ignored. At some point he dozes off on the sofa with a book, and when he wakes, something's weird. He sits up, hears a distant mew.

The apartment's dark — *fully* dark. He can't see a thing.

The lamp clicks unresponsively. Feeling his way to a window, Oliver looks out an awesome sight: beyond the glass lies an opaque landscape. There's barely a light on anywhere as far as he can see, just a few emergency beacons on the tops of distant towers and one partially illuminated building that must be a hospital. He slides open the balcony door and feels cold wet wood underfoot. Creaking trees, sirens. Someone's patio chimes dinging. He waves his hand in front of his eyes. It's barely discernable.

A feathery touch on his ankles makes him start. Oh shit, the door, the cat! But Mimi doesn't bolt. She swirls her tail around his leg, pushes her face against him. Carefully he squats down and holds out his hand. She nuzzles it, purring.

"Hello sweetheart," he coos. It's amazing how invisible she is, just a furry warm body under his hand. He starts to hum quietly to her, a made-up melody. Then he guides her back inside, closes the door. He sits down beside it on the floor. Mimi walks under his hand, flops on her side against him.

All the petty spats he and his mother got into, he misses them now. He runs his hand along the cat's belly. This would be a hell of a night to be alone.

GABE WANTS TO SEE him but not to come over. She's been inside for days grading exams, she says with a groan. Can they do the park again? He agrees, trying not to sound disappointed. He wants her here again, like before. He wants to cook them dinner. It's not about moving them toward sex (though that would be very welcome), but being alone, private. He can't think of how to say that without sounding awkward or pushy, though. She suggests they meet again at the same place on Ossington, "our place" she calls it, which is something, though it also feels like going backwards.

When they meet, she's lovely. She's wearing a dress with ankle boots, her legs bare underneath, and as they're waiting in line she takes his hand. Maybe he shouldn't get hung up on an idea of direction, whether forward or back. It's been ages since he dated. Maybe he doesn't even know what forward means.

"Your bruise is looking a lot better, and kinda interesting too," Gabe says after they sit down. There's a yellow ring with a bleeding-purple border all around his eye.

"I am technicolor."

"Actually, you look like a moth. Or half of one."

"The perfect date?"

She giggles, smiles. "I think so."

When they stroll in the park after eating, he tells her about his conversation with Rosh. "That's really scary," she says, "the fracking plans themselves, and what they're doing to make sure no one knows or can stop them." She looks up at him. "Are you going to get involved? Help him out?"

He's a bit startled by the question. "Me? No, I don't think so. He's got his group."

Gabe says nothing more about it. She's still holding his hand, but things feel more distant between them.

In the short time since they were here, the trees have flowered. They pass tulips and daffodils in bloom, and violets emerging on the grass. They descend the stairs to the dusky, grassy bowl they visited before and sit on the slope where the yellow light of Gabe's "castle" spills through the branches from above. Yet she sits with her arms around her knees.

"The political climate's changed since I was writing years ago," he says, feeling the need to elaborate. "Everything's become more polarized, riskier." New legislation has framed protest activities in criminal terms. He tells her he's read that individuals and organizations have been labelled "multi-issue extremists" by the RCMP, whose new term for peaceful protest is *non-violent attack strategy*. "Peace equals war, violence equals peace, and Orwell must be spinning in his grave."

Gabe says she's read the same things.

"Somehow I feel like I'm not meeting with your approval."

She leans against him, chin on his shoulder. "It's not disapproval. But you said it yourself: things are getting worse. I guess I've come to more of a seize-the-day philosophy. Rosh is basically on your doorstep, and you like him."

"Hmm. Does your philosophy apply to us?"

"Ah, touché." She straightens. "I'm struggling with that, for sure! I'm sandwiched between the end of term and my fieldwork, which begins in about two weeks. So it's not exactly an ideal time to start something new, and to be honest I'm kind of freaking out, because I want to see you very much, but it's like, when's that going to happen? And what can I give?" She waves her arms frantically.

But she wants to be involved with him, *very much*. That's all he needs to hear. The rest is logistical details, which seem pretty manageable.

"Your fieldwork's not going on forever," he says. "Just the summer."

"But it's a good couple of months and it'll be extremely busy."

"Can you visit? Could I visit you?"

"Uh, I don't think the latter. Not sure of the former at all. Maybe? Hopefully?" She plucks at the grass.

"Let's walk again," he suggests. They rise and climb the stairs and meander toward the park's perimeter, where Gabe left her car. "Look, I think the best thing is to just be relaxed. I'm in no rush, understand? I'm thrilled with how things are going." Which is mostly true.

She squeezes his hand. "Me too. It's just that slow has never been my best gear, personally. I think it confuses me."

He stops so she turns to face him. "Hey," he says, "*you* can rush all you want. Do whatever you need to, barrel away! But when it comes to you and me, just don't stress about pace on my account. I'm not going anywhere."

Her eyes shine. He pulls her close and kisses her brow. "And one more thing? For shit's sake, come over for dinner once before you go."

SHE VISITS TWICE. They make out like teens and she even sleeps over the last time, yet they don't get naked. *Neither backwards nor forwards.* The last night she brings him a gift.

The mercury's hit twenty-five degrees, though it's not quite May. After Gabe sets down her bags by the door and embraces him long and kisses him beautifully, she reaches in her jacket pocket and brings out a small plastic container, the kind used for medical samples.

"I've brought you a friend."

He takes it and lifts it to his face. Inside appears to be a fat snowflake.

"Here, open your hand." She eases the lid off the container and taps it. The snowflake tumbles into his palm, then stands up on four legs. A shiver goes through him.

"What *is* it?" he whispers, eyes wide.

Perched on his skin is a furry little creature that's so white, and so perfect, he can scarcely believe it's real. Its thick body sits atop delicate white legs. Velvety wings lie folded on its back, adorned with one black dot each. A white kittenish ruff encircles its head, and from that protrudes two silver antennae shaped like horns.

"Is this . . . rare?" It looks so regal, a fairytale being.

"Not at all. I found this little guy on the screen door last night. *Spilosoma virginica*. Your friendly local Tiger Moth."

"I've never seen anything like it."

"You could try looking in a garden. Do you like him less for being common?"

"There's *nothing* common about this." He's still gaping, fascinated by the furry face that seems to regard him. The moth's antennae gently probe. It steps about with a tickling touch and vibrates its wings.

"He's starting to get antsy. The fridge kept him drowsy. We'll put him out soon."

"Why 'tiger'? That's all wrong."

"I know. The common name describes the caterpillar, sort of." Gabe looks amused, watching them both.

They go downstairs to the front porch, the moth riding on his hand. Outside she tells him to touch the tip of his finger to its wings. The moth shivers, then takes flight. Oliver sighs.

"I think it's love," Gabe says.

18

A SPLASH. A sucking *thunk*.

In her sleeping bag Gabe stirs and opens her eyes. Faint starlight. The tent walls swelling and relaxing like lungs. She lies listening to the shrill chorus that's been singing since dusk, wondering what woke her.

Kuh-plunk.

Ah. Yes. The beavers' nightly spree. They sound like boulders. She imagines them doing belly flops, cannonballing.

Her friends who own the farm warned her they'd make a racket, offered her a space in their bunkie until the cabin was ready. But when she arrived late yesterday, she opted to sleep outdoors. Out here on the edge of the property it's a kilometre to the house, another quarter to the road. There's no human noise, not even an electric wire hum. Woods hug the beaver pond on three sides and extend into a county-owned forest. All this — the stars, the noisy darkness — is hers, and there's nothing solitary about it, not with a host of love-hungry peepers, bleating nightjars and piping whip-poor-wills, plus two rowdy, tail-slapping *castorae*.

She rolls over, stretches, and lets out a contented grunt. The meadow grass grows so long and thick by the pond that she had to fold and tamp it down like matting before spreading the ground sheet. Even so, the tent more or less floats.

Months of winter, months of ceilings and sealed windows have sprung open like a skin dried and fallen away. Now she wakes under heaven's vault, along with all the other lives stirring.

~

IN THE MORNINGS just before seven, Gabe wades through the grass to a sun-bleached picnic table and heats water on the portable stove. The air's still. She brews black tea and sits down with it and a notebook, awake but not thinking. Cloud shadows glide dimly across the pond. A crow lifts from a tree. On the table, a globe-eyed dragonfly perches by her hand.

Awake but not thinking. The sun breaks the cover of trees, strikes the water. A breeze stirs ripples; the grass sways. Then everything quiets again except for the aspens twirling and flashing their sequined leaves, showing her true sensitivity.

Oliver was surprised by her plan to come here a week before her fieldwork begins. Nor did he understand, until she explained, why she can't just zoom back and forth to the city during the study like she did for classes. She knows this from years as a hiker and camper and from working in the Park: it takes time to adjust to the land. Travelling's easy; arriving is not. You can't just parachute in and expect to learn, like a student who shows up for one or two lectures in a term. Every day this place opens to her a little more: she'll hear a bird she hadn't yet distinguished in the morning chorus, notice a tree or plant suddenly standing out from the green. And only now, after camping here all week, has she started to shed the civilized tension accumulated in the winter months. She could spend a month or two out here and probably feel the same way.

There's no changing the schedule, though: the cabin's ready. The project awaits.

After breakfast she strikes camp and loads the car. From the pond a track runs along the back field then bends toward Rachel and Tad's house. She follows it until the roof of the chicken coop comes into view, watches for the gap, and makes a sharp left onto a narrow, less-used track that tunnels into the bush. Bumping along, she passes rusty equipment tangled with wild grape and a pasture shed's splintering remains. The hundred-acre farm once kept cattle and grew commercial crops, but her hosts have let much of it go wild. Their coop, greenhouses and gardens provide plenty of work for a family of two humans and three dogs.

The track bends and starts down a steep ridge. Shadowed by oaks, the gravel's damp and slippery here from yesterday's downpour, so Gabe creeps with her foot on the brake. She's never seen this cabin, which Rachel described as "basically against the lake." Until yesterday Tad was still repairing screens and plugging gaps in walls. As she descends, the water comes into view through the trees, then a small, dark green structure raised on cinder blocks. Gabe pulls up to it, parks, and steps out.

The cabin's nestled in a long and shallow cove on Rice Lake's south shore. Rachel was certainly correct about the location: a strip of grass, not much wider than this picnic table sitting on it, is all that separates the front steps from the water. No beach or dock, no natural or human-made entry point to the lake. Maybe there once was and it's been overtaken by the wall of bulrushes taller than her. Gabe climbs onto the table. Wind stirs her hair. Navy-coloured water undulates. This perspective is unfamiliar: though she can see one of the lake's bushy islands, a point of land to the east cuts off her view of the north shore, where the Serpent Mound lies. Perhaps one day she'll hike out to see it from this angle.

The two-room building is serviceable and plain. After quickly unpacking, she heads outside again with a daypack slung over her shoulder. The traps don't need to be set up until tonight. She hikes up the ridge and heads into the woods, bushwhacking.

Knowing the names of moths is one thing; being able to identify their pupae and larvae quite another. Her goal today is to practise those much-less-honed skills — and see what's awake and about too. Attracted by an oak with some low branches, Gabe pauses to cast her gaze over it in a casual, unfocused way. The trick to finding caterpillars that don't want to be found lies in looking not for the creatures themselves, but their traces: chewed or drilled leaves, odd shapes that stand out in the mass of foliage. The ground beneath the tree might also hold clues, such as debris from feeding. Though she can't see any caterpillars she finds many such signs: whatever's dining here, it's a popular spot. With a nub of white chalk she tags the trunk by drawing a spiral symbol. She'll return at night when caterpillars tend to be most active.

Searching is slow, patient work. The sun heats the woods, the temperature climbing. She wanders, keeping her sense of direction by the sun and the lake, swatting at the gnats eagerly companioning her trek. She's decided to concentrate on silk moths, just to have a focus. Yet even so, many caterpillars of the regional silk moths resemble one another, so she keeps turning over leaves and referring to her guidebook, trying to identify the various creeping, arching, and motionless wormy creatures, each unique if you take the time to look closely; and of course the majority of the larvae she inspects aren't from silk moths but other moth species, and often they're dull and brown and bare and kind of turd-like, just pitiably soft pieces of flesh clinging to leaves. It's a treat to find a Woolly Bear or the tufted white larvae of the Banded Tussock and tickle their backs.

After an hour she circles round and heads west again, toward the cabin. These woods seem healthy if young and thin, probably cut in the last eighty years. There's a lovely floor of leaf litter and aromas that change and pips and twitters and croaks. It feels so good to be enfolded by life! In the city, as the avenues turned lush and green this spring, she kept noticing all the absences: puddles where no skimmers skated, solitary swans and gulls, flowers without bees tending them, mere huddles of birds. Birds, bees, insects — how deep and far will the diminishments to life go? So many populations are disappearing, and no one really knows how to stop it or even what it will mean. Today's temperature has soared, it must be nearing thirty — high summer weather, though it's barely mid-May. Only last week she slept fully clothed inside her bag.

The seasonal cycles have entered a wobbly state; it feels like the turning and spinning of a great global gyre is slowing, losing power.

Sometimes she imagines a sheet of ice descending.

More often she pictures fires.

Or just a spreading dustbowl for millennia . . . until the gyre changes course.

Studies won't change it. Even hers. Meanwhile so much is still unknown! The world teems with mysteries, each a necessary thread in the weave. In some weeks' time one of these marvels will reappear: the cicadas. Then if she does this walk again their husks will be everywhere stuck to trees. The husks aren't the same as a snake's shucked skin or a moth's abandoned pupae. They are *discarded forms*.

Of all the physical transformations she knows of, the cicada's is the most spectacular and inexplicable. Unlike the moth, which metamorphosizes from larvae to adult in its dissolving, pupal state — a radical enough event — the cicada grows a completely new body within a still-active one. These two different forms — one juvenile, one adult; one beetle-like and flightless, the other twice as large and winged — operate together, somehow, until the moment of separation and emergence. And what a moment! The Big Night arrives: inside the ground, where the juvenile cicada has lived for months or even years, the beetle tunnels up and onto the surface for the first time in its life. It crawls toward the tree whose roots have nursed it, or a fencepost (any vertical shape will do), then up it climbs.

How to comprehend what happens next?

The living beetle splits open. What was just walking becomes a spent shell as the new being pushes out. A new head rises from the old cracked skull, new limbs pull free like fingers from a glove, wings unfold with a shiver. Only the eyes are the same, the eyes are not exchanged.

From such outrageous acts, maturity is born.

If she could write the thesis she wants, that's the title she'd choose: *Outrageous Acts*. She'd talk about the journey of the cicada, the transparent wing-windows of Polyphemus and the eye-spots of the giant Madagascar silk moth, *Antherina suraka,* which replicate a lemur's face as a form of defense. She would ask the questions that to her need asking: What mind or minds create these designs? What are we, in relation? And then, how can we best learn from them? The answers wouldn't suit a graph line or evidence-based argument.

Look up, Gabe: there's a spider on a filament sailing past.

While she camped by the beaver pond, she sketched out some notes toward a revised methodology that might address the Supervisory Committee's objections to using live moth counts. But her notes shanked off into opinion; the fact is, she doesn't know how to pull an argument against collecting together in a persuasive way. All winter it's eaten away at her, this compromise she's had to make. She kept hoping she'd hear something in a lecture or read a study that would give her solid objections to put before the committee members. She spoke to other students about it too, and discovered a few who felt the same moral discomfort and also at a loss about what to do about it. Still there seems no other way, not if she wants to remain in grad school and learn to practise science.

Returning to the cabin, she strips off her damp clothes right there on the grass and steps naked through the rushes. Their sharp leaves brush her. Is this what a caterpillar feels? The cold water makes her cringe, too. There are weedy shallows and she feels exposed as her feet search for footing, the wind touching her everywhere, though no one can see. As she wades slowly in, the water rises up her legs like an icy blade. When it reaches her thighs, she plunges.

It's damn cold, but tolerable. She twists and rises with a kick and a gasp.

Once she's caught her breath, and worked up a bit of energy with her limbs, she takes a deep inhale and dives. The amber sunlight dims, the temperature drops. She touches the water that the sun's not yet warmed, the body within the lake's skin.

NO ONE KNOWS for sure why moths fly to lights. Many moth traps, like Gabe's pair, are homemade: a plastic garbage bin lidded with trimmed corrugated board, a circle cut in its middle to hold the funnel, narrow end blunted for extra width. Underneath, a strip of wood suspended between two cut holes in the plastic holds the electrical socket for the moth beacon: a mercury vapour light bulb. Moths are especially partial to this type of light. The bulb protrudes from the funnel, luring them inside.

That evening just past six, Gabe drives back to the beaver pond and brings out one trap. She places it beside the picnic table, snakes the electrical cord through the exit hole in the bottom, arranges the egg cartons inside. Beside the bulb are two slim metal brackets: these support the clear glass bowl she places over the hot surface, to keep moths away from it and protect it from moisture. The cord plugs into a portable battery with enough juice for an all-night moth draw. Lights up! It's showtime.

Then she's back in the car, trundling up the track past the house and onto the main road.

The other trap sites chosen for the project lie north and south of Peterborough, meeting point for the two bioregions her study will compare: the granite-dominated, thin-soiled Canadian Shield to the north, and the Carolinian-forested plains in which the farm lies, part of the Peterborough Drumlin Field. She set up the study this way to ensure a wide sweep in terms of species diversity, though it will make for a great deal of footwork. During each sampling period, which lasts nine days, she must set two traps per night, one in each bioregion. The six sites rotate and repeat over the period to ensure sufficient breadth. After one period ends, she'll have two mad weeks to log the contents of eighteen separate batches – and write her thesis – before she does it all again.

Following the committee's feedback on improving her site selection, in March and early April she scouted other potential locations and swapped out three of her six original choices for sites that have been overtly disturbed, one by fire, two by logging. The committee was satisfied. Tonight's site is the first of these, a wooded area on the north side of Rice Lake. East of the Serpent Mounds Park, she cuts off the highway and onto a gravel road heading south, back toward the water. The land slopes steeply here. Poplars and maples hug the road, fields and farms behind them. The road bends and follows the shoreline, hidden a kilometre or two away. She reaches the site, a lonely place of burned skeletal trunks and charred ground. Sets the trap. Is happy to leave.

It's close to seven-thirty, and she flicks on the headlights for the return on the gravel road. Perhaps that's why she passed it the first time. There, in the ditch: milkweed! She pulls right over. Stepping out, she catches the sweet lilac scent of *Asclepias*, named for a healing god. Though its flowering season is still weeks off, a few of the pink, nub-like blooms have opened.

The sole food of monarch butterflies, milkweed is also beloved of hawk moths. One enchanted evening back when she was just getting to know Hugh, she witnessed him catch a hawk moth using a butterfly net and a flashlight. The memory makes her smile: Hugh swinging his headlamp around in the dark and leaping into the milkweed patch they'd found. It was some Indiana Jones move, and she'd been duly smitten at the dexterity of this lanky, middle-aged naturalist. He turned around proudly and she waded in after him. Caught in the mesh was a gorgeous Hog Sphinx hawk moth, the pale and olive green of its kite-shaped wings so vivid that it might have emerged that hour. They held it between them like a jewel before carefully freeing it from the netting.

The light picks up their eyes, Hugh explained. She would never try using a net herself; one poor swing and the damage would be done. Yet she can hang here awhile to see if any come to feed.

Flashlight in her pocket, Gabe crosses the gravel to the ditch where the milkweed grows. There at the edge she assumes a familiar stance, relaxed and motionless. On the other side, a cornfield of perhaps five acres extends north to black woods. Night is deepening. There are no lights along the road, no sounds of machinery. This place is a pocket of darkness and safety and almost peace, where a beautiful creature like a hawk moth can still live, nourished by "weeds" left to themselves.

And then — something.

It emerges from the woods and floats through the air above the field like a dandelion wheel. It's a pale yet steady white light.

Huh?

Slowly Gabe turns to look at it straight on. The flying light draws closer, its course a zigzagging path that suggests a male moth searching for a mate. It's largish, the size of a silk moth. It is — indeed — a moth. It has to be! But bright? Impossibly so. Luminescent.

The moth has reached the milkweed some distance from her. Softly she approaches, closes in, comes almost alongside. At two arms' lengths away she can see white wings, with no apparent markings. Why doesn't she have a net? Reaching into her pocket she grasps the flashlight, raises it, switches it on.

Contrary to expectation, the moth doesn't approach the light but lifts higher and starts moving off as she follows, now trying to catch it in the light just to see it better. Oh wait! It grows agitated and flutters away. She plunges after it across the field, but it's too dark and she loses it behind something. At the edge of the woods she stops, frantically searching.

She remains there — pacing, standing still, wandering about, even sitting on the ground — for as long as she can stand it. Hours. Her stomach aches, her mouth's gone dry. There's water and snacks in the car but she refuses to leave.

Later, when a sickle moon has risen and moisture breathes from the ground, she gives up and returns to the road and sits in the car in the dark. Her head's pounding. What just happened makes no sense, no sense at all. Moths do not glow, not anywhere on Earth.

19

BEFORE THE NIGHTMARES STARTED, he would have said that worry woke him in the lonely hours. Fear. How little he understood. It's been searching for him this whole time. It's been waiting: the Black Rider.

Some nights he sleeps only an hour or two before it finds him. Then it doesn't matter how tired he feels, there's no sleep to be had in the basement again. Even with the lights on, like a little boy. He heads upstairs, dragging his blanket with him. Goes down to the river with Reggie as long as exhaustion allows, then returns to wait it out, dozing cautiously on the living room couch. Relocated upstairs he's still not completely safe, not until the first pale light burns the night to ashy grey; then he feels its departure, like smoke drifting out a vent. As long as it's dark, though, the Black Rider is there.

It enters through sleep. Or it enters through darkness and penetrates sleep. Either way, he's never alone.

When dawn comes he sleeps hard. Sometimes he misses breakfast and wakes disoriented and alarmed by the empty house. Naomi's merely taken Gwynn to school, yet he sips coffee nervously, unable to concentrate on work or even the news on his tablet until she returns.

He's fucking losing it.

Nothing's changing at home; Naomi seems to have moved on with her life and he can't talk to her because he's not sure anymore what he wants. Love, basically, but can they make each other happy again? He looks around this house, all the money time years that's gone into it. The slog. The stress. The delusional "must-haves." What the fuck was he thinking? He *knew* better than to fall into this trap years ago! And now? How the hell do they wriggle out? Will Mom Suit Naomi accept a lifestyle downgrade? Has he lost her to the comfort he wanted for his wife and continues to pay for? What kind of meditation retreat charges $500 a day?

The dreams. The terrors. They started after he visited the ticket office, like he'd touched a tripwire. At first he blamed the excessive high, but he's stayed off junk for days now and the dreams haven't stopped. It always begins the same way: asleep on his foam mattress in the basement, he wakes to see that the ceiling lights are on, shining brightly. As soon as he looks at them, though, their light dims. There's nothing threatening to be seen in the faintly illuminated room, but oh, can he feel It.

From the shadows comes its voice: weary, despairing, malevolent. It's the entity that hooked onto his crystal plane and came back down with him, dark angel, his own Black Rider.

See, it whispers. *See.*

And Justin sees that the lights have failed because they will fail. Night presses against the windows, bearing something immense and suffering within it. The last lights are dying, the glass cracking, the room sinking into gloom . . .

The dream ends there. Yet when he wakes for real and turns on a lamp that works, he can still feel the Black Rider. At times he thinks he discerns a faint hazy presence, a distortion of air.

Drugs don't help. He takes them anyway, though they plunge him into further isolation, too messed up to work, too nervous to interact with Gwynn or anybody else. When Naomi returns in the mornings, he retreats to the basement and channels his agitation into playing Drag Racer and Helicopter Escape and Prison Breakout and Bowman Avenger for hours, starting up from these trances when the Xanax and crystal wear off. He does banking too, lots of it, for his mother's estate has finally cleared. He pays off everything he can: his and Naomi's credit cards and lines of credit, the loan for Leverage. Clean slate. All the money his mother nurtured carefully for years, his big, once-in-a-lifetime inheritance: a Get Out of Jail Free card.

And he gets the Oakville house on the market. It receives an offer on Naomi's birthday, which they celebrate awkwardly for Gwynn's sake. That evening he opens a special account for Gwynn's future, planning to put their portion of the house sale into it. He will put the money Oliver pays him to buy out his share of the island house toward their own mortgage.

And then?

In the past, such a financial blessing would have made him feel secure about the future. Now it feels like tying up loose ends — the few he can reach.

Going into work is almost unbearable. Like a troll surfacing he scowls at staff and shuts himself upstairs. He wants to see no one, especially Kurt. If he needs help he calls down to the kitchen for the Kid (*Sherwin*, he has to remind himself; the name just won't stick to that Korean face), who comes upstairs with his kind, defeated grin.

At times in his office at Ace he sees that same brownish murk in the atmosphere. Don't be fooled: the Black Rider is here too, just not at its full power. It feeds him disturbing images: hanging himself, jumping in front of a subway train . . . a moment of agony to find peace. But he has ties. His girl needs a father, not a wraith.

"Fuck off," he mutters, sitting at his desk. He swats the air. "I'm not your butt boy."

The Black Rider doesn't like this.

One night, it follows him upstairs from the basement. On the couch he feels observed, and when he nods off he has an experience so vivid and potent that he knows it's of a different order than "dream." It begins with him returning to the basement, though that's the last place he wants to go. In the floor there's a hole: a man hole. He can't see anything inside of it, yet knows that he must go in — it's the only way.

He lowers himself, gripping the edges tightly, and suddenly he's sucked in. The upper world vanishes. He plummets for miles, an impossible distance into the Earth.

He pops out in a lit, cavernous space.

A creature walks by. It's like a small troll with a long nose and floppy ears, and it glances his way.

This is Hell! How will he ever get back?

An alarm must have been raised, for suddenly a troll horde descends. They grab his legs and drag him into a cell and cast him upon a heap of ashes and clang the door shut. There's a cold, faint light. The ashes contain the debris of former lives and also large, roaming beetles. They don't bite; they're occupied with their own pursuits.

He lies in the cell. He ages. His skin peels. He's lain locked in this hopeless, timeless place for centuries, maybe millennia, and his heart touches a loneliness so vast and terrible that he starts to scream. And the door flies open and the creatures barge in and roughly turn him upside down and bury his face and shoulders in the ash heap so he can scream no more.

His screech brings Naomi pounding down the stairs.

"What is it?" she cries, bending over him, looking nearly as afraid as he.

He can only cry out. He's reversed on the couch, lying the opposite direction from the one he fell asleep in — a fact that further convinces him, in the moment, that the dream was real. He thrashes about trying to rid himself of the prison, and such is his state that Naomi catches his arms and pulls him up and across her thighs, where he weeps, clutching her hips, his face in her warm groin, weeps like only a man sprung from damnation could.

At some point he hears her whispering to Gwynn, feels Reggie's muzzle against his ear. The whole gang's come down and then they go, except Naomi doesn't, even after he settles down and grows drowsy. She lies with him on the couch so he can smell her fragrance and feel her slender cool hands, smoothing his face.

~

THE FAMILY EATS breakfast together the next morning. It's not a full reconciliation, far from it, but it's a reinstatement. Naomi serves freshly made juice in tumblers with ice. As Justin sips the sweet liquid, the cold breath of the ice soothes his lips and nose.

"Are you working at home this morning, Jay?"

He nods, his heart lifting. He understands her signal and suggests a walk by the river. "We can pick up coffees on the way," he says, and it's like they've made a date. Naomi even changes her clothes and puts on lipstick, though Justin knows better than to be too encouraged, strolling with coffee being a pastime of friends and business partners, too.

Whatever her reasons, after plunging into Hell, a walk with Naomi under any circumstances floods him with gratitude. It's a shockingly beautiful May morning, one of those days that emerge in Toronto in late spring: the air blossom-scented, the trees newly leafed, and green suddenly enlivening the worn dreary places. Naomi too seems to feel her own peace, for she says little as they head up the river path that he knows better by darkness, except to point out a bird or flower to him or respond to his occasional comment. The water rushes and gurgles. The morning grows warm and humid. He removes his winter trench coat — with him always these days — and wipes his brow.

At the end of the paved path is the gravel trail where the trees thicken and the opposite bank rises into a wild-looking slope. Here she asks about the dream. Telling it makes his voice tremble. He's become so weak, he really has fallen out of the saddle, another warrior downed by his inability to ride with the times. As they talk Naomi's hair waves in the wind. Her face shows the question she doesn't ask — was he high last night? He doesn't offer an answer and the question passes, released.

If they could just keep walking. If the path could keep leading further into the green.

They linger, yet finally turn back. On the way she takes his arm and lets him lean into her a little so he feels lucky, because whatever her failings she's a good person, beautiful and strong, and a kind of balm comes from her body. Whether it will revive him or allow a gentler death, he doesn't know.

IT'S NAOMI who suggests he try sleeping *outside* to break the pattern of nightmares. She's washing pots after supper that evening while he sits at the kitchen island, enjoying the goodwill that's stayed between them today, and she looks up and this idea comes out of her mouth. It's an unusual one, yet sincere: she's not casting him out of the house, but speaking from a source of wisdom that he recognizes right away. It's also the first thing they've agreed on for some time.

The night's warm and inviting. Justin sets up camp on the lowest part of the back deck. He takes a few slugs from the flask he rolled into his bedding, grapefruit juice with vodka to help him ease off Xanax.

Naomi visits once he's lying down. "How is it?"

"Brilliant. You're brilliant." *I love you,* he wants to add, but doesn't. Those words were part of a relationship now exploded, and might or might not return to them again.

Saying goodnight, she turns off the deck lights. Soon he becomes aware of the yard's other occupants: birds cheeping, and a spotted cat who creeps onto the deck and freezes in surprise before trotting away.

In contrast to his dream, where the darkness felt suffocating, here there's a sense of release. Overhead lies the Big Dipper, and a thin yellow moon gleams through the trees. Drifting clouds and the city's murmur create a continual gentle motion, and like a child being swung in a cradle, his eyes glaze over.

During that first night outside he wakes often, but not from bad dreams. Each time things are a little different: the sky clears, the stars change positions, the moon sets. Once he's woken by a cool stream of air blowing on his face, although the night remains warm. Puzzled, he feels his nose and chin: the cold's still on his skin. It had felt like the breath from the ice when he drank the glass of juice.

At dawn a faint steam rises and the bedding feels damp. In a room nothing changes unless you change it, but outside, things always shift. Flow, movement – and no nightmares. Maybe he's been the one exuding vapours? Maybe outside his stress actually *goes* somewhere instead of choking up the room.

Naomi's suggestion is so successful that he continues backyard camping. After the first night his sleeps deepen, and even when he wakes up for a while in the small hours, he doesn't mind, for the quality of the sleep itself has changed: it's less like conking out, more like a draught of fresh water. Once on a trip to visit his in-laws in Calgary, he and Naomi went hiking in the Rocky Mountains and he stooped to drink with his hands from a stream, the only time in his life he's not drunk water from a tap or bottle; the act felt casual in the moment, and he thought mostly about whether the stream was really safe or might be infected with beaver fever. Yet this memory has often come back to him over the years, like the echo of a much more formative experience. It comes back to him again on the deck.

After his move outside, life returns to something more normal at Baby Point. Naomi says she doesn't know about their marriage, she needs time. He gives it to her, satisfied to prolong a decision while he weans himself off crystal by returning to his three-day routine and reducing the Day One dose. Perhaps they really will recover. Or perhaps this is the "new normal" fantasy that things will work out — like the new normal fantasies that the economy will recover and our government is working for our best interests, the cameras and drones and security are simply there for your safety. He doesn't know; he just wants peace.

He works, he does bullshit. Sleeps outside and kicks junk entirely. Naomi orders cushions for the new sunroom's custom banquette built by Casey. The cushions are coming from France. He sucks it up. Soon they'll be able to enjoy their favourite space again.

It's during this time that Oliver calls. His message says that he and his architect are discussing house plans, and he's meeting with a few contractors to get estimates on the job. He wants to know about the timing of the money from the Oakville house sale and such. Justin tells Naomi about it over a glass of wine.

"Oliver and contractors, that's bad news," he says with a groan. "Apparently the entire place is getting rebuilt, and he's got nothing to draw on but Mom's money. He'll be fucked if he doesn't find the right person."

"The inheritance probably seems like a fortune to him," Naomi says.

"It is." Justin sighs. "In a sane world, it would be plenty to build the simple kind of place Oliver wants. But it's going to be tight."

He remembers Oliver's visits to Ace, his look of anxious desperation. Oliver knows as much about construction as he does about building a rocket. He's a babe in the forest, a juicy target for any shady operator who'll inflate the costs. Oliver needs guidance. But that would entail going to meet with these contractors himself, sparring with Oliver's ignorance and insecurities, even going out to the island, and he doesn't have the energy or will yet to take any of this on. Plus he hates the island.

He calls him. Oliver's pissy, like he's surprised to hear from him at all. Justin ignores that.

"It sounds like you've got things really organized," he says. "I was thinking that I could take a look at those bids for you, when they come in. I've had to deal with a lot of them over the years. Know what to look for."

"I imagine it's straightforward," Oliver says, oblivious to how utterly, stupendously daft this sounds. "The architect recommended a few people she's worked with and knows."

"Well, that's good, but you'd be surprised at what can happen. Prices can be wildly different. Some guys are experts at hidden costs, all kinds of traps you have to be on the watch for. And things just get overlooked too. Not saying that your architect and her people aren't professional, but building is complicated. You want to comb through what you're buying carefully before the shovels hit the ground."

Oliver doesn't say anything for a moment. When he does, it's to ask about the money from the house sale. He's being brushed off.

"Silly little prick," Justin mutters once they've hung up. Little brother deserves what he gets.

IT'S A SATURDAY MORNING of heavy skies, rain predicted. Naomi's going to Pilates, Gwynn to a friend's birthday party. After devouring blueberry pancakes, he and Gwynn have declared a Storm Watch. They sit at the dining table, their sticky plates pushed aside.

"I hope we do storm watches at Parrybourne," says Gwynn.

Justin looks her. So does Naomi, who's filling her water bottle at the sink, though she quickly hides it.

"Parrybourne?"

Gwynn's hesitation is brief, her recovery impeccable. "I mean if I ever go there."

"Is that so?"

Parrybourne is a Muskoka summer camp with a private-school price tag that Naomi once ludicrously suggested for Gwynn. He vetoed it outright.

Naomi turns off the tap. "I enrolled her for July," she says, as casually as she might confirm with him a plan for tonight's dinner. "I thought it would be good for Gwynn to have a change of scene this year."

To get away from us, her face says.

To get away from you, he hears.

Without a word, he rises and descends into his study. The transaction's easily located: ten grand removed from their joint savings, an account he doesn't monitor closely. Five hundred and change left.

A deep quiet befalls him as he stares at the screen. That it has come to this: lies and manipulation for such petty decisions. He remembers Naomi's mockery of him on the phone. This lack of trust is an illness, a disease between them.

He used to know better.

How many of his so-called neighbours send their brats to Parrybourne? To hang out with other rich kids taught tennis and yoga and photography by industry professionals. What bothers him about such a place isn't just the price tag — it's this aspiration toward a rotten symbol, a rotten dream: a royal, white-linened cult of superiority. *What was he thinking?* Hasn't this proven its falseness again and again? Isn't it so yesterday?

"I want the receipt right now," he says, back upstairs.

"It's in my files — why?"

Justin tells Gwynn to wait in Naomi's car. When she's out the door, he slams it shut.

"Because she's not going. And you will be the one to tell her that."

"She *is* going. She deserves it. I get to make decisions for her too."

He advances. "So you lie? You get our daughter to lie? What bullshit were you going to feed me when she went?"

Instead of falling to her knees, Naomi glares at him defiantly. "I was going to tell you before, of course! If I'd asked first, you would have said no."

He wants to slap her. Burning energy courses up his back.

It takes huge willpower to speak calmly. "Junkie man here is still a man, dear, still *a person*. We decide things together."

She starts to argue so he advances another step and she stops, eyes glittering.

"I don't want to hear your excuses. You're undermining us. No, this disrespect *undoes* us. He pauses, his breathing heavy. "You are ignorant and arrogant. Smart, I'll give you that. Sometimes brilliant. But also treacherous in ways you refuse to fucking own. Maybe I've just been way too tolerant of you." His words feel shattering. "That money is going to be put back in the account, and we are finished. Done."

Naomi's eyes widen. "Done?" she says, with an incredulous smirk. He might just go nuclear if he hears more so he turns and opens the door and steps outside.

Gwynn's moony face is bent over her phone. He slides in the driver's seat, snaps an answer to her question. They travel to their destination in silence. It's one thing to refuse a wish, another to take away what's been promised. He'll be blamed for this.

WHEN THE CAB pulls up with the Kid, Justin's sitting in the Audi's passenger seat. He's been there since returning from Gwynn's friend's. The Kid (*Sherwin!*) shuffles up the driveway thumbing his phone. Chunky with sadness, as usual. Practically bashes into the car and still doesn't notice his boss.

Justin whistles.

"Hey Mr. Leveridge." That soft, late-night radio voice. "You're all ready."

"I'm *so* ready."

Opening the driver's side door, the Kid slides in. He takes in the Audi's stitched seats and eucalyptus finish. Sets his hands upon the leather wheel with chrome stripping.

"Uh, Sherwin? You can feel the pedals through those monster running shoes, right?"

"Yes, no problem." Twenty-three and working two restaurant jobs and living at home. No idea why this intelligent, well-mannered kid is so boxed in. One of these days, Justin'll learn the rest of his story.

"Thanks so much for calling me," Sherwin says. Justin nods. Tells him to ensure his phone is off. Sherwin presses a button and the screen goes dark.

After a quick orientation to the car's controls he starts the ignition, which turns over so effortlessly it's beautiful, and they roll out of the driveway just like that. The house recedes, just like that.

They drive toward downtown. A few drops of rain spatter the windshield on the way, but otherwise, the morning stays dry. At Dupont and Spadina Justin directs them into a convenience store lot, tells Sherwin to wait, gets out. From the sidewalk he glances back at the car. Its colour is called "Cappuccino X." How crass it looks against the stained parking lot, before a business where employees earn minimum wage. One of his own white-linen objects, evidence of his twisted dreams.

He picks up a free daily from a newspaper box. The café isn't far from where he and Gwynn saw the play.

Baseball cap pulled low, Fluke sits near the back staring at his phone, wires sprouting from his ears. The paper's set out already. Justin sets his own paper down with the money tucked inside, then picks up Fluke's.

"Hang for a minute, man."

"Why?"

Fluke lowers his voice. "'Cause you just arrived and I want to keep using this place."

Justin pulls out a chair. Fluke's safer than buying from Kurt. How careless that was! Kurt needs to believe that his boss is clean.

Fluke returns to his phone. He's another oddball: athletically poised, despite the eruption of acne and circles under his eyes; he looks like a reject from a Russian ballet academy, and maybe he is. Justin idly scans the establishment. Behind the counter a dark, kohl-eyed woman with long black hair is arranging sweets inside the display case. Painted on the wall behind her in sepia tones is a rough outline of a map. Perhaps intended to connect to the café name, Arabia, or leftover from a former business, the map shows the notched edge of a continent, while in the parchment-coloured space beyond, an old-fashioned galleon in full sail presses through a wavy line toward him.

Justin approaches to buy a pastry. Smiling, the woman retrieves it with tongs and slips it into a paper sleeve. Pride in work. She looks his age, a mother and wife, and he's sorry he can't smile back. From him there will be no smiles today. He's on the other side of the glass.

He drops a few coins into her tip bowl and leaves, pressing the newspaper under his arm.

At the corner he turns north, descends into an underpass and rises again, then enters the lot under the hydro towers where he parked that winter night. Clear sightlines and no security cameras, he remembered. Hiding in plain sight works best.

On someone's trunk he opens the paper, crumbles a bit of the crystal into the pipe's bowl, then strolls to the lot's rank, littered perimeter and ignites.

When he yanks the car door open, Sherwin's fallen asleep.

"Do we need to take you home to bed?"

The young man apologizes with such shame that Justin bitch-slaps him on the shoulder. Then sighs. "Did you close up last night?" he asks, attempting to sound jovial.

"No, but I stayed up late."

"Online?"

"Yeah. And I couldn't sleep."

"Ah, so you're pie-eyed. Turn left on Bathurst."

They drive south, pass Bloor. "I never drank coffee until I started at Ace," Sherwin says.

"Now you drink coffee more and more."

He grins. "And still feel tired."

"And have bad dreams."

Sherwin smiles politely.

At the park Justin tells him to wait for his call. Then he passes through the familiar gates.

This is right, this is his territory. He's more identified with this triangular zone defined by the park, Walnut Avenue and Ace's location on Queen Street than anywhere. The Walnut apartment was the first place he ever lived on his own, before, during and well after he got Ace going, a flat so small you could practically fry an egg from the shower. Yet the parties! His narrow study was often occupied by a friend who needed it and he wasn't bothered in the least by living that way, working like mad. He was joyful.

The park's busy, people camped on the grass and benches with takeout food and picnic lunches. He descends the steep slope into the doggie-run bowl. Away from the main dog area there's a patch of dense foliage. He sits down there screened on the hillside and gets out his dope.

One strong haul on the pipe, two. Smoke swirls into his lungs and his heart goes crazy. Retching, holding his chest, he slumps over. The ground tilts. He turns cold, breaks a sweat. He's going to puke.

But the surging eases, drops down.

Suddenly — violently — he has to shit.

Clutching his gut, he starts up the slope. Won't make it! The pressure —

Wedging himself within the brush as best he can, Justin drops his pants. A long sputtering fart . . . heralds the first spurt of a thick ooze that emerges convulsively, through stabbing contractions, and puddles hotly between his feet. His anus burns. With each racking expulsion he gasps, trembling and damp with sweat, his pulse throbbing in his ears.

Then stillness, and a weak but true sense of relief. The sounds of the park return: a bicycle ticking past on the path above, the huff of a dog. Human voices too, like the chatter of birds. He's never thought of voices like that, yet with his eyes closed he can picture a forest. How long he squats there, feet and calves straining, he doesn't know; the evacuation recurs in waves, his gut cramping to expel more waste into the poo pool. Then blinking rest, gentle clarity, and the next build up to a spasming burst.

At last his bowels quiet, and he searches for something with which to clean himself. Finding nothing he topples forward and crawls, gets onto one knee and pulls up one pant leg, switches sides, pushes himself up.

Sherwin drives him to a coffee shop where he uses the bathroom, tossing his soiled underwear in the garbage. He washes his face, buys water and drinks it immediately. Where to next? the Kid wants to know, but he's out of ideas. They're parked outside the coffee shop on Queen West. Barely one o'clock, and all he wants to do is crawl under his blanket on the deck.

He takes out his wallet, counts bills and passes them across. "You can head back to work. I'll take it from here."

"Thanks, boss. You sure you're okay, boss?"

Justin nods, not meeting his eyes. The Kid's kindness could make him weep.

When he's gone, Justin seals the windows and locks the doors. He rests his head on the glass, still in the passenger seat, and watches people pass on the sidewalk.

How could Naomi have been so stupid? Lies. Hers and his. He refuses more lies.

He holds the lump of crystal against the light. Hard to see through tears. Wipe. You did your bum, now your face.

He focuses again: the crystal is opaque, a cloud to get lost in. Only the Black Rider knows how to navigate that space.

Pain in his chest. Heaviness creeping up his arm. He's got Pain Creep.

Justin pinches and crumbles the lump into powder, elbows the door open and sweeps it into the gutter. Shut and re-lock. Possibly never leave this seat.

His eyes flutter closed. The sun's out now, so much for the forecast. It's bright on his retinas, a red black. Tears, gentle and warm. Let them come, the little streams, hot then cool on his skin. He listens. All around are voices, the voices of the people of the city. Do they know they're really people of the forest? In their noise lies music waiting to take shape. He hears it in that woman's goofy laugh, hears it . . . It just needs to be recognized, people need to know what they can do in order to try to do it. If only he had a giant mirror, one that revealed Beauty . . .

The voices fade and return. The pain blooms in his chest now, causing a sound in his throat. *And the husbands, dancing with joy as they flew . . .* A line from a fairy tale he used to read Gwynn. About birds coming home to their nests, was it? Or butterflies. But there's no such flight for him, no making it to the other side — wherever, whatever, the other side is.

20

WHEN THE DOORBELL RINGS, Oliver's not asleep. His phone woke him a while ago, the call bearing an unknown number. *Gabe?* he said hopefully. Heard a noise like great pistons, like his caller was standing at the centre of the Earth. *Wei?* came the reply.

Now his doorbell, insistently pressed at two in the morning. He peers outside. A light rain's falling, and there's no SUV in sight. Rosh perhaps? But not at the front door, and Gabe's out at the lake.

He pads downstairs and speaks through the wood. "Yeah?"

"It's your brother."

Oliver slides back the bolt. It's true. Under the porch light stands a wet and pasty Justin, hair stuck to his forehead. He's wearing an unseasonably heavy overcoat. Dirty and rain-stained, it hangs off his shoulders more like a blanket than a piece of clothing.

"You gonna invite me in?"

"Of course! Come."

His brother brings a damp dog smell over the threshold. Oliver locks the door behind him and leads the way upstairs. In the kitchen Justin stands uncertainly, eyes on the floor. He looks like he's come off a flu or bender.

"What can I get you? Water? Tea?" Should he offer him beer?

"Actually . . ." Wiping his face, winded from the climb. "Maybe a coffee?"

Oliver presses the button on the coffee maker preset for the morning. In the living room he straightens up the sofa cushions and Justin slumps down, staring into space. His face is shiny, like he's been outside for a while.

"I'll get you a towel." Oliver darts away, his mind awhirl. He puts together a snack too and clears the books from the coffee table to make space for the tray.

"Black, right?"

"Stop fussing," Justin complains. He gives his hair a couple of half-hearted swipes with the towel then just holds onto it. He's still not removed the wet coat.

Oliver takes a chair. "What's happened?"

Justin's gaze wanders over the crackers and cheese. "That's a very good question, one I'll try to answer. Just . . . getting my bearings. It took me a while to find this place again." He takes in the exposed brick wall, the wainscotting. He's never actually come inside, just given Oliver a lift home a few times after family events.

"Cozy place. Hey, it okay if I borrow this fine couch tonight?"

"Of course."

Thumbs-up. "Thanks, you're a star." He reaches for the steaming mug, and his lips tremble like an old man's when he tests the liquid. Oliver looks away, a lump in his throat. He's seen his brother hungover, depressed, furious, sick, and disappointed, but never frail. Never. Dread seeps into him.

Justin sighs. "That's nice brew, Bro. Strong." His gaze roams again, stops at Oliver's desk. It's actually two desks pushed end-to-end along one side of the living room, with his computer on one and the other for books and papers. Sitting there propped on a document holder is a sketch of the bungalow rebuilt, which he picked up just this week along with some initial drawings, and which he hopes Justin doesn't ask about. Entering this process alone has been nerve-wracking to say the least, and he can do without his brother's scrutiny.

But Justin's focused on something else.

"Hey, who's that?"

Also propped near the sketch is a picture he took of Gabe that day on the island. He printed it after she left. She's smiling at him from the bow of the canoe.

"That's Gabe."

"New girlfriend?"

"I think so."

Justin nods. "She's a beauty. What's her background?"

"She's from Peterborough."

Justin closes his eyes. "I meant ethnically."

Oliver ignores him and goes to get a beer. Justin's always pushing his buttons.

From the living room his brother calls out: "You're whispering to yourself!"

"The Whisperer still lives," he says when Oliver returns. "Guess I'm making you jumpy."

"Sorry." Rattled and scared and irritated all at once. "It's just . . . I don't know. It's not easy. It's never easy."

"Talking to your brother?"

"You and Mom. There's always been these —" He makes chopping gestures. "Angles, obstructions, like everything gets bent no matter how straight you try to aim it."

"Ah. Yes."

Connie once described this chemistry precisely using astrology — and in fact, he was drawing on her geometric metaphor. It was something about squares in mutual (was that the word?) charts. Among her vain attempts at getting him interested in astral influence, that conversation stuck a chord by neatly articulating what he'd always felt to be an inexplicable roadblock in communication.

"But you and Mom never seemed to have that problem," he says.

"No, that's not true. I think I could just connect with Mom on her terms more than you could. She liked to think she 'got' me. And mostly, she did." Justin finally notices Mimi, who's been sniffing his pant legs intently. He leans over to scratch her head. "Hey, speaking of Mom, it was good of you to take her cat. She probably smells shit. I had an accident earlier."

"What?"

"Got caught in an urgent situation in Bellwoods Park. I walked out on Naomi this morning." He leans back as this shockwave rolls over Oliver.

"Holy fuck."

"Yeah."

"Has this happened between you before?"

"Never."

Justin says he'll have a beer after all. Oliver gets one, hands it to him. He takes a long drink, then rests his head on the cushion. "It's basically a fucked situation. It's been that way for a while." He brings the bottle to his chest. "You know how it goes. You try to fix this and fix that, but you're just patching it and then things get worse and *ppfftt*. It all collapses."

Yes, Oliver does know how that goes.

"Until this winter, I didn't think the trouble was too serious," Justin continues. "But it is. It's been obvious that things aren't working. Weakened at the core. Maybe it was like that right from the beginning and I didn't see it."

"I don't know, you two always seemed solid to me," Oliver says. Justin's always been so proud of his family. Still, he wasn't acting like a devoted husband that night at Ace.

He rises and pulls the balcony door open a little. Moist, fresh-smelling air touches his face and he breathes it deeply. He's trembling, he realizes, trembling with utter disbelief that his brother is *here*. Not at a hotel, or a friend's, or at Ace. He came to find him, after all this time, and despite all their bullshit.

"Does she know where you are?" he asks gently.

"Nope. Haven't talked to her since. What happened to your face?"

"An incident. Maybe you should let her know?"

Justin's eyes move to the ceiling. They look empty, defeated. Then he blinks, raises the bottle. "You got another? Don't get up, I can do it." Lurching off to the kitchen, opening the fridge. When he returns he stretches out with his heels propped on the sofa's opposite arm, the beer on his chest.

"I hope things work out for you and your girlfriend," he says. "Is it serious? Big love?"

"Don't know yet. It could be, but it's early days."

"Well, I hope so." Justin yawns, his jaw popping. "Love is it, nothing else comes close. My little girl . . . I love her more than anything, sun and moon and stars. Too bad wives are so much harder. Too much politics. I don't know about them anymore.

"I always thought it could be something truly creative, marriage, if you both had the right attitude. Great music. You got to be on cue, though, sharp and loose . . . responsive. You can't keep repeating the same steps for years, got to bust through the calcifications, or else. I guess we didn't. It's easier to follow the dance everyone else is dancing, even if it's fatal. Story of the human race."

He yawns again, wipes his eyes. Mimi jumps up and starts kneading the couch, staring at him. He runs a hand down her back.

Oliver leans against the wall by the balcony door. That Justin and Naomi might split up is something he's never contemplated. His own heart, his own grip on the world, feel weakened.

"I'm really sorry," he says.

"So am I." Justin takes a drink, thinking. "I've learned some important things lately, though. One is that women can become as violent as men. Rage is a disease. It eats things up, including the host." He looks at Oliver. "It's true. It's just that women are innies and we're outies, usually."

"Psychological versus physical violence, you mean?"

"Passive-aggressive, you got it. That's why it goes unrecognized. No one will punish you in a court of law. No one will present statistics. And you know what? The State is onto this big time: the innie way is being used on us all these days, to render us weak little babies. It's Big Brother meets Mad Auntie. Watched for our own good. Strangled by 'safety' measures for our own good. Privacy? You don't need it. On the other hand, you demonize aggression. Because it's dangerous, you know, if you're *angry*. An angry person might hurt somebody."

Oliver sighs. It's not the time for a political discussion. "Naomi's always had a temper," he says gently. "So do you."

"Yeah, well, temper is alright. It's when temper is deemed 'bad' that things go wrong. When you *can't* be passionate or disagree without there being repercussions. When the bullet-proof glass goes up between you. That's the end."

He closes his eyes. His speech seems to have run its course, and after a moment he looks half-asleep, the cat curled by his side. Oliver gets out a blanket and unfolds it over him. He sits down in the chair. His nerves are humming.

"What are you doing?" Justin says.

"Just relaxing here for a bit. I'll go to bed soon. Get some sleep. Things usually seem better in the morning. You can talk to her."

Justin shakes his head. "I don't know how anymore. I can't keep playing the old way. Games. Bullshit. Perpetual tug-o-war. It all hurts too much, he versus she versus he. You versus me." He raises a hand from Mimi's back, drops it again. "It's destroying us. It's been killing me, and I'm done."

In a moment, his breathing becomes rhythmic. A breeze pushes in through the door, cars swish past on the street. Justin's lips part and he makes a soft gurgling sound.

Oliver watches him. Everyone has a child's face when they sleep, their mother once said. A lifetime has passed since he saw his brother at rest. Those storybook nights in the tent — such estrangement between them then was unthinkable.

He turns off the lamp and continues sitting up in the dim room.

~

FUCK OFF FUCK OFF FUCK OFF!

Oliver practically leaps from the chair. It's still night. The couch is empty. His brother's standing at one of the windows, peering out.

"What is it?" Oliver hisses.

"Cops!"

"What?" Oliver goes to the other window. There's no police cruiser, not even the SUV.

"I think they've gone around back." Justin faces him, grinning bitterly. "This is beautiful! Remember what I said about feminine violence? Here you go."

"I don't follow."

"The car. It's Naomi's. I took it this morning." He points out a vehicle parked on the street. It has a crushed headlight.

"Were you in an accident?"

"No." Justin paces, the coat disappearing into the kitchen.

Then Oliver sees them: two men emerging from somewhere near the house. They could be people leaving an apartment. They could be the men who tried to break in. Anyone.

He finds Justin at the bathroom window. "I think they're in your yard now," he says.

"They're on the sidewalk. Look, it doesn't make sense that cops are here about the car because Naomi doesn't know where you are." If anything, he thinks, they're here for Rosh.

"They were all over it checking it out while you were snoring."

"I do not snore. So they're curious, or they're thieves."

"You don't get it! I smashed into Stanko's car."

"What? You said you weren't in an accident!"

"It wasn't an accident. I smashed his car." He grins again. In the bathroom standing uncomfortably close, he looks like a maniac.

"Are you out of your fucking mind?"

"Oh, calm the fuck down! I'm not a *murderer*. I just had to do it. It was time."

Oliver glares at him. "Why didn't you tell me this before?"

"Because there was nothing to tell. His car was parked at Ace. As far as I could see he wasn't in it, unfortunately."

"Jesus Christ. Can we get out of this bathroom now?"

"Yeah, I don't see 'em."

They return to the living room, where Justin takes up his post by the window. The two men are still outside, talking on the sidewalk. "If they have ill intent they're being pretty casual about it," Oliver observes. "I'll go and see."

"Don't. For all we know these guys are Stanko's friends."

"That's . . . No. They're not. I'll just go —"

"Don't! Let's just keep cool."

"Like we are. Fine. You stand guard." He flops onto the sofa and gathers the blanket. A vengeful Naomi, landlord thugs . . . it's five a.m. and he's losing patience. Work's going to be hell.

"The Whisperer!" Justin says. "You're doing it again."

"Wake me when they storm the building."

His brother replies, but Oliver doesn't catch it. He's drifting already. *The Whisperer.* It was the nickname their father gave him, because when he was little he was so shy around guests that he'd hide behind his dad's chair and whisper in his ear. His father would pretend to pass on Oliver's comments, except they'd be his own humorous observations.

Can't be at ease in our own skin. Was that it?

He feels a current of air on his face and smells damp wool, but he's too shagged to open his eyes.

When he does, hours have passed and the apartment's cheerfully sunny. He's alone in the room. Rising, he checks the bedroom. Empty. In the kitchen the bottles are lined up on the counter and there's a note written on the back of an Ace business card: *Hope you slept. Sorry to bother you so much last night. J.*

Oliver troops sullenly to the gym. He'd been putting in weekends to make up time spent at Oakville, and this was a day he promised to Foroud. He slumps over his desk dizzily, certain he'll soon faint if he doesn't get a proper night's sleep.

He can't justify a sick day, though, so on his lunch hour he takes a cab home and lies down with the alarm set for forty minutes later. When he wakes he goes straight to the window: Naomi's car is still outside, just as he thought. He must have noticed it earlier, but it didn't register. Why would Justin leave it behind? A yellow parking ticket's clamped to the windshield.

Justin doesn't answer his phone. Over the afternoon Oliver drags information from one small square to the next in the Excel spreadsheet he's interminably updating with membership data, feeling a queasy unease that blooms into full-out guilt and regret. His brother's in crisis, for fuck's sake. He shouldn't have gotten cranky. He should have told Justin to stay as long as he needs to. He should have left him a key.

He calls Ace. A staff person says Justin's not been in today. He sends another text: "What's going on? Worried. Can leave the place open for you tonight. Dinner if you like. I promise not to be a grump."

The car's still there in the evening, but no Justin appears. Maybe he went home and crashed? Left the Audi so Naomi wouldn't see it. Maybe he's been home all day.

After a sandwich supper, he pets Mimi for a little while and plays a game he's discovered where she likes to run for the cat toys and cat treats he tosses. This routine seems to matter to her, she'll start nudging and swatting his feet if he forgets. Usually half a dozen treats. He waits until nine, then calls the house. No, Naomi tells him, Justin's not here.

"This is kind of awkward," Oliver says, "but he stayed over here last night. And your car is parked here too."

"Oh." There's a gush of running water. "It's Uncle Oliver, honey. We're just doing dinner. It's been quite a day."

"Have you heard from him?"

"No, but that's not entirely unusual these days, as maybe he told you. Gwynn had to get a ride home from piano today, didn't you, sweetheart? Honestly, Oliver, I have no idea. But he's got the dog, so we'll probably see him tonight."

"The dog? So he came home today?"

"At some point he was here."

Weird. Maybe Justin lost the car keys? Still, his brother seems to be planning on going home. Just in case, he sends him another text reiterating that he's welcome, et cetera, and leaves his phone on and close to the bed all night.

There's no word, and he assumes that Justin's deep into it with Naomi until she texts him around noon the next day. She's coming to retrieve her car, she says. Justin didn't come home and hasn't called.

He replies and leaves work and waits for her outside to pull up in a cab. She smiles, even though she's visibly upset; she's always been friendly to him. He gives her a quick hug.

"How's Gwynn?"

She shakes her head. "Don't get me started. I'm trying to keep up the good front, you know? Offer a reasonable explanation as to where Daddy's vanished to?"

"What do you think?"

"Oh. My. God." She's seen the headlight. "Look at this. What do I *think?* I think my husband's gone bananas. Did he tell you about the drugs?"

"No." That night at Ace, though.

"And the women? Uh-huh, I thought not."

236

Monday evening passes. Tuesday. He checks in again with Naomi. She says she doesn't care where Justin is, he's probably "off being enraged" somewhere. On a bender.

"Has he been to Ace?"

"Nope. They called me earlier."

"This isn't good."

"Tell me about it."

But Naomi's speaking a different language. Oliver sits at his desk for a while after their call. Justin's been doing crystal — a lot, according to her. Shadowy henchmen still seem improbable, but not a drug overdose. He starts calling hospitals. Why didn't he think of this earlier?

By Wednesday, Justin's officially missed two days of work and slept somewhere unknown for three nights. Sounding shrill, Naomi concedes that something might really be wrong. Things are "extremely upset" at home, she says. He tells her he's going to the police.

He bikes to the nearest station and goes inside and tells his story to the person behind the desk, then takes a seat to wait. He can't believe this is happening. Justin came to *him*. He needed *help*. And what did he do? Acted like an asshole. Fell asleep! Let him go off alone, his poor, damaged, heartbroken brother.

Gone. Very possibly dead. Dead brother.

Oliver holds his hand over his mouth. His parents. How can he ever, ever, live up to them if things go down like this?

After waiting a long time he's admitted and sits in a cubicle with an officer. The woman's questions, though reasonable enough, lash his conscience. *Was Justin noticeably unhappy? Did he speak about problems with work or at home?*

Was he abusing any substances? Which ones? For how long?

Did he ever speak of suicide?

Yes to everything. Didn't he say that his problems were killing him? That he was "done"?

He goes home. Wanders the apartment. He was supposed to get together with Rosh and cancels. Cannot bring himself to reach out to Gabe.

He cycles through memories of Justin over the decades. All the chances Oliver had to *be* a brother. Why did he let their differences become such a huge deal? His own pettiness and pride and immaturity appall him. It's as Connie always said: he's isolated himself.

That night, on the balcony, Oliver closes his eyes and sends out a silent message, the closest thing to a prayer he's ever made: *Justin, Justin! I'm sorry I wasn't a better brother, but I really want to be. Come back. Please. We need you. Come home.* He imagines his plea rising like the Tiger Moth, fluttering over the city, searching tirelessly for Justin's scent.

21

SIX O'CLOCK ALARM. An overcast morning, steamy, the sun a pink smudge. On the cabin's front steps Gabe sips coffee, listening to the voices in the air: pileated woodpecker and white-throated sparrow, robin, cardinal, crow. Geese and cormorants pass over the water. A blue jay eyes her from a nearby branch, swoops to a bulrush tip and balances acrobatically, takes flight with a shrill call. Last sip. With a thermos and knapsack, she's in the car.

The first trap's set up in the Northumberland forest, on the edge of a small clearing off the Black Oak Loop, about ten minutes in from the parking lot. She chose this spot so she could ID in good light. After unplugging the bulb, she moves the trap from the shade and sets it down, trying not to disturb the rue-anemone and trilliums. Nestles the tape recorder in her shirt pocket securely, tests it.

Easing off the trap's lid, Gabe peers inside. Egg carton bottoms, circularly stacked, form a tiered, Escher-like space where moths lie nested in hollows and grooves. A handful flutter away, but most don't stir. She presses the record button, reaches in, removes the uppermost carton and re-closes the lid, then begins speaking the names of the residents aloud, talking with practised precision as her eyes travel the length of the paper. It's a strange, rolling recitation, a kind of liturgy to creation offered to the inhabitants of the woods:

Spring Hemlock Looper
Gray Furcula and Black-spotted Prominent
Maple Looper, Oak Besma, The Herald
Toothed Somberwing
Maple Caloptilia
Brown-bordered Geometer, Clover Looper
The Brother
Box-Elder Leafroller and Grapevine Epimenis
Many-Dotted Appleworm
Striped Eudonia, Festive Midget, and Comstock's Sallow . . .

And she must proceed rapidly yet take great care. She's well practised, though, this is her zone, and once she falls into a focused rhythm she can keep going, moth after moth, carton upon carton, hindered only by moths that confuse her. Almost all are swiftly identified, though some micros need to be nudged into more revealing positions. Completing one carton, she lays it on the ground and reopens the trap and removes the next. Again a moth or two escapes, which she notes on the tape.

Sunbeams reach through the trees. Grey cartons clutter the area as moth city deconstructs. Some moths, aware of their freedom, crawl groggily on the paper nests or meander into the trees, though most remain asleep. When the trap's empty she gently shakes each carton until the moths whir about her like leaves or seeds, landing on her hair and clothes, finally fluttering off.

Back at the car with the trap in the back seat, she drinks a cup from the thermos. The process took two hours, and out of the eighty or so moths logged there were seven she couldn't identify, now in plastic containers. Yesterday, the first day emptying the traps, only three stumped her. Hope welled: maybe she'd not have to freeze any. She'd ID them all! And indeed, two of them she identified easily at the cabin with the help of a calming hour in the fridge and her magnifying glass. That left only one: a snouty Grass-Veneer, whether the Common or Leach's she couldn't decide. The golden-brown Grass-Veneers drive her a bit batty generally. The Pasture Grass-Veneer, the Double-banded, the Wide-stripe, the Mottled and the Eastern, plus the Common and Leach's, are so closely alike that she's always straining to discern who's who, and at ten to fifteen millimetres, even magnification can fail with a restless moth whose colours are faded or wings ragged. She squinted and nudged and puzzled over that poor creature, looked to the freezer, changed her mind. It was just *one* moth. She took it to the front step and let it go.

But seven today, from a single trap, with the second to come. Brimer was right: the time spent IDing these at the cabin will add up fast.

So will the dead, if she follows through.

She takes another swig of coffee, though it burns her mouth. What does she even mean, "if"? Stop fooling yourself, Gabe. You won't be able to ID everything and you can't release *all* the moths that elude you, deceive the committee or suddenly change your method. They could fail you. And they'd be right, too, because you agreed to their terms. No one's making you do this.

But she didn't sign up for killing moths! And why? Why must it be this way?

Peering at the side profile of the Grass-Veneer last night, she could perfectly see its eye. The shape and liquidity reminded her of a fish's. Within the golden iris lay a black dot of pupil. The moth peered back.

On the highway to the next site, two trucks pull out and race past her. She's got to watch her speed; despite the coffee, the last two days are catching up and her impulse when tired is to slow down. The night of the luminescent moth she was up until almost three, at the field then at the farmhouse afterward researching bioluminescence online, bouncing around moth forums, naturalist news and even paranormal sites in search of an explanation. Yesterday, after freeing Grass-Veneer, she was at the house again until late.

Two traps a day, rotating through the six sites over three days. Three such rotations for each counting period, for a total of nine sampling days per period of the project. This is only Day Two of the first rotation of the first sampling. In the afternoons she's supposed to transcribe the day's log onto the study's spreadsheets, while in the evenings, if the logging's done, she should work on her thesis or review her index cards and hit the hay early. None of that happened after Day One, nor will it today.

Instead, she's going to be saving what she can this afternoon from an icy grave. And then, she's going back to that field with a moth sheet, a camera, and a prayer that whatever that unearthly creature was, it will show up again.

ON WEBSITES and discussion forums devoted to moths, she's put out feelers: have there been any sightings of white giant silk moths? No one has shared one yet. And since none of the known giant silk moths in Ontario is white, responses to her query have been frustrating if predictable: that she saw a Tiger or Leopard or even a Luna – as if she'd make such a rookie mistake.

Sharing that the anomalous moth *glowed* is out of the question.

The common European Ghost Moth takes its name from the white male's habit of eerily hovering in midair to attract a mate. Gabe thought of it after her encounter with the luminous moth, yet the Ghost doesn't shine. No, there are no glowing moths on Earth. There are not even any other insects that resemble fat, buttery, silvery shards of light. She's looked.

Why are there no glowing moths? Because like so many small creatures, moths survive by camouflage. They want to hide, not stand out.

So here it is: somewhere near Rice Lake lives a moth species so expertly cloaked it's eluded human detection for hundreds of years, but at the same time, it calls attention to itself through light.

Make sense?

"Not at bit," Gabe mutters, pulling into the farm's dirt driveway.

An albino moth? A genetically mutated moth?

There's the famous example of the Peppered Moth in the UK, which adapted for dark-coloured spots in drastic numbers during the Industrial Revolution, in areas most affected by air pollution. This tactic of melanism aided the moth in blending into sooty trunks. Perhaps a similar adaptation today would involve a moth lightening its colour in an area of high light pollution. Yet her moth came out of the woods. And *glowing* is not at all like changing colour.

It's not just unprecedented, it's fantastical. Inexplicable, like sighting a UFO.

A radioactive moth?

Such a moth would be dead.

The usual reasons creatures have for emitting light — defense, solicitation, signaling, predation — make no sense for moths. They have superb defenses already. They call by scent. They locate each other just fine in the dark.

She reaches the cabin just after one-thirty p.m., the travel to the day's sites and trap recording having taken seven hours. Out of the car, she heads wearily to the picnic table with her bottled water and climbs onto it and stands looking out at the undulating water, shadowed by a few cumulous clouds. The catch at the second site near Big Cedar Lake, north of Peterborough, was leaner than in the forest this morning, but she jarred ten moths nonetheless.

She retrieves the collection box and brings it into the kitchen. All the moths in the jars are micros. The distinction between micro- and macrolepidoptera isn't exclusively size; in fact this division of moths is not, strictly speaking, scientific, but a useful and convenient vernacularism that stuck. There are taxonomic differences between the groups, and in general micromoths – the various Miners, Casebearers, Fairies, Concealers and Scavengers, Cosmets, Twirlers, Lichens, Sedges, Diamondbacks and False Diamondbacks, Falcate-winged, Leaf Blotch Miners, Ribbed Cocoon-Makers, Ermines and Needleminers, Fungus and Tubes, Cochylids, Olethreutines, Phycitines, Moss Eaters, Grass-Veneers and others – are the most primitive, in other words ancient, of moths.

With a jar plucked, Gabe slides the box into the fridge. Under a magnifying glass it's a cinch to identify this moth as Iron-lined Olethreutes. She records it. Some classmates found her use of a *tape recorder* amusingly old fogey. "What if the tape breaks?" "Can you still buy the insert things – cassettes?" But in her experience, nothing beats the ease and efficiency of a pocket recorder.

The next two moths are also easily ID'd. Then she finds one that isn't. It's a Leaf Blotch Miner the size of a sharpened pencil tip, but the colours and markings just don't line up with her books. Age could have faded them, or this individual might simply be a bit different. After all, if we could see more deeply, if our senses were as powerfully honed as other creatures', we'd surely be astonished by the uniqueness of every moth – of everything – and admit that much of what we lean on as knowledge is generalization.

Half an hour later, after wrestling with various views, and even photographing and enlarging the image on her computer, she's still unsure. She replaces the moth in the fridge and keeps going.

During moth nights at the Park or species counts the staff periodically conducted, she would offer IDs as near as she could make them using only her eyes, or the camera zoom or magnifying glass if needed. No one expected perfect accuracy; when it came to moths, her species knowledge and ID skills so exceeded the resident naturalists' that they were a treasure to the team.

Yes, Brimer, you were fucking right: there isn't time for this extra work. The day's transcription (which takes hours) isn't even started. Should she skip her outing tonight and work through the evening on that and these remaining moths? But she's already given them all she has. Of the seventeen, eight remain undecided. The others are freed. It's almost four, she's fried, and in two hours she's got to drive out and set the traps again.

Perhaps leave the moths in the fridge until tomorrow? But by then there will be more. Just stop dithering! They'll be dead soon anyway, outside or in; it's not like moths live for very long.

Since when did her needs become more important than the moths'? Wasn't the whole point of this degree to "offer herself," as she told Oliver in the restaurant? How laughably high-minded of her. Why didn't she try harder with the committee? Why did she continue with this fucked up degree! But if she quits now, then what? Isn't at least seeing things through better, for her and the moths generally?

You either do this now or you walk away. Go back to Jenn's. Press restart.

With a sick feeling, Gabe opens the freezer and places the box inside. She shuts the door. Turns her face aside. She can't believe this. This is such bullshit. Bullshit! Yet with effort, she releases the handle and walks away.

Outside, she stands on the grass. After a moment she takes off her clothes and wades into the cold lake and pulls herself down into its silent depths.

~

CARRYING EQUIPMENT in both hands, Gabe negotiates the ditch. Stalky mullein and purple thistle, fern-like yarrow and milkweed nodding with flower heads – in her headlamp they jump out from the dark looking startled, estranged from their daytime selves. She scrambles up and lifts her things over the old wire fence.

Tender young corn plants occupy the field, so she walks along the rutted edge. It leads straight to the woods and she can move without the light now, which she switches off. There's also some need for caution: a lone farmhouse lies west along the road, and although she's seen no sign of the owners whose land she's traipsing across, who may or may not live in that house, she wants to keep it that way.

At the field's north end she turns and passes in front of the woods. Partway along she finds a grassy nook screened by the roll of the land and trees to the west. Soon the white cotton sheet has been raised between the portable poles. She stabilizes the tripod in front of it, attaches socket and wire, inserts the light bulb — black, to attract less human attention — and connects plug to battery. A soft purple radiance fills the sheet; it reminds Gabe of a seminar room screen when someone's about to give a presentation.

Next, tree sugaring. She opens the lidded pail of moth broth: a funky mix of browned bananas, sugar, molasses and stale beer. With a paint brush she slaps it generously on the trees nearest to the light. Satisfied, she sets the pail aside and settles in her camping chair. Now it's watch and wait.

The night's clear and warm. Nine-thirty and she's not even wearing a jacket. All month the weather's been ahead of schedule; today it was close to thirty degrees again, July temperatures in late May. On the west coast drought continues both south and north of the border, even in BC, the land of rainforest. Images of infernos and smoldering homes fill the news, the "summer" wildfire season begun. On the phone to her parents in Victoria, she listened to descriptions of smoke-filled skies and sore throats.

Gabe sips iced tea. Distantly, a fox or coyote yips. At her back like an open door, the forest breathes cooler air.

Every quarter hour or so she inspects the sheet. Many are coming to perch on this fabricated ground, all manner of light-enchanted things: beetles, flies, moths, and nameless winged specks so slight and translucent they seem barely to hold form. They remind her of krill, the krill of the air; she's read that insects swarm in the upper atmosphere, which teems with unimaginable life — or did once.

Headlamp on, Gabe looms in to look. There's a stubby Sigmoid Prominent, *Clostera albosigma,* its rolled wings and erect forewing tuft mimicking a twig. And a Linda's Wainscot, *Leucania linda,* with its chain of modest black dots at the postmedial line. Out early. A demure Grateful Midget, *Elaphria grata,* patterned like leaf litter, with two black dots dropped inside an hourglass-shaped reniform spot. She scans from left to right and top to bottom, her presence having no obvious effect. Some moths perch motionlessly, others intensely vibrate their wings.

Headlamp off, slump down. Another gulp of tea.

Slowly the time passes. She paces around the field, stands under the trees, swings and slaps her arms to keep alert. Midnight, one o'clock . . . by one-thirty she's nodding off so often in her chair that the vigil's falling apart. It's a washout.

Pack up, return to car. Come back tomorrow. For how long? She's considered that she could have been mistaken — yet there was truly no doubt at all. Yes, dammit, she'll take it to her grave: *she saw it.*

With the car loaded she reverses and sets off. Climbs a hill canopied by trees — and up ahead, just to the right, is a small point of light.

Gabe brakes and kills the lights.

The glowing thing's bouncing above the ditch. It travels a few feet then abruptly disappears. Rationally, it looked like someone walking with a pencil flashlight ducked behind a tree.

Easing off the brake, Gabe inches over the crest. The light's reappeared on the other side, up ahead and still to the right. It's dipping and rising. Searching.

In a moment she's out of the car, camera in hand. For perhaps fifteen seconds she observes the light as it snakes a tight route. Cautiously she follows.

There's no field at this point on the road, just the woods coming right up on either side. The moth's very close to the outer trees. She approaches, she's a car length away —

The moth zigzags restlessly. Its vectors grow erratic. *No no no! Stay!* But it flies into the woods and is gone.

CELL SIGNALS at the cabin can be spotty and there's no internet there; for that she works at her friends' house, often after they go to bed, though they don't mind her intrusions either. Late the next morning, after emptying the traps at sites five and six, Gabe pulls up on her way in. Tessa, the old brown Lab retriever who's going blind, noses the screen door open and shuffles down the steps with a grin to greet her. No one else seems around. On the couch in the screened porch, Gabe shoves aside dog toys and newspapers and opens her laptop. A riot of messages pours into her account and she scans from the oldest up, tagging and deleting and looking for Oliver's name. They were in touch every other day the first week she was here, but it's been several since they exchanged messages or texts — not since her sighting of the luminous moth has she reached out. This morning she woke feeling deeply alone and longing to hear his voice, to talk to him about everything that's been happening.

Nothing from him.

Disappointment steals over her. Is he just giving her the space she said she would need? Should she be grateful? And why expect him to write or call, when she hasn't?

All the old emotional crap.

Fuck this. She's on her feet and out the screen door, striding away with her phone. She stops by the chicken coop and calls. He answers.

"Oliver! Hi!"

There's no warmth or excitement; his tone tells her right away that something's wrong. He's working, he's irritated, she needs to hold on. In the background the sounds of clanking and voices quiet.

"Okay. Yeah. I'm afraid things aren't good here, not at all." He takes a breath. "Something's happened with my brother and it's bad, really bad." And he tells her: his brother is missing, has been missing for four days.

"Oh my god. Does he have a family?"

"Besides me, yes." He tells her about the calls with his sister-in-law and filing a missing person's report. She can barely believe what she's hearing.

"And I could have stopped it," he says bitterly. "He came over, the last night . . ." His voice cracks, there's a pause, then he speaks firmly again. "He came to me and I didn't see how bad things were with him. I refused to see. I refused to see it all along."

Harsh as that sounds, it doesn't seem her place to deny it. "There must have been a lot going on in his life," she says.

"Of course there was. But I didn't want to know, even when it was right in my face."

"Did you talk that night?"

"Of course we talked! We fucking *talked*, but I didn't tell him what I should have."

"Oh, Oliver." She sits down on the ground with her back against the coop, watching a few hens scuff about. "I'm so, so sorry. Yet you don't know what his real reasons were for — leaving. He didn't say he wanted to leave town, did he?"

"No. He didn't leave town, I know it. He would never leave his daughter. No, I do know what's happened, only I don't want to go there, I can't. I'm as afraid as I was."

The noise returns, someone speaks. Oliver says he has to go.

"We'll talk later, then? I can call you tonight?"

"Sure. Do. Or maybe not — I'm not in the mood for talking much. I think I'm going to Naomi's later. I don't know. I don't know what's happening anymore."

And on that note, their call ends.

Back at the cabin, Gabe sets the latest box of jarred moths on the table (fourteen today) and sits staring out the window at the rushes. She can't tell if she needs a nap or exercise. Wrecked and wired she is – from three days of late nights and early mornings, from the driving, from the mind-blowing experience at the field, from peering at moths so they don't become little frozen carcasses. Wired and wrecked.

Now this: a missing sibling. She can only imagine his terror. Even hearing about it second-hand, she feels like the air's gone out of her entirely.

If she were in Toronto, she'd rush to Oliver immediately. And she wants to, feels she should because it's not right that he's alone. But there's six more days in this study period. And there's the field. What will he think if she doesn't go? Will it seem understandable or selfish? Uncommitted. And really, where *does* she stand? Is he truly the big deal she thought – Love, Home – or another one of her fantasies, a fabulous distraction?

She closes her eyes.

Part II

Outrageous Acts

22

NOISE. HE OPENS HIS EYES. This pattern of darkness familiar. Listens, but noise now gone. Heart racing, though. He reaches for the dog and kneads his warm, loose skin. The dog isn't large yet his crown can support a grown man's hand. Reg raises his head at the touch, then lowers it with a snuff. Whatever the noise, no concern.

Sometimes things just fall to the ground.

Noise in his own head, perhaps. The voices can shout him awake. It's happened, they can be a crazy chorus, though at least they don't talk over each other anymore, just one at a time. Distinctly. One sounds like an older Southern Black gentleman and another a jacked-up Scot, and there's an English guy, clever intellectual type. All men. They aren't cruel; they just seem to have a lot to say, and they get most active at night.

Rolling over onto his elbows and knees, his head low and torso sagging between the four points like a bloated bag. Bison position. He likes this one. The ground's vapour gets into his joints, but a few moments in bison takes away the ache. He can even doze like this. Bison sleep on their feet too, though they don't sag.

At first he could only listen to the voices' chatter: commentaries, opinions, questions, outbursts of passion, like a radio program dedicated to monologues. He has no clue where these people come from – what does he know about Black gospel? Or this guy's complaints about his job? He – Justin – was so awfully, awfully, *awfully* tired, so tired he wanted to weep and sometimes did when they kept him torturously awake, sleep breaking in at last like a relapse, collapse.

Then he made a discovery: when he's not so tired, he can assert himself and be part of the radio show, like the host. They quiet down.

He must have dozed off on his hoofs because now there's a faint light and twittering bird. Gentle, gentle. This is the kindest time. He sinks onto his haunches with his face to the ground. The easiest time, this and the twilight with its oasis blue. Salvation blue. The soft transitions. Twitter twitter, sweet. Where is it? What colour? *Oh what is that birdie out the window,* they'd sing to baby Gwynn.

Now he can sit up, though his gut hurts. Reggie licks his face. He massages the dog's jaw, whispering an apology for going to bed hungry. He wanted to eat – his hunger is almost as strong as the cravings for crystal – but they have only a bit of food left and need fuel for the trip into town.

The garbage bag is undisturbed and he tumbles the stones and earwigs aside. A hunk of convenience-store cheddar, some pita, the last of the kibble. He feeds Reggie from one hand, eating his own breakfast from the other and focusing on the food and the birdwood, not his whirly thoughts. It's okay. Such presences at dawn grow indistinct.

When the food's gone he rolls up his coat and slides it inside the garbage bag and hides it again. It's a journey to reach the street. The most direct and private route is right up the slope of the ravine, a stiff climb through brush so that he bends over often to use his hands for balance. That's okay, he's not above being on Reggie's level, and when he feels too wobbly he rests. There's plenty to see sitting under a tree that he's not had time for in ages: old walnut shells halved open to reveal fire-blackened caves, for example, and snails and caterpillars galore. Here are droplets of eggs pinned to the skeleton of an old leaf, placed there by who knows what. And the ravine has mini-toads the size of his thumbnail. Who knew? He wonders if the eggs belong to them before recalling that toads birth tadpoles.

The memory takes him back to high-school science class, and to echoes of good feelings that pass through his mind with faded pictures: the classroom with counters instead of cramped desks, working sinks and wooden-top metal stools. The science room was a place of action – such a relief from reading and writing. Science and music were his favourite subjects. Later, his interests changed. And a long time passed. Now he's a man twirling a leaf who's been sleeping in the park for days.

On his first trip to the street he didn't have this luxury of thinking. That was the day after his first night down here. Or maybe several days, he's not really sure. It was the first time he felt a bit less sick and confused. Something had happened between Oliver's and home. He'd gone outside that night for some air – no, because there were men. Or was that before? He strayed somehow, felt lost. Saw a cab, and homing instinct took hold.

Still before sunrise. In the taxi, the pain creep and familiar dread. Those gothic gates at the Baby Point entrance. Knew it was a bad idea.

Then on the path to his front door, he met it: a force field. What haunted him in the basement had grown bolder. He'd circled around to the back of the house, thinking to resume his outpost on the deck, but It lay in wait even there: malevolent, engulfing. He remembered Naomi's cold unlove, his bowels emptying, the nightmare. Despair welled and who knows if he would have made it through that moment? The Black Rider was winning. But a motion caught his eye: Reggie standing eagerly on hind legs in the sun-room, watching him.

Grimacing at the back door he punched in the code, cracked it open. The dark energy pounded over him as he waited long seconds with teeth gritted, Reggie's nails ticking across the kitchen tiles until he rushed out. Shut the door and back off – quickly! – through the yard and to the street with the Rider tearing after them. Holding Reggie in his arms now because he might spook, and fleeing toward the trail head, puffing, arrows in his chest and the Rider blowing heat at his heels.

And he reached the junction, descended the path. When they emerged by the river, the energy was gone; it couldn't pass through this barrier. Looking behind, he witnessed a blue streak in the east slicing through shadow.

Free! He went on until he met the gravel path, thinking he'd walk until daylight, but then dizziness, stomach-bowels churning and the park blurring, something wrong with his vision. Wounded in battle. Found the Sleep Tree, surrendered there.

At the top of the ravine, a property fence forces him to bush-whack. It's a stretch to Dundas Street, but the terrain's level now. Going this way beats taking a public path, and nothing could be as bad as that first journey when the sun was hot, after lying sick. His thirst had sent him to drink from the dirty river, gagging. But then he bathed his feet and head, and later, made it up to a street. Blue bins bulged with garbage bags, stench. His senses on overdrive. A man walked by him and spoke with a cruel smile. Not the Black Rider, but one of its servants.

He knew he had to be fast, then, for he was so vulnerable. Found a store. Glimpses of his cloaked figure in confectionary glass. No phone, left somewhere or lost. Keeping his eyes on Reggie. Then retreat to the river, his burrow.

How many days ago? Three? More? Now when he finds the street he remembers the direction of the store. There it is. Stay close, Reg.

Coffee, a large. And more cheese, bread, water, apples, dog food.

Nowhere to breakfast except out back, which will do: sugared liquid magic on his tongue and a dumpster casting shade.

He falls asleep against the brick wall and wakes when the steel door swings open. The clerk, emerging with empty boxes. Justin apologizes.

"It's alright," he says. Tosses in the recycling then pulls out a pack of smokes. Lights one, warily returning Reggie's stare.

Justin gradually stands. Neck in a crick, clothes frightful. He smooths his hair.

"It's okay, finish your coffee," the man says. "Is your dog friendly?" He waves at Reggie, who thumps his tail.

Justin encourages Reggie to visit and he does, nosing the offered palm. Justin picks up his bags.

"Have a good day," the man says. "It's a weird one. Lots of sirens."

Justin listens but doesn't hear any.

On his return to the ravine he rests in a bus shelter by a cluster of newspaper boxes and eats a packaged cheese sandwich, reading windowed headlines. The obsession with oil, wars in faraway lands. Oil to make the plastic wrap around the sandwich and to make the bread factories run. To ensure the soybean harvest for the mayonnaise. Whirly whirl whirl. *That's not the end of it, is it mate?* For mixing the ink on the price sticker, pulping the paper. Pumping water for crops — which need insecticides, fertilizers, tractors, produce trucks. The operations. The communications. Requiring extractions of ore, minerals, rare earths. The food for the workers. The drugs for their diseases. *And we're still on agribusiness.* Look at the aluminum newspaper box, your shoes. Everything's greasy.

Hands shaking, he swallows, focusing instead on his meal. He's read enough for now.

Things are going to hell in a handbasket, Mom liked to say, a phrase he never quite understood, though he loved that other one of hers: *Bullshit baffles brains.*

Mom was usually right — about him, too.

For a long time he thought she'd invested in Ace because she believed in him; then he saw that what she believed in was the soundness of her own idea. She placed confidence in him because he was indeed a force, though one that needed to be pointed in the right direction. He's not so good at that — sensing direction. He should have listened to Naomi about Leverage. Didn't like her ideas at the time, and they were smarter than he acknowledged. Basically he's a good soldier who shoulders the work no matter what, marches the long march despite doubts and rebellious sensitivities, goes forward, forward, while the world crashes around him and his troops die and his body sags until his own heart gets blown out.

Not that it's Mom's fault.

He thinks of her as he watches traffic on Dundas Street, holding Reggie on his lap. A blessing, he supposes, that she didn't live to see him now. Though he's starting to really miss her. The place she occupied in his life, always vague or maybe too vast to discern, has been coming into focus with time, like a rent in fabric.

A young woman joins him at the bus stop and he pushes the last crust in his mouth and sets Reggie down. Sirens: he realizes he's been hearing them now for a while.

The walk back seems long, having to edge down the slope with his bags. Beneath the Sleep Tree he curls up under his coat, dizzy and sad. When Reggie disappears, he doesn't even have the strength to call him.

THE VOICES HAVE gotten quieter. Mostly there's his own voice now, satellited by ghosts: Gwynn. Naomi. Leverage. Ace. Sweating and drooling like a peaceful madman in the woods, dining beside dumpsters.

Though he's not eating from them, at least.

Levy, don't be an eejit.

It's true, he deserved that. Other men he's also seen in the park who seem dedicated to wandering here, perhaps like him have found a protective place. Always alone, marked by grime and by a certain semi-feral stare. So they don't have homes. So they eat what they can find. So he's among them. Location, location! Don't believe that bullshit, *bullshit baffles brains*: all through the city people are breaking down and freaking out, in condos and hotels and even the basements of Baby Point.

At sunset mosquitoes hunt and he hikes the coat over his head, snorting in and out of sleep. Naomi, Gwynn, Ace . . . Will Naomi turn his daughter against him? Can she be turned?

Reggie returns. They eat hungrily, then sleep.

At sunrise he feels clear enough to face a basic decision: this tree has guarded him, but it's time to find a drier place. The last several nights have been wet. Scouting for a new tree becomes his goal for the morning, and then retrieving his food and the blanket he also found, an old yellow fleece.

He still has energy. This might be the day.

In the same bus shelter, later. The bus pulls up with a pneumatic wheeze and he starts to tremble as he waits to board. The owner of Ace, a smelly man.

"Let's go!" the driver shouts.

He turns and walks way, feels stung all over. Can't happen.

On foot he and Reg cross the bridge over the river ravine and continue. Up ahead, a box store. Glass doors bolt back, stench like rubber. Too many people. Up the street again, a plaza, rusted sign — better. He requires a tarp. Zero eye contact from the cashier as she makes change, tears the receipt, and he leaves thinking about the obscure archival history that's just occurred, cuneiform rendering of a moment in his story.

He can do this much. He picks up several more items and, safe again at the river, rests.

He's weak — still too weak, that's clear. The Black Rider will consume him in this state. To make sure that doesn't happen, to be

259

confident, he needs more than just detox: he must dig out the gravel he keeps slipping on, which has something to do with how he's seen things and himself, illusions about priorities and what matters plus the missions he only too willingly signs up for until he's blind.

All of this passing through his mind in a kind of breeze that moves him.

The new tree is a chestnut, well away from any paths. Gratefully he rests propped against its trunk with Reggie's head on his leg while daylight pales and the Earth exhales until only one bird is left singing.

Moonrise. He removes his clothes and enters the river where it shoals and wades upstream, knee deep, waist deep. The water's malodorous taint no longer bothers him; the river's another victim of the age and it accepts him because you don't need to be whole to love. He wades until he can sink to his shoulders. The cool current breaks over his chest and fills his ears with its trickle. His mind stills. Overhead, the moon calls down to his bones. When he spreads his arms into the pearling current, she turns them ancient.

23

"OLIVER. MR. ATHLETE." With a weak smile, Naomi gestures to come in. The house is refreshingly cool. He removes his bike helmet and Naomi, barefoot in a short grey dress, leans in for a shoulder-embrace, dry cheek against his hot one. He pats her back.

In the sunroom she's laid out an antipasto tray with cold cuts and cheeses. She's drinking white wine, offers him one that he declines. Gwynn, tucked up in a corner of the banquette with a tablet, stares at him and doesn't return his smile or hello.

"Do you mind if I stand for a while?" He's sweaty and pumped up from the ride. It's over fourteen kilometres from the gym to Justin's, and it's been a long time since he biked this far.

"Whatever you like." With a wave Naomi leans back, reaching out to touch Gwynn.

"How are you?"

"Very busy, actually," she says brightly. "Meeting with staff almost daily. Have to keep things afloat, right?" Her look suggests she means more than the business.

"Anything I can help with?"

"Oh, I don't think so. It's pretty under control." Another fake grin. He's getting impatient. He's not here just to buck up the home-front façade.

"Shall we step outside?"

"Sure." She tells Gwynn that they'll be on the back deck.

"Can't I come?"

"Uncle Oliver and I need some grown-up talk time alone."

"But *why?*" She seems on the verge of tantrum or tears. Naomi smooths her hair, kisses her brow. Then with a nod she rises and heads to the back door.

It's hot and bright under the late afternoon sun and he shivers because his clothes had started to cool. Naomi goes to the deck table and starts cranking open the umbrella.

"I called the police today to keep the file updated. That's what they suggested."

"Shit, I forgot my glass. Shall I get your water, or do you want something else?"

"I don't care." She stops and looks at him. "Look, I'm sorry, but we need to decide some things. I've made up the poster." He brings one out from his courier bag, still slung over his shoulder, and places it on the glass. A photo of Justin in a suit, handsome. It might have been taken at the funeral.

LAST SEEN IN THE AREA OF GREENWOOD AND DANFORTH. PLEASE CONTACT 647—OR THE POLICE AT—

His own phone number.

Naomi frowns and sucks her bottom lip. Her eyes have gone filmy and red – or were they that way before? "I don't know what to say. I'm getting my drink."

She's gone a while. He paces on the deck, listening to the trees shushing and birds calling. They seem far off, below or above he cannot tell. His life teeters on the brink of a precipice, he feels attached with a single guy wire like those tourists edge-walking on the CN tower. Justin's been gone six days. Six fucking days! Last member of the incredible shrinking family.

Finally he notices her in the sunroom by the table. She's texting.

When he enters the kitchen, he can tell by her bent head and a sniffle that she's been crying. He slides into the banquette, picks up the miniature fork and stabs an olive, a slice of tomato. Gwynn's tablet bleeps and blings as she scores points on whatever.

"That was the manager at Leverage." Naomi joins him and places the phone on the table. The sunlight reveals lines and slack skin on her face that he's never noticed. She sighs, and her voice shakes a little when she speaks. "It's just that, I'm thinking this through a bit differently. I don't think you're seeing this for what it truly is, Oliver. It's called abandonment."

He thinks he understands; probably he'd feel the same way. Still, it's not Justin's style to slink away. "We don't know everything," he tells her. "There might be illness. Reasons."

"Doubtful. Where's Reg?" She takes a sip, considers, then speaks firmly. "I don't want notices around this neighbourhood. Or Queen Street West."

He gapes at her. "What's that, like NIMBYism? The whole point of them is to be seen."

"What notice?" asks Gwynn.

"Put them up on the other side of town. It makes sense to start on the east side anyway." Naomi's switched to her bright tone again, like they're discussing where to hang a painting.

"Fuck that. No way."

Gwynn looks to him. "What notice?"

"We're trying to contact your dad, sweetheart," he says, while Naomi glares.

"I know where he is."

Naomi turns to her with a frown. "Where, honey?"

"Hiding."

"Well, I sure wish he'd stop. Don't you?"

Gwynn shrugs. She slides off the cushion and lies on her belly on the rug in the dining room with her game.

"Okay, I'll start on the east side," he says. After a while, Naomi clears the plates. While she's busy in the kitchen Gwynn gets up and drops wordlessly onto the banquette beside him and curls up with her head on his lap. Astonished, he drapes an arm over her. She pretends to be asleep.

~

SIX DAYS SINCE Justin evaporated like a gust of rain. Naomi said the dog would come home if something had happened, if he could. He's a smart dog. For these reasons she retains her shaky conviction that Justin's holed up somewhere, trying to get his shit together, or possibly with someone else. He'd not hurt himself, she insists. He'd never abandon Gwynn.

Perhaps. But suicides aren't always intentional.

From Baby Point Oliver cycles east to Dupont, jogs south to Bloor, passes through Koreatown, the Annex, U of T campus, crosses the Yonge Street dividing line and reaches Jarvis. Then it's downhill to Queen and east to Parliament. Though he's still far west of Greenwood, this is where he wants to start.

He walks north, guiding his bike. About forty minutes of daylight left, and even so, there's nothing to stop him postering at night. He comes to a community bulletin board and opens the bag. Position. Staple. He smooths the paper needlessly after it's mounted.

Next stop is a utility pole. Half a block, then another. Should he do both sides of the block at once, or return? Better to get max coverage now. He crosses the street. Down the block, staple, sometimes tape, head back. Strange trail indeed, his brother's plight repeating along the street. A few passersby glance at him curiously.

So this is how it feels to leave pieces of your story behind, everywhere. To broadcast your woe.

Filing a missing person report, he's learned, is just that. Justin's profile has been added to MissingPeople.ca and the Toronto Police Association website, but there's no investigative policework involved in this kind of situation unless there's reason to suspect foul play, or the missing individual is ill, underage, demented, a danger to themselves or others. "It's not a crime to run away," a young, sympathetic constable explained to Oliver when he visited the station again yesterday, thinking that rattling someone's cage might do something. "People drop out of sight. They have their reasons."

A streetcar squeals as it jerks onto Gerrard. A gathering of sad faces in the dirty parkette. A bike courier shouting to a driver backing in. As Oliver crosses into Cabbagetown, familiar places reach out to him. This was why he needed to start here, his neighbourhood from all those years ago, where he lived when he returned from grad school single and hyped up with his own potential. The Pear Tree restaurant. Jet Fuel Coffee. Suddenly there it is: a film-clip memory of Justin and him at the apartment on Berkeley Street, late at night and laughing like fools. Justin was single then too and used to turn up after work unannounced because that didn't matter. Soft tread on the back steps, his brother always surprisingly light on his feet. Hours they'd spend just hanging, listening to music. The time! How did they have all that time?

He didn't tell Naomi about the Facebook page. Later. He reactivated his long-dormant profile to create it. *Justin Leveridge hasn't been seen by family or friends since the night of May 21. We're very distressed by his absence and hope he's alright.* On the page he loaded a few photos: Justin as a teen holding a guitar, huge hair. Justin at the opening of Ace, at some Christmas dinner where he looks drink-jolly. How few pictures Oliver has; most came from boxes packed in Oakville, their mother's archive. The page is a bit of a fake history of brotherly care, though the sentiments are real. *We love Justin and ask that anyone with information on his whereabouts contact us.* His number and email again.

After activating the page, the next step felt almost as strange: sharing it with his former "friends." When he checked it again he was astounded at the number of comments, shares and even a few private notes; moved to tears by the warmth and sympathy offered.

Colleagues, grad-school pals, mutual friends of his and Connie's (who called right away). He'd no idea what to expect, but it wasn't that kind of support.

Twenty-five posters. He'd like to do forty today.

Wellesley. St. James Town and the cemetery. Late in the day he reaches the top of Parliament and his quota. The skin's sore on the back of his neck and he's all trembly. Traffic races past toward the viaduct. Cumulus clouds drift over the city, filled with golden light. He gets on his bike and pedals east and onto the bridge that spans the valley. It opens beneath, green and paradisal from this height. Six days. His legs ache. The bridge has been strung with suicide-prevention wires and glints and gleams like a musical instrument.

It's dark when he gets home. He showers and puts on clean underwear. Shirtless, he stares before the mirror. The bruise has completely healed. He refused to see what was happening with Justin. He turned away. He's been turning away for years. But not looking didn't make things better. He should have seen these punches coming — all of them. Should have mended the old hurts in himself and between them, should have been better prepared.

Gabe's call yesterday caught him at a weak moment; he was scattered, overwhelmed and inelegant to boot. She's left two messages since. What must she think of him? That he falls apart in a crisis. That he can't face the tough stuff — can't rise to the occasion. Just like she thought in the park when they spoke about Rosh and his group. She didn't say that, but he'd felt it.

He's been a coward and a fool. For years. Yes, things went south with Connie and his career — but not everything. He still had his mom and Justin; he had the gym and Foroud and could have reached out to some friends. He could have even tried again with his book. Little Angel in the house: perhaps he chose that role because it came with the lowest stakes.

THE NEXT DAY the power goes out in the neighbourhood. Oliver notices the light dimming around three in the afternoon when his computer screen glows brighter. Rain patters the windows, and in a moment it's drumming on the roof.

There's a gunshot sound and the screen goes black. Groans from the gym.

He stands and opens the office door. Foroud's pointing out the front window and talking about a blown transformer. "Blue sparks!" He calls to Oliver for flashlights for the locker rooms so members can retrieve their things.

"Got it!" Oliver shouts back, glad for the excuse to leave the back room. How invigorating to have the skies open and the silos get broken! He helps members pack up and trainers unplug the exercise machines, then joins staff at the front desk. Foroud's taped one of the posters to the door. Everyone's seen it and expresses their concern. Most want to help, and he ends up giving out many of the posters he's printed, moved and humbled again by this community he'd not realized he has. He'll have to return to the copy shop.

He thinks about the posters from yesterday on his wet walk home. Might need redoing, though obviously not tonight.

To his surprise, the power's on along Greenwood and his street. Lights shine in Rosh's apartment — he's back again from another short trip — and on the way upstairs Oliver badly wants to knock, see how Rosh is doing, hang out instead of racking up another evening alone. But he's never just popped by. He could conjure ten reasons why he shouldn't, including "not bothering Rosh," but they amount to one stupid truth: he's scared. He's not made a new friend in years. With Gabe the desire's too powerful to be denied. Well, what would she make of him now? A coward and a fool.

Taking a breath, he raises his hand and raps.

Rosh opens the door wearing a phone headset and smiles and waves Oliver in like he's expected, gestures to sit and holds up five fingers twice, still grinning. There's a small sofa, an upholstered chair under a reading lamp, and nearer the desk, a padded bench set with colourfully embroidered pillows. Oliver sits there. An elephant in beaded headdress. A jumping fish. On the desk, two large monitors wired to a laptop. Rosh scrolls through a website on one while continuing to discuss what sounds like *Fracking Up the Future's* opening title sequence. The other screen seems to be running a digital rendering program.

"Oliver!" Rosh speaks sotto voce, fingers over the headset mic. "Do you want something? Beer's in the fridge. Or tea? Kettle's on the counter." Oliver feels weird wandering into Rosh's kitchen so just waves the offer aside. "Water?" Rosh persists, before called back to the screen. There's a water glass to one side of it, almost empty, so Oliver picks that up and finds a glass for himself and fills them both from the tap.

Rosh has finished the call. In his usual upbeat manner he says it's good to see him and asks about Mimi.

"We've progressed to open cuddling."

"I never doubted it would happen. And you? How's Gabe?" Raised eyebrows.

"Out of town for her fieldwork now, but we're in touch."

"Right on." On the way home from the bar that night, after they'd said goodbye to Gabe, Rosh had teased him about plucking a damsel from the crow's nest. Oliver swore it wasn't his usual M.O.

He nods at the screens. "How's the project? Sounds like you're pretty far along."

"Yes and no. Come see for yourself."

Rosh opens a minimized page. On it a video is paused: the chaotic image shows a road, protestors and police facing off in smoke-filled air. The protestors are shouting. The police wear caps and hi-vis raincoats. In the foreground a woman bleeding from a head wound has slumped to the pavement, held and shielded by two others. Blonde hair, raincoat, it's difficult to tell her age. Without noise or movement the scene could be a painting, a tableaux. A war.

A raid. There's something sickeningly timeless about it, and Oliver wonders briefly why people keep inflicting such hurt, why history keeps repeating. Then Rosh presses play, and a din of shouts and scuffles bursts into the quiet apartment. The woman on the ground starts breathing, crying, as her companions look about anxiously and call for aid. A tear-gas cannister arcs behind them, spinning bluish smoke.

"This was New Brunswick last year," Rosh says, "a seismic testing site blockade. Emily LaViolette — we interview her later. She's a math teacher. It's good to have teachers."

"Was she okay, then?"

"Not at all — she got a concussion. She recovered, though."

As the injured woman's helped to her feet and away the camera follows them, then swings as commotion erupts offscreen. A dense line of police, drawing close. People back away, past the camera. The person filming enters the group at the front, where grey-haired elders flanked by younger faces hold signs — FRACK OFF — UNCEDED MI'KMAQ TERRITORY — and wave flags. One raises an eagle feather like a protective cross. Behind the police line a van pulls up, then another as the officers press forward using ends of batons to prod people away from the blockaded site. Mostly they don't speak, though they seem to grumble. No — they're chanting: *move back, move back, move back* . . . The protestors steadily lose ground. A young man keeps shouting that the cops have no authority here. One reaches out as if to clench his throat while another cracks his baton on the man's shoulder. A woman screams. The popping of rubber bullets erupts. Wails in the crowd, police pushing past someone in a wheelchair who turns and shakes a fist. A dog barking. The camera pivots to the roadside, where two men in army fatigues stand in the grass holding machine guns, one gripping a chain on a lunging Rottweiler.

"My god," Oliver says. It's hard to watch. An unarmed man edges up to the soldiers, arms spread, and goads them to shoot. A woman intervenes. Rosh presses pause.

"Yeah. It started to rain just then, so there's not much more that's good. But as you can see, this speaks pretty loudly to what's happening. We've included some of it in the trailer, which we were almost done, but now with the report, everything's kind of unsettled."

"You mentioned your group was divided about it."

"Not on its importance, obviously, just how to most effectively use it. The thing with a report is it's *boring,* words on a page. Like, I've done this —" He pulls up another window, plays a clip showing a close-up of a page, type highlighted, while a voiceover reads. "Pretty standard doc stuff, though."

"What about getting interviews with the authors — the scientists?"

"That would be fantastic, but . . ." He shrugs. "Lots of footwork. Time and money." He shakes his head.

"That sucks."

"Yeah."

He suggested the interviews automatically, force-of-habit thinking, but now the possibility seems to hang in the air. Oliver doesn't know whether Rosh feels it too or the tension comes solely from his own conscience, but it makes him suddenly restless. Mimi's waiting to be fed. He wants to call Gabe. Check for messages on the poster.

"My brother's gone missing."

Rosh turns to him.

Is this a confidence or excuse? "He's been gone for six — seven — days now. I've got a poster up —"

"Your *brother?* And we've been watching *this?*"

"It's good to get my mind on other things. Important things. I've been pretty, I don't know . . . it's really intense. His family, the police . . ." He starts describing what happened. Rosh asks about sharing the Facebook page, about postering the neighbourhood. He offers to do some of it on the weekend. "That's really kind, thank you," Oliver mumbles, awash with too much emotion to say more. He's suddenly incredibly tired. They've been standing through the conversation and his back throbs.

Upstairs, he's too weary to cook dinner. After seeing to Mimi he writes down the messages on the poster to follow up in the morning, checks the Facebook page, answers Gabe's texts, pours himself a huge bowl of cereal and climbs into bed.

IN THE DREAM, he's building an egg. It must get finished. Its ribbed frame stands before him, reaching well above his head, a skeleton lacking organs, an outline needing paragraphs . . . But he's stalled, confused as to what happens next. Boards lie scattered. Tools wait. Must get finished! He bends to scribble figures on an offcut, panting with exertion. Drums pound in his ears. He doesn't have time, he'll never fucking make it –

There's no sleep left in him, and before dawn he's up reading the news. He learns that yesterday's blackout or blackouts affected the entire Lake Ontario metro region, west past Hamilton and east as far as Port Hope. Power has been restored to most areas, so he along with millions of others can count on hot breakfasts courtesy of the nuclear facility at Darlington and the coal-burning plants in Hamilton that the *Arctic Sunrise* sailed here to blockade.

He turns on the radio – more blackout reporting – fills the coffee pot with purified, fluoride-free water from the Berkey filter (an investment from his journalistic days), pours it into the machine, grinds fresh beans, and presses a button. The irony isn't lost on him. Though is it irony, really, or simply denial? Refusal to see.

Talk radio moves on from the blackout to a traffic incident in the eastbound collector lane of the 401. But on the island listserv, which he recently joined, the conversation about the rains and this year's water levels is raging. Oliver scrolls through photos of broken trees, eroded shorelines, submerged beaches, standing water – all taken this spring.

This is something else he's been avoiding. Several climate resilience strategies for the bungalow have been suggested by his architect, from storm-rated windows, roof and doors to rain barrels and solar panels. But the main one concerned elevation: raise it off the ground. This cannot be done with the existing house. The foundation needs replacing and redesign.

She suggested a meeting and he's not followed through. And of the three contractors she put him in touch with, only one will consider a project on the island. That too is stalled.

He should be talking to Islanders. A community meeting's been called for this Sunday.

Remember the Toronto Regional Conservation Authority's shore management plan? one listserv commenter asks. *The one that went nowhere?* After a mega-storm hit the city in 2004, the TRCA's plan posited erosion safeguards for the island that have yet to be built.

We need to start sandbagging. This is just the beginning.

~

EIGHT DAYS. The copy shop has put one of his posters on the counter; more unexpected kindness. As he bikes around the neighbourhood, Justin's face taunts him from utility poles, bus shelters, shop windows. Calls have started to come in. *A man who looked exactly like that photo only with a shaved head asked me for change at a bus stop . . . was sleeping on the sidewalk at Royal York and Bloor . . . stood behind me in the No Frills checkout . . . lives with my sister in Scarborough . . . walks his dog past our house . . .* He returns every call. If the tip sounds worth it and doable for him to check out, he rides his bike or the subway there.

The summer ferries have been brought out of hibernation, and on Sunday morning he travels on the *Thomas Rennie,* its two decks crowded with tourists pointing phones. Even with his knowledge of the situation, he's unnerved by what he sees as they approach Ward's: the eastern breakwater, a crumbling cement spit jutting into the harbour, has vanished beneath the water's surface. So has the semi-permanent sandbag dike that protects The Cove, a vulnerable section of Ward's. The shoreline willows with their great shaggy crowns rise like surreal eruptions from the lake.

They dock and the ferry empties. Ward's Café has opened and is doing a lively business. Near its outdoor tables and ice cream stand, the soccer field has become a mirror. Children are running through the water – no, not running, *surfing*. They have boards and launch themselves screaming.

The meeting's at the Algonquin Island Clubhouse, tucked into the woods just down the lane from his place. Walking his bike on the busy road, Oliver passes more ponding water and a group of muddy millennials playing ultimate frisbee in bathing suits. He crosses the bridge and passes the vacant bungalow. The key's in his pocket; earlier he thought about going inside, attempting some cleanup, but that too seems like more denial. He knows what has to happen now.

Bicycles clutter the pathway to the clubhouse entrance. This is the first time he's gone inside, at least that he can remember. He chooses a backrow seat among the folding chairs.

"Oliver, nice to see you again." It's Susanna, his neighbour to the south. He met her and her husband the day he visited the bungalow inside. They occupy one of original bungalows as well, though theirs has been lovingly kept up. He's noticed her posts on the listserv – she's one of the "political" members.

"Seems like a good turnout," he says.

She takes the seat beside him, waves her husband over. "Hmm, the usual suspects mostly so far. Ah, *that's* interesting." She nods archly, he can't tell at what or who. "Yes, we might be in for some heat."

"Wonderful," her husband says with a groan. He gives Oliver an exasperated grin.

A grey-haired man dressed in a rumpled shirt and jeans approaches the podium and regards them over the rim of his glasses. That's David, Susanna tells him. Oliver searches his memory for that name on the listserv as the room quiets. After a brief greeting and call to order, he moves to the meeting's purpose. "As we all know by now," David says, "we've got a real problem. Wet winter. Wet spring. And if the weather continues like this — as it's supposed to — our problem will get a lot worse." He lets that sink in. "What we're here to do this morning is discuss actions we can take. We don't have much time, there's a wedding coming in for set up at noon today, so I ask that we please be focused, and that the discussion stay *positive*. This isn't the time to rehash our grievances, though these are many. We want to leave with a plan for next steps before we meet again in —" He looks to a woman standing nearby, who holds up two fingers. "Two weeks, that's our target. Actions for the next two weeks."

One resident raises her hand and stands. She wants to share research that she and others have been doing. "We're all learning about the lake, about the whole system of water," she says. She describes how the level of Lake Ontario is connected to what's happening upstream. Montreal, at the confluence of the St. Lawrence and Ottawa Rivers, is highly vulnerable to flooding. A regulation plan governs flow-regulation through two major dams to protect that city. The needs of all the shoreline municipalities downstream, of shipping and hydro also, are affected and juggled by these flow decisions. Unfortunately, the current plan doesn't take into account increased high water levels in the spring freshets, or abnormal increases in levels occurring.

"So *we* get flooded," someone says.

"Yes. And we know it's bad. On the one hand, I look at it like we all need to share the pain. But we also must keep up the political pressure so this plan is updated to reflect the changing weather. We need to work with the water."

Another speaker stands. He reminds the group that tax money has supported park facilities on the island, not erosion safeguards. The Toronto Regional Conservation Authority's protection proposal is only a paper plan. "Consultants got rich, and our shoreline's still degrading." These comments inspire many nods. The city — the fucking city! From the earliest days the island's been targeted by its schemes, and every resident lives with a certain justifiable fear of what the city could spring on them next.

"An Islander never forgets!" mutters an old man sitting near Oliver.

"My friends, we can spend all morning rehashing everything that's gone wrong. Probably all weekend." It's the woman who was standing near the podium before. Elke, Susanna says. "But we really *must* make some decisions. Time is ticking."

Some feel they should contact the Toronto Regional Conservation Authority after all. Others suggest calling on the provincial government. And isn't there an emergency preparedness body that can help? Their MPP, and sympathetic city councilors . . . A man standing at the back raises his hand. "Seeing as in this situation our interests are the same," he says, "why not also approach the Toronto Port Authority and petition together for help?"

A ripple of emotion. The TPA operate the island airport.

The white-haired elder turns in his chair. "You mean shake hands with the devil?"

But enough agree with the idea to keep it afloat. Discussion winds round, eating up time. With fifteen minutes left, Elke and David return to the podium and declare a stalemate. They propose forming an Emergency Response Committee to consider options for this summer. Residents should approach them to volunteer immediately. Oliver wonders if the committee already unofficially exists.

"Oh yes," Susanna confirms, "today's just to ignite people to join. That's always the problem. Two kinds of Islanders." She shakes her head. "If things keep on like this, we're heading for a breaking point."

"With the floods?"

"That, yes, but I meant the community. It's going to come down to a fundamental question of what we're about here. Are you in or out, and what does that mean? You know?"

"The cottage crowd doesn't care," her husband says. "The ones who live elsewhere, who use this place like their mini-Muskoka."

"The offshore holders are to blame, but so are lots of residents. They have their city jobs, and the island's just like a cute suburb. There's no shared philosophy or responsibility — that has always been the problem here, and it might be our end." Susanna sighs, then clutches Oliver's elbow playfully. "I sure hope you can swim."

THE *THOMAS RENNIE* chugs him back to the city. From the upper deck he watches the willows recede, the island shrink and thin. Ever since that day he learned about the bungalow, he's held onto an image of himself back in that house: his bookshelves in the front room, woodstove ticking as he reads by lamplight; staking tomatoes in summer, walking the beaches, canoeing. A peaceful, gentle life. A life in beauty. How could he have been so naïve? Beauty's getting swallowed by global disaster. It's getting choked, it's getting blasted to smithereens. What a fool! He's *known* this; he knew it long ago. Retreat is neither possible nor right, if it ever was.

At home he sits at his computer and searches for the shale-rights maps Rosh spoke of in connection to the leaked report. An energy company's website offers a PDF of a presentation called "Leveraging Today's Shale Gas Opportunity." On the assets map, Lake Erie — the lake shaped like a sweet potato, he always thought — has been sectioned into a grid. Hundreds of little squares: most blue, but about a quarter are yellow, and these are peppered with black dots. Proposed drill sites.

He prints the map in colour and props it up. He writes Rosh an email: *I have some ideas for you. Can I read the report? Can we speak?*

Then he gets up to check the latest phone messages from the poster.

24

THE NINE-DAY May sampling period is over. And now she should return to campus with her portable morgue, and with the help of a taxonomic expert like Brimer or Ochoa-Rodriguez, identify these snowflakes to species level based on external morphology, genitalia features and the available literature. Then log and dispose.

What's done is done. Suck it up.

Gabe saves the sampling data file, copies it to the external hard drive, leans back in the chair. Half a day spent entering the last of the May data from her tapes. She gets up and kicks the screen door open and there's the world, being rolled by a brisk breeze: leaves seethe, rushes chafe, water curls and foams.

And what of the luminous moth? Seven nights out at the field. Is she delirious? What if there is no glowing moth? Certainly that's what every entomologist would tell her, should she dare to speak of it. Because this moth *does* seem a lot like a made-to-order excuse: another bright decoy for her to chase after, another ungraspable dream to keep her from sticking with the plan, from growing the fuck up.

Even if it exists, it might be too late to find the luminous moth anyway. Moth life cycles range from entire seasons to mere weeks;

given their elusivity, the illuminated moths could have been born and danced their bright lives toward the next generation all within the month of May.

And yet. She could go out there tonight or even today, perhaps. Maybe there's something about those woods? Driving to campus is about as appealing as going to a mall. And she's sick to death of the computer. You have to be *out* in the world to catch what's going on. You can't be holed up in a lab or library or pinned to a screen. At some hours, certain things step forward.

There's a good four hours left until dusk. She packs her small knapsack with food and water, brings her laptop in case she wants to check email at the house later, and drives out.

~

MOTHS CAN BE highly regional, with some species living only in certain valleys or other ecological niches. Could the woods by the field possess a unique feature? The most likely is undisturbed ravines, deemed too difficult to farm or build on. Topographical maps have been unhelpful except to show her that the woods extend farther than most in this fragmented region, joining up with a designated wilderness area in the northeast.

Chalk in hand, Gabe begins at the southeast corner of the woods where it meets the field. Young alders, blackberry and raspberry bushes crowd this edge, but when she works past them the forest floor opens: white trilliums whose flowers have almost finished for the year, violets, mosses, ferns and ropes of wild grape — foliage easy to walk through. She gazes about the canopy. Maple, ash, fir and oak. Entering a wood is like coming up from that first dive into the lake: you need to catch your breath, adjust to the temperature, sense the currents. Her entrance here creates ripples, and at first the woods are silent. But then a blue jay calls, a robin twitters a thought, two squirrels race around a trunk.

Within sight of the cornfield she marks a blaze on a tree, the first sign that will be the last on her return. She proceeds north-east in a gently meandering line, pausing every minute or so to mark the trail and occasionally, though not often, overshooting her sightline and doubling back to locate the last blaze. She has a good sense of direction, always has, and the compass in her pack rarely sees action.

Boulders, mossy and dusty with old leaves, hunker here and there like scattered ruins. The ground starts to rise after a time and at the top of a steep slope she finds herself under oaks that rise above an almost trench-like ravine. Water glints in the green below. She edges down carefully, feeling the quiet deepen. The air grows pungently moist, druggishly verdant. She tests the spongey ground before leaping the rivulet. Then a slog up the other side. Locate the last blaze, chalk the next.

She's been hiking a half hour and the woods seem to continue in every direction, cresting and sinking. Drumlins – of course! She's in a drumlin field. When the glaciers that scoured and gouged the Earth here retreated, they left great humps of gravel in wave-like deposits. Drumlins became the islands of Rice Lake; around Peterborough they mound farmers' fields like barrows, entombed whales. And they move through this wood. Could this be the fea-ture she's looking for?

Gabe skirts a creek bed scored with damp black trails where water ran recently. Another chalk mark. And then another ravine edge. Heading down, slipping on leaf litter, pausing at the bottom. There's a presence, a kind of *density* to places long undisturbed. Some trees have been taken, yes, but not for many decades and this place was never thoroughly logged. It feels like no human has done anything but lightly pass through here for a very long time. Abruptly she looks up: far overhead a pair of vultures are spiraling, round and round each other, two fragments of a circle.

Where was her last mark? She's a tad lightheaded. She scans the top of the slope and can't see one. Did she forget to make it?

Opening her pack, she takes out water and drinks, then eats a handful of walnuts. There's the mark: right where she was looking.

Working up the next slope, she reflects on the woods being *undisturbed*. The idea is an illusion, a joke; she thought that because she was looking with her eyes only. If these leaves and soil were tested, they'd tell another story: heavy metals would be present because they travel everywhere, and then there's tritium, a radio-active waste product from nuclear reactors that's being vented in Peterborough. Only recently, from Rachel and Tad, did she learn about a local factory's use of tritium to make glow-in-the-dark signs, and its legal or semi-legal release of this toxin for decades. Rachel and Tad have to test the produce they grow on the farm for tritium concentration.

No, there's not a place on Earth safe from human *disturbance* today, no matter how remote or unpopulated — and "disturbance" itself is a euphemism, a word-lie that should be left behind; she will strike it from her thesis. Tell the truth. Polluted. Poisoned. Damaged. Defiled.

We're a disgrace, she thinks, huffing as she climbs. Look at the humble milkweed: it offers food and medicine to moths and other creatures — including humans — with its whole body. Does the milk-weed not teach that our gifts are not to be kept to ourselves? People could be great healers, magicians of the natural world. Is that not the human role?

Down again. Up again. Hiking until she can just see her last mark, drawing another. She's not sure what she's searching for. A site, maybe, where she can come in for the night? Signs of cater-pillar feeding? A vibe?

The carcass is suddenly at her feet: grey doe, body ripped apart.

Gabe takes her in. The doe's head, neck and front legs are intact, but beyond them there's nothing but naked spine, the vertebrae capped with tufts of fur. The skeleton looks almost aquatic, arcing from the front to the hind legs and a stiff, flattened tail. Her head's been savagely bent as if she was dragged by the neck – strangled, in the manner of cats.

Gabe finds her handkerchief and pats her brow. This is interesting. Big cats are sighted every year in the area, usually unconfirmed and dismissed as fantasy; still, she's met sober naturalists who've witnessed cougars and their tracks as far south as the fringes of metropolitan Toronto, and Rice Lake lies much closer to the wild.

She bends and scoops leaves and lays them gently over the doe's face. At least hers was an honorable death.

The ground rises and falls and rises. She plods along panting. Usually she can hike all day, but she's running on sleep deprivation. Atop the next rise she clutches at a trunk woozily. What she sees when she looks down is daunting: a near-vertical plunge to a distant, thicketed bottom. Impossible to get there without rope.

Try another direction or return to the field? As she's pondering, a wood thrush starts to sing. The lilting, flute-like phrases repeat, curiously modified, over and over. The bird is somewhere below. Listening, Gabe's heartbeat settles, the mental fog lifts.

The ravine pulls on her. Its inaccessibility. Its secrecy.

Walking along the ridgetop, she discovers a place where trees grow closely enough together to serve as grips for a descent. She cautiously edges over, hanging onto a trunk and squatting to keep her weight low. The next handhold's a bit farther away than she thought, but she lets go and sort of half-skids, half-falls toward it. She catches the trunk fine, though she slams against it rather hard and swings a little.

A voice twirps in her head as she reaches for the next trunk – not the thrush, but Jenn. *You're your own worst enemy,* she's always said, usually when Gabe presented another blossoming bruise or wrenched ankle. But her strategy's working! She's about one-third of the way. In truth that was as far as she could clearly see earlier, so it's a bit of a concern that the next tree's so distant, but she can make it.

She lets go, skids, and misses.

Balance thrown, she hits the ground. Instinctively as she starts to tumble she scrabbles for a hold, trying to dig in with her heels and catch anything she can. But she's sliding fast. Her foot snags and she jerks to a stop, dangling headfirst with her ankle and leg twisted, shoe caught in a root. Her own weight pulls her free and she tumbles helplessly until her hip smacks a horribly hard thing.

The pain is white fire.

Hurt. Oh god, hurt.

Hurt to breathe. Breathe . . .

The world fades back in. Explosion subsides to agony. She's lying against a tree, about three-quarters of the way down. Wincing, she wriggles her toes on each foot and tests each leg. Not broken. That's something. She wipes tears from her eyes and pats the trunk that stopped her fall. She could have cracked her head.

Eyes closed, she rests. Pain is a daze, or a haze. How she will walk out of here is not clear but moving seems a faraway thing. Good to rest, lie on the forest floor, let it hold her.

The thrush resumes whistling.

The thrush — probably a wood thrush — is a bird she's never actually seen. Her images of it are based only on photos and drawings and a handful of glimpses: a dark form taking off from a branch, a ruddy-brown blur. The wood thrush lives for her through its song.

The quizzical, flute-like notes move around in her thoughts. Her body opens to them; a numbness is spreading into her hip, natural painkiller — what's it called? — and in a torpor she lies listening to the melodic inflections. She imagines the thrush's song as a flight path curving through the trees . . . and then this path becomes the scent trail of a female moth. Her moth. Her scent would travel like bird song, like a radio signal, perhaps in sensual eddying whirls or a fractal pattern. And faraway the male moth detects her, and starts honing. Yes. Even now. The female's scent could be mingling with the thrush song and the jays and warblers right here, mingling with all the calls and noises of the woods, one note among thousands, yet still uniquely itself. If only she could tune in and locate the frequency. Become the receiver.

Eyes closed, she gives it a try. I'm listening. *I'm here to listen.*

In her mind there's an energy like static. She pictures the moth as she saw it that first night: flying over the milkweed and aglow like a tiny moon. As she concentrates on that image, the static diminishes.

I am listening.

Her mind calms. Like a lily on dark water, the moth floats there.

I am here to listen.

She slips back to the memory of that night, the field where she frantically searched and waited. Again she focuses, isolating the moth from that context. The lily-still image returns and she pulls it closer, as if the moth were perched on her hand. She brings it eye-level.

I am here to listen.

For the first time she sees past the illumination that obscures the moth's body. Scalloped wings – a Sphinx moth! The sturdy, bumblebee-like torso tapers to a blunt rump, and its wings are not flat or folded, but held erect and angled away from the body – an arms-out, airplane pose unique to the sphinxes that she's always felt suggests their legendary flight capacity. The moth isn't plain white, either, but white with silver, and its head looks almost grey. The forewings are gorgeously rippled with silver, butter, and pale blue-grey bands, and through these wind deep, rose-pink lines like hints of flame. Finally, along the wings' scalloped fringe runs a terminal line of fierce, electric blue.

The moth has the colours of sunrise and cloud, of the moon in the afternoon sky.

All the time she's looking *I am here to listen* thrums in her mind. *Listening, listening. To listen, to listen. Here, here. I am, I am . . .*

The moth's filiform antennae gently probe.

If it's a type of eyed sphinx, then its hindwings will tell her. May I see your hindwings?

The creature rotates and its forewings fan open to their full reach. Two crimson patches with owlish pupils appear, glaring. Gabe gazes at them with awe and respect, for a moth's underwings are its most intimate secret, concealed beauty and defense.

Thank you.

The view rotates again, and she looks into the moth's soft, alien face. Furred snout. Dark insect eyes. Antennae curving from its brow like feathery horns.

The moth looks back. Gabe wonders what it sees.

USING THE TREE she pulls herself to sitting, gets her left leg under her, stands. Her right leg bends fine but the hip stabs pain when she puts weight on it. She looks for a possible staff. Can't use one on the slope anyway. And there are so many slopes. The maps showed the woods elongated north-south; she walked in northeast, so if she heads directly east she might get out quicker. But that would mean not following the blazes. Best to stick with the trail. Try.

She can hobble and limp, slide down and crawl up. She can even cry a few times. But she must get out before dark.

When she emerges the sun's beneath the horizon and swallows flit over the field. She stands uncertainly, swaying, weak with fatigue and relief. The cabin, the loneliness — she can't face them. She needs safety and rest. She wants to go home.

Where is that?

Oliver.

And she hasn't seen him. She's been here, while his life's been upended. How alone he must feel!

Here is where she had to be, she thought. Her fieldwork, the moth — has she been wrong to stay? Oliver is not really her partner. Technically, they've not even consummated coupledom.

Relevant?

A male moth flies through the night to find his mate. Though he's never even seen her, he knows who she is. Dating protocols don't matter to him; he's going home.

SHE CALLS HIM when she's parked outside his place. Lights are on. If he doesn't answer she will just keep calling, she decides. But he does. He's surprised, obviously, and says he'll come down. After sitting she gets out with difficulty and the pain winds her. She waits by his door.

She expects him to look haggard and needy but he doesn't: he seems only curious and startled and shyly happy; she's the one who's a mess, with her scraped skin and stained clothes, favouring her left leg.

When their eyes meet, her chest starts to heave. It's just so, so good to see him.

"Are you okay?" he says.

"Yeah." She smiles. Oh god, is she going to cry? "I just fell."

He's taking her in. And she realizes that in coming here like this, she's casting off, sloughing off a way of being that's familiar yet constricting and she's got to be free of it. Awkwardly. Gropingly.

"Um, remember that stuff I said about this not being an easy time for me to start something? And that understanding thing you said about going slow?"

Oliver nods.

"Well, that's still true, but I think I need to get over it. Could we speed up a little now?"

25

DEEP IN THE NIGHT when the air becomes cool, worries and woes used to snap at him. Hour of the Wolf, now it's a welcome, holy time.

They rise and he bathes in the river, dresses, then starts walking. At this hour the blue herons and egrets like to coast down the river corridor one at a time, always midstream, arrows heeding only their own intention — maybe the same Intention that pushes the current and also him. Taking only some kibble, he and Reg follow the river north. Behind them on the opposite bank, electric lights cradle the condo hatchery, but at this hour there are no juddering drivers or collisions of steel, and after he's walked some ways even the perpetual purr of traffic mutes. He enters a pocket of silence. He's become sensitive to these secret pockets; where he sleeps the planes whine overhead long past midnight, but now he has this pocket.

The official Humber River park ends at a footbridge guiding people across the water to the west bank, but a dirt path continues on this side through the woods. It's very dim in here and he can imagine himself an explorer like Étienne Brûlé, first white man in this land.

But no, he doesn't want a name, at least not the kind belonging to King and Country. Perhaps the Sleep Tree will give him a name; it knows his dreams.

The dusky night's lifting. Up ahead lies a golf course, leveled and tended ground. A brown hare stands on its haunches to observe them until Reg lunges and the hare darts away.

A creek joins the river here, flowing inside a concrete culvert trenched into the land. The culvert heads east and this morning he skids down the concrete bank and follows it, wondering at the effort and expense to contain this one creek. The water runs fast and seemingly deep, but the culvert's broad shoulders accommodate them both. They pass out of the golf course, under a road, and into what seems to be another park. Feathery willows droop in pink morning light. Lifting Reg, he climbs the concrete bank to see what's up there and finds a vacant road curving through trees, lily-covered marshes, water sluicing through hidden grates. He wanders slowly, marvelling. Sharp-nosed turtles poke their heads through weedy surfaces, small fish flit beneath. Frogs gulp, a sound like bubbles popping. A pair of night herons regard from a branch. This complexity and lush beauty bewilder him and a new truth pushes into his mind — for he's never had the time or inclination to see the city as *land*, as a living world before pavement and everything else. He's never paused to imagine the obvious: that people had to come into these places and get rid of them to build the roads and plazas. The flowers were ripped out, the turtles crushed. It all had to be demolished.

Where the road rises out of the ravine he returns to the culverted creek. Past the wetland it tunnels under a wide road and he discovers a gallery inside: bright pictures painted on the walls by the running water that narrate the dreams of the present age, and these seem to him not so different from those prehistoric cave paintings of horses and bison and mystical half-human creatures. There's a life-sized female angel with dark skin, a dragon, fantastical beings, human figures bearing weapons, songs and prayers.

They emerge to find a great meadow opening on the south side, apartment towers clustered beyond, and on his left through twisting sumac he glimpses traffic lights and rumbling vehicles, close yet distant, like that world is streaming on another channel. The culvert is more weathered here. From its concrete seams sprout dandelions and thick grass, even saplings flagged with ragged plastic. After a while there's another surprise: a water junction, where the creek bends north and meets a little stream. The stream flows out of woods to the east, banked with wildflowers and grasses of tender green. The place feels fresher, more alive, and he changes course to follow its sandy, entangled banks until he comes to a tree: it's a willow, the largest he's ever seen, with a massive triple trunk gnarled and knobbed like some warty old giant.

How long has it stood here? Centuries, perhaps. The great-great-great guardian of the stream, maintaining its connection to a time of purity. And there is no one and nothing else here. Another secret pocket.

They rest awhile, and he stores his coat before they leave so he doesn't have to lug it around in the sun. A trail of hand-placed stones spans the water and leads to a path behind houses, then a hill, a street, and another path up into a ridgeline hydro corridor. The stream's now flowing down below and a hard city smell meets him: the stench of rendering and chemicals like magic marker, solvents maybe. Behind thinning trees rises a box store and in minutes he meets a road with transport trucks rumbling in clouds of dust, construction zone fencing. It's part of the Stockyards development, an industrial region transformed into residences and a retail destination. Except for their signage, the new retail outlets are indistinguishable from the old meat-packing plant around the corner; the same trucks enter and depart.

In this exalted region of iconic names and furious mobilization, a merchant grilling Polish sausages on a trolley with a yellow umbrella offers a welcome landing place. He stops to eat, grateful to taste hot food, fresh onions. His appearance attracts no notice as he sits on a bench among the construction and factory workers.

On the other side of the Stockyards he searches for the stream again, but comes up against an endless fence. There's a railway corridor beyond, and it doesn't take long to find a large gash made in the wire. He knows what this place is: the northbound track winds up from Union Station and at the Junction meets the east-west line. He steps through.

The hole in the fence leads into a wide expanse. No traffic, no people, just the tracks reaching far. Signs warn of danger and trespass, but clearly aren't serious. The east-west corridor, he discovers, holds two operational tracks with a wide, brambled border on either side, and he finds two more derelict and overgrown tracks half-hidden. The walking is rough, with constant sharp stones and attention to footwork required. Reggie can do it but there's broken glass too, so Justin carries him until the old tracks disappear and the stones give way to gravel.

They continue east, parallel to Dupont Street. The tracks take them over bridges he's driven under all his life without realizing what's up here. Passing a supermarket he sees through the fencing people carrying and loading grocery bags into cars, an employee making a call out back just beyond the wire, oblivious to him. Different channels.

The railway corridor pulls him on. How far does it reach? He wants to find out. As he walks he occasionally sees other people in it: a bent-legged old man in a baseball cap; a younger man with a camera; a teenaged couple; two men chuckling over a bottle in a makeshift camp in the shade. Then there are three Asian women right in his path.

They're digging up dandelions. Under the trees by the edge of the tracks they squat with hand spades, wearing straw hats and gloves, tossing their harvest into baskets. When he pauses to watch, one of them turns his way.

"They very good." She smiles with shyness or perhaps feels their activity needs explanation. "Very special plant. Good for blood. Clean the blood."

She holds out a freshly unearthed plant, flower nodding above a raw, red-veined root. He stares at it lying in his palm. The petals yellow as the sun, the leaves sharp, soiled root a tentacle curling. "Best eat now in springtime. Eat whole thing or part." The woman makes a circle with her hand. "All of it good."

He thanks her and plucks at it as he walks on, starting with the flower and then the leaves. Wildly bitter tastes. Earthy. The true flavour of the land.

It's grown hot and they've been travelling since before dawn, but he keeps going. A kind of protection has fallen over him, like he carries the pocket of silence from the river. Or maybe it's held in the rhythm of his feet. Within the pocket, he's still very tender. Speaking feels strange and difficult; words have become distant, he has to pull them back. Were he to go home now he'd be taken to a doctor, who would want to give him drugs. A diagnosis. A narrative. But out here there are no words to label him; his life's his own. He can watch the city feeling like he's watching his old self: there's a man with his wife, talking and not looking at her as he drives. And there's a child, which he once was.

They walk and walk, stopping to rest, continuing. That Toronto can be navigated this way — off road, alternating woodland, waterway and railway routes — is a revelation. From deep within the city he sees it from the edges. It feels like he's seeing it turned inside out.

By late afternoon they've crossed all the way into the Don Valley, where he drinks from its brown and stinking river. Reggie does it first and Justin follows because here too is the flavour of the land. If the Don River flowed into every household tap the collective purge would remake consciousness. Take that to City Council.

They head south, on the paved path that leads under the Bloor Street viaduct, and at sunset he reaches the Gardiner Expressway, where he counts sixteen traffic lanes meeting. It's like a symphony of chainsaws, and he pauses to let them chew away at his soul. Flavour of the land.

He emerges from the valley onto a street: people, cyclists, the glaring sun making a white light in his head. At an intersection a woman stands hitting herself in the face, a mechanical gesture like she's gotten stuck in a loop: *Stupid! Stupid!* A group of punked-out kids hover near her, visibly upset.

It's okay, he tells her. He doesn't hesitate to touch her, setting a hand on her shoulder. He wants to share his pocket of silence.

"We didn't do anything!" says a boy.

I believe you.

The pocket works: she quiets and without a word moves on. It seems a sign, what he has been seeking without knowing. He can sleep now.

THE VALLEY SHELTERS THEM. Next morning they retrace their route along the railway to the stream and his coat, the culvert and finally the path along the so-called Humber (who or what is Humber?). They return footsore to the Sleep Tree, and that evening once the park is quiet and empty, he goes into the river and gives thanks for his life. Bats flit above him. When he fingers the water with love, he's not the only one moved. The river doesn't need his companionship, yet his companionship isn't wasted: it's perceived, it matters.

The ravine system, everyone calls this place. It was one of Naomi's selling points for the house in Baby Point, a phrase to excite her like a possession: *It's on the ravine system!* But it wasn't just her, he had the same views.

That night he sleeps fitfully. Something's agitating him and when he wakes at the holy hour he knows what: he must return Reggie. He can manage without him now, and Naomi and Gwynn need his love and protection too.

He rises immediately and goes south for the first time since that night, to the parking lot vigilantly lit despite its emptiness and then the hillside path that he fled down and up into his neighbourhood, which looks stable and unchanged. When they reach his street and he sees the darkened house, he kneels for a moment and pushes his brow to Reg's, skin to fur, bone to bone, pulse to pulse. Then they go on.

He heads to the back door like before but without incident, and presses in the code hoping she hasn't changed it. The light on the lock turns green. Reg is wagging his tail and dancing. Justin calms him. Then inches open the door, and sniffs. The house smells like it did when they first viewed it before purchase, a clue he dismissed at the time: stale and sad, either due to the previous owners or the mortar, wood and stone it's made of. Perhaps the ground itself is the problem, an Indigenous village abandoned or razed, an early French settlement torched. Tears of loss and war. Or maybe too many turtle marshes and coyote dens and fish-filled streams were obliterated here, and that's when the shadows crept in. Naomi was right that there's something toxic in the house, though new carpentry and décor won't fix it.

Holding Reg by the collar he steps over the threshold and carefully closes the door. It's darker inside and he's aware of the basement stairs yawning on his left, from which seem to seep an unease like weep from a wound. He leads Reggie to the kitchen, gives him water and commands him to stay with a look.

Papers are spread out on the dining room table. He can just make out the print: statements of accounts, assets. As he picks one up a new voice speaks: *All this in time.* The paper feels like dry skin in his hands and he sets it down.

Climbs the stairs.

Both bedroom doors stand ajar, and on the landing he can feel a change in atmosphere from the main level, the vital breath of the sleepers that dissipates the heaviness. Noiselessly he goes into his daughter's room, where the wooden chair waits in the corner. He fills the seat like a piece of the darkness.

So as not to wake her, he doesn't stare. He doesn't need his eyes to feel her all around him, to smell her and sense her dreaming. He is her father bonded with her beyond breaking; his wild little girl, his heart. His whole body surges to be near her again — and he realizes that he's always been afraid of this love, afraid that it could be too much, that he should be more reserved. That was his mother, yes. Cool strength. But not Dad. Oh, not their sweet father, with his soft low voice that was never raised . . . And he left so soon. And something got busted, in all of them, and he's always been afraid to be too gentle, too much like him.

Now he sees the man in his mind's eye here in the room, smiling at him. His father is here, radiant and whole. His mother is here, radiant and whole. And he knows that the love he so wanted was and will always be here, within. He hears Gwynn sigh, and he closes his eyes and lets the great warmth of love bloom in his chest like a burn, a white, consuming flame.

~

SOUNDS OF THE PARK coming to life with people wake him. It's mid-morning and stuffy under the blanket. He pushes it aside and lies blinking and sweaty.

They will have read his note. He wrote little, only that he was very sorry to worry them, that he misses them and will be in touch as soon as he can. But Naomi — how will she react? And Gwynn. He doesn't want to be any further away from her. Yet what kind of father can he be if he no longer fulfills the old promises?

The Sleep Tree rustles and lifts. *This too, in time.*

He misses Reg. He wraps his arms around himself.

IT MUST BE AFTERNOON when he wakes again, though it's cloudy and hard to tell. He goes to the river to freshen his face. Low grey clouds have moved in and through the trees he can see a storm front approaching from the lake. The wind's picked up. He returns to the tree to store his few possessions and eat.

The air cools, grows static. He sits on the tarp away from the base of the tree.

The storm rolls silence before it. No more dog barks or bike bell dings; a hush falls, with only the condo construction noises continuing until these also cease.

Thunder drums softly. Wind swirls the tops of trees and sets branches swaying. Then it picks up for real and the woods ripple while leaves, bark, litter, seed pods and dirt whirl and scatter into his face. Rain patters and clatters and then it's pelting and roaring in a non-stop screen. Leafy fronds from the canopy drop like offerings. The ground glistens.

He's draped the tarp over himself and squats, mud-splashed and chilled, his shoes soppy. The rain rains, rains, rains. It drums away thought. He's a blue-hooded gnome with straining ankles.

A man comes through the woods. Is it a man? Broad-shouldered and tall, he wears a dark hooded cloak, shining wet, and walks with concentration. He's not following a path and passes without looking in his direction.

When his ankles fail he sits on the wet sheet, which isn't as cold as the ground. The storm carries on. At times he hears or thinks he hears bangs, thuds, cries. He imagines the strange man shouting and hurling stones.

When the rain finally stops it's very late and he can barely see the gap between trees and sky. Pain stabs his legs and feet as he stands. His pants and shoes are heavy so he pulls them off, but it's too dark to locate his bundle. He crawls around for a while, getting poked and bug bitten, gives up and makes for the river, finds it and sits on the bank.

A breeze gradually dries his face.

He thinks about the woman who gave him the dandelion and the woman who was assaulting herself and how a plant fed him the strength of earth, sun and rain.

You will find your way home. There is always a path.

He lies back on the grass. When it's light enough to find his bundle, he'll retrieve what he needs, thank the Sleep Tree, and set out.

26

HE'S ALIVE. The text is from Naomi, 6:47 am. It's close to nine-thirty now. He must have been out on the balcony with Gabe or seeing her off when the message came in.

He calls immediately. "You've heard from him?"

"Yes." His hand goes to his chest. "Oliver, he came *in* here in the middle of the night." Naomi's voice shakes. "He came in and walked around and left muddy prints. And Reggie. And a fucking *note*."

"He came home and left again?"

"You got it!" A laugh like an injured yelp. She woke up to the dog with his front paws on the bed beside her, excitedly wagging. Aside from stinking like a sewer, and missing his collar, Reg seems fine. A search of the house yielded no husband, just the note. "It's short and useless. He's sorry, blah blah. Who fucking cares? He tells us nothing. Promises nothing."

"But it *was* him? So he's okay." His mouth opens in wonder. *Alive!*

"Yes, I'm sorry, I know how worried you've been. He is. He's okay."

"Thank god." He's choking up, his eyes wet. Naomi's also crying.

"Does Gwynn know?"

"Of course, because Reggie's here. But I never suggested in any way to her that Justin might be . . . gone. I only said he was away from us. I've always known that."

He sits down at his desk. "Tell me everything again?"

She does, but the story of Justin's midnight skulk is as puzzling as his disappearance. "What kind of a person *does* this?" Naomi asks, her bitterness returning. "Like, now he's gotten tired of caring for Reg, so he sneaks in and dumps him here? I can't believe this is happening. I can't believe he's this cruel."

Oliver doesn't answer. The gesture seems more pathetic to him. His brother might have left the dog out of kindness, because that's all he has to give.

He asks if he can see the note. He needs to hold it in his hands.

AS THE DAY WEARS ON and the new reality settles, Oliver's confusion grows. He thinks about the posters and the possibility of Justin seeing them. Does his brother hold their last conversation against him, or did it mean nothing at all? Naomi's anger seems more and more justified.

When Gabe returns from campus, she holds him. He called her earlier to share the news. She's staying one more night before heading back to the lake.

"I think you should try to give yourself a break from worrying, from trying to figure it all out," she says gently. "Compared to what you feared yesterday, this is the best possible news."

"I know. I just wish . . . I don't know what I wish. I'd just like to take back the times I didn't listen, I guess. But that's pointless to say."

"What's not pointless is everything you've done lately. You'll see your brother again." She leans over the chair he's slumped in and kisses his brow, then the cheek that was injured, then the other.

"Thank you for tri-point balancing me."

"That's exactly what I was doing. You're welcome."

They eat on the balcony, chairs pushed together so their bare calves touch. A breeze flutters the maple tree and stirs Gabe's hair. Over dinner she relates the full story of the moth she believes she's discovered, which she shared only briefly before. An impossible moth, a moth that emits light. "A freak or a miracle," he says. She frowns at that, thinking.

"I'll tell you another story." Her toes press onto his, cool and soft. "When I was little I used to try to capture night in a jar. It's true: I'd set an open mason jar beside my bed, and when I woke up in the dark, I'd clap on the lid and close it really fast. When this didn't work, I threw a towel over the jar too, and I'd peek to make sure I'd really got it before going back to sleep. I was convinced night was in there, it just kept slipping out."

"I don't know if that's incredibly sweet or lamentably stupid."

She laughs loudly, pleased to have amused. "I was only three or four, you understand."

After dinner, when they've settled cozily, he tells her about the leaked Ministry of the Environment fracking study and the plans for drilling throughout the region, which he and Rosh believe motivated the break-in. "I'm reading the report now," he says. "I've decided to help him, to join the cause." He has? He is? Saying it aloud brings a surge of apprehension.

"You mean you'll work on the film?"

He takes a deep breath. Once more unto the breach. "I want to interview the authors of the study — assuming I can get them to talk to me, and that Rosh's group agrees to it."

"That's fantastic!"

"You think?"

She takes his hand, eyes shining with affection and pride. His fingers close around hers. "You inspired me, you know?" he says. "The chances you've taken by going back to school. Your dedication to what you love. I admire it a great deal."

For a moment she drinks this in. Then she squeezes his hand, lets it go, picks up her iced tea. "Tell me more about what you're planning."

He describes the seismic exploration map of Lake Erie and the film and what he's seen of it so far. Then he talks about the flooding on the island, and attending the meeting, the plans for building dikes, and how the bungalow must be demolished and rebuilt. And finally he talks about his book, the book about water pollution, and all the collapse that happened in his life so that he stopped writing it.

They stay up late, and once they turn in he can't sleep. The bedroom feels boxy. Gabe turns restlessly and the cat makes noise in the living room, stalking along the windowsills behind the blinds. He goes out to the balcony, moves aside the chairs and lies on the wood with a cushion as a pillow. City night sky through the maple tree's branches. After a time Gabe appears. She brings the duvet for them to lie on and takes his right side so she can sleep on her left with an arm draped over him. He drifts off to leaves shushing and the smell of lilacs from the yard below.

The wind's rippling the tree. His eyes open with animal alertness and he turns to nuzzle Gabe, moves a hand to her breast. She arches into it, nipple hard under his fingers. In a moment they're moving together, she on top with her mouth on his, his fingers digging in her hair, both of them panting. T-shirts off. Underwear. *This is going to bruise,* he thinks as they clutch and thrust, rolling against the wood, and it doesn't matter.

Close to dawn: that darkest of dark hours, when unknown stars communicate in hieroglyphic frequencies to the Earth. Gabe's back in bed. Naked, Oliver stands on the balcony alone, looking up at the hints of constellations through the clouds, then down at the quiet street. His cock feels raw, his mind on fire. The police who entered the building, the men who tried to break in — they might come for him next. He's chosen a side, declared himself. He feels like gouging his name into the railing and adding the date.

~

THERE SEEMS TO BE no return to spring. The city's hot and smelly and noisy, day after day. Asphalt bakes. Glass blinds. Troops of landscapers saw trees and blow dust and spit grass, while construction-choked streets fill with traffic, fuming to infinity. The gym, like most public buildings, becomes a giant refrigerator. Humming fans pursue him everywhere (he runs two in his apartment) and another damn plane is always snarling across the sky.

City summer is a nightmare.

There's the lake, of course: cool and beautiful and right there, with its floating plastic bottle caps and algae blooms. Risk-level notices are posted along scrappy ribbons of beach, where people lounge with their picnics and SPF lotions to gaze at the horizon. Occasional rogue individuals enter the water to piddle around or perform a few moves.

Oliver hasn't swum in the lake since childhood. In fact he's rarely swum at all. He never took to pools, with their chlorine sting, dank changing rooms and rusty lockers. In Oakville he learned to equate summer with suffering. When he goes over to help build Ward's dike, though, he stands with his toes in the sand, the water to his thighs, and feels strangely soothed and reassured even as he works to keep water from engulfing their home. At the end of the day he washes the sweat from his body and dunks his head.

Most evenings he still returns calls from the poster. He's discovered that those who notice it — who pick it out from the thousands of other things vying for attention on city streets — have usually lost someone too. Some haven't sighted or believed they sighted Justin; they just call, wanting to share their story, hoping it might help or needing to unload. Offering advice. Their story might have a happy ending, or it doesn't but they learned things. He plunges into life histories with these strangers who are moved to act. He listens. It's what he used to be good at: listening for the stories waiting to be told.

Then a cold dinner. And when the dishes are washed and the coffee maker set, he continues reading *Impact Assessment: Water and Air Pollutants at Hydraulic Fracturing Sites.*

Water, always water. There with him from the beginning.

Water took him down. How could he have expected otherwise, once he'd aligned himself with it? Toronto, a city of water, denies water. Creeks and streams, brooks and freshets and rivers — the veins and capillaries of the land converge *here*, at this great heart. The Don, the Humber and the Rouge rivers. Mud Creek and Yellow Creek, Black Creek and Lavender Creek. Highland, Market, Castle Frank, Rosedale and Garrison Creeks. Walmsley, Massey, Taylor, Burke, Cudmore and Russell. Taddle Creek, Mimico Creek, Etobicoke Creek. A history of settlement in waterways, and all of them bent into new shapes, blocked up, or buried.

The heart has become a stagnant pool.

It's in his research: how in darkness unobserved, water passes beneath the city's neighbourhoods and shopping malls, office towers and highways. Half a dozen creeks gurgle beneath the financial district alone. Their fates aren't really known. Some were buried wrong and might be dead, while others were driven into new courses that have never been mapped. He hears them trickling and gushing as he walks the streets. *Here. Hear.* Ancient verses echoing from storm sewer grates, still being sung.

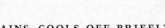

IT RAINS, COOLS OFF BRIEFLY, rains again. June has become one enveloping waft of moisture, like the lake's evaporating or a primeval rainforest is taking root beneath the office-condo towers multiplying like pillars to progress across the land. Oliver speaks to the contractor about a demolition date. He sets up a meeting with Rosh and his group. He sleeps with Mimi on the balcony on an old foam mattress, swathed in memories of Gabe's last touch. He returns calls and sometimes rides out to look for his brother.

He leaves the posters up, yet decides not to make more for now. They're rain-tattered. Soon the print will be unreadable.

A professional dog walker contacts him, claiming to have seen Justin in the Don Valley. "He was sitting by the river, burning something," she tells Oliver when he returns her call.

"How did he look?"

"Dirty. Like a homeless guy, you know? But he seemed peaceful. He had his eyes closed, and was kind of muttering. I think he was praying."

"Right," Oliver says crisply, and pencils a question mark beside the location he's just jotted down: *West side by fish ladder. N. of Todmorden Mills*. When the call's over he puts down the phone and sits staring.

All year it's been this emotional rollercoaster, starting with Auntie Fiona's call the day after New Year's Day. He wasn't made for this. His mother was. She could withstand anything, think her way out of jail if need be. Read a book, ten books. Take a course. Then practise. What did she do when she wanted extra money? Learn securities inside out. Join an online poker league, become top player.

And this? What would Mom do?

He's got time before tonight's meeting to check out the lead. He'll bike the westside trail north then double back, maybe all the way to Lakeshore. His brother won't be there, he knows, but he can't not try.

THE PUB'S EAST OF Greektown in the grungier strip of the Danforth. As hoped he arrives first, orders from a server and opens up his laptop to *Impact Assessment: Water and Air Pollutants at Hydraulic Fracturing Sites*, 327 pages read and notated. If the Wild Water Alliance team agrees to his plan, he'll be getting to know the report even better.

Reading it transported him to the days when he was researching water pollution. In the process known as fracking, methane and benzene and a slurry of other chemicals are blended with water. Pumped into the earth under extremely high pressure, this liquid spew fractures shale rock. Great volumes of water are required. Such water becomes toxic waste. And the spew leaks underground, of course, poisoning groundwater.

Up above, fracking vents methylene chloride gas and other toxins into the air. The hazardous, spent liquid needs to be transported, processed, and stored. So much water. The study documents degraded human health near fracking sites: higher incidents of cancer, respiratory illness, congenital conditions and lowered IQ scores. There are similar damages to animals, and evidence that fracking increases seismic activity due to destabilizing the earth.

Oliver flips through his handwritten notes. He's not thoroughly checked out all the references and corollary studies yet, but even so, Rosh was right: the study's devastating.

He's sipping an ale when the group starts to arrive. Rosh comes in with Charlotte, the ex-director of the Wild Water Alliance who got audited. Then former board members and staff, seven people all told not including him. Rosh has briefed them on Oliver's background and interest in the project, and everyone's friendly, if a little standoffish and preoccupied. There's a lot to talk about tonight.

Once they've gathered and ordered and been introduced, the first topic is budget: the film is scheduled for release this September – the start of fall film season in Toronto – and they're out of money. Should they try tapping their small donor base again, or launch a crowd fundraiser to see them through? The latter will mean going public with the project, which may or may not be a good idea.

Oliver stays attentively quiet during this discussion. Charlotte, a measured woman with shoulder-length salt and pepper hair and Asian features, clearly carries the most weight with the group. There's an obvious age gap between those advising the organization and the ex-employees, who tend to be much younger; yet this doesn't seem to skew discussion, which is clearly between bonded peers. When they decide to solicit private donations rather than crowdfund, everyone agrees to support the choice even if they didn't initially. Oliver's encouraged: these seem like people he can work with.

The second issue on the table is what to do with the leaked study. Because it came to them unexpectedly, and so late in the project, they've been unsure how much presence it should have in the film. Rosh and the film's editor have inserted information from the report, which they present on a laptop: the same shots Oliver saw at Rosh's, showing the study with key sections highlighted as a voiceover reads them.

"It's flat," one of the board members says.

"There's no drama," adds someone else. Everyone feels there must be better ways to present such explosive material.

"It's also way too nice."

They turn to Oliver. It's the first time he's spoken since the introductions.

"I think you need to go much further," he continues. "Put the study front and centre in the film. Get the scientists responsible for it on camera and get those who commissioned and buried it to explain themselves, if they dare."

The group looks uncertain. "I agree with you in theory," Charlotte says, "but the legwork will be significant, we'd likely have to re-edit quite a bit, and we're already maxed and working to deadline."

"Not if I do it," Oliver says. "Self-funded, I might add. That's why I'm here."

Charlotte nods, considering him. "Well, from what I've seen of your writing I've no doubt you can do a good job interviewing, Oliver. And you've certainly taken it on the chin — or cheek — for us, which we're deeply grateful for already." The others nod eagerly, and Oliver realizes now with their eyes on him that their stiffness earlier arose in part from shyness, even a bit of awe or guilt at what he'd done.

"Rosh," Charlotte continues, "I think this ought to be your call, if everyone's okay with that? You obviously feel confident about Oliver and you've paid the biggest price for the film of all of us, that's for sure."

"Everyone's paid," Rosh says. "I think we should do it. I think we can't *not* do it. I can work with Oliver over the summer. We won't alter our deadline, we'll just get everything we can get done by then, that's all."

"You'll have to work fast."

"Hey, we live in the same house."

"That's handy!" one of the youngest men chirps. Linkin Park T-shirt, tats on both arms. He was the warmest to Oliver when they all shook hands earlier. "It'll be like having an HQ again. A secret HQ."

"Not secret enough," Rosh reminds him.

"No," Charlotte says, "I'm afraid that our time of true secrecy is done. Ben, maybe you could help the guys with tech?" Ben says he's game. The group sets a date to review progress in a couple of weeks.

On the sidewalk after the meeting breaks up, Ben approaches Oliver and thanks him for coming on board. "You're like the new wind that's gonna take us to the finish line. This film's gonna be wicked. I can't wait!" Oliver smiles. He feels rather stunned at how well things went and what he's just committed to. But he really liked Charlotte and the others. He and Rosh bike home together, coasting down darkened streets, a quiet whir of wheels and blinking lights.

Rosh comes up to debrief and talk strategy. He recently attended an anti-fracking demonstration in the US. "A tense scene," he says, describing armed blockades and constant surveillance. "Probably my last trip south for a while."

"Too nasty?"

"Yeah, though I'd go again in a heartbeat. But I got a friendly call from CSIS afterwards." Oliver gapes. "I kid you not. The guy was very upfront and polite, introduced himself right off the top. At which point I started recording him on my phone."

He takes it out, powers it on, and plays back the file: one creepy and confused conversation. Where the recording cuts in, the officer's asking to meet Rosh for coffee. When refused, he says that he has questions about Rosh's recent trip to the USA. Specifically, what he was saying to people about Canada? Rosh answers truthfully: he was discussing fracking. "Is there a problem with that?" Rosh asks. "We have a problem with misrepresenting the truth," the officer replies.

After this suggestive statement, the caller insinuates that Rosh left Enbridge for reasons that might cause people to doubt his credibility "if they really knew."

"He's trying to smear you!" Oliver cries.

The call concludes at that point: Rosh says he's heard enough and has nothing to say.

Rosh shuts off the phone. "Honestly, if this guy had showed up at the front door or accosted me outside? I don't know what I would have done. I was furious. Fucking furious!" His eyes blaze. "So, I thought you should know what you're getting into, my friend. There's still time to back out."

"No way." On the bike ride home he mentally wrote the email he plans to send the first scientist on his list. "I'm starting tomorrow."

"Alright. Well, it's been a really good night. Everyone's excited again now, you gave them a real boost." He slides his feet into his sandals, opens the door. "We've got tons of work ahead. This summer's going to be —" He shakes his head.

"'Wild'?"

"I was thinking crazy, but that'll work."

ON THE SUBWAY HOME from his monthly massage therapy treatment, Oliver thinks he spots Justin. It's Monday, past seven p.m. His eastbound train has pulled into Castle Frank, a station busy only during rush hour, so the stop will be brief. Across the tracks and further down on the westbound platform, the man he saw when they rolled in occupies a bench. But however Oliver twists and presses his cheek to the window, he can't quite make him out. Still, those shoulders. That hair.

He stands as the chime sounds and the car doors slide closed.

They rumble across the Don Valley, suspended between its slopes. They meet no oncoming train so there's still time. At Broadview station he dashes out and across to the westbound platform. He boards the lead car and peers through the front window as their passage resounds through the vaulted bridge. Castle Frank station appears and grows. The train pours in. Only a handful of passengers are waiting, and there's no one on the bench.

He hurries along the length of the platform to the stairs. Commuters wait for a bus outside, and he makes sure to see each face.

Descending to another train feels unbearable. He sets out across the viaduct on foot, glancing down through the suicide veil at the lines of river, trails and traffic. Justin always had this longing for a freer life, a life of creativity and expression that he thought he could find through music. Yet he let that go. What has he found now? Is there ever freedom in escape?

At the viaduct's eastern end he waits at a red light. Across the street at a pizza outlet on the corner, there's a familiar figure sitting by a window, angled away. That head and shoulders. That hair . . .

Oliver crosses the road and walks up to the glass and raps it. The figure turns: mutual astonishment.

The other is first to lift a hand and motion: come inside.

Dazedly, Oliver enters. The man's leaning on the table now, watching him, and Oliver falls toward his gaze. At the table they sit staring at each other. The face, the eyes — are Justin's, but a different Justin.

Oliver finds his voice. "Were you just sitting in Castle Frank station?"

"No, but I was just thinking about Castle Frank station," Justin says. His speech is calm, articulate and completely sane. "I was wondering who Frank was and why there's no castle." He pushes a paper plate toward Oliver. The slice on it is mostly intact. "Care for some pizza?"

"Where the hell have you been?"

"That's a bit of a big question, Bro."

"I have time."

Justin gazes out the window. "Okay, maybe you should come to my camp. Fill you in there?"

"You've dropped weight." Twenty pounds at least. Even with Justin sitting down, Oliver can tell. Though the leaner Justin looks younger and healthier, his eyes clear and the puffy bags beneath them diminished.

"Yeah?" His brother looks down at his belly. "That's alright, I could stand to. Actually, this isn't agreeing with me." He nods at the greasy slice. "If you don't want it, we can go."

"Where's this camp?"

"In the valley."

"How far?"

"I'm not sure, really."

"But —"

Justin's standing, so he does the same yet he can't just *leave*. He glares at his brother, still shocked and begging for answers.

"It's good to see you, Bro. You gonna wrap up the slice?"

27

IN HER BASEMENT ROOM, Gabe unpacks her few things then lies on the bed. Her hip throbs from sitting in the car and her whole body feels achy and sore. Neck, shoulders, back, legs — she slowly flexes and stretches each joint and limb. As she moves, memories of lovemaking and tenderness with Oliver flare like embers, like pulses.

Oliver's her hearth-fire. *Shhh* . . . she'll keep that close for now. She's come back to Jenn's because she still can't face the cabin. Something broke when she took that fall in the woods: a shield that had formed with the return to school, the intimidation, the loneliness and self-doubt, the accelerated atmosphere and grad-school specialness and institutional heft (which can work for or against you), and then — and then — the killing. At day six or seven of the nine-day sampling period she tried to stop tallying the number in the freezer, to set her jaw and just get on with it. Wasn't that the idea? Killing's necessary. Unavoidable. Justifiable. It's a bit messy and emotional at first, but one gets used to it.

Lying on the ground in searing pain, she knew that she didn't want to.

And she followed the thrush's voice. And her mind's eye saw.

In Toronto while Oliver was at work she limped into Robarts Library and spent a day rereading the completed sections of her thesis, scrolling through the data entered for May, and reviewing all of her project notes – a reckoning. She felt that sinking sense of a path not leading where you expected to go. So much has been poured into this project: her hunkering and dedication this year, plus the assistance from the university and her teachers, yet really, what will the thesis amount to? A set of lists: a ledger of moth populations like some environmental assets sheet. A "deliverable." On its current trajectory the study will fit into the scientific literature in style, form and content, will serve a handful of researchers (at best) and act as a stepping stone to her next job or degree.

The June sampling period's approaching fast.

From the bed Gabe gazes at the moth web spreading across the walls, a tapestry of colours and shapes. Wincing, she stands and moves close to study the pictures. A Morning Glory Plume moth, wings tight and tapered as a glider plane. A Large Paectes in the extreme-yoga resting position of the species: body bent and raised into the air between its wings. A common Meal moth, dusky and demure against a green leaf. All of these photographs she took herself over the years: individual moths sighted in different seasons and places and weather, each one splendid, vital, unique.

Yes, creation works in patterns – in designs and forces too grand ever to be fully grasped – yet patterns consist of individuals, whether in species or materials inert as stone. Every moth here in the web represents a species *and* itself. Every moth in the cabin's freezer too.

They died because they're small. Because they're puzzling, these ancient beings. They died so they could be named – with one hundred percent accuracy! – in a study whose purpose is, ostensibly, to help prevent more death.

Populations aren't harmed by a few nights of collecting, Brimer asserted (or did he say "disturbed" or "impacted," or "affected," some other euphemism like "collecting"?) There's no evidence that collecting hurts the entire generation of moths born to a particular species that year.

No harm to a population, just individuals.

Her committee didn't see this as a problem. Why would they? In all the studies that she's read for her research and literature review, not a single one discusses the ethics of researchers killing their own subjects. The closest thing to acknowledgement she's found is the use of the word "sacrifice" instead of "collect." In some of the lengthier moth studies, *thousands* of moths and other insects are thus sacrificed for research. The dead whisper from the pages of scientific journals. And every time she reads these studies she hears them, and feels sorrowful and disturbed, and pushes these feelings down. She heard the moths as she stuck them in the freezer to die. She still hears them.

She recalls *The Voyage of the Beagle,* one of her most cherished books. How Darwin, who speaks against slavery and rough behaviour, and whose mind opens in curiosity and wonder to everything he encounters, pivots from describing a beautiful or strange new animal to noting next what he found in its gut. This glossing over harm, this sleight-of-mind maneuver — it was there also in guest presentations she attended with other students this winter. Such coolness or heartlessness seems to be the shadow of intellect. Maybe even a badge of honour. Does this detachment make possible pinnacles of accomplishment like Darwin's? Certainly it enables specific paths of action. But detachment must also influence the results — what is learned, in the end, and who one becomes through the learning.

It seems a paradox of science: that passion for life isn't nurtured through indifference to death. To senseless death. To doing harm.

There must be another way. At her desk, Gabe opens her laptop and starts typing.

Lessons of Asclepias syriaca, Milkweed:

That's it — the first principle.

> Asclepius, the Greek hero-god of medicine, gave to us the most fundamental principle of medicine: Do No Harm.
>
> Notably, this first instruction for medical people was not about diagnosing correctly, or relieving pain, or even about offering a cure. It is a command to protect and support life. In biology, the study of living things, Asclepius' principle should surely apply.
>
> Harm creates trauma. At the least, harm diminishes vitality — life. Yet harming life, whether through manipulation (capture, confinement, testing, etc.) or outright killing (referenced as "sacrifice" and "collecting" in entomology literature), continues to be standard practice. Harm is done either to the subject being studied and/or to other organisms affected by the study.
>
> Doing harm also creates emotional disconnect within the biologist — for how can one seek to learn about life and protect it, when one has harmful intent? What is the cost of such disconnect, such cognitive dissonance, for researchers and all those building upon their example?

Can she say this to her committee? It's way outside the scope of conversations she's had with any of them, even with her fellow students.

She starts a message to Hegyi, deletes it. Although Hegyi's her supervisor, Brimer's opinion carried most weight with the others.

Dear Professor Brimer,

My fieldwork has been an astonishing experience — such that I find that my views of this project have changed, and I want to find another way to study moths without collecting them. Before, you said this wasn't possible. Yet while I remain passionately committed to the work, I cannot continue with the method as agreed.

Below are some of my reflections. They are perhaps too philosophical and I hesitate to share them, but I greatly respect your work and want you to know my reasons and my seriousness. I'd appreciate speaking in person or on the phone as soon as possible.

Sincerely, Gabe Flynn

There it is. She rereads the message. How she wishes she'd said this earlier! Yet she's saying it now, at least. Better late than never.

~

"SO YOU'RE STUCK on this again." Brimer doesn't hide his grumpiness. He's hunched inside a tent in the dark somewhere in Indonesia, face lit ghoulishly by the screen, and he sounds and looks like a man who's spent a month in the field already and still has to hold middle-of-the-night meetings with people back home.

"Completely stuck, I'm afraid," Gabe says with a smile. "I can't get past it, so I'm hoping we can work something out."

Brimer frowns, thinking. "Well. I don't know what you have in mind, but you can't do a diversity sample. If you want to do a study that doesn't collect, it would be some other kind of study. You could look at all kinds of things, I suppose."

"You mean start over? Totally?"

"Yes."

Did her email offend him? Or is there really no other way? "Can't I rejig this somehow? I'm out here to do the fieldwork already. I'm partway through."

"But you want to change the *method*. This means starting over. You can't change the method partway through a study and carry on the same course, right?" Gabe nods; what he's saying is logical. "So, you have to come up with a different proposal, one that goes with the method you want to use."

Six months' work going up in smoke.

"Wouldn't I have to get that approved and all?" Her voice is small; she finds it hard to speak. What would she even propose?

"You would. We could try to fast-track it for you so you could still get in your fieldwork now. That is, if you know what you want to do."

"I don't."

"Huh." He looks around for something, seems distracted. She fears he's going to abandon her. But he picks up a blanket and wraps it around his shoulders.

"Is it cold there, professor?"

"Yes, and wet as hell. And this tent's lousy. It blew down last night and it's still damp."

"Oh, I'm sorry."

"Yeah. This is better." He pulls the blanket closed over his chest and holds it there with both hands. The ghoul's become a guru.

"I wish I could bring you some hot soup," she says.

"That'd be some magic." He offers a weak grin. "So you're out in the field and you don't know. All you're clear on is what you *don't* want to do. But that's just a negative. You're passionate about the work, I believe that. So what are you most interested in finding out? What needs finding out?" He stops speaking and peers at her.

The questions are reasonable, yet staggeringly vast. Framing her interests in the language of a study means thinking like a scientist, even a budding one. "I guess what I'm stumbling on," she says, "is that I'm interested in so many things. How moths live, and our relationship to them. I feel that we have so much to learn from moths, and it's urgent to do so, but I don't know how that fits into a study. To be honest, the studies I've read are all so horribly dry and technical, even when they're propelled by critical issues like species extinction. Maybe the problem for me is the data-driven approach."

"Science is about gathering data," Brimer quips. Her face flushes. Of course it is; what a thing to say. "Still, I think you were getting somewhere for a moment, until you fell back on what's *wrong* with science instead of articulating what *you* see needs to change, why and how."

"But . . . that's kind of huge."

Brimer opens his hands. "But you want to do something different, challenge practice." *So you better come up with some solid shit.*

Her mind reels. "Can I think about it for a few days?" she says, though she honestly doesn't know what difference it will make.

"I'd advise that."

There's a last question she doesn't want to ask, but needs to know. "And the May sample? Might I still be able to use it?" She tries not to whine but can hear how fragile she sounds. Maybe that's why Brimer grimaces a little, sighs. In the gloom beyond the screen there's the clank of metal followed by a murmured question. His eyes flit up in the direction of the tent door, she guesses, and he nods and answers in another language. "Honestly, it's a shame, but it's hard to see how. My guess is that you'll have to revise your lit review too, as well as the introduction and methodology, obviously."

Return to trail head, start again. The moths in the freezer died pointlessly.

Brimer blinks, rubs his chin vigorously a moment. "Look, it's not all bad! Speak to Professor Hegyi, I'm sure she'll agree with the change. You'll salvage what you can and you can send me or us your proposal draft. We can get things moving again."

Gabe smiles weakly and they say goodnight. Then she lowers her head to the desk with a groan.

28

THE TICKING OF bike wheels announces his brother. "Hey, I was wondering if you'd make it."

"It was looking doubtful earlier, but I caught the last of the light."

"Glad you did. Need a hand?"

"I got it." Oliver leans the bike against a tree. He's wearing a cycling jacket, T-shirt and shorts, and his face gleams with sweat. He lifts the first of two bulging panniers from the rear rack and sets it down.

Another squall tore through the city this afternoon: electric flashes and cataclysmic booms, nailing rain and spooky light. He was up top at the time – buying water, ironically. Water cascaded from rooftops and rivered in streets, spouted from sewers.

The whole week's been like this. The swollen, turbid Don has flooded much of the lower valley and even brimmed over the foundation walls into traffic. Some days the expressway gets closed for hours. He can't see where the traffic goes, but the gridlock must be spectacular. The men who call the valley home have shifted their camps to higher ground: Leaside, Crothers Woods. He's aware of them, among them, though each of them lives apart.

A hot, fuggy air hangs over the camp. Wet drips and drips from branches. Above, what was solid cloud has loosened into a billowing, drifting mass, slowly tearing apart. Denser grey depths give way to ripening orange and ribbons of blue. He pulls wood from under the plastic sheet. While he builds a fire — to deter bugs — Oliver unpacks and lays out supper on a dry tarp. There's a veritable feast: home-made baked tortilla with olives and red pepper, a salad of green beans and cherry tomatoes, salsa, hummus, and sourdough bread with butter.

He thanks Oliver and they fill their bowls in relaxed silence. He hasn't eaten this much or richly and takes it slow, savouring the tomatoes' sweetness, the olives' salty kick. It's all a bit over-powering. His favourite thing's the bread and butter.

Oliver gazes around the clearing. He looks worried. "I do not understand how you're managing out here," he says.

"It's easier than you think. I've still got cash in my pocket. When I go up top it's usually for coffee, I miss coffee after a few days. And water, I don't have a system for it. Sometimes I grab cheese, or a pizza slice — fortunately."

"Hey," he continues, "I found a treat for you today." He stretches and picks up the bag where he keeps his food. The mushrooms are protected in an old paper cup inside. He hands it across.

"Morels! Oh my god." Oliver holds one up, his eyes shining. "I haven't eaten these in, I don't know. Remember picking them with Mom and Dad?"

"Out by the lighthouse woods. That's how I recognized them."

He's been remembering other things too since Oliver found him. The times they camped in a backyard tent on hot summer nights, just like now. Oliver small for his age then, skinny and ham-pered by shyness, but he loved to sing. Once they snuck out to the lighthouse at midnight, probably every island kid did that, to see if they could catch Radelmüller's ghost moaning. And of course he hid and scared the shit out of his younger brother.

Would those morel patches still exist out there, pockets of the old and wild? It's hard to imagine, with so many visitors tramping around. Yet they're here in the urban woods, just as Oliver's here tonight.

His brother packs up the morels with the leftovers. The woods have sunk into gloom, shrinking their world to the fire's radiance. Oliver sits at the edge of it on the tarp, removes his glasses and wipes his face with his T-shirt. "My god, I'm sweltering. How can you stand those clothes?"

He's wearing the same long-sleeved shirt and jeans, his coat and T-shirt rolled up. The shirt's better protection against mosquitoes. "Guess I'm kind of used to it," he says.

"Used to it," Oliver echoes. He puts on his glasses and peers through them pointedly, checking for spots. He sighs, and his mouth tightens. "I've not spoken to Naomi about seeing you, yet. But I feel like I'm lying. It's not right."

He nods. Oliver's a man of integrity. He shouldn't be put in this position.

"So can we come to some agreement?"

"If you have to tell her, I understand."

"No, *you* have to tell her."

"Not yet." He rises and starts to tidy the camp, covering the firewood for the night.

"Justin, *please.*"

A rumble approaches — another plane, ascending from the airport due west. The machine comes on tediously slow, blinking lights marking each stiff wing. It passes over them with a long, grumbling wake. The planes pass overhead every few minutes. They're supposed to stop after ten p.m., but wake him often in the night.

"You've been gone four weeks," Oliver says. He's come by every evening since they met, sat by the fire, and he's been very gentle and kind and undemanding, even wanting to sleep here tonight.

Justin re-stacks the wood. He often does this to pass the time, enjoying the different shapes, grains, textures. Oliver's right. He doesn't want to keep hurting his family. And in any normal sense, this camp isn't *living*, just surviving on the fringes. Yet he felt so terrible before, on the fringes of himself. This place has sheltered him – not only Crothers, but this life outside, the life apart. Here he's not felt on edge. Here he's at the centre, with everything else. The birds. The trees. The wind. Dawn to dusk, cloud to rainfall, the world carries them all.

"I've had a thought," Oliver continues. "What if you came home with me? You could stay as long as you want."

"Your place is pretty small, as I recall." He's thinking of Oliver's tolerance, not his own. Oliver's monkish lifestyle seems a smart choice to him now.

"Yeah, but it's summer and it's practically twice as big then. I think it would be great. What if you just gave it a try? Come back with me in the morning?"

"Tomorrow!"

"Just for a few nights?"

Fuck. But he can't think of an argument, so he nods.

As the fire burns low, they lie head to head. Camp is a scrub clearing he discovered around a concrete plug. The plug looks like an alien turd here. Sometimes he's wondered what's underneath it. The trees have stayed away from it and so has he, sleeping at the clearing's edge.

"Look, you can almost see the Big Dipper."

Justin follows his brother's finger. It takes him a moment to find the Big Dipper's bowl. "You were always interested in the stars," he says. "Do you still use Dad's telescope?"

"Not in years. Too much light pollution. It's frustrating."

"You could still use it. Here's the Big Dipper."

"Yes, you're right." He sighs. Takes a guzzle of water from his bottle. "I read an article the other night about a planet they think they've discovered inside the Oort Cloud."

"The Oort Cloud?"

"It surrounds our solar system, theoretically. A vast cloud of ices, comets, asteroids, planetismals, all the matter from which our solar system formed, swirling around on the outermost fringes of the sun's gravitational pull. Inside they found this enormous, gaseous planet – like Jupiter, only bigger. A new planet for us, if it's really there. I thought it was interesting that we might end up with nine planets again after Pluto's demotion. They've named the new planet Tyche – like 'psyche' but with a T. Anyway, I got enough on my plate right now. I need to keep focused on the basics."

"Such as?"

"Focusing on what needs to get done. Letting go of all this fear of failure, like you have."

"That's quite a compliment to a man who sleeps on dirt and hasn't had a proper shower in a month, brother."

In the night, it feels like only a couple of hours later, he wakes from sleep hearing his name. *Justin. Justin!* That terse Oliver style.

"What?"

"Listen!" Oliver's whispering.

There's crickets, the city's mechanical hum, a bird, and then an odd kind of huff. It's a deer blowing; he knows this only because he ran into a buck recently, maybe this same one, and was amazed when the fellow just stood there and snorted. Only the toughest bucks survive this jungle, he thought.

The sound repeats: a huff, a pause, another huff.

Oliver's twisting around. The fire's just coals. They can see nothing but the rough outline of the woods against a milky sky.

"You hear it? It sounds like a fucking pig!"

"Maybe it is." He's trying not to laugh.

"No really, what the hell is it?"

"Beats me. Wild boar?"

His brother lies down again. There's a distant clank, probably a car wheel hitting a loose sewer lid, but no more huffing.

323

"I hope Tyche's for real," Oliver says. "I'd like some good news for a change."

"How would finding it make any difference?"

"Finding *her*. My ex, Connie — you remember her? She came to Mom's funeral. We've been in touch off and on for years. Anyway, she's really into astrology, and she told me that every discovery of a planet in our solar system evokes a shift in our conscious evolution. Uranus heralded the Industrial Revolution. Pluto the splitting of the atom. Tyche was the Greek goddess of luck and prosperity, called Fortuna by the Romans. She governed the destiny of cities too."

"Fortune could be in our future?"

"Maybe. She's associated with risk, too. Sometimes she worked with Nemesis. Maybe her attitude depended on how people received what she bestowed."

His brother settles down again, but Justin lies awake.

IN THE MORNING after lukewarm thermos coffee, they strike camp and head south. As the land descends from Crothers, flooding diverts them to Bayview Avenue. There's no sidewalk, they must trudge along a muddy, debris-strewn shoulder as traffic speeds past. Then Pottery Road, the river running high underneath the bridge.

On the valley's east side they climb up to O'Connor and reach Danforth Avenue. Oliver rolls his bike ahead and periodically glances behind. Restaurants, produce stalls. People looking down at their phones, busy and tense. Yet sometimes Justin sees or thinks he sees feathery streams of light energy waving and curling about them.

At the apartment Oliver cooks lunch while, out of consideration mostly, Justin uses the shower. It feels less welcoming than he imagined. Over the tub there's a window, frosted except for one pane that opens to vent steam. He peers out: a red brick wall, another bathroom window, coloured shampoos. The water rills down his calves, splattering.

He regards a stranger's face in the mirror. Not a bad face, not wasted, though he does look tired – or maybe just tender. The valley's been hot, wet, noisy. A great seam treated as an urban trough and carrying way more load and garbage and damage than its west side sibling. The men there hurt. Tough place for a new leaf.

After taking Reggie home, he travelled north with the creek. Slept by its banks. There was often no path, yet there was always a way. He was most active in the night, like a coyote, going through the gloaming by his nose. He wandered up to the city streets, their breadth fascinating, a world beyond his world, a time unlike his. Eventually, though, he lost the water. It disappeared for good into a steel tube. He searched for it in a patchwork land of residential streets and industrial parks, abandoned acreages and malls. Wildrose Glen, Heather Vista, staked saplings and clipped grass. Hiking up traffic ramps to search for the creek's sign system, bulrushes and tall grass. But he never did find it again. He made his escape through a hydro corridor that went on forever, spanning some bygone city border like a skeletal fortress, and then he went down, down into the forest hugging the Don River. Different river, same river.

He naps after lunch. It's hot, and when he wakes up the fans have gone still; no power, though the sky's a scrubbed summer blue. Lying on the couch, he wafts air at himself with an envelope, watches light and shadow pattern the walls. Oliver emerges from the bedroom in his boxers, opens the freezer with a groan and packs something into ice. A puff of the gas element being ignited, his brother whispering.

This living within walls and ceilings – over fifty years he's been doing it. What does that mean? He's always needed an open window, even in winter – arguments with Naomi about it – and even this afternoon he slept facing the balcony.

Out there his brother has set up pillowed chairs and a table, flowers and a cat box. He joins Oliver as he reads the Sunday *New York Times* and offers him sections, but he doesn't want them, the death tolls, the endless arguments, voices gabbering. Bubbly white clouds tinted mauve float over the city now. He unhooks seed pods from the cuffs of his pants and gathers the little claws in his palm. He rests his head against the Muskoka chair.

The sliding door stirs him. Oliver, bringing out small glasses of beer.

"You're an excellent host, bro."

"Well, it's nice to have this weekend time. Here —" He reaches out, and they clink glasses. "To reunion." Oliver holds his gaze for a moment. "And to good days and years ahead."

Days and years. He likes the sound of that, though he's still getting through this day, which has seemed very long already. He takes a sip. The beer's bitter yet light, like something distilled from a streambed. Sunday dinner hour; he always cooked it for them.

"I'm going to have to leave you on your own tomorrow. I'm doing an interview in Hamilton, so I'll be gone early. Then I've got another late in the day."

"You're writing again?"

"Not exactly, but I'm involved with a project. Actually, I've got to pop down to my neighbour's in a bit — we're working on it together." He winces. "Also, there's trouble. I just learned that the dike we've been building on Ward's breached."

He remembers those dikes: spring floods on the island some years, their parents and neighbours out sandbagging. Back then it made him furious that they lived out there under threat and with all the stupid inconveniences instead of safely ashore, with the sane people.

"What are they going to do?"

"People are already repairing it. They worked through last night, but they really need help. There's talk of temporary evacuation. I have to get out there asap. Obviously not tomorrow, but the day after."

"What's going on with your house?" An architectural drawing is still taped above Oliver's desk.

"We've finalized the new design but otherwise, not much yet. We set a demo date, but I'm wondering if this contractor isn't going to bail. Between dealing with the ferry and the weather, this has to be the worst project of all time."

Mosquitoes find them at dusk, so they move inside. Oliver lights candles. He brings out old coffee-table books for Justin to look at, like he's a sick child: *The Great Lakes — An Illustrated History; Britain, Its Mystic Places* ("For my skeptical Ollie, love Connie"); *The Moon and the Planets.* Lying on his couch-bed, he flips through while Oliver's downstairs. Then the smoke detector lets out a shrill beep, the fans start whirring, the fridge rattles into action and the printer whines and clanks — all at the same moment. The cat jumps onto his lap and starts pawing his thighs, staring at him. A bright drop of drool appears on her chin.

When Oliver returns he asks if he wants to use the computer? It seems a weird question at this hour and after so much time unplugged but he doesn't put much weight on it.

"I'm good, Bro."

"Will it bother you if I work? I've got some prep for tomorrow still."

They say goodnight.

Here he is: back in the world. Oliver's bedroom light stays on for a while and then he talks in his sleep and gets up several times in the night. The fridge gurgles like it has cancerous lungs. Heat lightning strobes the city; he feels like he's in a spectral kingdom. Anxiety starts up the old thought-spin cycle. What will he find at home? New locks? A punch in the face? Divorce papers, surely. And what's Naomi been saying to Gwynn about him? How ugly might this be?

From the open windows comes the smell of grass. He can feel the woods, the river, and the men in the valley in their make-shift burrows, the inverse of those dining under patio lanterns on the Danforth tonight, men like he used to be. Club owner. Restauranteur. Pay to stay. And now?

He can't live in the urban woods, not with a daughter to raise.

He falls back to sleep, and when he wakes in the night and rises he notices the clocks on the stove and coffee maker blinking, waiting to be reset.

29

KENSINGTON MARKET, happy hour, a hot June day: cars, pedestrians, delivery trucks and cyclists cram the narrow streets; sidewalk patios spill music and laughter, and punks drink beer in the park. Fish stores reek, bakeries vent. Weed is pungent as joss sticks at a shrine. Oliver, swerving around merch stands and sandwich boards and curbside garbage, hopes he isn't late. DON'T RAGE IN AN OUTAGE, WE'RE OPEN! BLACKOUT & FUEL UP, LIMITED MENU/CASH ONLY.

Alexandra is only steps behind him when he reaches the café. They opt for sitting inside where it's relatively quiet. Having spoken on the phone at some length, they keep preliminary chat brief, get their coffees, and he hands her a paper copy of the fracking study.

The City, in conjunction with Hydro One, has announced plans for rotating power cuts. Spurred by the blackouts and continuing stormy weather, the cuts are expected to last all summer. Not everyone has reacted as playfully as the denizens of the Market; the media, predictably, are hyping everything that might go wrong and who's to blame. Yet there's also been praise for the precautionary decision, for many have recalled the great Northeast Blackout of August 2003, when power went down across Ontario and the northeastern US for two days and more in some places. That time, buggy software created a vulnerability in the grid, and summer energy demand broke it.

While Alexandra reads, Oliver checks the weather forecast again. That little symbol of the sun tucked behind a raincloud with lightning bolting from its belly seems to be permanently stuck to the daily predictions. So far today they've been granted clear skies, but he's worried about the island.

Alexandra hasn't touched her coffee. She scans through *Impact Assessment: Water and Air Pollutants at Hydraulic Fracturing Sites* without breaking concentration, not even jotting a note. It's odd to see the study in anyone's hands but his, he's come to know it so well. It felt even odder to contact her, a veteran CBC journalist who represents everything he once hoped to achieve. He thought it a long shot, yet she replied to his email the same day.

He's drinking a second glass of water when she finally puts the study down. She stares off for a minute, then seems to remember her coffee and knocks it back.

"Wow."

Oliver holds his breath. Maybe it was just really good espresso.

"I can't wait to read your interviews," she says.

"I can share them as they come in. The first today went really well. He wouldn't agree to be filmed, but was lucid about the study." Riding the GO Train to Hamilton this morning, watching the lake race past, he'd never felt more nervous about a job — and this one he's essentially paying to do. "I expect at least a couple of the others might, though. They've been very responsive. Angry, I think, that their work was ignored."

"That's great." She removes her glasses. They're a shapely blue plastic, attached to a silver chain, and probably cost as much as his laptop. "The thing is, unfortunately, I'm not sure it's a good idea for me to write about this, much as I'd love to. This is extremely important information — no question. But with things as they are now, the political climate?" Her lips press together. "Even if I got a green light, I worry that the story might get killed from higher up. I don't have the latitude I used to, there's incredible scrutiny, it's really quite frightening. So I could try, but it might just be wasted effort." She sighs. "Actually, that's optimistic. It would be most likely be so."

Oliver's gut churns. The crumbled Wild Water Alliance needs connections and friends. Alexandra, who's covered environmental issues for years, was his top and perhaps only choice for a high-profile journalist who might help break this story.

"I'm sorry to disappoint you," she continues, "but I actually think this track is safer. These days, this kind of thing has to come out in other streams first — alt media, DIY. Once it gains some traction with the public first, a bit of exposure, then I might safely step in. Wrong as that sounds, which it is, I'm just being frank."

"Yes, of course." How will they gain "exposure" without her? He thanks her for taking the time. "Perhaps, later, we could work together?"

"I hope so. I meant it — I'm really interested in what happens as you pursue this."

He expects her to leave then, but she wants to hear more about the film. They discuss it and his interview for some time, and then the conversation naturally branches to their shared experiences as writers, what's happening in the biz — and even with all the bad news it's such a pleasure to talk shop with a colleague again, let alone one of her calibre: smart, dedicated and a little maternal, which he doesn't mind at all. Out on the sidewalk, awkwardly because he likes her and might not have another chance, he gushes something to this effect.

Alexandra laughs. In the sunlight the skin on her face looks papery, like an old bill folded and refolded and smoothed out again. "Contact me anytime and I'll do what I can. Often I wish I were free-lance again, like you, able to tackle things my way."

He wants to ask why she isn't, but can guess the answer lies in a remodeled house, children in university, benefits and pension plans, or who knows what obligations and difficulties she shoulders. He takes her extended hand and she wishes him luck.

She moves away with the stream of pedestrians, leaving him pondering the emotions he saw in her face. Regret, but also confidence and enthusiasm and hope: that *he* will make something happen.

~

AT HOME he stops by Rosh's to fill him in on the day, including Alexandra's response. Rosh isn't much fazed that she turned them down; he's more excited about the interview.

"I'll transcribe it tonight and send it over."

"Great! Charlotte's coming by to talk money. It'll help cheer her up."

"How's the fundraising going?"

"I try not to ask, since I got my hands full enough. But if she's coming over, that means she needs encouragement."

Oliver heads upstairs, thinking of the work to be done. He finds Justin in the kitchen making bean salad and something colourful with rice noodles. His brother seems tired, sad and preoccupied though reassures him that he won't take off in the night. *But have you spoken to your wife?* Oliver wants to ask.

Instead he feeds Mimi, unloads his knapsack, then sits down at his desk to check the latest news on the island listserv. Ponds have appeared in places that water doesn't normally collect; there's a large one near the school. "Off-Islanders" are being openly criticized for not pitching in with sandbagging. Dike building's set to resume tomorrow at ten a.m.

He's got to get out there, and not after work. Bad as he feels for taking another day off, he texts Foroud: this is an emergency. The gym has to wait.

Outside on the balcony he's aware of gobbling his dinner and tries to slow down, match his brother's pace, but his mind keeps lurching about. Thousands paid to the architect. The contractor given a deposit for the demo. Should he have waited? "I was thinking about your builder problem today," Justin says, as if tuning in to Oliver's thoughts. "Have you considered alternatives?"

"In what way?"

"You might be able to have the house built in the city and floated over. Save the ferry hassles for your builder, not have to worry about him bumping or dumping you."

"I never thought of that." It sounds wildly difficult.

"It's probably doable. It might just be easiest, though, to modify your plan. Go for something less complex."

"Than *that?*" Oliver points to the drawing. "That's virtually the same footprint as the old house." He resisted pressure from the architect to enlarge it, in fact, and is proud he stuck to his guns.

"You could still scale it back."

Says the guy with the 3,000-square-foot house! Oliver snorts. "Into what, a fucking yurt?"

Justin considers, then grins. "With a loft."

There's no time for this now. He retrieves his laptop and returns to the balcony to work. Justin moves inside, hovering by the desk and scrutinizing the plan on the wall.

Down below, children play Frisbee in one of the front yards while adults watch from a candlelit porch. Some people are already keeping lights off to conserve energy. A pod of cycling teens whizzes past, the sounds of gears clicking. "Mind if I look at this?" Justin calls from inside. He's picked up the fracking study from the desk.

Oliver's pleasantly surprised. "It's not exactly bedtime reading, but sure, knock yourself out."

The evening passes in quiet intensity: he transcribes, his brother reads. An email comes in from Rosh: tapping donors isn't panning out, Charlotte's not hopeful about crowdfunding. Will they even be able to use these interviews?

Morning brings smoggy and humid weather. The UV index sits at eight, classified as "high risk." *High levels of pollution are expected today. Keep outdoor activities to a minimum,* advises Environment Canada's website. *Children, seniors, and those with cardiovascular or lung disease, such as asthma, are especially at risk.* The advice makes him snarl. *Keep your life in a box! Don't expect more!* And so much for the lives without that choice.

Justin emerges from the bathroom with his hair wet. He asks if there's an extra backpack and water bottle, and maybe an old pair of shorts?

"Sure, but — you mean, you're coming with me today?"

"I thought that was obvious." A puzzled look.

At mid-morning the lake is dark, fetid. The boat crossing brings no refreshing breeze, just heavy heat and particulate matter they feel in their chests. On the north shore of Ward's, facing the city, the new dike rises like a fortress wall: sloping sides leading to a wide, flat top. It's far thicker than the dike he helped put in before, and as they dock he watches lines of people add bags from a mound on the grass; behind that, a hillock of dumped sand. For reasons he doesn't know, this vulnerable section of Ward's was never bulkheaded like the north edge of Algonquin. Houses sit close to the shore here, and now they almost touch it.

"They studied plans this time. From New Orleans, apparently," Oliver tells Justin as they stroll over. Now they can see that plastic sheets have also been layered between the rows of bags.

They're welcomed warmly if hastily by half a dozen people he worked with last time, then they get down to it. The sandbags weigh thirty to forty pounds. Not everyone can capably lift them, so others work to fill bags or refresh the drinks and snacks table or help reposition the bags on the dike. There's even a young girl dolloping noses with sunscreen. And yet, his quick count puts the number of volunteers at under fifty, youth included, from six hundred residents.

Over the first hour he adjusts to the rhythm again, reminding himself to hold the bags low against his belly so the weight distributes into his gut and butt, and to keep his knees bent and hips engaged and feet planted. Then, to swing in one smooth motion to pass the bag to his brother and to turn – not twist – and to not fumble. They don't talk, just pass, swing-turn the weight, pass. From time to time someone near the head of the line calls out as they send along a new bag, a sound like *yip!* or *hep!* like you might use with a horse. He digs it. He needs it, as his muscles start to ache and his clothes dampen and his breathing grows laboured. Yet he starts to lose himself in the motions too: the line moves as one animal, one mind, and his own calms.

They break as a line, rest in the shade. The table offers lemonade, minted water, iced tea, hot coffee and baked goods. He doesn't care for the food; he just wants to drink everything.

Later, as a change from the line, he and Justin help lift up and position the bags. Now they can stand in water, which is refreshing. Use different muscles, sort of, to hoist the bags up and to slosh along when one drops and heave it up from the water.

They labour as long as they can, extending their breaks between stints, but by mid-afternoon he's spent. Justin nudges him and points to the sky, which has grown ominously dark in the east. "Why don't you show me the place now? We can always come back and do a bit more here, if we're up for it."

Agreed on that plan, they rub the sand off themselves then set out. Justin's quiet on the way there, taking it all in. On the boat earlier he said that he's not been to the island since he and Naomi took Gwynn to the amusement park on Centre, years ago, and even then, he didn't visit Algonquin or Ward's. He never showed them the old house.

When they arrive at the bungalow, Justin surveys the dwelling and yard for some moments. "Hey," he says at last, "I remember that shed."

"And the chestnut tree?"

"Nope. But I remember that pine. Cones used to peg our tent at night and freak you out." He smiles a little, walks onto the grass and around the side of the house, Oliver following. "This is actually larger than I thought."

Grateful not to be facing more scorn, Oliver's quick to agree. "It's a modest place, yet roomy enough."

"Certainly."

There's a sudden gust of wind and a bang — someone's door slamming. A soft deep rumble comes to them, sounding very remote, like the reverberation of a mountain breaking apart in some corner of the world. It goes on for a moment, stops. They examine the sky. The sun's still bright.

"Should we go?" Oliver says.

The rumble repeats, followed by a rushing, windy swell. The trees start rippling, first this way, then that way. Oliver checks his watch. If they hoof it, they could make the 4:15.

"I think we should go. If it storms the ferry might not run."

"But we just got here." Justin heads up the front steps and opens the screen door. He steps into the enclosed porch and does exactly what Oliver did on that first visit: turns around, faces the street.

Oliver walks to the laneway and looks north. The stormfront hangs low over the city: clouds like wildfire smoke, unholy metallic light. White caps are rolling across the harbour. Around him trees seethe and a dark thing flies past with a squawk. It looked like a cat. He jogs up the path and joins Justin, who's foraged a couple of shitty plastic chairs. Lightning shocks the sky. Thunder peals. From the porch they watch the rain sweep in, and soon it screens everything from view.

The air's gone cold. Goosebumps cover his skin. He counts the seconds between each crackling peal until he's too rattled to think. The dike! Will it hold?

Water drizzles through the battered roof, seeps in by their feet.

TIME PASSES SLOWLY. Just when the storm seems to be blowing itself out, it surges with new vigour. They keep shifting their chairs on the porch, vying for dry spots. He calls the ferry service: six rings and an automated message saying service has been temporarily suspended. All those tourists stuck. Ward's dock has only two small shelters, and one has an old piano in it.

For a long while the weather's too intense to talk over so they simply sit, side by side, like two old bachelors who've never left. The Leveridge brothers, fixtures of the laneway. Would the picture amuse their parents, he wonders.

When the worst seems truly past and the rain has relaxed into a steady downfall, he asks Justin if he feels like looking around inside the house. Slouched in the chair staring fixedly for ages, his brother rouses himself to decline, flicks water from the chair arms, returns to his brooding repose.

It's after six and the ferry service isn't answering, their outgoing message unchanged. Candlelight wavers in the house across the lane and at Susanna's next door. On his phone Oliver logs into local news: extensive blackouts reported in the metro region, all of downtown affected — which means the ferries probably won't run until power's restored. There's a small fleet of water taxis, run by a handful of individuals who mostly pick people up outside of the ferry's limited hours. Yet everyone on the docks at Ward's, Centre and Hanlan's will be trying to get one.

"Nothing to do but wait," Justin says at this update. He closes his eyes.

Evening deepens; the rain continues. First night in my new-old house, Oliver thinks glumly. His stomach growls. Hunching over the phone, blowing on his fingers to warm them, he thumbs through news and wishes he'd eaten some of the banana bread on the table when he had the chance. He texts Gabe, but she doesn't reply. What will Islanders do if the dike doesn't hold? How will his contractor ever work out here with this chaos? He should have left

337

Rosh a key so he could feed Mimi. What's going to happen if the film can't get finished, and the drills invade, and this mad enterprise hurtles into reality?

If the fracking deals-in-the-making go ahead, the water of the Great Lakes will be siphoned off even more than it is for the nuclear plants and industries and cities along the shores. Another mouth to feed, and more poisonous puke in return. Water will be used to blast through Lake Erie's own foundation. Could that correctly be called shooting oneself in the foot? That lake will be forced to shoot itself in the foot.

Rigs by the hundreds. Pipelines, wastewater cauldrons, open-air pits. Oil, Earth's digestive bile, sucked and slurried into drums. Water becomes weapon in the demolition of Earth. Elements forced to do battle.

An image comes to him of a great wave rising in the lake: an epic, survival-reflex heave of mud and plastic and writhing eels, dumped junk and sick salmon and revenant sturgeon. WATER CLAW, the ultimate excavator, demos the city and all human bullshit from here to Hudson's Bay.

Around eight-thirty, Justin gets up and goes inside with their water bottles to refill them from the kitchen. What's going to become of him? His marriage? His mental stability? How flimsy are these threads! Why can't at least one thing in his life feel fucking secure?

"The rain's letting up for real," he observes when his brother reappears, trying to sound hopeful. "We might get a water taxi now."

"Let's check out the harbour."

In the dusky light they walk to the north end of the lane, where a boulevard runs along the bulwarked shore and a few benches face the city skyline. Clouds still obscure its upper reaches, and they stand gazing at dark buildings as far as they can see. Evening's last light is fading; silently, rapidly, night falls. His brother becomes shadow, and the grey city fades like something vanished into jungle legend or deep space.

A water taxi's lone headlight moves across the harbour like a comet.

Cloud cover shifts, points of light emerge: red emergency beacons atop towers, the odd spot of shining white.

It's growing warm again. Justin removes his wet clothes and shakes them and Oliver follows suit. It's much more comfortable to stand naked in the soft breeze, letting it dry their skin. The taxi's purr fades as it disappears. The lake slops against steel.

"So quiet," Oliver says.

"The real deal."

Voices reach them. Flashlights bob up the lane.

They hastily pull on their shorts. It's a small group of Islanders out on patrol. They bring news that the residents on Ward's living closest to the dike have gone to stay with neighbours.

"My brother just texted from Hamilton," a man says. "The power's out there too." It's out in Scarborough, Oshawa, Oakville, Burlington, Markham, Richmond Hill . . .

"Where's it *not* out?" Oliver asks.

"Not sure yet. I had to stop web searching. It's draining my phone."

"The blackout's big, that's all we know," a woman tells them.

"So much for the rotating cuts."

Someone snorts. "Too little too late. The grid's as shaky as it was in '03."

"It's never not been," another says. "People just forget." Peering into the gloom, Oliver thinks he recognizes the speaker as David, who co-led the clubhouse meeting. "You two going to be alright? You can try for a taxi, but there's still quite a crowd waiting at Centre, we've heard."

"We're okay. Mostly just hungry."

"Susanna's got some burgers on for us. Just ask her, she'll set you up." He'd not thought of that. The patrol departs, heading to check on the seniors' residence and people living alone.

Three water taxis are skimming across the harbour now, with hours of work ahead. He talks it over with Justin, who's likewise not inclined to wait in line yet and face the search for a bus or cab on the other side. They stretch out on the wet grass.

His brother blends into the night. Oliver can barely see his own hand when he raises it to his face. Lulled by the water and darkness, he finds himself moving in and out of a sensation of floating, adrift on the lake. The wooden egg from his dream comes back to him — the great egg that never gets finished. How did he not see? It's not an egg. It's an ark.

He opens his eyes. A rift has appeared in the clouds, revealing black space dense with gathered light. The stars look like seeds, like glowing spores.

"You awake?"

"Yeah." Oliver raises himself. Egg-ark. He's been so desperate to come home to the island, to make things right again here, yet everything keeps going askew.

"What's up? You're muttering again."

"I'm muttering because my life keeps unravelling just when I think it's coming together."

"Nah, you're just anxious."

"You're the one who said it before, that night in your office. Hopeless. Doomed. That's what you said about the bungalow."

"That was harsh. I was probably influenced by my own situation. But I don't think I was wrong, either."

"Thanks a lot!"

"You've *got* to make things easier on yourself."

"How? I can't just snap my fingers!" A wide section of sky has opened. Oliver gazes at the stars, his heart aching.

"This is a good place," Justin says after a moment. "I was wrong about that part before."

"You mean this wretched, godforsaken, sinking island?"

Justin laughs. "There are good people here, and more. Much

more. I was thinking, maybe I could help you out, kind of hold it for you. Then you wouldn't have to worry anymore, you could concentrate on your project."

"You? What do you mean?"

"I'm not sure, I just think I can help. But this house you've got planned — you *do* have to forget about it. That project *is* doomed."

Forget about the bungalow rebuild!

"It's wasting your energy, Bro. It's sucking you down. And believe me, I know all about that. Leverage undid me. Don't make that mistake. You've got far better and more crucial things to do now, you've got your friend, who seems like a very solid guy, and whatever you're doing with that study — well, I looked through it, and that's serious stuff. You've got this new woman in your life too. You're just starting out, actually, so let it go already! Put the house out of your mind — at least for a good, long while."

Oliver hears him stretching out on the grass. He flings himself down likewise, feeling utterly bewildered. Let it go? After all this time, money and effort? How on earth is that possible? *How how how?*

From the darkness, a warm hand reaches out and covers his.

30

A GLOWING BAND, as from a curtain slightly parted, has appeared in the east. Sitting below the Serpent Mound at the lake, Gabe watches the band widen and gain hue as colour seeps into the darkened world. The sky breaks into iron clouds, inky blotches suspended in a pale grey wash. Slowly the print transforms to a blue-on-blue landscape that seems to originate from the fiery horizon, as if unfurled by the emergent sun. Lake answers sky with a rippling reflection, and the bristling tips of trees sharpen into an outline, yet for a while longer the lands of Hiawatha nation, and the cottages and measured acreages of farms, remain invisible.

Behind her the winding Serpent looks over the water. Eight eggs nestle near her, ovular burial sites. For over half a millennia she's lain here, the only one of her kind in this vast country. She was here when financiers of a young nation sent men to dig the Trent-Severn waterway, a three-hundred-kilometre trench that so altered water levels it almost destroyed this lake's namesake: the wild rice that nourished the First Peoples here. Transport tech changed, the waterway rapidly lost its utility, and the descendants of those peoples still beg access to their own diminished lands.

The Serpent bore witness to another boom-economy scheme: the trestle bridge that crept out from Harwood across the water. Like an incoming vision of the mania to come, the bridge of several kilometres ate up a forest. Locomotives raced across it like missiles. Tourists joyrided. And in a handful of years the bridge fell, hammered by ice and human neglect.

Gabe sets her hands on the sun-scorched grass. By afternoon it will be hot and prickly, dry as old bone, but at this hour it's soft and faintly fragrant, revealing the life held within. This morning as usual she brought walnuts, carrots and birdseed to the Mound. The offerings are always taken. Most of life happens beyond our view; we see surfaces, traces, effects. Yet twice in the dark of the field and once in her mind she's seen the impossible – a freak or a miracle, Oliver said. Maybe its season has passed. Maybe she'll never see it again. Maybe it's just a lure of her own making! But sitting here, she knows this isn't so.

How?

There's no evidence, no data. She can't even hedge a hypothesis to explain the luminous moth's existence. She's got no legit answer, just *knows* that it's real. And that she's got to get back to the field, raise the sheet.

Now with the sun reddening she rises and heads back to the car. Earlier this morning, in the basement's opaque silence, she dressed and packed her knapsack (still the same scant items she took with her the afternoon she left to hike in the woods; in the city Oliver gave her a new toothbrush, loaned her boxers, T-shirts and socks, all endearingly baggy on her). She looted Jenn's smorgasbord-stocked kitchen for a few days' supplies and moth sugaring ingredients, scribbled a note. Despite the lurid bruise on her hip, climbing into the car brought only a twinge; negotiating the milkweed ditch with her gear will be fine. The last few days – spent churning over her dialogue with Brimer, and trying to work up the scattered reflections in her fieldnotes to something like a new research question — have not led anywhere. Something's gotta give.

The cabin feels sad and neglected when she arrives, as if holding a grudge at her abrupt absence. Clothes cast over chairs, books piled askew, terminal flies on the sills. After setting down her things, Gabe finds a clean glass bowl and strides to the fridge. The dead in the freezer are stacked in paper sleeves. She opens each and taps out the contents. Moving quickly outside, she plucks a few sprigs of pink flox and buttercup, then wades into the lake, where she tilts the bowl to empty. The water's still quite cool, and for a moment the bodies float near the surface before being released from their icy encasements. She casts the flowers over them.

~

SPENDING NIGHTS mothing at the field alters her sleep pattern. She rests from dawn until noon and devotes afternoons to "the thesis," which grows ever more vaporous. It's mid-June and over a week since she talked to Brimer. Heygi, Gabe's official supervisor, has been understanding yet anxious on her behalf.

Meanwhile, the fucking sheet hasn't worked, sugaring's been a dud, and she's out of ideas. Not all moths fly to light or will feed on baited trees; some respond only to the scent of their own species, and the moth catcher must use a species-specific pheromone lure. Of course she doesn't have one for the luminous moth.

After a fourth defeated vigil, she decamps early (around two a.m.) and heads back to the farm, where she stops at the house instead of continuing to the cabin. She's depressed and awake enough that she might as well go online. A few emails (a note to Oliver, phrased to sound more optimistic about her work and less impatient to see him again than she feels), a few tours of moth forums and blogs, a scroll through unexciting social media, and she's done. Laptop under her arm, she switches off the lamp and steps outside.

Her hosts don't keep property lights on at night, so it takes a moment for the farm's various structures to distinguish themselves: chicken coop, cistern, greenhouses and the bunkie-office where Rachel sorts the heritage seeds that she sells — slowly Gabe makes them out against the sky, and the shoulders of the county forest to the north, past the fields. The night's warm and gloriously starry; at the car she finds herself leaving the laptop on the seat and carrying on, surrendering to the galactic river. The buildings fall behind. She goes swimming in the dark.

Croaks, cheeps, the occasional hoot. Nightlife abounds, but there's something else out here too: a palpable current, like thought — or rather, many thoughts — that fins about her. Trailing her fingers along the leaves by the path, Gabe tries to sense the current's threads, as she did when she lay listening to the thrush song and seemed to catch hold of the luminous moth's scent-thread. Moths' ability to find each other over long distances through scent alone seems almost miraculous (or freakish), yet they do. And their ability is not, actually, unique: every creature has ways of communicating to its fellows that are mysterious or indiscernible to others. Elephants and other mammals use infrasound calls that travel several kilometres. Whale songs reach through oceans. Species from termites to trees use chemical messaging.

In fact it strikes her as strange, even highly unlikely, that humans with their celebrated cleverness would lack similar abilities. Yes, most of life lives beyond reach of our immediate senses, particularly our sight, but that doesn't mean beyond our *range*. We've made tools for distance communication, including written speech, yet these are relatively recent developments. Could people once have communicated over distance by other means? Wouldn't staying connected to one's fellows from afar be crucial to survival in the prehistoric world? Might not such abilities reveal themselves in telepathy, pre-cognition, and other so-called paranormal phenomena? If such abilities exist today, Gabe considers, they'd inevitably be latent or even vestigial, obvious in only some of the population, perhaps, like the Occipitalis Minor or Darwin's tubercle.

She's overshot the sidetrack to the cabin. Bringing the flashlight would have helped. She turns and retraces her path.

But why illumination, why *light?*

That's the constantly circulating question. Light is a force of energy biochemically emitted by virtually all living things – including people, though typically in wavelengths invisible to the naked eye. Most bioluminescent species live deep in the ocean.

A new sound comes on the wind: coyotes, calling to each other or just howling at the night. She pauses to listen, feel the threads.

At the lake, the bulrushes are chaffing. She sits outside on the table. Lights stand out along the opposite shore, wavering like souls crossed to the other side. And then it hits her. Oh, the irony. The luminescent moth *is* the bulb. She, the trapper, is the one who must be lured.

THE NEXT EVENING after a late supper, she drives out to the field. This time she brings only a blanket and her small pack. At the place where she usually hangs the sheet and goops the trees, she simply sits on the ground.

Listening.

It takes focus to quiet her mind, relax, and move into a state of alert receptivity. After a while, a tingling in her brow starts to come and go. Sometimes the sensation grows warm and pulse-like, then fainter, like a spider's thread tickling. Coming and going. Near and far.

Listening.

One of the marvels from *The Voyage of the Beagle* that's always stuck with her: the *Beagle* has anchored in the great estuary of Rio de la Plata, many miles offshore, when the rigging becomes coated in thousands upon thousands of spider strands, each from the arrival of a single tiny spider sailing in with its fellows on a thread.

"Little aeronauts," Darwin calls them, this throng of travellers voyaging as if by dream-spun volition. The spiders touch down on the ship for a rest, then cast off to the horizon, out of sight.

Is the sensation she's experiencing now a thought- or sixth-sense connection to the moth, or just her own grasping for one? Maybe the tingle's nothing but heightened sensitivity, byproduct of a meditative state or something blander: stress, nerves, fatigue. Or the opposite is true: heightened receptivity has made her *aware*, finally, of what's been present all along.

Gabe tips to the side and frees one stiff leg from under her, tucks in the other. The ground's hard from being tilled, probably for decades, and her hip dully aches.

Her mind wanders again, she can't help it, and she thinks about trapping. Moths have such brief lives; the Polyphemus lives only one week. And since it rests during the day, landing in a trap overnight can, effectively, steal a seventh of its life. Would she give a dozen years of her own to inform a moth about herself? Should she even *be* trapping? Maybe asking the question — letting it be asked — makes a difference even if she can't answer it now. At the least, she should be more mindful of trapping and grateful to the moths.

At Jenn's the other night, watching TV with one of her nephews, she saw a commercial featuring a glowing, animated moth that flew into a bedroom and landed on a sleeper. The moth was neon green, the ad for a sleeping pill called Lunasta. The advertisers were evoking the Luna moth as deliverer of rest. And she wondered how many people have actually seen a Luna, one of the most regal and fairy-like of moths, formerly commonplace, now diminished while its image gets yoked into product service. There's a kind of spirit theft in that, a fate worse than death. It seems to her a deep perversion the modern age has spiraled into, this continual replacement of the living with virtual images and commodified replicas, part of an ever-growing, technological confinement enveloping humanity and creation like a toxic cocoon.

She takes a deep breath and returns to *listening*. The tingle, the pulse. Coming and going. Near and Far. She sticks with it for a while, but nothing more happens. Maybe this approach isn't right? Or it is, but it's not going far enough.

In the car for a break, she flips through her notebook under the dome light. Periodicity has been a question also. Certain cicada species emerge every thirteen and seventeen years. The Northern Oak Egger moth in Britain has a two-year cycle, as does the Pine Resin-gall moth. One subspecies of the latter has adapted this cycle to three years. Could her moth also follow an idiosyncratic cycle? Could that account for it not being seen?

The book's margins are busy with her doodles. Pupae dangle from branches; caterpillars entwine like lovers. Moths perch and fly. They bear flowers, they bear scrolls. They blow trumpets and wear coronets. Some carry riders with human-like faces.

Gabe clicks her pen and writes:

Communication is integral to the natural order of life: everything communicates, whether within ecosystems or cells.

Since all biological communities exist interdependently, communication must occur between organisms and species continuously. We know that trees seem to communicate with some insects and frogs who will then accommodate so as not to overly predate the host species [insert citations]. Interspecies communication should be the natural state of things. What if it is, but humans have lost awareness of it? (Everything from industrialized life to culture and education could account for this loss.) What if species are sending us messages all the time?

Communication is fullest with an open heart, an open mind. When inhibitions are present, communication is always partial, frustrated, distorted, or absent.

Manipulation creates barriers. Freedom — mutual freedom — is the best way, the only way, for robust communication to occur.

She stares off for a moment, remembering her fall, and her injury, and the moth coming in the darkness of her mind. How did she not see? It was showing her what she's needed to understand all along.

The moths teach us: dissolve old forms, let go of what binds you.
She shuts the book.

~

THE FOLLOWING NIGHT she returns to the field without even a blanket. At the edge of the woods, darkness seeps like a tidal mark reaching toward her feet. Now that she's standing here like this, the truth seems so obvious. Perhaps her heart's known all along, but she couldn't surrender to it.

She steps toward the trees. A white moth with dark patterning flutters up, perhaps a Hapola. In a moment it's gone. Black columns of trunks rise before her, the corn field light by contrast. She steps through the brush bordering the canopy. She crosses over, goes in.

Darkness envelops her. Gabe takes some slow, relaxing breaths. Then, holding her hands in front of her, she steps forward again. Being effectively blind, her instinct is to shuffle, but shuffling will lead to falls. Lifting her feet with care, she progresses by swaying one hand before her side to side like a trunk or antenna, the other raised behind it.

No path, no guidance. Step, step, step . . . When she looks behind, the field's gone.

A swimmer always wants a point to aim toward, even if that point is the horizon. Here she has nothing. In her small pack there's water, a compass, an ankle brace, bandages and painkillers, a raincoat, and a flashlight not to be used unless absolutely driven to. Really it could only help her bandage a wound and see her other things. No chalk.

Her hand feels ahead for the next tree and the next, her safety posts. Groping through black emptiness rings a deep, primal alarm, a sense of being swallowed alive or trapped and not moving at all. Her senses seem confused. She hears leaves shushing right beside her, it seems, reaches out for the tree and touches only empty space. She cannot tell distances; everything seems on an equal plane. A tree jumps out where it wasn't on the first sweep with her hand. Her own footsteps seem to come from elsewhere.

She's not forgotten the eviscerated doe. She is very aware that everything out here has its own purpose, and there might be something whose purpose she serves quite well. There is no such thing as being alone in this world; alienation is a human concept, a human possibility, a human-made horror. All around her, though it's a relatively windless night, the woods creak and crack, and things scurry about the ground. A heron passes overhead with a garbled croak. She starts to long for more birds, like the night-hawk's measured, friendly *peet*, but mostly it's mosquitoes who visit, whining suddenly in her ears like tiny heat-seeking missiles and startling her out of proportion.

Whenever she touches bark, her palm smooths it gratefully. Each bole is a checkpoint, reassurance that she's progressed. Even if she's travelling in circles they'll be imperfect ones, loops that take her somewhere. No moth flies a straight line.

Moving this way, stumbling occasionally. Overhead, a scattering of stars.

Closing her eyes, she clears her mind and visualizes the moth and the thread-like connection between them. *Listening*.

The tingling in her brow begins almost immediately, stronger than ever.

A dull thud up ahead freezes her. It sounded like something heavy dropping to the ground, probably just a branch, but she can't move. The thread's gone.

She reaches behind her for the tree she just left, steps back and wraps her arms around it. Minutes tick by as her ears and nerves strain. *Listen!* But she can't.

She thinks of Oliver and the picnic he packed for them the day they went to the island, sandwiches wrapped in wax paper. Three different kinds. How she laughed when he brought them out, which was kind of rude. She laughed because those sweet sandwiches made her heart crack open: this was devotion. To her. She remembers the strength she saw and felt welling up in him after his brother disappeared, his bravery in the face of that crisis, and how he's finding his passion for justice again.

With her eyes still closed, Gabe calms, and finds the thread again. When she leaves the tree she imagines sliding along it *listening*. After a time she can open her eyes without losing the connection. She can't see anything in the woods but at least the stars are visible and it feels more natural, and easier, to move this way.

Another trunk, another temporary outpost. How long has she been walking? She's still not reached the first drumlin. The ground seems to have risen steadily, then leveled off.

Listening. She breathes deeply, feels it thread steady, casts off again.

As she proceeds she tries an experiment. *Can the connection be stronger?* she asks. There's no change, so she tries a simpler thought: *Help. Stronger.*

The sky flashes: heat lightning. The thread has become a pulse.

She lets herself be pulled by it until something hard and cool blocks the path: a boulder, an outlier from a drumlin. On the other side, steeply rising ground. This is the trickiest walking yet, for the angle of the slope means she can't climb and feel her way ahead at the same time. She ascends sideways and stooped so she won't smack her head.

At the top she pauses. The pulse has intensified. Her brow aches. It feels hot.

She sinks to her knees from weariness and nerves. It's good to be on the ground. She presses her hands to her face, massages her temples, and when she looks up again, a small silvery light is moving through the air not far from her. The light flits as her star-tled eyes follow, then is joined by another. The two flutter together, dancing or playing or courting or speaking. They're close enough to see their scalloped wings. In a moment they rise and lift Gabe's gaze up to the forest canopy.

The air is full of snow.

The moths are like moondrops. Radiant thoughts. She can't count them, there are so many.

Closer, please?

They descend in a chaotic spiral and pass before her face. Skim the ground, her legs. One lands on her arm, its light softening. It is exactly what she saw: a type of Sphinx moth the colours of snow and cloud, dusk and dawn.

Beauty! Her brow still pulses almost painfully. Though she longs to leap up in joy, she keeps herself motionless to let them approach. Wings brush her cheek. Glide against her hair.

How?

She had not meant to ask but did, and an answer comes: not words, but impressions like words that she receives as clearly as their touch. She sees the moths emerging from their pupae as if from their perspective: feels their eagerness to work free and their elation to be alive and in the world after so long a sleep. So long a sleep.

Why so long?

An ache, nauseating as a humming headache. It's what the moths feel: the world is *wrong*. The night, the darkness, the air, the land – sickened.

There is still joy in living, yet everywhere they feel what's been done. The world is not the same. The trees know. Everything knows; all of life strains. So they sleep longer and longer, as the years pass.

She's flying. Over the corn field, out to the gravel road. Senses the lights on the farmhouse up the way, then Peterborough, a hori-zon glow. The humming straining ache and another feeling she can't quite name. Astonishment? Confusion?

Why light?

So you see.

The moths are no longer visible, though she feels the creature's weight still on her arm and senses them whirring about her. Emitting light saps energy. It's like shouting. Oh — *that's* the feeling: a dizzying disorientation from the light pollution, which to them feels like noise. Cacophony. Like everything's shouting, so they have brightened in response — shouted back — to gain attention. A desperate measure they cannot sustain.

I understand.

More images and sensations. She's flying through the woods at night, but not night as she's ever perceived it: the woods are alight with strange colours that flicker and flash like heat lightning, in a spectrum of hues that doesn't make sense. The colours are *dark*, as in invisible, yet perceptible. Is this some further human damage to the atmosphere, as the moths see it?

Our songs!

What?

Our songs.

The colours shimmer, beautiful and complex beyond imagining, like the shades and patterns of the moths themselves. It's like the pictures of nebulae, star clusters birthing and whirling. Their songs. The songs of moths. And of other creatures as well: birds, flowers, trees . . . She sees, she understands: humans, in losing touch with the subtler senses, perceive only emptiness. They have filled the world with their own noise — and in so doing are draining it, like bloodletting, like removing colours from a weave. The new generations are scanter, the pulse of creation weaker.

A moth flutters against her face. Gabe starts to weep, overwhelmed by the vision and pain of it and the sensation that envelops her on the hill with her companions, tender and sweet and powerful as the stars: love.

~

HOURS LATER, awake in the woods with the birds and early light, she sits up and brushes debris from her hair. With morning clarity, the answer comes to her: the study method was the stumbling block, so make the problem the solution. Her study's purpose can be to field test a new study method that doesn't rely on killing moths. She will use a combination of moth sheets, sugaring, and very limited trapping. Maybe compare results. All three eliminate harm. The sheet causes some interference, but little, the trap more. The real advantage of the first two methods, she thinks, is that they require the individual to be present throughout the process, not in bed or on a computer while a trap does the work. That seems crucial.

She gets to her feet, stretches and slaps feeling into her chilled limbs, opens her pack and rummages. Drinks deeply from the water bottle. There's a pale light overhead, enough to walk by, though to read the compass she'll need the flashlight. Stuffs it into her pocket. The lake lies south, the gravel road parallel to it. No chalk, no markers to lead back to this hill. No lazy shortcuts. Compass in hand, she sets out.

31

THE CAB'S SPEED startles him. First they're cruising with cyclists at street level, then they've left the east end and are flying toward downtown on the expressway, curving past the financial district, where the towers stand empty. He lowers the window, closes his eyes, and feels the wind on his face.

It would have felt better to return to Baby Point on foot, but he's taken so much time. At sunrise when he woke on the island, he knew the moment had come. He wanted to call Naomi then but Oliver's phone couldn't find a signal, and they still had to get back; when they did there was no landline to use at Oliver's and still no cellular signals or power. The entire metro region was blacked out, and still is. Oliver's neighbour friend, Rosh, came up and told them that the blackout covered the whole Great Lakes region, the north-eastern seaboard states and parts of Quebec. So yesterday in the late afternoon he went to Ace, knowing it would be closed. He'd lost his phone during that flight from the house, but not his keys. He let himself into the dim building, climbed the stairs to his office, opened the balcony door for light, sat at his desk. Considered his legacy, not just to himself but to others. Then he called home.

~

357

HE'S WEARING ONE OF Oliver's shirts with the sleeves rolled up, and otherwise the same jeans and shoes, cleaned up as best as possible, with his coat on his arm. He'd have liked to arrive with gifts, considered one of the bouquets in plastic tubs at a corner store. The flowers looked stale and made him sad, though, and nothing else is open.

On the driveway once the cab leaves he regards the house. Morning light falls softly on the windows. There's nothing amiss to his senses: the grass is green and the garden blooms. He rings the bell.

Naomi opens the door. His arms spread and he wonders if she'll just keep staring. Then she presses into him, warm and real, her breasts against his chest, slender back under his hands. She feels thinner and he touches her head, hush, a moment of peace. When he pulls back she wipes her eyes and there's Gwynn, emerging from her side: this sad child, wavering. He bends and sweeps her into him.

"Oh my girl," he murmurs.

Reggie's there also, dancing and yipping and grinning.

Gwynn chatters and clings to him in a way that makes his heart hurt. She wants to show him the new bedspreads Naomi bought when he was away — including one on their own bed — then play with her new soccer ball. Naomi nods and seems even pleased, and joins them to watch in the backyard. They have a lively game with Reg, who tries to jaw the ball when they kick it. There's lunch on the deck after, coffee made on the gas stove, and he's grateful though declines when Naomi offers him a plate.

He has to hold his head and bends over in his seat.

"Justin? Justin."

"I'm okay. It's easier to breathe this way."

"Want to go inside? It's cooler."

"Here is better." It feels like someone's standing on his chest, but to reassure her he sits up again and tries to smile.

"Are you still sick, Dad?"

"A little, Pumpkin, but I'm getting better." Gwynn comes to hug him, and he pulls her onto his lap and holds her there, wincing as she leans into him. He kisses her. "Let me and Mom talk for a bit? Then I'll come see your new bedding?" She nods.

"How are things here?" he asks, once he and Naomi are alone.

She shrugs. Her mood's been subdued and remote since their embrace. "Surviving, as you can see."

He looks down. Reg is lying between them on the deck, pretending to sleep.

"I know this is going to take a while —"

"What 'this' are you referring to?"

He takes a breath. "This transition, whatever it is. But I want to talk to you today about something that I hope you think about. I want to step away from Ace and Leverage, permanently."

Her eyebrows arch.

"And I wondered if you would like to have them. Oliver told me you've been managing things, and I'm sure you're doing a great job. Though that doesn't mean you enjoy it. I'm saying, if this would be enjoyable to you, truly, then I hope you consider it. Otherwise, there are other options."

"You'd actually sell."

"Yeah."

"And do what?"

He shakes his head. Don't know.

"Are you saying you want to sell them to me? Like in some kind of settlement?"

"Of course not." Resentment flares in him. But maybe it's an understandable question. "I'm saying I'm not in charge anymore. You can decide. Whatever direction you feel is right, that's what we'll do."

Naomi's leg starts to joggle. She stops it, shoots him a pissed off look. "Well! This is kind of unexpected, Jay, though I guess that's the way of things these days. I can't decide right now, I'll need time."

"You don't have to."

"That's easy for *you* to say. We'll need to reopen when the blackout's over, deal with the food rotting in the freezers, et cetera. I asked staff to take what they could, but . . ."

"Right. I'll help with that — if you want me to, that is."

"And what if *I* don't feel like doing *any* of it?"

He's inclined to say that he often didn't "feel like doing any of it," and they wouldn't be sitting here in this yard with this house if he'd decided not to. Then he thinks about that. Indeed, who knows what would have happened if he'd made different choices? Maybe Naomi would have been running Ace for the past decade, or through necessity, found a new passion? Maybe they'd be sitting somewhere else having a happier conversation.

He pulls himself straight and resolute. "If you wish for me to step in to help in the short term, then I will. But not for long, that's what I'd say. A few weeks, a month tops. No more." He will not give it more of his blood.

It's hardly a complete reckoning between them, but for today, Naomi seems satisfied.

LATER, he heads down to the basement office. Naomi's been working here, it seems; she's put away his bedding, removed the piles of paper crap from the desk, added an essential oil burner to clean the air, and of course the sliding door's open. He cannot sense the Black Rider, yet the room still feels like a tomb: like visiting his own crypt, and witnessing gestures made by the living to his memory.

Summer's End

1

SEPTEMBER'S THE MOST BEAUTIFUL MONTH in Toronto, "the city within a park" — or so many say. The wilting humidity and summer storms have abated, and with them the smog; as the sun's roar mellows, the air gains a freshness and clarity that brings lighter thoughts. Grapes and tomatoes pull heavily on their vines. Baskets of squash, corn, potatoes and beans cram the markets. It feels like the whole year's promise has finally been delivered. Nights are cool and days filled with golden light.

A calendar whiteboard has replaced the bungalow rebuild plans above Oliver's desk. Among busy notations of tasks, due dates, meetings, calls and other events this month (including Rosh's court appearance), the release of *Fracking Up the Future* on the 21st is boxed in red. Fall equinox also happens to be Zero Emissions or ZeDay in Canada. Less than two weeks to go.

On the sofa Gabe lounges with Mimi stretched alongside, laptop and notebook on the coffee table next to a crumbed lunch plate. "Could we leave soon? Otherwise I might feel obliged to do something work-like, and I think the cat will protest."

"We don't want that. I'm almost done." He's been updating the film's budget spreadsheet. Although he's overseen the gym's accounts for years, he never put these skills to work for anyone else. It didn't occur to him that this kind of thing *was* a skill. Now he's taken on accounting for the project so others can concentrate on promo. It happened naturally over the summer — after he offered to pay for the film's post-production, using money he was going to spend on the house. With the interviews done, he also has more time in the evenings. He's even been given credit as a co-producer.

They bought Gabe a used bike this week, got it tuned up and equipped with a basket and bell. They ride together to the ferry, coasting down Greenwood all the way to the lakeshore path, and take the two-thirty p.m. sailing to Ward's. His brother and niece have gone over already and are out in the water when he and Gabe arrive. Oliver waves, and Justin points them to where they've laid their towels and packs on the sand.

The summer crowd's toned down to a couple dozen people lounging and splashing in the water. Most visitors go to Hanlan's beach these days. At Ward's there's not much left of one anymore: just a strip, still scarred by ashy pits from fires lit during the black-out. Fires sprang up all around the lakeshore during those nights, like tribal encampments. Once he and Justin made it back to the city, Oliver arranged for Rosh to care for Mimi, packed his old tent and supplies, and returned to work on the dike for four more days. Justin joined too when he could. Parts of the structure had caved in or loosened during the storm. They rebuilt them and widened the dike further. Water levels have receded somewhat since, and the dike's held.

"You coming in?"

"Soon. You go."

Gabe charges into the lake and dives. When she surfaces she whoops and waves, cajoling him to get off his ass and join her. Her brown skin gleams like it did on the hottest nights in his place when they lay side by side in bed, touching impossible, so reading to each other before seeking the balcony, with its tree cover and breezes, where they keep the foam mattress. No one can see them there. The benefits of that balcony just keep expanding.

He watches her join Justin and Gwynn, game around a little. The remains of Ward's beach. He's not swum here since their family left. Just east, the Leslie Street Spit juts out far from the mainland. Its shoreline trees stand pale, denuded from generations of nesting cormorants dropping guano. The flock shrieks, a sawing background drone, and lines of the sleek black birds undulate over the water like moving script. The birds have always been here, making this music, inscribing the wind.

The film keeps eating up his money. It's not clear what will remain of his inheritance, and sometimes this makes him panic. Interest has been building with the release of the film's trailer: acceptances in festivals into the new year, requests for interviews. Several of the report's scientists agreed to be filmed. The interviews are damning. The film could be ignored, or ignite a public scandal. Being co-producer will place him on an activist watchlist for the rest of his life, no doubt, and with the increasingly militant approach to governance these days, he'll be lucky if that's all it does. Oil drives the engine of this civilization; those who profit most have the most to lose. He's already glimpsed what they're willing to do.

So when he wakes in the night, he still often feels like he's gonna lose his shit. But this panic doesn't last. A few tours around the apartment, a few pages read and it's gone, unlike the specters that kept him sleepless and miserable for years. Then, he thought only of his own failure to make a difference, to protect the water. But there's more to it, he now knows, because no matter what happens, he can still live for the water. After all, he owes it his life: water holds him like it holds the island, the ark in the lake, the chance at a future worth living for all. That's what he lost touch with. His mother's gift — this reminder.

2

TREADING WATER, Gabe watches the lights of Hamilton Harbour shimmer in the west. On a tall slim tower amid smoking black trunks burns a bright, perpetual flame. Ignited more than a century ago, it remains unextinguished. Coke ovens burn 24/7 in "Steel City," Oliver told her. Below, under the water of that harbour, lies Randle Reef: a miasmic bulge of industrial contamination so severe it's been given a name. The reef thickens year by year, spreading across the lakebed.

She's never called Toronto home. Still can't quite see it. And Oliver's place is not exactly spacious. But since returning to Ontario last year, she's gotten used to fitting herself into corners, moving about as needed. And even here, when she quiets, she can sense the threads. Oliver. The birds. His brother and niece.

Regarding her thesis on the new method for studying moths, the committee members' reactions have been mixed, to say the least; she's got a month of revisions to go before handing the final draft in, though nothing so daunting that she's worried. What comes after puzzles her more. Hegyi wants her to apply for a PhD; Brimer, to hook her up with a colleague researching night ecology in Algonquin Park. Ochoa-Rodriguez, with whom she's had the least contact all along, called her draft "exceptional and important" and has urged her to try to publish it.

She said nothing about the luminous moth in it or to them. If she spoke up now, assuming she was believed, the moth would be cast into the standard species narrative: assigned a Latinate name, a place in the taxonomic order; studied for its unique adaptive strategies. At this point she doesn't even know where the moth lives, exactly. Every excursion after that first — over a dozen now — she's made in the same way, and she doesn't always end up at the hill. The last time, fewer moths were present; their season's drawing to an end. She will have to wait until spring next year, possibly longer, to see them again.

There's so much more to learn — and to unlearn. It's urgent yet can't be rushed. The world stands on the edge of losses so radical no one can fathom the consequences, while possibilities for reconnection and renewal wait to be discovered in the dark. Once she hands in her thesis, she'll read through the many notes accumulated from her visits to the moths. The drawings too. There's a story needing to be told — the moths' story. Science can describe only part of it. The story includes her experience too. It requires an artist's eyes, a musician's ears, a diplomat's humility, a healer's heart. A great expansion of perception, and more people listening.

Perhaps this degree will prove a stepping stone that leads away from academia. Perhaps her struggle with it *was* the stone, the block that had to be dissolved within.

She keeps listening, sensing the next step.

She dives down to the sandy bottom, pushes off. At the surface again, she spins to face the shore. Oliver's wading in toward her. He looks really serious. She flings drops at his skin, and when that doesn't budge his composure, chops water to drench him. A smile at last — then he two-hands a wave in her laughing face.

Many silk moth species are born without mouths. The caterpillar eats greedily; then it stops, and when the moth emerges from that long night of undoing, it doesn't need to feed. It carries all it needs for a brilliant life.

3

THE CORMORANTS keep passing overhead, their wings making a sound like an airy whistle. Today, the many-mooded lake swells a jewel-like blue. Justin ploughs through the cool water that pulls against his thighs, bearing Gwynn atop his shoulders like the figurehead of a ship. He sets her down on the beach.

They dry off, dress, and start toward Algonquin with Oliver and Gabe to look at the bungalow site. The demolition crew finished earlier this week. He and Oliver salvaged a few items only; the rest they left to be taken.

To make things easier on Gwynn, he's been staying at the Baby Point house. He bunks in the living room. It helps him and Naomi too, since she still has many questions about Ace and Leverage, and lingering doubts about her ability to successfully run them. He reminds her that in business, like life, success depends on much beyond one's control (though privately, he hopes she closes Leverage). The other day he went to Ace again for the first time in weeks, to sort through his office. He's much better at moving between worlds now, and Ace has shrunk to quite a small one, so he wasn't uneasy even when he saw Kurt behind the bar. It was actually a relief — he'd been thinking about that friendship, spoken to Naomi about him — and it was Kurt who looked awkward and nervous. Justin invited him up to the office, and when Kurt politely made an excuse, told him to come. They didn't speak long. Kurt, being himself, was wary and defensive. Still, Justin said what he needed to: that he hoped Kurt could find his way free of this urban racket without too much body and soul damage; that if he needed a plane ticket to Regina (who knows?) or something else to help, even just to listen, he could call Justin. No judgement.

They've come to the laneway, the site. Bulldozer treads track across the lawn to — nothing. Depressions where the bungalow's foundation blocks used to sit, but since there was no basement there's no hole, just an imprint on the ground, bare and pale. Where walls once stood wind blows and gnats gather. They stand looking, and he finds that his eyes are wet. Oliver puts an arm around Gabe.

Justin tells Gwynn this is where the tiny house will be, the house on wheels that's coming on the ferry this fall, where he will live for the next while.

"I'll live here too," she says.

"Whenever you want. Now, tell me, where's a good place for a bird feeder?"

The sun's setting. The leaves on the chestnut tree have begun to yellow. The morels have finished for the year. Soon the caterpillars will be spinning into their winter shells.

ACKNOWLEDGEMENTS

This novel was over a decade in the making; it took me on a long, winding path. At the beginning I felt rather alone. My gratitude goes to the rivers and woods, lakes and lands, and all the marvellous beings who dwell there, for their beauty and for nourishing and educating me over the years: Toronto Islands and Lake Ontario, the Humber River watershed and Black Creek, Rice Lake and the Serpent Mounds, to name only a few. *See us. Speak for us. Come home to us,* they said. This was the best I could do in this way.

Without my beloved husband, Kevin Connelly, there would be no book. His wisdom, insights and stories, particularly from being a musician and tradesman in Toronto, helped shape its characters and directions. But it was really his love, belief and understanding that held me and made this book possible, as well as his grit in enduring my absences from home and marathon stretches of preoccupation and unavailability. My deepest love, astonishment and gratitude for you, always.

Profound thanks to my parents, Douglas and Shirleyan English, for unwavering support and patience. "Revenge of the Moth People" took much longer to emerge than we all expected. Thanks to my brother David Lawrence and sister-in-law Sharon Lindala for the always-bracing political conversations, drinks and shared research.

Many writers have helped sustain and inspire me over the years. In particular I want to thank Patricia Robertson, twin soul, for her friendship and deep insights into writing during a time of ecological crisis. The writers and editors at the crucial Dark Mountain Project, particularly Dougald Hine, Paul Kingsnorth, and Charlotte

Du Cann, and Sharon Blackie at *Earthlines* magazine, have been constant way-showers and a community afar that has meant much to me. Loving gratitude also to Deena Metzger, dearest mentor and friend, for writing and teaching the literature of restoration, and to the editors of *Dark Matter: Women Witnessing*, Kristin Flyntz and Lise Weil, for making a home for it. A final acknowledgement to the late Barry Lopez, whose writings about our kinship with and obligations to the natural world, and the example of his life, first opened this door for me and continue to shine light on the way forward.

Moths came into this book for reasons mysterious to me. I'm forever grateful for their guidance. When I started this project I knew nothing about these nocturnal creatures, and any inaccuracies about them here are wholly mine. I'm immensely grateful to "Moth Man" David Beadle, whose photographs, blog, research, fieldtrips and extraordinary passion inspired and educated me. I also want to thank the hosts of the overnight moth nights and the folks at TEA, the Toronto Entomologists' Association, for their fieldtrips, events, publications and dedication to protecting and celebrating insects.

Books that were particularly or fundamentally useful to me in my research were *Peterson Field Guide to Moths of Northeastern North America* by David Beadle and Seabrooke Leckie; *Moths and Caterpillars of the North Woods* by James Sogaard; *Moth Catcher* by Michael M. Collins; *More Than an Island: A History of the Toronto Island* by Sally Gibson; *Toronto: An Illustrated History of its First 12,000 Years* by Ron Williamson (editor); and Christopher Bryson's harrowing and lucid *The Fluoride Deception*. The analogy of technology as a toxic pupae comes from *How Soon Is Now?* by Daniel Pinchbeck. Nancy Windheart's essay "Saved by Whales," in Issue 4 of *Dark Matter: Women Witnessing*, helped me contemplate animal communication, as did, in a different way, Steven Harrod Buhner's *Plant Intelligence and the Imaginal Realm*. Research published in

2020 by the Flood Committee of Toronto Island helped confirm and clarify what I understood from previous reading.

I'm very grateful to Robert Hilles for his generous work as my editor prior to placing this book with a publisher; his insights into the story — and belief in it — helped structure and focus it immensely. Thank you to readers at various stages for their attention and advice: Chris Bucci, Jacky Sawatzky, Kevin Connelly, Leanna McLennan, Becky Vogan, Roz Spafford (who suggested the current, better title), Bonnie McElhinny, Andrea Most and Sasha Chapman. For inspiring and encouraging my hand-drawn maps, thanks to Steven Heighton. For conversations and faithful interest that helped me to persevere, loving thanks to Mike Barnes, Mariana Grezova and Mary-Lou Zeitoun.

For financial support, my grateful thanks to the Canada Council of the Arts, the Toronto Arts Council, the Ontario Arts Council and the publishers who recommended grants through the OAC: Biblioasis, Key Porter Books, the New Quarterly and Thomas Allen. My thanks also to Cynthia Messenger and Charlie Keil at Innis College for keeping me gainfully and meaningfully employed.

A funded residency at the beautiful and dynamic Anderson Center in Minnesota helped me start this novel ages ago. Thank you to co-founder Robert Hedin for his invitation and gracious presence. The short-term studio rentals offered by Artscape Gibraltar Point on Toronto Island provided me retreat space countless times; what began as a convenience became integral to this story, and the old island schoolhouse will always feel like another home. My thanks to the wonderful staff and management there for their hospitality.

The crew at Freehand Books have been a writer's dream team, enthusiastic, professional, devoted and gracious at every turn. My deep thanks to you for giving this story a home and helping to shape it into its current form. Heartfelt gratitude to my amazing editor, Deborah Willis, for her superb insights, tact and fiery energy; to Natalie Olsen for managing to transpose the book's themes into a gorgeous cover design; and to Kelsey Attard for her exacting copy editing and great warmth and support throughout the management of this project.

The names of places used in this novel are different in Indigenous languages. This book encompasses regions traditional to a number of First Nations, some covered by treaties and some unceded. I wish to acknowledge that the Mississaugas of the Credit, of Hiawatha and of Alderville Nations, and the Anishinaabe, Chippewa, Wendat and Haudenosaunee peoples in Ontario have cared responsibly and lovingly for these regions, their homelands, for millennia; that they continue to be displaced from their traditional territories and thwarted in holding their ceremonies there; and that for settlers, the urgent work of being accountable to our history, the land, and relationships past and present with Indigenous peoples in Canada is both political and personal.

At the end of this journey I feel buoyed and humbled by all these gifts, including what I have learned. A final thanks to Spirit, and to the dreams, animals and ancestors who helped show me the path.

SHARON ENGLISH comes from a long line of mostly Scots settlers and grew up in the suburbs of London, ON, Canada. She's written two story collections, *Uncomfortably Numb* and *Zero Gravity*, which was longlisted for the Giller Prize, shortlisted for a ReLit Award, included in the *Globe and Mail's* Best 100 new titles of the year, and recently translated into Serbian. Her fiction and essays have appeared in *Best Canadian Stories*, *Canadian Notes and Queries*, *Dark Matter: Women Witnessing* and *Dark Mountain* in the UK. After decades of living in Toronto, she now makes her home in rural Nova Scotia.

www.sharonenglish.net